The Fovean Chronicles
Book Four:Indomitus Sum

By Robert W. Brady, Jr.

I0685167

Sometimes victory is simply the absence of defeat.

The Fovean Chronicles
Book Four: Indomitus Sum
© 2014 by Robert W. Brady, Jr.

ISBN: 9780979367977

Cover art: Adrijus Guscia

First Printing

10   9   8   7   6   5   4   3   2   1

Dedicated to Ralph Fisher

Who gave his life in service to his country, not on the battlefield but in the aftermath, with courage and distinction befitting a member of the armed services.

A better man than I.

The Map of Fovea

Prologue

The man-god Steel stood atop the Iron Mountains, sadly watching the city called Steel, filled with people who didn't even know this city had been named after Him, *not* after the ore carried out of the adjacent mines. Steel watched soldiers marshalling on a practice field, girding themselves in armor and weapons, making ready to kill others barely different than themselves.

Steel's mother, Life, had birthed him after she coupled with one of these. Life had created all manner of things on the face of the god Earth, alongside the goddess Water, who lay forever asleep in His arms.

These two had birthed Life, after all. Steel was born of an exotic and powerful line.

Atop the mountains, the goddess Weather, a lesser god, pulled at Steel's salt-and-pepper hair. She begged him, "Worry not. The machinations of Men, of Uman and Dwarves, of Slee and Swamp Devils, Scitai and Uman-Chi, are nothing in the long stretch of things. War might think Himself ascendant, but in fact he's just another storm, on a planet where there's ever sunshine."

Steel knew better. Unlike the Fovean gods, He was himself part Man, and this could sometimes give Him insight into mortal things. The god War had brought forward His instrument from another reality, and had sidestepped the Rule of the Gods; He could speak to Lupus the Conqueror. In retaliation the All-Mother, the goddess Eveave, had brought forth two others from the same place, not to face War's instrument but to counter His plans.

And then had come a song, and the song had been Steel's own creation. The song, sung by the Uman-Chi Glynn Escaroth, forewarned of the coming battles, the events about to shake Fovea and the world it lay on.

"On Fovea, on Fovea, seek a noble young and old,
A foreigner among his kind
A hero, fate foretold
One who fights as does the Sun
Waits in a sacred place
A guardian will bring you there
With a devil born and raised"

"Through Fovea, through Fovea, over you shall watch
One who eludes prying eyes,
With one who can't be touched.
So shall they come together
Heroes of the land
Together to oppose the One
While all apart they stand."

As loudly as He dared proclaim it, as directly as He dared push against the Rule of the Gods, which bound Him loosely as half a Man. Six for fighting against the One, to work with Eveave's champion while they could.

Steel wept, watching warriors march on the plains below him. So many of these would be lost, and for what? More influence to the god War? More power to War's father, the god who *called himself* Power? A bloody feast at the table of the lesser goddess Destruction?

When the first living beings, the Cheyak, walked upon the face of Earth thousands of years ago, there'd been a balance. The gods had been content to watch, to tinker, to push idly without real concern about the outcome of Earthly things. Then the god Power had found this other *Earth*, domain of the *One God*, and found a way past the Rule of the Gods. He'd heavily influenced the Cheyak and, in the end, destroyed them. That had led to the thousand-year reign of the god Chaos, the formation of the new Fovean nations, the ascendance of Fovean peoples such as the Andarons and the Confluni and, finally, a great peace brokered by Life's sister and brother, Order and Law, which stifled the fighting in the name of Adriam, the All-Father.

That peace had lasted less than one hundred years. Now the one called 'The Conqueror' ruled the nation of Eldador in the name of War. Now all nations rallied to the clarion call of fear; fear of War, fear of His instrument, the Conqueror, fear there would be a return to the days of their great-grandfathers and the reign of Chaos. Fear of the losses of War.

For this Steel wept.

He'd interfered. He'd done His best. He'd sent the Almadain, the mighty stallion from Life's cherished herd, to soften War's instrument. The Almadain had birthed half-breed sons and daughters which, in time, could aid them, but even now the instrument of War moved forward with a plan to take Fovea.

That, Steel knew, must never be. That would usher in a time of blackness even He couldn't see the end of. The Conqueror knew his god's will, and such a person was capable of monstrous things, yet even War's instrument had no concept of what his own successes might usher in.

Eveave countered him with Her Instrument, the woman called Raven, perhaps greater in her way than the Conqueror, however Eveave would *never* let her instrument know her will, and so this Raven would *never* know the absolute commitment of a true follower.

Steel did not believe the Raven could prevail, and so He'd set his prophecy in motion. His prophecy put a whole new set of rules, a whole new set of possibilities in play. Should He be wrong, then War's darkness might intensify one hundred fold, and live to the time when Life became unwelcome on Fovea.

If successful, the best Steel could hope for was a dim time, not a dark one. His best hope, his brightest dream, was for a time of only gray.

Sometimes in the world, victory is simply the lack of defeat.

Chapter One

Secrets

"Blast!"

"Blast, blast, blast and damnation!"

Thebinaar had seen the Duke, in these last twelve years of his reign in Thera, in various states of joy and anger, but not like this, not in court where everyone could see him.

Def Namek nudged him in the ribs. "Think he's angry?" he asked.

The Master at Arms had a strange sense of humor, even for an old Man.

"I wouldn't make that comment to him," Thebinaar responded, dry as ever. An Uman, he had a longer view of things than a Man.

Andarons at their best could be difficult.

"Def!" Two Spears roared, bellowing like a bull on his Ducal throne. He sat atop a raised set of four stone steps, still a powerful Man in his thirties, a little grey at the temples of his long, black hair, the black mustachios wagging under the chin of his otherwise clean-shaven face. The courtiers in the gallery were already stirring and the two Wolf Soldiers before him were so rigid at attention that they *must* be in fear for their lives.

"Your Grace," Def said, stepping forward on the platform to the left of the Ducal throne. Thebinaar and Def served as the Shem Hannen of Thera, much as the three who served the Emperor in Eldador. In old Cheyak, the term meant literally, "The Wise Ears."

In all things they were opposites. Def stood stick-figure thin, old for the race of Men, in his late sixties. His wiry hair stood out like the whisps of an old brush from his head, revealing a spotted scalp.

Thebinaar, on the other hand, was less than ninety, middle-aged for the race of Uman. His people were fair-skinned where Def was ruddy and the Duke olive-skinned. Thebinaar's hair was close-cropped and white, but it had been white his whole life.

The Duke fixed the Master at Arms with furious brown eyes, the nostrils flaring in his hawk-like nose. "My sister has been captured with my nieces by the Bounty Hunter's Guild," he said. "My nephew's whereabouts are unknown."

"Yuh—your sister, the *Empress*?" Def spluttered.

Well, that should make for interesting conversation at every table in the Empire over the next week, Thebinaar thought to himself. *Why not just surrender to Conflu?*

"Of course, you imbecile," Two Spears bellowed, hammering the wooden arms to his throne. He'd broken them one-per-year for every year of his reign and Thebinaar didn't hold out high hopes for this one now.

The gallery was abuzz. Courtiers were already glancing furtively at the doors. Some of them came here from other nations. When Rancor Mordetur had been a Duke, he'd helped to make this place one of the most important cities on Tren Bay for culture and commerce, and since then Two Spears had been at least as successful.

"We—by War's Whiskers, your Grace, shall we take this out of the court?" Def at least tried to contain the situation.

The Emperor had some cliché about closing barns doors once horses escaped, but Thebinaar couldn't recall it at the moment.

"I want three thousand Theran Lancers on the marshalling field by the time I have my armor on," Two Spears demanded, "and I want a message sent to the Aschire that I need as many archers as they can spare. Send a fast horse to the Emperor in Uman City and let him know that, when I have my sister back, I'll be sending her to him."

"Your—your Grace, shall we not—"

A fist like an anvil shattered the arm of the wooden throne.

"By the wind in Weather's hair," Two Spears swore, red faced, "if I have to repeat myself I'll let my scimitar do my talking for me—I think it's about time we cleared out this court of those who can't do what I tell them to, and when!"

"Im—immediately, your Grace," Def stammered. Thebinaar held to the better part of valor and his tongue, not that it saved him.

"To me, Uman," Two Spears said, standing. "We have a few things to set straight. Def Namek—War better be right at your shoulder if you tell me anything but that you've done what I need of you, when next I see you."

Def nodded. Thebinaar glided out after Two Spears, so enraged that he didn't even bother to dismiss the court.

Let the courtiers sit until their courage caught up with their hunger, Thebinaar thought. The longer it took them to spread this bad news, the longer the Empress would be alive.

"Your Grace," Thebinaar said, soft as a whisper, as one might to a spooked horse, once they were away from the throne room. "How may I be of—?"

Two Spears turned. He stood tall, almost as tall as the Emperor, broad shouldered and heavily muscled. The corners of his brown eyes showed the wrinkles of both age and worry. Being a Duke in Rancor Mordetur's Empire was no easy job.

"My nephew took eight men, and they're following the Bounty Hunters," he said, softly, a hand on Thebinaar's shoulder.

"Vulpe?"

The boy had seen eleven springs, no more. Thebinaar had rarely spoken to him, but for a child of Men he'd shown amazing intelligence. At six, he'd actually sung at the Theatre au Thera, and so beautifully even the Uman-Chi had given him a standing ovation.

"He took control of a squad, he's given his orders, he sent for reinforcements and he's looking for a way to get his mother back."

Thebinaar was actually dumbfounded. "At eleven?"

Two Spears nodded. "The Wolf Soldiers are calling him by his first name, and you know what *that* means."

Wolf Soldiers referred to the Emperor, the boy's father, by his nick-name, 'Lupus.' It was their term for respect and obedience, and they hadn't shared it with any others.

"Your Grace…"

Two Spears nodded, and started stomping back to his personal chambers, where once the Emperor had slept with Shela, Two Spears' sister. That same sister had picked the Duke out an Andaron wife from the Wolf Rider tribe—the one that had made Rancor Mordetur an Andaron.

She waited for him there, tears in her eyes, Two Spears' armor already waiting for him. He'd given up the familiar Andaron leather for Eldadorian plate—some of the finest in the world, a gift from his brother-in-law.

"Oh, Tali Digatishi," Wanigey Digitolay, his wife, greeted him. In her Andaron tongue, it meant 'Soft Eyes.' "The estate is already seething with it—"

He took her in his arms. The Empress had picked this woman out for her brother, another custom among their people. She was everything Two Spears never let himself be—soft, loving, caring.

On her first day here, she'd disappeared and they'd found her in the inner city, helping wash peoples' clothes. When asked why, she just said, "Well, it needed to be done."

Thebinaar himself admitted his own heart swelled with love for this dusky woman with long, black hair and eyes the size of Tabaars, colored golden brown.

"I'll have all four of them back before Weather's end, and the skins of the Bounty Hunters dripping on the walls," Two Spears promised. "Wani—I need you to run the city while I'm out."

She turned her soulful eyes to Thebinaar's. She laid a hand on the upper curve of his gigantic belly and asked, "You'll help me, wise one?"

I'd walk across hot coals to bring you your wine, he thought to himself. "I am forever at your slightest service, your Grace," he said.

Love or hate the Emperor, he knew how to pick good people, Thebinaar thought to himself. Thera was the bulwark of Eldador's economy, and her people loved their Duke and Duchess so much, they'd do anything for them.

An Uman-Chi poet once wrote,
"The thunder of Theran Lancers
"So like the thunder of God,
"Rings not so loud as Theran coin
"In every purse abroad."

"You see, 'Tisha," she said. "I am all well. My love, you *must* find them."

"You claim your nephew…" Thebinaar intervened.

"And what was *that?*" Def burst into the room behind them.

Two Spears grinned wide. His wife already had his blouse and breeches off, and was dressing him in his armor.

"You liked our little play?" Two Spears asked him.

Def fumed.

These Men*,* Thebinaar thought. *Like onions. So many layers and, when you peel them back, all you get is tears.*

"You know every tongue in the Empire—" Def began.

"Will be wagging," Two Spears concluded for him, "and woe to any who see these scum on our soil."

"The Bounty Hunter's Guild—"

"Has an agreement with the Empire," Two Spears said. His wife was sliding his greaves up his shins. "Do you know the *real* reason why they stopped trying to kill the Emperor?"

Yes, Thebinaar thought to himself, *I know exactly why. It was my idea.*

"Because the Emperor swore that, after the next time he was attacked, he would declare all out war not only on the guild, but on anyone who did business with them."

"And no nation wanted the animosity of the man who sacked Outpost IX," Two Spears said. "And if the Bounty Hunter's Guild believes their own members have taken the Empress—"

"Then they will do everything they can to get her back," Thebinaar said. "But, of course, only if they *know* she is gone."

Def just fumed.

"When next we spar," he said, finally, "I am not going to go so light on you as before, Tali Digatishi.

"I used to despair of damaging your brain, but now I hold no hope for it."

***

Nina found herself left all alone, waiting in the semi-darkness. The night before, the Wolf Soldiers had taken the city. Someone had cast a torch into the room. It landed on a couch, which started burning. Nina wondered, struggling against her bonds, if this would be the end of her, her message undelivered.

Aschire live their lives in harmony with their forest. The plants, the trees, the animals, the rocks; are all *the Aschire*. An Aschire is born into a crowd and lives in one. For her to restrict herself just to the royal family had itself been a sacrifice in her life.

Where normally her power would have freed her, being abandoned here had left her so rattled she could barely douse the torch, and even then only after several tries. She'd always favored flame.

That morning her heart leapt when someone kicked in the green door. She saw the guard still lying dead in the alleyway beyond it. Kor had seen its share of bodies before him.

"What have we here?" a Wolf Soldier sergeant demanded? He stepped up to her, took her jaw in his hand. She almost melted into his rough palm, welcoming the touch of any living thing.

A moment later she knew from the look in the sergeant's eyes that the battle lust was on him. He'd probably raped already and wanted to do so again. Lupus encouraged his men to be merciless.

"Nina of the Aschire," she informed him, straightening in her bonds. "Guardian Protector to the Princess Lee, of the House of Mordetur. Mistreat me on your life, sergeant."

The sergeant sneered. Another behind him put his hand on the Man's shoulder.

"She's who she says she is," he said, a Volkhydran. "I served two years with the First Millennium. I've seen her many times; I know the Mist—I know the Lady Nina."

"My pardon," the sergeant said. "You there, cut free her bonds. My lady, I beg of you—"

She waved it off. After what she'd suffered, he been almost kind to her. "You're the fifth out of Vrek?"

"The eighth," he corrected her. "Under Major Gevenal, we've taken the city—"

No time for it. "Did the Druid Dilvesh come with you?"

The sergeant nodded. "Aye—said he had someone to meet—"

She nodded. "That someone is me," she said. "Take me to him. I have to speak with Lupus before he mobilizes his armies."

As the ropes fell away she was on her feet, her slender fingers in the collar of the Wolf Soldier's leather cuirass and her grey eyes inches from his.

She hadn't missed what the other Wolf Soldier had nearly called her—the nick-name she hated most of all, used only by Wolf Soldiers and, oddly, the Emperor's direst enemies, referring to her.

The Emperor's Watch-Bitch, *Mistress of Pain*.

She flipped her purple hair. Her heightened Aschire senses let her actually smell the fear flowing off of him. Nina of the Aschire had made an oath on her life to guard the children born of Rancor and Shela Mordetur; an oath she took seriously.

"The victory you think you've had," she informed him, "means nothing if I don't speak to the Emperor."

* * *

Karl rode an Eldadorian mare, feisty like all Eldadorian steeds. Even if they weren't from Lupus' Blizzard, it seemed they all wanted to be like him.

This one must be coming into heat, having what Karl's father would have called a 'mare moment,' balking at every move he made, every sound she heard, and every smell in the air.

Some people liked a testy mount, but not Karl. He liked people and animals both to do their jobs with as little fuss and difficulty as possible.

That would have served them well in the defense of Kor; but the Emperor's warriors had planned too well. Perhaps the infamous Duke Ceberro himself had come to take the last free city, the pirate capitol of the Forgotten Sea. It had been a miracle Karl had gotten his friends out alive.

Supposedly the troubadours were calling it *The Battle of Heroes*. Karl hadn't stuck around to hear the songs; he'd been too busy fighting for his life, a sword in his hand, his Volkhydran comrades beside him. Not just the crew of the ill-fated *Sprite*, but the Volkhydran visitors to the port, the buccaneers and pirates and heartless merchants who frequented a place like this—they'd heard *the Hero of Tamara* was standing in defense of the city, and they'd joined in to brag later that they'd fought beside him.

His friend Jahunga had done no worse. Toorians frequented the last free city, where they could sell not only their own wares but those they came across on the Forgotten Sea. They'd flocked to Jahunga, the unbeaten warrior. The dark-skinned Toorians in their traditional white robes, the Volkhydrans in their furs and shaggy hair; when the Wolf Soldiers swarmed the gates, the Koran Guard, a mish-mass of every race and people, had pretended to fall before them and the others had swarmed in from behind.

Wolf Soldiers battled from their orderly squads, forming a defensive circle, their pikes bristling, their huge shields an impenetrable wall which could part on an order and meet flesh with

Eldadorian steel. The Toorians and the Volkhydrans had driven them back out of the city, but hadn't been able to slaughter them.

And once past the cover provided by the archers in the retreating Koran Guard, they'd met the lances of one thousand armored Angadorian Knights.

Duke Tartan Stowe, the son of the former King, Glennen, had swept in and slashed the defenders with their lances, killing dozens and driving the rest back into the shattered city gates.

From there it had been attrition, nothing more. The Wolf Soldiers swarmed, the arrows fell. They advanced and fought Koran Guardsman in patchwork armor, wild-eyed Volkhydrans and cunning Toorians. If they pushed deep enough into the city, the horse engaged and slaughtered. If they withdrew, the same.

After a week, the exhausted defenders buckled before the veteran Wolf Soldier army. People from the city either threw down their weapons or scattered, fighting from alley to home through the city or scrambling over the city walls into the relative freedom of the Salt Wood. Karl and Jahunga knew then that they could do no more. They abandoned the city behind the advancing army with their friends.

From there it had been another week in the Salt Wood, hiding from patrols, avoiding refugees. Karl had thought to hide among them but the Scitai ambassador who'd brought them here countermanded him.

Why, Xinto had asked, would refugees have horses, armor, gold? They didn't look like refugees, and they didn't act like refugees. Therefore, they wouldn't blend in with the refugees, they would be a beacon, very easy to find.

Karl admitted after the fact Xinto had made the right decision. His yakking countrymen would have found it impossible not to get drunk and spill their tale at the first opportunity. Instead they hid, moved slowly, and crawled out of the Salt Wood under the cover of darkness.

* * *

Glynn Escaroth guided her small party back in the direction of Kor, across the wide expanse of the Eldadorian plains southeast from the Lone Wood. She and the Man, Jack, rode their prospective horses. The Swamp Devil Zarshar, the Black Adept ran between them, and the dog which they'd adopted ran either before or behind.

The Druid woman, Vedeen, road a large roan stallion behind

them, her blonde hair flying out behind her, her white robe and brown overcloak billowing around her. Her blue eyes sparkled, taking in everything they passed, lighting on a flower here, a cloud up in the sky, or perhaps nothing, just reflecting a thought in her head.

The Druids were strange, but the idea they'd been included in the prophetic song she'd sung, the message from the goddess Eveave that guided them, filled the Uman-Chi's heart with hope.

The Druids were ancient and powerful. One of them was an ally to the Emperor, the One whom they fought, whose coming threatened the land of Fovea. Vedeen might neutralize them, might even turn them to Glynn's side.

She'd crossed the Eldadorian plains, thinking these thoughts, when the dog, running before them, dropped into a crouch. She was an ugly beast, this dog. Jack called her a mastiff—she was wrinkled from her nose to her tail, bearing a wicked underbite and slavering jaws, green eyes that knew neither sympathy nor fear, her fur brindled almost blue, making her invisible at night.

Glynn raised her hand and the other two stopped. Jack dismounted and held up a hand to her, to help her to dismount from her side-saddle.

The Swamp Devil, ebon-skinned and heavily muscled with red teeth and eyes and a black mane that touched the ground behind him, dropped to its belly and crept the distance between them and the dog, drawing up beside it.

An army, thousands of mounted and armored warriors, between us and the Salt Wood, Glynn heard in her mind. The Devil used his magic in order to speak to her in quiet over the half daheer between them.

She knew these troops—Angadorian Knights. The sub-nation of Angador resided to the south of Eldador, a part of the Empire ruled by the Duke Tartan Stowe. The horses they rode were a breed unique to that region, their training mirrored Andaron, Wolf Soldier and Theran influence.

And Tartan Stowe had trained under the Emperor himself since his father, the former King Glennen Stowe, had died. They'd fought together when the Empire had conquered the southwest of Andoron and taken what was now called 'Wisex' and 'The Black Lake,' at the joining of the Safe and Mid Rivers.

We do not want to provoke those troops, Sirrah, she warned

Zarshar. *Please return with the dog.*

Glynn turned to the Druid and Jack. "We've encountered thousands of Angadorian Knights between us and the Salt Wood," she informed them. "We must needs either circle 'round them, or wait their passing."

Jack looked to the East. "They'll have scouts," he said. "We should stand pat—um, we should wait here and watch them."

"I agree," Vedeen said in her ethereal voice. "With my feet upon the Earth, I'll know if any come near, and we can avoid them."

Zarshar and the dog approached from the east. The latter trotted over to Jack and rubbed her side against his.

Glynn weighed her options.

Chapter Two

A Near Meeting

Xareff, a Man who once called himself 'The Duke of Thieves,' stood in what used to be his throne room, in a port that used to be called 'Kor,' in front of what was once his throne, made of stone, on a cracked dais of thirteen steps, where a Druid named Dilvesh sat now.

They'd let him keep his pants on—that was more than he usually did. Strip a man down naked in front of others and he was more vulnerable and more easily intimidated. He'd had two Toorian bodyguards, but they were just bodies now, laying to his left in bloody puddles against what used to be his rough, wooden gallery.

An Uman named Narem stood next to him, bleeding from gashes in his arms, chest and face. His brown eyes were fixed on the dais' bottom step, blood was matted in his short, white hair, his lips were fixed in a thin, pink line. Narem had been the captain of the Koran Guard which had protected the city, but there wasn't much of that left now.

Dilvesh didn't say anything; he just…looked at them. He sat in white robes with a green hook symbol under a dot on the front of them, a brown over cloak open, framing him. He looked regal somehow—more regal than the former Duke of Thieves, anyway.

Xareff knew of Dilvesh—everyone did. A member of the Daff Kanaar and an ally of the Eldadorian Emperor, he'd come here with 2,000 Wolf Soldiers and another thousand Angadorian Knights, and he hadn't just sacked port Kor, he'd conquered it. His troops held the whole city. Those who hadn't bent a knee to the Druid in the Emperor's name were dead.

That made for a *lot* of dead. Kor had been a pirate haven and the last free city in Fovea. People didn't give that up easily, no matter *what* squalor they lived in.

To Xareff's right he recognized Duke Tartan Stowe of Angador and his Duchess, the Lady Yeral. The former dressed out in Eldadorian field plate—a plain, steel breastplate, sleeves and greaves, a full helmet clipped to his hip and a long sword over his shoulder. The latter dressed as if for court in a full green gown with a voluminous skirt—Xareff had a hard time imagining she'd seen combat, but then, why was she here?

No one spoke—it was nerve-wracking.

Xareff heard a commotion behind him. He turned reflexively—you didn't make it as far as he had in life without your reflexes responding on their own. Marching in through the shattered double-doors behind him he recognized Nina of the Aschire, her purple hair streaming out behind her, her black leather pants and vest smudged with white dust, her face with black soot.

Roughly two weeks ago it had been she standing before Xareff, pleading her case. Now she marched past him, two Wolf Soldiers stopping at the throne room entrance, as if he weren't there.

The Druid smiled wide. His brown eyes followed her under green eyebrows and curly, green hair. Supposedly Dilvesh was the only hybrid of Men and Uman, but that never rang true to Xareff.

"Green One," she addressed him.

"Nina," Dilvesh said, inclining his head.

"Thank you for coming," she said, her back to Xareff now, so he couldn't see her expression. "But I didn't mean for you to sack the whole city."

Dilvesh shrugged. "The city was going to be taken eventually," he said. "If our enemies were planning to use it, then it made sense to do that now."

Nina's shoulders relaxed. "Not like you had something better to do?" she said.

Dilvesh chuckled. "That's what *he* would say, yes," he said.

Xareff could guess who *he* was. It was a strange expression.

Nina turned. "And these?" she asked, turning. Her grey eyes travelled up and down the former Duke of Thieves. "I have to be honest," she added, "he was decent to me. He could have hurt me and he didn't."

"That's good to know," Dilvesh said. "I was going to hang him—maybe not now."

Nina's eyes travelled to the other, the Uman, Narem. "Who's this one?"

"I'm the captain of the Koran Guard," Narem almost spat at her, looking up from the bottom of the dais.

"That's a hard thing to be," Dilvesh said, "seeing as there isn't a Kor any more, much less a Koran Guard."

Narem looked him in the eyes. "You slaughtered them all?"

Dilvesh shrugged. "I'm not sure," he said. "I don't recall them calling for quarter."

"About one hundred did," Tartan Stowe piped up. All eyes turned to him. "I'm holding them outside the city. They've asked for this one—they claim the Guard serves the city, not the leader, and if we run things now—"

"If you think you run things now," Narem interrupted, "then we'll serve you like we served him."

The throne room went quiet. Glances flew between Narem and Dilvesh.

"We don't need 'em," Tartan Stowe said, finally.

"I tend to agree," Dilvesh said.

"I don't," Nina inserted.

Dilvesh regarded her. She half-turned so she could face the group of them.

"His troops know the city," she said, "and it will take us a long time to do that. They can fight, they're peace keepers, we're warriors—they know how to do things we don't, like hunt down criminals and contact important people left in the city."

"Not many of those," Tartan said, a smirk on his face.

"But some," Dilvesh countered. "You don't know this Uman, Nina. How can you speak to his loyalty?"

Nina turned her face to his. "Are the Wolf Soldiers any different, before they take their vows?"

Dilvesh sighed, closed his eyes and opened them.

Nina turned to Narem. "Your solemn vow?" she asked him.

Narem met her eyes. "Given to the city," he said. "The Koran Guard—"

"There is no more Kor," Dilvesh interrupted him. "This is the port city of Lupor, of the Eldadorian Empire. Where is your loyalty now?"

Narem looked sideways at Xareff, then back at the Druid.

"On my life, on my honor," he said, "to the Port City of Lupor, of the Eldadorian Empire, 'till the gods take me."

Nina smiled. Her eyes shifted between Narem, Xareff and Dilvesh.

The Druid nodded.

"And now, the other one," Tartan Stowe said.

* * *

Shela Mordetur lay bound with her hands behind her over the back of her gelding—the same one she'd ridden off of the plains with her husband, then her master, when she'd met her Yonega Waya more than a decade ago.

They'd been travelling south slowly. By her best estimates they were at the edges of Thera's provinces now. The Bounty Hunters who'd captured her, her daughters and prince Hectaro, son of the Duke of Galnesh Eldador were complaining there were Eldadorian patrols everywhere, and debating whether they were looking for this group or not.

She knew better. Her husband was in the process of collecting his forces in Uman City for the War months. Roads from Andurin and Metz, from Galnesh Eldador and the wealthy port cities came through here.

Any of them would have *someone* who'd recognize the Empress of Eldador, and the Bounty Hunters knew it. They were keeping their heads down, as her husband would say.

Her husband, the Emperor. She'd betrayed him. She'd known better, she'd *known* better than to leave on her own with her children to track him down on his way to Uman City and inform him she'd ordered the Druid in Vrek to march on Kor. It was a relatively unimportant adjustment to their plans which could be handled with a message, but she wanted to be with her man, and any excuse seemed reasonable.

Now she'd turned herself and those children over to his enemies—and not just any, but Clear Genna, the woman they'd left for dead in Conflu more than a decade before, the one who'd loved him before he'd come to Andoron and they'd met.

They hadn't known Genna was a Bounty Hunter, but it made

sense now. Her resourcefulness, her effectiveness as a guide—they should have suspected this of her all along.

Now she had these hostages, and she'd use them to force her husband to surrender to the Bounty Hunter's Guild or, worse, to her. She and her children were likely as good as dead anyway—she'd tried to kill them all and failed before they'd subdued her. She'd do it again now if she could.

She couldn't—she had to speak the words to use her magic to kill her children, and they'd gagged her. Now she pretended to be asleep, unconscious from the poison they put into her blood stream when they'd ambushed her and killed her guards. They'd reapplied it to her lips but she'd neutralized it—changed it to salt water. She acted like an unconscious woman, she'd even soiled herself and left herself for her older daughter to clean as best she could, and she waited.

They'd make a mistake, and she'd act. Oh, how she'd act. They'd know the full fury of an Andaron Sorceress, the most feared on Fovea, when she got her chance.

A thousand years from now, people would shudder at the fate of Clear Genna of the Daff Kanaar.

* * *

Jahunga had insisted he and his seven remaining Toorians scout ahead of their wandering band from Kor. The Salt Wood wasn't the same as their native jungle, but tracking and scouting didn't change anywhere.

It had been the right decision. Defassi, his good friend, knelt down in the dry brush next to him and surveyed the Eldadorian plain beside him.

They'd left one thousand Angadorian Knights behind them at Kor. They hadn't expected to find another 3,500 here between them and the Lone Wood.

"That is more than we can sneak past," Defassi informed him, as if he needed to. "Especially with this lot."

Jahunga nodded. They were in the camps the Eldadorian soldiers made. The trash around them, the cess pits and the refuse from their fires, told him they'd been here in this same place for more than a week. They didn't look like they were packing up now—they were running drills and they were practicing charging and their turns—this group was going to remain right here for a while.

"We can cross to the north," he said. "We can avoid their

scouts, circle past them—"

"The one called Raven," Defassi argued, "she said to the purple-haired witch that we'd go north."

Jahunga closed his eyes and nodded. "You're right," he said. They'd wanted their enemies to think they were heading to Andurin. Not wise to go that way.

"South, then," he said. "Just as good."

"It's not," Defassi said. He pointed south and continued, "Their supply train runs south and they guard it."

Jahunga shook his head.

He'd been wondering at their logic, at keeping with these people. They'd gone to Kor and that was pointless. They'd divided their forces for no reason, either, in his opinion. Their song told them to go to a sacred place and find the one who 'fights as does the sun.' It didn't say they couldn't all go, just that certain of them had to. It would have been wiser to stay together, but they hadn't listened to Jahunga.

The Scitai, Xinto, and the Uman-Chi, Glynn, had appointed themselves as leader. Why not Jahunga? In Toor his council was among the wisest. Here, they thought of him as just another warrior with a spear.

It was hard not to be angry over this.

"There!" Defassi said, pointing past the army on the field.

Jahunga squinted, the setting sun behind him, and painted by the dusk light, four individuals, one of them a hulking giant, another an overlarge Man, and the third a slip of a figure in a dress. A fourth dressed in some sort of robe or cloak—it was impossible to tell more in the dying light.

Roaming at their feet, apparently something the size of a small lion; behind them three horses, one of them huge.

They could have picked up the animal, but there was no mistaking Zarshar or Little Storm. Magee, the Uman-Chi witch, had probably found them by the beacon Karl carried. Jahunga watched as they ducked back behind the hill they'd topped, to let themselves be seen.

They couldn't let this army see them; neither could they let their allies miss them. No one of the race of Men would have marked them in the Salt Wood, hidden as they were, but Uman-Chi eyes worked strangely.

Or they might have been there for a long time, exposing

themselves a few times a day. It didn't matter—Jahunga needed to report this back to the mainstay of their group.

* * *

Dilvesh dined with the Duke Tartan Stowe, his wife Yeral and Nina of the Aschire at what passed for a dining room, in what passed for a palace, in the port city now called Lupor, the newest of the Eldadorian Empire.

It used to be known by another name. It used to be called 'Outpost III' when the Cheyak lived here, but that was more than 1,000 years ago. Dilvesh kept this secret to himself. The Daff Kanaar had once been a group focused on selling mercenary services to the rest of Fovea, in an effort eventually to eradicate the Fovean High Council and pave the way for Ancenon Aurelias to reunify the nations under his banner. That had quickly changed to the wolf's head banner of Lupus the Conqueror, and that had changed again when that same Lupus had started to discover the lost Cheyak Outposts. Lupus knew of almost all of them now, and the Daff Kanaar were very focused on reclaiming and looting them.

Not for their gold, but for the knowledge still hidden within them. Lupus had an amazing and exceedingly fortunate fixation with history and the collection of knowledge, and that played right into Dilvesh's hands.

As they dined on a mean fare of pork and old vegetables, the Druid called 'the Green One' collected more of that information now.

"In fact," he answered Nina, who sawed on a piece of over-tough pork before her, "no one ever saw Genna fall, so of course we were never sure she'd died. I'd always had my doubts."

The Duke and his wife kept their own council, just listening. Neither of them had ever met this lost member of the Daff Kanaar.

"She confessed to me she'd left to Conflu," Nina said, "but not just to escape the Emperor."

"And that's what I find troubling," Dilvesh said.

"The timing does *not* work," Yeral added. She was a plain woman with a freckled face and over-large bosom. She tried to style her hair but it tended to fall back straight and dish-water blonde. She been paired to the Duke, but her family had once ruled Uman City, and her father had been deposed. She'd served as a lady in waiting for the Empress and elevated from common to baroness without lands, with only that to legitimize her marriage to the son of the former King.

Lupus might seem to sit secure on his throne, but he'd clearly still felt the need to neutralize the old Stowe line.

All eyes turned to her. This woman had, in the last ten years, all but created the infamous Angadorian breed of horses, the most coveted by Angadorian Knights and Theran Lancers. Her worth was in her mind—she'd made her husband a wealthy man and, ultimately, a Duke with her ingenuity.

"Assuming no dalliance with her during his relationship with the Empress, then his slave," she said, "she'd have birthed a child before the Battle of Tamaran Glen."

"There was a period when Genna rarely saw the rest of the Free Legion, before she set up the meeting between Lupus and my father," Tartan Stowe said, holding a pile of withered vegetables on the end of his knife, before him. "She may have birthed it then."

"Or she may be lying," Dilvesh said. "Genna has done worse to slight Black Lupus."

Nina shook her head. "I looked into her eyes," she said. "I heard her words. I also saw her body—let there be no question, Genna birthed a child, and she believes in her heart the father of that child is Rancor Mordetur, Emperor of Eldador. She *also* believes this is his *eldest* child, so she must have birthed it during that time when she was away from the rest."

"Or lied," Yeral reasserted.

"Regardless," Dilvesh said, "we must contact the Emperor with this and let him know he has Genna's machinations to consider."

"This couldn't come at a worse time," Nina complained, putting her ragged piece of pork in her mouth.

"I don't see why," Tartan said, his brown eyes shifting between the persons at the table. "Lupus could have a thousand sons and all of them could be older than Lee and Vulpe, and it wouldn't matter. The Eldadorian law is not that the leader's eldest son succeeds him."

"Or else you would sit the throne," Yeral added.

She exchanged a glance with her husband. Nina regarded both of them and returned her attention to her meal.

Dilvesh thought *these* feelings were of more concern to the Emperor. There had been a time when nobles in the Eldadorian nation might have considered changing their laws and putting Tartan on the throne. That had been a time when Black Lupus, then just become Emperor, had nearly provoked every nation in Fovea to attack him. Many of the Dukes had shown concern that the new ruler took on too much, assumed too much, and they'd all pay for it with their lives and the lives of their people.

Then Black Lupus had won a decisive naval engagement with the Uman-Chi called *The Battle of the Deceptions*. After that, Eldador could boast decisive sea power in addition to the most feared land troops on the planet.

No one wanted to alienate Eldador. Now Black Lupus was starting that whole process again. It might be a good time for an ambitious Tartan Stowe to seek his future, if he wanted more than he already had.

"And so," Dilvesh said. Nina opened her mouth but Dilvesh interrupted her.

"However I know Clear Genna," he said. "And it doesn't matter to her what the law is, what the rules are or what protocol might dictate, not when it comes to Black Lupus. What will matter is that she has some imagined slight, she has some imagined cure for it, and she will focus a great deal of effort to secure that cure, especially if she believes she's entitled to it, which I'm sure she does."

"Making this something the Emperor needs to know," Nina said. "Do you have access to Central Communications from here?"

Dilvesh shook his head. "Central Communications is set up between specially tuned rooms between the key cities in the Empire," he said. "It lets Wizards communicate by sight and sound between the cities, but I can't just invoke it from here. It will be months before I can choose a room and tune it to Central Communications."

"Then I need to go to—" Nina said, but Dilvesh was shaking his head.

"No," he said. "You have an immediate mission, and you need to complete that."

Nina lowered her eyes. Yeral straightened.

"Messengers to Uman City should suffice," she said. "We can send a full Century if need be."

"I think that would be excessive," Tartan countered.

Dilvesh considered.

"You claim this group you're following split up, and now they'll try to get back together in Andurin," he said.

Nina nodded.

"And they have a beacon, made by the Uman-Chi, to allow her to find them again."

"Yes," Nina said, her eyes on him now.

Dilvesh smiled. "I don't suppose you can use that same beacon to find them?" he asked.

She shook her head. "I don't know how it's tuned," she said.

A Wizard would create a beacon to emit a call into the infinite aether, the stuff of the universe which contained all things and nothing. The Wizard would then look into the aether for that specific call. Because the aether is infinite and the things that resonate into it many, one looks like the next and someone who didn't know what he or she was looking for could find another Wizard, an enchanted weapon or a duck that swallowed the ingredients to a complicated spell.

This bellied methods more simple.

"I don't suppose the Salt Wood is overrun with magical beacons, created by Uman-Chi," he said. "I would think the beacon would have to be very powerful, and relatively near to us."

Nina frowned and looked into her plate. She closed her eyes, hummed for a moment, and then opened them, a smile on her face.

"I believe the Duke and his Lady could now be of great assistance to you," Dilvesh said.

**

"So they're out there waiting for us on the other side of an army," Karl said, repeating what Jahunga had told him.

Typical of the race of Men, Xinto couldn't help thinking.

"To the south their supply train stretches back to either Vrek or Angador," Jahunga said. "Perhaps both. They expect us to go to the north."

Xinto nodded. Karl with him.

"To the north, then," the Volkhydran said, looking to Xinto for approval.

The Scitai nodded.

"But that might put us—" Raven protested.

"That will put us right where they expected us to be," Xinto said, cutting her off. "And then they will think we are doing just what they expected us to do, and they will move past us and cut us off."

"Because with that many warriors, it's easier to ambush us

than to chase us," Jahunga said.

"They'll spread out to our north, while we double back in a day and come right back here," Karl said. By the time they realize we're not coming, we'll be gone to the west or the south."

Xinto nodded.

Clearly his intelligence was rubbing off on them.

Chapter Three

One Man's Sacrifice

For a day and a half, their little group of Volkhydrans, Toorians and whatever someone decided someday to call the rest of them travelled north toward the city of Andurin in the Salt Wood. For a day and a half they travelled back.

The Angadorian army shadowed them the whole way.

"They know we're here," Karl informed the rest of them, as if he needed to.

"Their scouts are poor," Jahunga informed them, "or we would be among them now, in chains. It will not be long, though, before they simply enter the woods and drive us to the ocean."

"I don't know why they haven't done so already," Xinto said. They were sitting in one of the many little glens that formed throughout the Salt Wood. The trees were mostly fir and pine, twisted by the wind that constantly swept in from the Sea. They tended to look more like tall creatures reaching for them, especially at night, and even more so in their current situation.

At least, that's what Raven thought.

"Okay," she said, "if they know we're here, and they aren't coming to get us, then it's because someone's telling them not to."

"Or no one has told them *to* yet," Xinto added. "They could be under command just to keep us here until the Emperor arrives."

"I don't think Rancor Mordetur handles things like this himself," Karl said. "He already sent Nina—she's the one who knows we're in the Wood now. If they're waiting for anyone, they're waiting for her."

"I've never seen or heard of Nina of the Aschire commanding troops," Karl said.

"But Tartan Stowe does," Jahunga countered. "I saw *him*

myself. If they're waiting for anyone, they're waiting for their Duke."

"They're waiting for both, then," Xinto concluded. "And if they aren't with their troops already, they soon will be. Then they'll come find us."

"But *how*?" Raven pressed them. This was frustrating. "And why hasn't Glynn come found us? She's some kind of wizard, why doesn't she just pull us out of here?"

"I don't think her beacon allows Magee to do that," Jahunga said. "When our own shamans use a beacon, it's to find those who might be lost—oh!"

All eyes turned to Jahunga. His shoulder slumped and he shook his head.

"What?" Xinto and Karl demanded together.

"The beacon," Jahunga said. He turned his face to Raven. "Where is it now?" he asked her.

"I don't know," she said. "I'm not supposed to touch it."

"Try and find it," he said to her. "Think about it, not for what it is, but think about the magic of it; look for something magical that doesn't belong."

Raven searched Jahunga's face, then shrugged. Nina hadn't taught her how to do anything like this. She knew a little of the nature of magical things, but not...

When she'd learned to manipulate the flame on the candle, she'd first watched Nina do it, and it was like she could imagine her finger touching the flame as Nina manipulated it. She did that now— she imagined her arm reaching out through all of them, the fingers of this imaginary hand touching them, touching their things, feeling their possessions.

Clothes, weapons, all of that just felt dead and plain. Their minds, their thoughts—she couldn't read them but she could tell they were there, little tingles of activity. She looked for more of that—but more powerful, more focused, more regular. A beacon would pulse, she decided. It would say, "I am here," so Glynn could find it.

She smiled. "In Karl's pack," she said. "Wrapped in a blanket."

"War's beard," Karl swore.

Xinto shook his head.

"So we're letting them know where we are, and Glynn probably already knows this and that's why she's staying away," he said.

"Or she is doing something to keep them from pursuing us," Jahunga said.

"Regardless," Karl said, "we need to send that beacon back to Glynn, and she needs to destroy it."

"Give it to Raven and let her destroy it right now," Jahunga said.

"And leave Glynn to believe we've been captured?" Xinto asked. "She'll be away from here as fast as her horse can carry her."

Raven shook her head. "Get it," she said to Karl.

He turned to her, then to Xinto. The Scitai shrugged.

Karl went to the pack on his horse.

"Slurn!" Raven hissed.

In a wink, the saurian melted out of the shrubbery. He stood up next to Raven and hissed at her.

"Do you know where Glynn and Jack are?" she asked him.

He hissed. Xinto translated, "He does, or he can find them."

Karl returned with the beacon—a simple steel rod. He handed it to Raven.

She stepped back from it and pointed to Slurn.

"Give it to him," she said.

Karl held out the rod. Slurn took it in his webbed claw, then transferred it to his teeth.

Without another word he was gone.

Raven called after him, "Be careful!"

Karl snorted. "We didn't even tell him what to do," he said.

* * *

Slurn slithered through the tall grass to the north of the Angadorian army. He held a steel rod in his jaws, one he'd seen many times before—a beacon for the Uman-Chi enchantress.

He had no magic among his people. They didn't cast spells, they didn't have shamans. Water, their goddess, gave her people nothing other than the promise of her return.

As the sun rose, the army rumbled awake. Pots and pans clattered, horses neighed, Men and Uman grumbled their good mornings. In his home, his mates would be packing their unhatched eggs with fresh mud, or teaching the newborn how to strain for minnows and frogs.

The plains grass whipped his scales and left him feeling dry.

He'd become stiff for lack of water, and testy. He didn't look forward to a meeting with the bullying Swamp Devil as he crawled up the ridge where he'd seen them last.

They'd had the sense to get out of the light, anyway. He found them on the dark side of a hill, Glynn, Jack, a woman of the race of Men, Zarshar, three horses and a dog.

He'd eaten dog before. He liked the taste. The thing growled at him as if in recognition of his fate as a meal.

"Slurn?" Glynn stepped away from her own mount. She was thinner than when he'd last seen her, and she'd been a waif then.

He hissed his greeting. She spoke the language of Water and Earth, his own.

"We sensed you on the other side of this army, then moving toward us," she said. "We'd hoped to attract you all. We fear our enemy has found us out."

He handed her the beacon, and informed her that their group also believed Nina of the Aschire knew of this thing, and had likely parked this army here to capture them. He informed her of Nina's capture, and of her educating Raven in the beginnings of her spell casting.

Glynn sighed. "Well, certainly, I can neutralize this," Glynn said, and stroked the beacon with her index finger. "I assume there is a meeting place for our two groups?"

Slurn informed her they had told Nina they were heading for Andurin, so in fact they could go anywhere else.

He hadn't been introduced to this new female. Typical of the Uman-Chi, who considered him an animal.

Jack shook his head and took the rod from Glynn. "Run and they'll just follow you," he said. "If I were the Emperor, I would have worked out a way for the cities to communicate between each other by now. They'll cut us off and we'll be caught."

"And your plan, Sirrah?" Glynn asked him.

"No matter what they have, they can't keep up with Little Storm," he said. "I'll run him just ahead of their army until I've gotten them all out from between you. You regroup back to the Silent Isle and I'll find you there."

Glynn's face was difficult for Slurn to read, but even he saw the scorn. "And how will you get to my homeland, Sirrah?" she asked him. "I think your mount cannot swim."

Zarshar sighed. Even that made Slurn's blood boil. To tolerate such a one, over and over, speaking in its arrogance, filled him with a gut-wrenching anger.

"Give him your gold," the Swamp Devil said. "I think he can muster the wherewithal to hire a boat."

"He is a hunted Man," Glynn protested.

"I'll be that no matter what," Jack said.

Slurn hissed his agreement. As the sun continued to climb past the horizon, he reminded them they needed to be off, and quickly.

Jack kicked his stallion in the ribs and reached into Glynn's hand and took the rod. Slurn was surprised—he didn't expect any of them to be so bold with the Uman-Chi. He felt even more surprised that she tolerated it.

"Is there any way for you to get a message to me, if you don't end up going to Outpost IX?" Jack asked her.

"I could find a way to use the beacon," Glynn said. "However, you must discard that as soon as you can. If I replace it, then our enemies will have you as soon as they derive it."

"Perhaps I might be of assistance," the other female said. "Extend your hand to me, Jack."

Jack pulled the reins to his left and Little Storm stepped up to the woman's charger. Jack reached out his hand to her, and she took it.

Without preamble, she pulled a curved dagger from her belt, concealed in her white robes, and pricked the end of his finger. He gasped as she pressed out a few drops of blood into her palm.

Slurn stood up on his hind legs in time to see the woman's palm absorb the blood. She looked up into Jack's brown eyes and said, "I've taken a small part of you into my person now. For three cycles of the moon, I will be able to sense you, and to send you images, while your bare feet touch Fovean soil. If you need me, then put your skin to the ground and think of me. If I need you, I will wait for such an event.

Jack nodded. He turned his head to Slurn and said, "Tell Raven I'm alright, and I'll see her soon."

Slurn hissed. Glynn didn't translate, but hardly needed to.

He turned back to Zarshar. "Look out for the dog—she'll want to follow me and she'll slow me down."

The Swamp Devil laid a surprisingly gentle hand on the animal, who warmed to him and wagged its tail. Slurn didn't expect that. He'd never known any sort of kindness from their kind, especially not toward a lesser creature. A Swamp Devil would be more likely to torture such an animal out of his own meanness.

"I admit I've grown attached to the thing," he said. "I suppose I could be bothered to watch out for it."

Jack smiled that frightening, toothy smile that Men did. "I'd be forever in your debt," he said.

A debt to a Devil is no less than the cost of your soul, Slurn thought to himself.

With no more preamble, Jack kicked Little Storm into motion and ran south, away from their destination.

Slurn could already see the changes among these people. Watching the Man ride away, he wondered what else would change.

* * *

"They're moving," Nina informed the Duke and Duchess, leaping into their pavilion through the tent slit. She'd already dressed out in her leather pants and halter, daggers on her thighs.

Duke Stowe stirred in his travel furs, his wife clearly naked under the furs beside him. He rolled over onto his back and propped himself up on his elbows.

Nina had known this man since Lupus had been elevated to King. She'd watched the changes in him, from beaten-down son of a drunken monarch, to over-taxed apprentice to a rising Emperor, to Earl, to Duke, to one of the most important men in the Empire.

With power had come ambition. Tartan stank of it now.

"I would ask if you would treat the Emperor this way, but I know from personal experience that you do," he grumbled. "When you say, 'They're moving,' I assume you mean these friends of yours?"

"You know I do," she said. "South, toward Angador."

That got his attention. "We've all but emptied out the garrison," he said. "With any sort of force at all—"

"Be calm, your grace," Nina said, crossing the pavilion and taking a seat on a chest. She didn't like this—too gaudy. Too much 'stuff,' too much work to move it. The Emperor slept in little more than a bedroll, perhaps a tent if he brought the Empress. He'd been a common once. He didn't see the value of opulence.

"They're only a few. If they recruited all of the rats of Kor, they wouldn't have a thousand. What could they do with that?"

"Wreak some bloody havoc," the Duke said. His wife sat up topless from her furs, saw Nina and, wide-eyed, covered herself.

"My lady," Nina inclined her head.

"Unannounced and uninvited," Yeral sputtered. "I know the Emperor keeps a loose etiquette—"

"Beloved, please," Stowe interrupted her. Looking at Nina he asked, "When did they start moving?"

"They have an hour on us, moving fast. Even if Little Storm can keep up that pace, they'll kill their other horses if they try."

Tartan stood, a loin cloth his only clothing, and pulled his hose from a pile next to the furs. "It will take no less than three hours to rouse the camp," he said. "Summon my captains—"

"Done," Nina told him, a smile on her lips. She'd campaigned with the Emperor before. "And fast riders out to try and catch them. They won't, but they'll leave a fresh trail for us to follow."

Stowe nodded. "Well done, Nina. If you'll excuse us, then…"

Nina nodded and stood, shooting a glance at the Duchess trying to wiggle into a cloth nightgown under the furs. The Lady Shela would have realized they had nothing amongst spouses and women to hide and just stood to greet her.

With a little extra swing to her hips, she sauntered out of the pavilion. Cooks were already scrambling to put together a fast travel paste for the warriors. The Wolf Soldiers had remained in Lupor, and the Angadorian Knights were no Wolf Soldiers, even if they had the training. More like Eldadorian regulars, not necessarily playing at soldiers, but not the soldiers others could be.

On an order from the Emperor, Wolf Soldiers would be marching in less than half an hour. They'd eat on the way if they had to, or do without, the pain giving them an edge.

She could still feel the talisman Karl carried, moving south. She'd have to tell the Emperor the Hero of Tamara had turned against them. She didn't look forward to that.

All the while, and off and on for these last weeks, actually a month now, she'd been flashing on that last encounter with the Emperor, where she'd defied him, where he'd beaten her.

She should hate him for that, she knew. She'd like to think Krell would hear of it and be at the Emperor's throat with a knife, however he'd be more likely to finish on her what Lupus had begun.

No one—*no one*—raised a hand to Rancor Mordetur. All

threats were destroyed. The Emperor had told her once, "Never leave an enemy standing. Destroy them, ruin them, make others dread their fate. There's no nobility in being struck back, it just hurts and makes you weaker."

But he'd left her standing, just hurt her. Afterward he'd sought her out, asked if she still wanted to be here, asked if she thought she had anything left to learn from them. Sent her on this mission.

Because he needed someone he could trust.

She'd wrapped her arms around his neck and lifted her feet up off the ground. Hanging from his shoulders, his arm around her middle, she'd wept into his neck and told him she wanted to be with the royal family.

She would always be Nina of the Aschire, but she was Nina of the Mordetur, too.

Whom he could trust, she thought. That one memory diminished all others. She'd looked into those blue, blue eyes and she'd loved him like any daughter of his issue. She pledged to return successful and he'd believed it.

"If you get in trouble," he'd told her, "there is Dilvesh, in Vrek, and there are the Stowes, in Angador. Dilvesh would die bloody before betraying me. The Stowes, I think, are more vassal than friend. I became a father to the boy whose father had betrayed him, and the one became the other."

She got that. When the time came, she'd done exactly as he'd expected, she felt sure. Now they would move south. Now she would complete a complicated but not inglorious mission.

* * *

"You let him go?"

Glynn was surprised at this Raven, gone so short a time. She sat straighter in her saddle. She had that confidence, that self-control, which marked a Caster of any kind. Nina had begun and then abandoned her training, and now the student had her own ideas.

"Indeed, there was no stopping him," Glynn informed her, once again. They had rejoined in the shadow of the Salt Wood, and already begun the journey west.

It had been Raven's first instinct to run off after her aging lover, but that might have proved suicidal with an entire army between them. Glynn had reminded Raven this was not self-sacrifice, but indeed self-preservation for them all. No horse alive save one could catch Little Storm.

Tears streamed her face. Raven clearly yearned for this Jack. She found the reaction on the face of the now-identified Karl Henekhson more interesting.

No wonder he hadn't wanted the Emperor to see him on that fateful night, when she'd met him in Galnesh Eldador. The Emperor would want long words with the Hero of Tamara, unannounced on Eldadorian soil.

Karl clearly had thoughts on this Raven. Glynn wondered if that could benefit her in the short and the long run.

"Do you think the gaffer can make it on his own back to Outpost IX?" Karl asked her, a sideways look at a stiff-chinned Raven. "I know the horse is capable—"

"Don't be fool enough to underestimate that one," Zarshar told Karl, the dog at his feet. "He's sharp as a claw and deadly as he needs to be. He'll make the lot of them look stupid and likely beat us to Outpost IX just to remind us who he is."

Where this affinity for Jack came from, Glynn couldn't imagine, but if it meant the Swamp Devil had abandoned the idea of killing them in their sleep, so be it.

"And now we have the one who fights as does the sun," Jahunga said, eyeing Vedeen. "A Druid of our own, to counter the one among the Daff Kanaar."

Vedeen smiled. "I think you overestimate me, goodsir," she said. "The Green One is not someone to counter. He is a friend to the world, as I am, and I might remind you again, before you write answers to your song, you must consider the proper questions."

That irritated Glynn no end. The greatest minds among the Uman-Chi, Angron Aurelias himself, had poured over the song. Druids may be wise, but a candle to a volcano compared to Uman-Chi wisdom, crossing centuries of Life.

The sun fought with the power of Earth and Weather, of course. It warmed and it cooled, it crossed the sky and left it darkened. It fought *eventually*, not immediately. Of *course* it was a Druid—she'd surmised no less when first she'd realized their destination was the Lone Wood.

D'gattis had informed her his might was no match for Dilvesh of the Daff Kanaar, in a battle of wills. However, in a battle to the finish, he knew he would prevail. Uman-Chi subtlety and the tactics of hundreds of years' studies would outmatch what Dilvesh could possible gather in his short breath of years.

So, too, with this Vedeen. She spoke for the Druids and had taken over Dilvesh's post as guardian of the Lone Wood, but in fact she represented no more than a sprinkling of power and knowledge, compared to her.

So as they rode north Glynn occupied herself instead with this weepy girl and her newfound powers, beginning Raven's re-training by asking her, "Girl, tell me—what do you *think* you know about spell casting?"

* * *

Jack rode all day and didn't sleep that first night they were chasing him, because he was pretty sure they would expect him to. He was one man, scared and tired. He had a horse to think about. He had the ability to be hidden and he needed the sun to see by. So he trusted to the moon, moved slowly and navigated by that, and he followed an ellipsis, not a straight line, using the compass he'd bought for himself in Lee's Hope.

By making a great arc away from the Forgotten Sea, his path would seem entirely random. Even when they picked up his trail, and he was sure they would, they would never know why he was following it, meaning they wouldn't get ahead of him.

When the sun rose he made camp, picking out what might have been a farm at one point, abandoned now, flat places in the earth with tell-tale lumps where someone had once built what settlers had called a 'soddy.' He hadn't heard any pursuit, no baying dogs, no thundering horses. Those following him would be back there, he felt sure, but that didn't bother him if they could never catch him.

If they got ahead of him, he was sunk, and that was what he couldn't allow. He still had his falchion but knew he wasn't good enough to fight real warriors.

Of all of the things he could be missing, he felt lonely for the dog. He hadn't had one in a long time—a little Springer Spaniel named, "Molly Malone." His wife had gotten her in their divorce. He'd actually created reasons to go see her in order to visit with the dog and throw a stick for her.

This new one had been wet-mouthed like Molly, less of a character but more of a companion. She seemed to have a need to touch people to be comforted.

Jack yanked the saddle from Little Storm's back and began to brush him down, working out the giant sweat stain from his back and shoulders and from the girth under his ribs. The horse had run quiet all night, the same pace, not a sound from him. Jack had rested him for what he considered to be about ten minutes every hour. For all Little Storm seemed to care, he might not have bothered, but an overworked horse could collapse or run himself lame, he knew, and his whole life depended on the mount now.

Little Storm began cropping grass the moment Jack stopped brushing him, letting him pick his hooves for pebbles. Jack spent a half hour poking around but didn't even find a woodchuck for company. Finally he lay down on his bedroll with his head on his pillow, closed his eyes to the rising sun and lay still, waiting for sleep to take him. He felt exhausted and expected it to come quickly.

"Good morning to you," he heard in his mind.

That gave him a start. He leapt up and saw no one, heard nothing but the stallion munching grass where he'd picketed it.

"We're resting," he heard again inside his mind. The voice was gender-neutral, he saw nothing but blackness in his mind. "I thought I might find you finally—you must have ridden all night."

"Who is this?" he asked himself. He had no idea if something or someone could hear him, but he didn't think that he should speak out loud.

"Why, who do you think it is, great bear?" the voice asked. "I told you I could speak to you this way, when your body touched the ground."

Jack felt immediately suspicious. The Druid would have just said who she was. This seemed like a trick Nina would play, maybe even Shela. He forced himself not to think of the Druid's name as he thought, "Glynn?"

He almost wanted to think, "Melissa," but that meant giving up her name, Shela might not know yet that Raven was spell casting.

"You are clever," the voice said. "But Glynn made no such claim. Think back to the moment behind the ridge, before you took the rod from her hand."

Okay, only Vedeen would know that. He felt his shoulders relax as he settled back into the horse blanket. "Why play games like that?" he asked.

A chuckle in his mind. "Because you must be careful in this world, my friend," she told him.

"Alright," he thought, "finish this: *In nomine patri, et fili.*"

Nothing.

"Still there?"

Nothing. Jack waited. He remembered the Swamp Devil's reactions to those words. Maybe he shouldn't have used them.

Maybe that was *exactly* what he should do.

His mind stayed quiet. He thought it might be a good time to get going, but in fact if his enemies were on to him, then this was the best time to stay pat.

Wondering these things, he drifted off to sleep despite himself, his last thoughts that he wasn't as young as he used to be.

Chapter Four

On the Run

Perched atop the sidesaddle of her Eldadorian charger, moving north to a ship and, perhaps, home, Baroness Glynn Escaroth had come to hate a word, spoken either in Uman or the language of Men.

That word was, "Why;" the favorite of her energetic protégé.

"Because magic obeys certain laws?" she informed Raven, sitting her own charger side saddle in her Andaron raider outfit, oblivious to the fact she was telling the world she thought she was pregnant.

Raven frowned. She had come to call this 'the waiting stage.' The girl would frown, as if angry at the power of the gods, and then restructure her attack, and come after Glynn on another front.

She had an odd mind, this one. The Emperor's people thought differently than those of Fovea. Born of another reality, Glynn would expect by definition they would not think the same way. How odd to be faced with that actuality before she could even explore the theory.

Raven shook her head, her long black hair flying. "No, no, no," she insisted. "You don't understand."

Glynn allowed herself a deprecating smiled. "Do I not?"

"No," Raven told her. "I mean, you understand magic, you don't understand my question."

"You seek to know the source of magic, and I informed you it was elemental," Glynn said. She let her eyes stray out across the plains. Loping half of a daheer ahead of them, Zarshar crossed the plain as their point guard. An equal distance behind them she could see Jahunga with his Toorians, running with spears over their backs. Karl rode either to the left or the right, presently the latter, his Volkhydrans opposite him. This left Xinto with the women, Glynn, Vedeen and Raven, to the center, and their dog and Slurn roving to any point of the compass. They'd spent two days on the road, Jack having drawn off all pursuit.

Since then Raven had been persistent in her eagerness to learn the craft. It was at first encouraging—Men are by their nature capricious in their quest for knowledge, taking little bites here and there and not sinking in their teeth to any one discipline. That Raven should commit wholeheartedly spoke of rare focus for her people.

Then she saw the other side of the mind of her people: savage, almost animal tenacity. It was very rare and terrible—Glynn could only assume the loss of her lover inspired her to greater efforts. The Emperor himself showed signs of this behavior. The race of Men possessed the ability to focus on one goal to the exclusion of all else, taking giant strides, even to the deterioration of their own health and well-being. Glennen Stowe had been such a Man. Now she recognized it in their Raven.

"But that doesn't *mean* anything," Raven insisted. "There is no elemental home of fire. It is like saying there is an elemental home of sand. I can get sand anywhere."

"Sand is the flesh of the god, Earth," Glynn informed her—again. The girl wasn't dense; she simply had strange and basically incorrect assumptions she had to work out of her mind, in order to move forward. Every mentor since the first student had needed to do the same thing, however Glynn had never mentored before.

In a perfect world she would have stayed Raven's progress until she worked these issues out for herself, either through study or meditation. This was far from a perfect world, however, and they enjoyed precious little time.

"No," Raven informed her, once again. "Sand is a mixture of chemicals, mostly silicon, which has certain properties, like when you heat it, you can turn it into glass."

"The eyes of Earth," Glynn informed her.

Raven sighed. The truth could be frustrating—not everyone

could absorb it.

"You think there is a place where fire is born," Raven said, "and you think that you can go there, in your mind, get some, and bring it back here."

"I have done so many times," Glynn said. "I discipline my mind to find the way, so I can travel there quickly, when I need."

"So how does a candle do it?"

"A candle can't, it must be lit."

"How about flint and steel?"

"They are opposites and hate each other," Glynn began.

"Oh, please."

"If you reject the knowledge, I cannot make you learn," Glynn allowed her irritation into her voice that time.

And then, the frown again.

"Okay," Raven tried again, "you understand how you get steam from boiling water?"

"Water rejects the fire's fury," Glynn informed her.

The destination would never arrive soon enough.

* * *

Tartan Stowe decided he would rise early rather than late for a change, and ordered his guard to wake him with the first dawn. He'd intended to run out to the pickets and conduct inspections of his sentries. Lupus had taught him long ago that it was better *he* should surprise them than his enemies.

He'd just pulled on his boots when a scream shook the camp.

His sword, still in its sheath, lay across a chest next to his furs. He grabbed it instinctively and swung it free of its scabbard as he leapt out into the dawn through his tent flap. Scrambling warriors greeted him, forming a circle around Nina of the Aschire, on all fours outside of her own collapsed tent, pounding the ground with her fist and shrieking.

He ran to her side, forcing himself through the crowd of blank-faced warriors, and knelt beside her. Blood flowed free from her nose and dripped down her ear lobes. Tartan had seen this before. She'd been casting, and something had gone wrong.

An Eldadorian wizard had taught him of what they called, "Blacklash," the return of energies directed out by the caster. One would send a simple query, a finding spell, something innocuous, and its power would be fired back as a weapon along the same conduit to the unsuspecting caster.

Shela's protégé should have been trained too well.

"Nina," he demanded, taking her by the shoulder. He'd been trained to handle this, as a commander of such people, because when a wizard fell it would be natural for all eyes to turn to him. Mere Men and Uman feared those so gifted.

"Nina," he repeated, shaking her as she screamed, pounding a bloody spot on the ground beneath her, her knuckles already raw. "Focus, Nina. Overcome it. You're on the Eldadorian plains, you're in my army. You're escorting me to find rebels to the Empire."

"I *know* where I am," she growled through gritted teeth. Even these were lined with blood. "I'd thought I found them for you, but it seems that this 'Jack' has more close to his vest than a big belly."

She stopped punching the ground, turned over on her hip, and sat. She raised her left fist between them, regarded her bloody knuckles and chuckled a little, curling her tongue over her pinkish teeth.

"What happened," Tartan demanded. Behind him, he could feel the Men and Uman part, and guessed the Duchess had found her way to them.

Nina looked him in the eyes. Tartan had so rarely seen eyes of grey, and Nina's, he admitted, had always fascinated him. They seemed full of chagrin now—one of the Emperor's "you got me" looks, where he lost a little and admitted it.

Nina considered herself his daughter as much as an Aschire. That was no secret to anyone.

"Last night I went out to look at the tracks we're following," she said. "Your clever scouts failed to inform you they are from one horse with huge hooves."

"Little Storm?" Tartan had been informed of the Emperor's gift to his kinsman.

Nina nodded. "He took their beacon and ran south, and we followed him as he intended. His allies are half way to Andurin by now, just as they planned. He knows that, on Little Storm, we'll never catch him, and eventually he'll run full out and perhaps even beat them to Groff's city."

"If he's for Groff's city then he's Groff's problem," Tartan informed her, standing. He extended his hand and she surprised him by taking it. Nina must have been sorely tested if she admitted weakness of any kind. "Inform Lupor's new governor what's happened, and we'll return to Angador.

She shook her head. "If we know where he'll be going then we can cut him off from getting there," she said. "We can spread our warriors west and, when he doubles back, we'll have him."

"First of all," Yeral said, stepping up next to Tartan, "these aren't *our* warriors, these are Angadorian Knights who answer to the Duke. Second, on Little Storm, no one of us will catch this Man no matter what we do. He'll charge our lines—"

Tartan found himself shaking his head, even as he saw Nina doing the same. Yeral had been an unfortunate choice for a bride for him, a woman of great mind but of no family. Now she grasped power whenever she could find it and did everything she could to poison him against the Emperor, a man she blamed for disgracing her father and her family.

In fact, Tartan didn't hate the Emperor, he merely knew he would never *be* the Emperor, and to a Man like Rancor Mordetur, such failure seemed unforgivable. Tartan could never learn enough, never know enough, and never be brave enough to do more than darken the Emperor's shadow.

Tartan Stowe's father had let a kingdom down, and never tried to teach his son to replace him, as a son should have. Lupus' crime was to attempt that training, only to realize Tartan wasn't up to it.

What Lupus had done to him was far worse.

"Little Storm is a fast horse," Tartan said, "but not invincible. The Man we seek is still old. He'll come north eventually, and when he does, he won't outrun our archers, especially on the plains."

He turned to Nina. "Go to the Emperor and tell him about this," he said. "Don't send someone, go yourself. We have our own wizards, but you have seen things the Emperor *must* know."

"I am assigned—" Nina began.

"I am the *Duke* of Angador," Tartan informed her. He caught his wife's smirk even as the Aschire girl straightened. "As the Emperor would say, this is 'my call.' You and I both know the only thing he hates more than failure is to be kept in the shadow."

"In the dark," Nina said, frowning. The blood was already drying on her face. She sighed. "You're right—it's time to get back to him. He'll have a lot of questions, and I have to answer them."

She took Tartan by his upper arm, and looked him in the face. Normally Tartan didn't like to be touched, but Nina, if not an actual friend, had known him longer than most. They'd both been schooled in some way under the Emperor.

"Be careful of him, your Grace," Nina told him. "He's more than he seems. Whatever he did to me, he almost killed me. I know Raven has learned some magix, but whatever this Jack has, he wields it like a hammer and he's hidden it even from the Empress."

Tartan nodded. "I'm not without my resources either, Nina of the Aschire," he said, and they both smiled to each other. "When we were living in Galnesh Eldador, it wasn't always *you* getting *me* into trouble."

She grinned even wider. It was a rare site from Nina of the Aschire, the watch-bitch of the Emperor's scions.

She turned and she sprinted towards the back of a horse, just being saddled. A natural acrobat, she placed two hands on its rump and vaulted into his saddle, taking the reins as the gelding reared.

"That's—" Yeral began, but he raised two fingers and quieted her. It was one of his personal horses, of the three that he rode during the day. If it bore her safe to the Emperor, she was welcome to it.

"I've more horses," Tartan informed her. Nina already had the skittish mount under control and was picking her way to the outskirts of the camp—the jess doonar or 'little city' that Wolf Soldiers made.

Tartan turned on his heel to find his captains and to inform them of the change in their strategy. Let the old man run, he thought.

He had one place to go, and it was through Tartan Stowe now.

Let him try *that* twice.

* * *

Damn!

There, on the edge of his vision, Jack saw Eldadorian soldiers, standing atop a hill, looking south for him.

It had been like this for three days. As fast as he could travel west, he'd seen Eldadorians on the prowl from him.

They hadn't gotten ahead of him, Jack thought, they just hadn't gotten out from behind him.

He'd come to reconcile himself to the idea that it had been Nina or Shela, not Vedeen, in his brain three days ago, and he'd tipped his hand to her.

Since then he'd dropped the beacon in a stream, making a little raft for it, in hope they'd go chasing it. No such luck! They were on every hilltop and in every valley, rooting through every farmhouse for him. They'd nearly trapped him a dozen times, and they had to know they were close to him.

He needed to send them in another direction, at least long enough for him to get through their lines. Once to their north, he could make a straight line to one of the little fishing villages on Tren Bay and then to Outpost IX.

Jack watched the patrol, but they weren't moving.

"You, there!" someone said from behind him, in the language of Men.

Jack's heart almost leapt out of his chest.

He turned to see an Uman farmer, a woman next to him, a pitchfork in his hand. They had a dog at their side, not a mastiff like the one he'd befriended, something more like a retriever, its ears pinned back, not showing his teeth but ready to.

"Good day, good sir," he said, inclining his head.

"Don't good sir me," the Uman said. "You're the one they're on about, aren't you?"

Damn it! If he ran, they'd yell for those soldiers and, if he didn't, then they'd turn him over to them.

"I'm, um—don't suppose you'd care if I'm unjustly accused, would you?" Jack stammered. A soft close, from his experience as a sales person. If you can't make the sale, then beg for sympathy and have them sell themselves.

The Uman shook his head. "If you're thinking I'm going to turn you over to the Empire, then you're a stranger to these lands. Just wanted to make sure I was helping out someone worth helping," he said, and his wife beside him, a skinny waif with long, green hair, smiled. "If you're smart, you'll walk that pony after me, and then at dusk we'll send you out by Milly's Gulch. Only locals knows that route; it'll get you out of our lives 'fore the next dawn."

Glynn had informed him, what seemed like months ago, the Emperor's subjects didn't love him. He'd spoken to the porters who feared the Emperor would hurt them just because he could. If these felt the same way then maybe he had a chance?

More likely they'd hold him until someone else brought that patrol around.

Either way, he might get a free meal out of it, and he was already starving. He dismounted.

"I'm in your debt, good sir," he said, and lowered his head.

His wife giggled. "Well," the Uman said. "You sure as don't

look like some threat to the Empire. My guess is you're just another Man, got into the wrong place when you least expected it."

Jack smiled, extending a hand to the Uman, "You have no idea," he said.

* * *

"Crap on a cracker!"

"Pardon?" Glynn's eyebrows rose over her ambiguous eyes.

Raven refocused her mind, and reapplied her will.

The sun was setting to their west, the sky turned pink and black, clouds floated above her with bloody fringes and the land around her had that unearthly dusk light to them. Their warriors or helpers or whatever they called themselves had collected a pile of dead branches and Glynn had asked her to light them with her magic.

She'd called fire before, but now she had all of these make-no-sense images of elemental planes of fire in her head, and she couldn't reach them, so she couldn't call the flame.

Maybe Glynn's real goal had been to neutralize her power. If so, she'd done a good job.

"If you aren't able…" Glynn said, as condescendingly as ever.

She felt a hand on her shoulder and turned to see Vedeen's sea-blue eyes. The Druid had her hair bound down her left shoulder in front of her, and that silly, serene look she always seemed to have.

"I think you've mixed your metaphors, sweet one," she said.

Beside her, the dog thumped its tail and seemed to grin up at Raven. The first time she'd seen it, she couldn't help thinking, "That is the ugliest friggin' dog I've ever seen." It followed either Zarshar or Vedeen everywhere.

"My—metaphors?" she repeated. She knew the word, but she didn't know if it meant the same in Uman as it did in English.

"You used to have an idea of what fire is," Vedeen said.

"The *wrong* idea," Glynn asserted. Raven just nodded.

Vedeen smiled. "The Uman-Chi focus their teaching on form more than substance," she said. "They achieve great power, this is true, but it is more important to them that they achieve it for certain reasons."

"Or else we'd be just—" Glynn began, but then caught herself.

"Or else you'd be just *Men*," Raven finished for her.

Glynn's silver-on-silver eyes could have been looking anywhere.

Raven straightened her back.

It didn't matter if flame came from an elemental plane of fire or existed as the transfer of matter to kinetic energy as carbon and oxygen molecules recombined.

In fact, in her mind's eye, she could see those molecules doing just that. She looked at a branch in the pile before her, really *looked* at it, and imagined in her mind all of the molecules it must be composed of, all of the atoms in those molecules, neutrons and protons and electrons flying around, crashing into each other but still holding form in a lattice that made this thing a branch.

In her mind, she broke the rule, and she took away a little piece of that branch, freed a portion of it from being wood, and let it be protons, neutrons and electrons, all swirling in a mass.

As she did this in her mind's eye, her actual eyes saw a corner of a branch waiver, then become a silvery globule pulsing and sparking next to the pile.

The wood, wet and dry, burst into flame.

"Gently, Raven, gently," Vedeen chided her. "You release all of its energy—but energy—"

"Cannot be created, and cannot be destroyed," she said, to the other women, clamping her will down with these mental muscles Nina had helped her to develop. "It can only change form."

"Or be sent to another plane," Glynn insisted. "Though even then, something must be drawn from there."

It would be pointless, Raven thought, to make the freed neutrons and protons back into wood. They had plenty of wood. Instead, she imagined the crystal lattice of a blood-red ruby. She'd studied the corundum in her last semester in college.

That brought back memories she had to beat back like flies from distracting her. The lattice of a corundum is actually a very basic one, which is what makes them perfect for lasers.

The globule coalesced, and she imagined the air around it, underneath it, couching it, then moving it to her on a pillow.

Like a shot from a gun, the ultra-hard surface flew at her. Vedeen plucked it out of the air before it caught her square between the eyes.

"Perhaps not ready yet to combine spells," she said, nonchalantly admiring the ruby. It was as big as a thumb, the facets cut at crazy angles; not raw, but perhaps the product of a jeweler who couldn't make up his mind?

Glynn gave a little grunt. "Couldn't be real," she said.

Vedeen raised her eyebrows. "Isn't it, though?" she asked. "Surely you know more about such things than I?"

"Give it here," Xinto waddled up from behind them. The other Men were watching, as well, from a safe distance.

Vedeen knelt down and stroked the side of Xinto's beard, much as she did the dog. Xinto took the ruby, held it to the campfire, then pulled a jeweler's loop from one of the many pockets in his robe.

Jimmy Hoffa has to be hiding in one of those, Raven thought.

"As real as it needs to be," he said, finally. He palmed the ruby for its weight. "Big as any Dwarf has found. Would you like for me to hold this?"

He looked up innocently at Raven, but she wasn't fooled.

"Be the last you'll see of it," Karl grumbled. He'd gotten his shirt off and walked past her in his breeches, grazing her elbow with his abdomen. He plucked the ruby from the Scitai's greedy fingers.

"Give that here," Glynn commanded him. He straightened, then looked at Raven.

Eventually they all had a look. Xinto tried several times to get her to let him keep it. Finally he admitted the stone was worth a Duke's ransom.

"You'd do well not to display that," Karl told her, the scar on his face ruddy in the firelight, once they'd all settled down. "Someone is going to convince himself he can get it away from you before we can catch him."

"Oh, let her," Vedeen said, smiling. She lay on her hip on the ground, close to the fire; her robes spread out in a blanket and dressed in a brown leather bra and skirt that she wore beneath. Xinto, pervert that he was, had positioned himself for a full view of her ass.

"It's so beautiful," she said. "I love the cuts—how did you decide on them?"

"Actually, I didn't," she admitted. Glynn was holding it now, its reflection in her silver-on-silver eyes. "I just thought of that plasma becoming a ruby, and it did."

"Plasma?" Vedeen said. "I do not know this word."

"Plasma is, well, hmmm—well, in my world, we study chemistry," she began.

"Chem–stree?" Glynn said. That had gotten her attention.

"You know chem–stree?"

Raven straightened on her bedroll. She had her raider's cloak where she could pull it over her when the night got cold, which it still did at this time of year, four days into the month of War.

"I studied it on what you call a *hoonar*—a place of learning for the young by the wise."

Vedeen nodded. "We have the Collection of the Oaks among the Druids—where the wise teach the novices."

"Among the Uman-Chi, we have apprentices and masters," Glynn said. "Mine was Chaheff—I was very fortunate."

"Well, we call it a college, or a university," Raven began but Glynn uncharacteristically interrupted her.

"The Emperor spoke to an Uman-Chi you know, D'gattis, about chem-stree," she said. "About removing the essence of wine and using it to kill something he called 'germs.'"

Karl nodded. "I remember that," he said.

All eyes turned to him.

He immediately looked uncomfortable. "Used to be," he said, finally, "more warriors died after a battle than during it. We thought evil demons fed on their wounds and left poison bile. You'd see fever, and sickness; healers would amputate arms and legs…"

He shuddered. "My uncle, he lost his hand because of a bad scrape. Lupus showed us that, rather than drinking strong alcohol, we could use it on healers' scalpels and in bandages. After the Battle of Tamaran Glen, we put witch hazel on wounds and alcohol on bandages, and the demons never came."

"Even we use alcohol now," Zarshar said, from across the fire. "I never understood why demons would feed on my kind. Chem-stree makes more sense."

Glynn leaned forward. "You know these secrets, then, Raven?" she persisted. "The Emperor claimed he could remove the salt from sea water, and now there is clean water in every Eldadorian city."

"That there is," Xinto said. "He laid huge pipes of clay and wood in the ground, and he builds a building of brick and steel that belches steam and pumps fresh water into those pipes, and now you can be in Galnesh Eldador, or Thera or Steel City or Vrek, and get water fresh as rain pumped right into your house."

"After he pumps it into huge towers?" Raven asked. Xinto nodded.

"Every city in my land, no matter how small," she said. "Now everyone lives longer and you have less—um, fewer babies die, yes?"

She didn't know the words for *infant mortality*.

Say what you would about the Emperor, she couldn't help thinking, he cares about his people.

Chapter Five

Surprises on the Eldadorian Plain

"Why would you help me?" Jack asked.

It seemed a pretty simple question.

The Uman farmer, Harkem, and his wife, Jeel, kept a small farm, a soddy and a wood barn, a crop of corn almost a daheer wide, a crop of hay even wider, a corral with aurochs, their retrievers to manage them, and a flock of children.

A lot to lose for a stranger.

Jeel had packed him full of food; Harkem had reshod Little Storm and tightened the stitches in his saddle. His saddlebags were packed with dried meat, peas and carrots. When the sun set, they took Jack out past their farm, and into a gulley between two hills. The way the landscape formed around it, you'd have to be standing right on top of Milly's Gulch to see it. They explained that, in the rainy season, it became a stream they tapped for irrigation. As they waited to be sure the patrols were all in, Harkem looked Jack right in the eye.

"I'm a vassal to Thera, my Duke is Two Spears, the brother-in-law of the Emperor. Do you know what that means?"

Jack shook his head.

"Twenty years ago this was all bottom land with very little clay. I settled here with my wife, we started this farm. I owed nothing to anyone, and I got nothing from anyone.

"Sometimes that meant I had to fight off raiders, but the neighbors banded together, and we lived."

Jack already had an idea where this was going.

"When Lupus the Conqueror became Duke of Thera, I

suddenly discovered my lands were his, and that I farmed them at his good graces. I was informed I had to pay him fifteen parts in one hundred of everything I grew here, but in return I would have Wolf Soldiers looking out for me.

"When the Confluni invaded Thera the first time, they tore up the farms of my neighbors and killed their children. We didn't see any Wolf Soldiers until they actually turned on the city. Then Lupus and his Wolf Soldiers crushed them, as he promised. He even spent a little of his own coin rebuilding our farms, although he couldn't replace the children.

"Then he became a King, and then an Emperor and we had this Two Spears. We who paid his way to the throne with our taxes were forgotten. Four years ago, Thera was invaded again, by twice as many Confluni, as well as Uman-Chi and Uman from the Silent Isle."

Jeel took her husband by the upper arm and squeezed. A tear ran down Harkem's cheek, and he looked away from Jack.

"I lost a daughter and two sons in that invasion," he said, and his voice cracked. "The daughter was raped, the sons strung up with the sons of others, t' draw out the Emperor and the Duke. We was something they could use t' get under a better man's skin, no more.

"This time the Emperor came out and met them in the field. They tore up my farm, they ran over my crops, and they charged over the dead bodies of my children. To get at them Confluni, the Theran Lancers done me and mine at least as bad as they done them.

"And afterwards, this time they didn't pay nothing. This time that Two Spears, he tells us he suffered so bad, and it cost him so much, he didn't have no more gold to help those whom the Confluni tortured and killed to get at Eldador.

"That was in War, and then in Chaos, he rebuilds his walls with cheap labor from farmers who ain't got no farms no more, and my daughter starves to death, crazy from what they done to her. He tells us we should be grateful he got us work at all."

"So you ask me why I help you, I tell you," Harkem said, and he gripped Jack's upper arm tight, "if they want you, then I want them not to have you, 'cuz maybe I can't do a lot about an Emperor, but I can do that."

"'sides," Jeel said, and patted the side of his cheek, "you don't look so bad. What could you o' done?"

Jack smiled to himself. "Well, nothing that bad," he said. "I'm sorry for your loss. I hope they found peace."

Jeel smiled and kissed him on the cheek. "Well, now," she said. "Well, that's nice—that's nice of you to say."

"You better git," Harkem told Jack. "You follow this gulley 'till it widens out, and you'll see a wash to the northeast. You follow that; you'll come to a flat part in the plains, maybe a tenth of a daheer across. Get across that and, right to the north, you'll find another gulley like this one. You get down that, and you'll be on the road to Galnesh Eldador, and you can go anywhere."

"Keep your head down and don't stop moving," Jeel told him. "They'll track you after you get to the plain, but you'll be to the road so fast after that, you'll be free. They'll never track you on the road."

"And don't ride," Harkem said. "Walk that pony—they'll see the top of your head otherwise."

"Thanks," Jack said. He took his horse by the reins.

"Life's good fortune to you," Harkem said.

Jack turned away from them and led his horse down the gulley. He could feel them watching him as the walls closed in like a blanket. He mulled their story over in his head as he walked.

He couldn't say that he'd have done anything differently from Lupus, given the circumstance. It's a wonderful idea to live free on the plains, but in fact, someone was going to come around who was larger, and take what they had eventually.

Granted he didn't approve of what Two Spears had done, but he could understand that he had to keep Thera safe or see the same invaders back again, and he probably *did* think he was doing the farmers a favor by employing them.

He couldn't really appreciate what it meant to be on both sides of an argument like this, but he could see why people could hate the Emperor, when they thought he just took their possessions to make his life better, at the expense of their own.

He'd never lost a child, certainly never in conditions like that. Would that change him? Would it make him act out against his government?

He had to ask himself again, as he had many times since he'd come here, if he was on the right side of this conflict.

* * *

When he'd been a child, an Uman kitchen servant had taken Hectaro into a pantry, and forced him to sit still and wait for his father, when he'd been caught stealing plums and fresh bread. He'd cried the whole time, and when his father had seen him, he'd ordered the Uman lashed.

"How can he steal what is already his?" Hectar had demanded of the Uman woman. "You serve at my pleasure, and you serve at his." Later, the woman had been transferred to the stables, and after that the barracks, where the women were notoriously brutalized by the Guard. In fact, Hectaro remembered seeing her carrying water less than a month ago.

Now for two weeks he'd been sleeping and riding with his wrists bound together, and thankful they'd let him keep his own horse. His sword remained sheathed by the bedroll behind him—a testimony to how little they feared him.

Beside him, the Empress was bound hand and foot across the saddle of her gelding. The Princess rode on his other side, her hands bound as well.

When he'd tried to speak, his captors had simply cuffed him. He couldn't identify himself; he couldn't demand the treatment due his stature. He'd seen Lee shift her eyes rapidly between him and his sword, but he'd just shrugged at her and said nothing.

He might have taken on one of them, but he didn't trust enough to his skills to take on this many.

They'd want gold for him. His father had gold. Better just to wait this out.

There were five—the Empress had managed to kill one before they subdued her. He'd at least tried to stand beside her. That would be worth something when they were all freed.

"Hold," one said, a woman. She led them. The others were all male, two Uman, both with short-cropped green hair and multiple facial scars, and two Men, a Volkhydran and a Confluni by the look of them, the first burly and strong, the second skinny as a rail, with tight leather armor and, like the woman, daggers all over his body.

The woman was of the race of Men as well, shortish, red hair with some gray, green eyes, a wild look to her, as if she had become used to being hunted.

The sun was rising. They'd been moving by night and camping by day, ever south, probably meaning to cut down into the plains and then west to Uman City and passage to Andoron. Excruciatingly slowly—they should have been to Steel City by now.

"This is a good place," she said. "Plenty of cover, we can get out through those hills over there, or those to the north, and any chasing us will be slowed down by them."

"Yes, yes," one of the Uman said. "We all know the terrain here—no need to explain it. You have the bitches off their saddles this time, then. I want to scout back our trail."

"I can't lift the Empress," she said.

"Then drag her off and drop her on her head," the Uman said. "When did a head injury ever change an Andaron?"

The rest chuckled. Hectaro had made the same joke himself.

"I'll get her, if you'll let me," Hectaro ventured.

One of the Men, the Volkhydran, raised a hand threateningly, but the female held up her hand. "Let him," she said. "I'll untie his hands and watch him."

"You think that's wise?" the other Uman asked.

"Well, you're all too busy," she said. "He's cowed enough, I assume. Maybe I'll make him take his pants off first, keep him from running."

Hectaro blushed crimson as the others laughed. The woman swung out of the saddle, the rest after. She held a dagger up to Hectaro where he sat Bastard.

"Give up your wrists," she said. He dutifully extended his hands.

She sawed the binds free. He flexed his fingers, letting himself look down the front of her tight, leather top.

Without warning, she yanked him from his saddle. Bastard snorted and bobbed his head, dancing to one side. She reached down and took him by the hair, and dragged him up to his knees. For a woman, her grip was like steel.

"Like the view from up there, 'my lord'?" she sneered.

"Um, well—er," he couldn't think of any answer that wouldn't get him into more trouble.

"Well, let's have a look," she said and, with one swipe, cut the laces from the front of his breeches.

His pants sprung open as she pulled him to his feet. Releasing his hair, she held her knife to his throat as he felt the cool air touch his thighs and nether parts.

The cold steel of a sharp blade touched him. "Well, seems to me you liked it well enough."

He looked away, and his eyes found Lee's. He could see the

respect she'd already lost for him.

Her father, he felt sure, would have killed them all by now. Her father wore a man's weight in armor and carried an enchanted sword, too.

"Fix those up, and get those bitches off their horses," she commanded him. "Then picket your horses away from ours, and feed them. Then come back here and ask me for something else to do."

"I—yes, I will," he promised.

The Men and Uman shook their heads and scattered. The woman took her horse to the other side of their camp and pulled the saddle from him. Hectaro hitched up his pants and stepped to the side of Singer, Lee's horse, and reached up for her.

"I can get down myself," she informed him, and did so, even with her hands bound.

"I'll get your mother," he informed her.

"Lay a bedroll out for her first, stupid," she said. "You don't lay the Empress of Eldador on the ground."

"Of course," he said and, stepping to the side of the Shela's horse, he pulled the bedroll from behind her saddle and laid it on the ground close to the fire. He returned to Shela's saddle and, as gently as he could, he pulled her from it.

Her body was stiff and, for a moment, he worried that she'd died on them. Her eyes were closed, her head didn't loll back as he expected. He caught a flicker then, and she saw him, and he knew she wasn't unconscious, just pretending as best as she could.

"Don't fondle her, move her," Lee complained. In a moment he'd gone from hero to low servant, because he didn't fight back.

Because he'd been cowed and weakened in her eyes.

Hectaro carried the now-limp form of the Empress to her bedroll, and laid her down as gently as he could. He straightened her head on the pillow, and laid her hair down gently at her side, where it wouldn't get in her way if she decided to act.

He didn't know if he could beat the woman to the side of his horse to get his sword. She'd told him to picket and to feed the horses. Doing that put him as near to his weapon as he wanted to be.

The woman with the red hair didn't think he was anything to worry about. The Princess no longer respected him. If he could be of any service to the Empress, however, he could redeem some of his lost honor.

Taking Singer and Bastard by their reins, he focused his

attention on that.

* * *

Vulpe had been shadowing his mother and her captors for fourteen days. These people were Bounty Hunters, trained in tracking, fighting and surveillance. He'd known of and hated Bounty Hunters his whole life, for what they'd done to his parents.

Had he trailed them, they'd had found him fast enough. That would be too easy. To east or west, he would have had better luck, but these people would have figured them out eventually. That's just another version of the same thing.

Grelt had trained with Karel of Stone, and could shadow these people from their destination. Those who are pursued will commonly follow in the footsteps of another, recent traveler, knowing their tracks can be lost in those before them, and the other will turn out any ambushers or patrols.

So by staying far enough ahead, they tracked their prey from their destination, and adjusted their path when their quarry did. Their scout behind was just another wary soul in Eldador.

A week earlier their scout before them had come across an outrider patrol from Thera, his uncle's men, and Vulpe had commandeered them, sending one back to report their position to his uncle the Duke.

Vulpe grinned to himself as Dunn rode beside him, twenty-seven Wolf Soldiers in their command, nineteen of them Theran Lancers.

He had done the right thing. His uncle should have been here days ago. He had to save his mother.

With 1,000 Theran Lancer's, they'd ring this little troop so thick they'd have nowhere to run. They'd release his mother, or suffer consequences so dire they could not imagine them.

The Emperor was ruthless when it came to his family. His son would be, too, but he didn't have the Lancers.

"Vulpe," one of his lancers trotted in from the direction of their quarry. Vulpe recognized an Andaron—Ochustee Owastah. His name meant, "Runs Alone."

"'Chustee," Vulpe nodded. He considered himself a Long Manes, so this man would be of his tribe.

"They camp," 'Chustee said. "They have a patrol out, almost caught us. They spent a lot of time looking at our tracks. I think they're getting suspicious."

"Damn it," Vulpe swore, then looked guiltily around him. No one flickered—their commander swore if he wanted to. He suppressed a guilty grin.

"Have to get out from in front of them," Grelt interjected. "We can go forward for the rest of the day, then turn east. We'll let them pass, try to see where they go, pick them up again. If the Duke shows up with his Lancers, we'll just ring them in like we planned."

"Or lose then," Dunn argued. "Anyone else, I'd say you're right, but these are Bounty Hunters. If they already figured us out—"

Vulpe sighed. These adults were no different from any others. They'd argue and argue, and never come to any conclusions. His father had told him once, if you let them, your warriors would argue themselves into defeat faster than victory.

"We'll keep going on in this direction," he said. "When they think we're still moving on, they'll rest. We'll double back and take them while they sleep—Lancers in first, then regular soldiers for clean up. We'll need to stay away—"

"Excuse me," they heard from before them, down the path they were following.

There he stood, larger than life, atop a giant stallion. His clothes were different, and he'd lost a lot of weight, but there was no mistaking him.

His warriors' swords leapt from their scabbards. 'Stupid,' was Vulpe's first thought. If this one could get this close to him, why not the Bounty Hunters?

Especially on Little Storm.

"I'm sorry," grandfather said, "but that isn't going to work."

* * *

For anyone else, the roads west from the Salt Wood would be straight, easy and safe.

For this band of vagabonds, Karl thought to himself, it would be anything but. They'd ended up turning north, and now a city called 'Metz' loomed in front of them at the center of the Andurin Peninsula—a city whose Earl was a founding member of the Daff Kanaar.

Metz, a city with a compliment of never less than 5,000 Daff Kanaari warriors, would find them in their first days on their territory. Volkhydran cities maintained outrider patrols, which could be bypassed or evaded. Metz's patrols, as any Eldadorian city, would run crossing patterns at a tangent to the city walls. You could not see a patrol for days and then see three of them. Unpredictable and efficient, the Emperor didn't need to get you right away; he just needed to get you eventually.

Of course, for most people, that meant nothing. So what if you saw even one hundred patrols, if you weren't doing anything illegal? They could actually be very helpful, and you knew you could sleep at night and not wake up with a knife at your throat or your horses missing.

For them, it meant they had to stay off of the main roads. Now Slurn and Jahunga's men were fanned out before them, looking for telltale tracks of the patrols that also didn't stick to the roads. Now his Volkhydrans fanned out behind, to cover their tracks and to protect them from any patrol that came up from behind. The rest of them clung to the center, staying small and compact, moving as fast as they dared.

"How much more of this?" Raven asked, for the third time that day.

"A lot," he told her. "We aren't even to the city yet. We pass north of Metz, then to Tonkin, assuming no patrols find us."

"You mean like that one?" Zarshar growled, pointing to the horizon.

Jahunga's men were already doubling back, and his Volkhydrans advancing. Karl saw outriders, Daff Kanaari lancers, only five of them, meaning they'd reduced the size of their patrols, or this one had seen some trouble.

Five daheer away and they were already trotting. Karl had tried to make lancers of his Volkhydrans in Teher, without success. He ripped his sword out of his sheath.

"Glynn, you women break to the north. Bring Xinto and my men with you. When Jahunga is within earshot, send him west with his men. The Daff Kanaar will follow them, if any live. Zarshar, you're with me."

"And you, Sirrah?" Glynn asked him. The Swamp Devil was already flexing its claws.

His eyes met hers. "No one lives forever," he said.

"Stupid," Raven complained. "I can already—"

"No!" Glynn, Zarshar, Xinto and Karl said, together. Xinto

added, "Use your power within fifty daheeri of Metz and there'll be a wizard trying to find out why. You want them to turn out the whole garrison?"

"I've been using my magic—" she began.

"Rainfall on the ocean," Glynn informed her. "Child, you must needs follow the direction of those who make war now. Attend me, let us away."

"But—but he'll—"

Karl kicked his skittish mount. She leapt forward, the Swamp Devil and the dog right behind him. He didn't need to hear a woman complain right then.

On horseback, the distance closed quickly. He'd passed the Toorians in just a few minutes, Jahunga nodding to him. The other warrior would know what this meant, what was happening. Someone had to address the patrol, to make it small enough that they could either follow, or report back to Metz, but not both. Had they attacked in force, they would have all lived, but then this patrol would have broken up and brought in reinforcements. This small a challenge, they would engage and try to take prisoners.

They broke out single file. The dog leaped ahead of them, running to the lance side, stupid animal.

"Looks like Jack is losing his pet," Zarshar commented, watching the loping hound.

"I don't know what she thinks she's doing," Karl said. He allowed himself a look over his shoulder. Jahunga had already broken west. Glynn and Xinto and his Volkhydrans were trying to keep Raven from coming after him.

He admitted to himself that he wouldn't mind being rescued by that one.

The lancers lined up in single file. Spread out, the Eldadorians would engage them fully exposed. One at a time, they would strike and break off, keeping the lengths of their lances between themselves and their enemies. Karl might have to sacrifice the horse's body in order to get a single strike at the lancer and then, unhorsed, he'd be on his feet.

To his surprise, the lancers actually turned away from the dog, not that it helped. She put on a burst of speed, her tail beating the empty air. *Probably thought she'd get her ears scratched*, Karl thought to himself.

But that wasn't what happened.

Picking his mount's trot up to a gallop, Jerrod held his sword low and leaned into the saddle. Skittish as she was, the mare was happy to oblige him. The Swamp Devil sprinted to keep up the pace, his talons bared.

The Daff Kanaari lowered their lances as one. Their hooves thundered on the plain, few as they were. The sun glinted from their steel armor and lance points.

The dog now at an all-out run leapt up from the first horse's side to knock the first of the lancers from its back, tumbling with him onto the ground. *Well, that was one*, Karl thought. *The dog will ravage him—*

But no—she disengaged and immediately leapt for the third, now from the other side. Quick as a wink, she had another lancer down, deftly avoiding his weapon as her powerful legs drove her up off the ground, crashing into the armored man's side. They were barely twenty yards apart now, and two had fallen.

The horse from the unmounted lancer ran to the left. The one behind him split his attention between his objective and the men behind him, and that was a mistake.

Karl closed on him, the lance passing before him, and drove his sword one-handed into the man's groin. The lancer screamed, dropping his weapon, and clutched his belly.

The dog was already chasing the fifth man, and Zarshar leapt for the fourth. The Eldadorian's lance shattered on the Swamp Devil's breastplate and Zarshar's claws separated the Man's armor.

The rider's scream was a horrible thing as the dog claimed her third victim, knocking him to the ground, her tail beating the air so hard it seemed to move in a circle, rather than back and forth. Behind him, an armored lancer tried to roll himself over onto this knees and elbows. Karl turned his horse into a wide circle and, on his second pass, ran the man down, the mare's hooves crushing head and arms.

Zarshar had already finished with his man and was homing in on the other fallen lancer. The dog had run from the last, whom she'd felled already, and took off after the horses. She made a wide arc away from where they ran and, much like a herd dog, she began to turn them in and collect them.

Karl trotted his mount, now much more amenable for her sudden exercise, to the last fallen man, struggling against the weight of his armor to get up off of the ground.

"I would lie still, were I you," Karl informed him.

The man squinted into the sun. The visor on his helmet had been left down, masking his face. He pushed his weapon away.

Not a mark on him. The dog hadn't fought; it had just knocked these men from their horses. She saw the whole thing as a trick or a game.

Karl's mind was racing.

"Well, have done with it," the man said. His accent was Eldadorian, but not Uman. He spoke the language of Men.

"Maybe you don't die," he said. Daff Kanaari weren't Wolf Soldiers. They might be desperate men, but they lacked that maniac edge, that belief that serving Lupus made them more than mortal.

"Maybe you tell us a few things, and you live," Karl informed him.

He could hear the Toorians running up to him from behind. The dog was growling at one of the horses that tried to shy from him. His Volkhydrans were trying to collect the nervous animals.

Having thought less than half an hour ago he'd be dead by now, Karl couldn't help considering it had turned out to be a hell of a morning.

Chapter Six

Family Reunion

Glynn arose from her prayers to find Karl Henekhson spitting another woodland beast, Jahunga laying on his back by the fire, chewing a twig, and her naked protégé frolicking with the dog in the shallow stream along which they'd decided to camp.

Jahunga's Toorians and Karl's Volkhydrans split the jobs of sentry and camp maintenance and guarding their one prisoner, and yet all found reasons enough to be within eyeshot of her. Glynn watched as two Volkhydrans crashed into each other, one with a load of wood, the other with an armful of green-cut hay, neither looking where they were bound.

The two Men shared a laugh and set about retrieving their burdens. Neither paid any less attention to Raven.

Glynn shook her head and rose, brushing dirt from the front of her blue travel dress. The outfit was already showing its wear, the front and seat discolored, a small tear forming under one arm. That she should travel with but one outfit made for burden enough without having to teach casting and morals to young Raven.

"Are you sufficiently entertained, Sirrah?" she asked of Jahunga, approaching their fire.

Jahunga looked up guiltily and pulled the twig from his lips, casting it into the fire. He sighed, pushed himself up to his feet, and said, "Perhaps I should make sure the sentries are split up fairly."

"What's that supposed to mean?" Karl demanded, looking up from the spit.

"Well, no one can question that my Toorians do more of the scouting," Jahunga said.

Karl snorted. "They did more of the running yesterday."

Jahunga straightened. "You call us cowards? You were the one who told *us* to run—"

"Like I had to tell them—"

"Goodsirs, *please*," Vedeen intervened. She'd sat herself down by the fire, where she mended a tear in her robe. "An it were me, I would appreciate the subtle evening more and the young lady less. In fact, I myself thought to join her."

"No, let them fight," Zarshar said, grinning. "The victor wins the argument."

"We won't have either beating either, Zarshar," Glynn insisted. The Devil sought the violence of its kind, which came as no surprise to her. In fact, the Devil probably believed what it was saying.

Xinto, whom she'd previously not noticed, reclining like a lump in a pile of Eldadorian saddles, added, "If it keeps them quiet after, then I say let them. When has it been in anyone's best interest to keep Men from fighting?"

"Perhaps the Fovean High Council might—" Glynn began.

"Irrelevant entity," Xinto interrupted.

"We *aren't* going to fight," Karl grumbled, and threw a bowl of water and spice herbs against the side on the spit. "Unless we decide to team up on one of you three."

Zarshar simply stood and flexed his muscles. Glynn stepped between him and the Volkhydran, knowing what was imminent.

"I think not, Sirrah," she said.

She knew she could count on Jahunga's good graces, and he didn't disappoint her. "We offer you no challenge, Zarshar," he said. "We have an agreement, and we honor it, of course."

Zarshar leveled his red eyes first at Jahunga, then at Karl, and then reseated himself. From the direction of the stream, the dog barked and leapt out of the water, shaking itself in a wide, wet spray. Raven, up to her hips in the stream, leaned her head back into the water to dip her long, black hair, accentuating her breasts.

"War's beard," one of the Volkhydrans swore. Glynn shook

her head.

"I'll take care of it," Karl said. He turned to Jahunga. "Can you watch this?"

"I think it better, Sirrah—" Glynn began. The last thing the girl needed was another male, ogling her.

"I bet you do." Karl said, and turned his back on her, grabbing a towel from the saddle pile. Jahunga stood and took hold of the handle on the spit, turning the side. Fat had already begun to bubble and pop on it.

Vedeen looked down into her robe and smiled, saying nothing.

"Better to leave this within the people," Xinto noted, leaning back into the pile of saddles.

"But, Sirrah," Glynn said. "They aren't of the same people."

* * *

Raven ran her fingers through her thick, wet hair, watching the dog run back and forth along the bank of the stream. The water was freezing, but it made her skin feel alive. Getting a pound of trail dust out of her hair didn't make her feel any worse, either.

The dog turned to see Karl approaching them and barked at him, its tail beating the air. She ran toward the Volkhydran, went down in a crouch, barked again and, its tail not missing a beat, charged back toward Raven.

She had to laugh.

"So," Karl said, as soon as he was sure he had her attention. "Are you trying to start a brawl, or is there a brothel you want into?"

She knelt down into the water until it covered her up to the shoulders. "None of them ever seen a woman before?" she asked.

"You want to wave it under their noses, go ahead," Karl informed her, holding up the towel. "They rape you in the night, don't scream for me."

She made a disgusted face and stood, exposing all of her, stepping out of the water. She knew she could dry herself in a second with her magic, but she'd been warned she'd draw the city's attention. They could see Metz' walls on the horizon now—there was no point in alerting them.

"I didn't know that was how your men behaved," she said, taking the towel and wrapping it around her. She felt Karl's fingertips brush her shoulders and suppressed a little thrill at their roughness.

He was gorgeous, but he still wasn't Bill. No one was Bill.

But Bill wasn't here, either. Bill had taken off on her. Bill was 'Jack,' and Jack had things to do.

So, yeah, she'd gone skinny dipping for some attention. It wasn't like they hadn't all seen her naked at some point, either getting into her bedroll, relieving herself, or what-have-you. She'd seen each of them, as well. She'd half-hoped that some of them would join her.

Maybe Glynn could have taken the opportunity to get the stick out of her ass.

"You can only push a man so far," Karl said. The dog ran up to him and nosed his hand. He ruffled her wet ears, then pushed her away. Reaching behind him, he pulled a dirk from his belt.

Raven watched him, drying herself off. She'd laid her leathers out on a large rock next to the stream, and turned her back on him, picking up her halter. "Better not hurt that dog," she said. "She took out more lancers than you did."

"She did, didn't she," Karl said, remaining behind her. She stepped into the leather halter, feeling it sliding up between her legs. She could feel his eyes on her ass. To her left, she saw their one prisoner, bound on his side, watching her.

"Never seen a dog do that before," he added. "And she didn't ravage them after—it was like a game to her."

"Jack would know more about that," Raven said, tying the halter behind her neck, under her wet hair. She thought about reusing the towel to bind it up, but being wet already, it would just make a mess of her hair and not dry it. "But I think there was something about knights and dogs and mastiffs and something that I remember from history."

"Yeah?" Karl seemed interested. She turned, and he was still holding the dirk. The dog had run off and was sniffing around Zarshar. They were buddies for some reason.

"Something about mastiffs being heavy and knocking knights off their horses," she said. "Seems to me that, once they were helpless, other knights had an easy time with them."

"Their armor traps them," Karl said. "People like the Emperor who wear heavy armor are helpless on their backs, like a turtle."

"So, then, if you taught a dog to do that," Raven said, stepping into her leather skirt, "you would want him just knocking down knights—lancers—because chewing them up is pointless."

Karl seemed to take a moment to digest that, giving her time to pull her boots on. She could put the raider jacket on, but at this point it wasn't that cold, and she'd taken to wearing it over her bedroll. She'd convinced herself it still smelled like Bill.

"So, what are you going to do with that?" she asked him, pointing at the dirk.

He looked at it as if he'd forgotten that he'd drawn it. She told herself that, in fact, he probably had. He'd been acting strange around her lately, and she wasn't sure she liked it.

"Oh, um—here," he said, and held the handle out toward her.

"You want me to have that?" she asked. She felt immediately on her guard. Men didn't give gifts like that and not want something.

"That pig sticker isn't going to protect you if we get down into it," Karl told her. "And any of these warriors could take it away from you in a second. If you're going to defend yourself, you better learn to do it right."

"I have my magic," she said.

He dropped the dirk and in one fluid motion, he had her by the throat. She felt her neck strain as he picked her up to her tiptoes with one hand.

"Errrk," she protested. She tried to kick him and couldn't. She dug her nails into his hand and upper arm but it didn't seem to affect him. As she started to see little spots, he pushed her and she landed on her butt.

"Sonofabitch," she swore, rubbing her throat and trying to stand. He shoved her by her forehead and she was back on her ass.

She stayed down, glaring at him. She itched to use her magic.

He extended his hand to her and, grudgingly, she took it. He pulled her to her feet and proffered the dirk's hilt again.

"Bet you want it now," he said a sloppy grin on his face.

She sure did. She took the weapon and held it up between them, admiring the blade, which had been blackened, even the edge.

"Let it rust and I'll take it back," he told her. "You need to learn how to use it, and how to respect it."

"Why?" she asked, looking into his brown eyes.

"A weapon like that will protect you, or betray you, depending on how you treat it, just like a dog, or a horse, or a lover—" he began.

"No," she interrupted him. "Why are you giving this to *me*?"

He frowned, looked down, then looked back at her.

"First off, I don't want to see you putting on a show like this again, understood?" he told her.

She straightened. "I don't have to do—" she began.

He snatched the dirk out of her hand by the blade and turned on his heel. She let him take three steps before she finally said, "Okay, okay. That was stupid."

"Yes, it was," he told her, turning. He stepped back up in front of her. "And one of those men was eventually going to get it into his head to join you, and then you'd have a hell of a time."

"All *right*," she didn't feel like being lectured like a little girl.

"Second, you need to be able to defend yourself," he said. "I've seen too many like Glynn, who have their magic but are useless without it. All they can do is run away. I don't think you are the run away kind."

He held out the hilt to her again, and she took it. Their hands touched, she looked into his eyes.

"You learn to use it right," he said to her. "You aren't the only woman ever to hold a sword. I've known a few. You have speed, you use your head; you can fight a man and live.

"I'll show you how," he said, and released the blade.

"Okay," she told him. "Don't I—um—don't I need a sheath for this?"

He smiled. "Yeah, girl," he said. "You can sheath my sword."

He turned and left. It took her a moment to get the joke, and then she wished she hadn't.

* * *

"Why are you here, grandfather?" Vulpe demanded of him. Jack saw the armed men, lined up behind the little boy—not looking so little with warriors forming a half-circle to either side of him.

He was almost twelve years old—kind of young for this sort of thing. But then, the average age of Napoleon's generals was sixteen.

Regardless, he'd bungle this good if his men just followed him against experienced warriors. Jack didn't know that he was any better qualified, but he was sure as hell no worse.

And the kid had called him 'grandfather,' and meant it.

"You're about to make a really big mistake, son," Jack said, keeping an eye on the men around him. "From what I've heard about your 'Bounty Hunters,' if they're on to you, then they'll come after you, not leave you behind. If I can get this close to you, they can."

Vulpe looked to his left and his right. There was a huge Man to one side, and an Uman to the other, and he clearly looked to them as his advisors. Jack knew that, if they resisted him, then he had no chance, grandfather or not. They were 'in,' and Jack had fought enough inter-office power struggles to know you don't work against an 'in' guy, unless you can take him out entirely.

"He *did* get past us," the Uman admitted.

"You should see what the gaffer knows," the other said. Jack felt himself straighten. "You never know what someone will pick up after a lot of years."

"What the gaffer knows," Jack said, and urged Little Storm up closer to the prince, "is that, if they think they have you, and you know better, then you don't want to make them think otherwise. They'll come to kill you, so you need to let them think they have a good chance of doing that, and take them out."

"You're saying just sit here—" the Man began, but Vulpe raised his hand. The Man instantly quieted.

The Uman smiled. "No," he said. "Draw them in, like flies to our web, we being the spiders."

Vulpe looked up into Jack's eyes. So young, so inquisitive, the eyes of a child with the responsibilities of an adult now. A kid trying to save his mom, if what he'd overheard was true.

"Show me how," he said.

* * *

Genna slinked forward, her belly to the ground, feeling the gravel on her skin. The land here consisted of scrub and pebbles, a wash, not good for farming. Usually with the spring rains this would all be flooded, but the spring rains were sparse this year.

Probably why she'd never married a farmer.

"See that?" the Man beside her, Jarf, told her, pointing to the center of the camp, where seven of the nine of them slept. Two stood guard, one on either side of the camp. Their horses were billeted close to the sleepers with a good-sized pile of green-cut hay.

"You mean that prince sitting there, bold as brass?" Genna asked him. "Asleep during the day with the sun shining, a collection of new-cut hay when there's none for miles?"

"A trap?" Jarf asked her. The man was a stone—a fighting Bounty Hunter, not a Stealthy one, like her. Of course, she was a little bit of both.

"I don't know that they're smart enough for a trap," Genna

said to him. "I just don't know that they're all there, and I want to catch them at the same time."

"If there are others, they'll come running when the fight begins," Jarf said.

"I know it," Genna said, and began to scoot back. Jarf followed. "Have Tuuren take out the one guard, and Pheeru the other. We three Men will sweep in at the last minute and kill the others. Take the prince hostage, of course."

"And if he fights?" Jarf asked her.

She knew Jarf. Killing children, women, helpless old people, didn't bother him any more than lacing up his sandals. Life meant nothing more to him than the light did from the candle.

"I want him alive," she said. "You weren't at the Battle of Tamaran Glen, I was. Kill a member of his family, and you will have the full force of the Emperor brought to bear against you, and he won't care what it takes or what he has to do to get his revenge."

"What do you suppose he'll do for all of this, then?" Jarf asked her.

Behind the rise from where they'd approached, she stood, Jarf with her. She'd made sure to scoot back even farther than she had to, knowing that Jarf, taller than she, would stand up the moment that she did.

"What will he do?" she echoed him. "Nothing—that's what. We have his family alive. To keep them that way, he'll do whatever we want him to do, and that plan is already in place."

She clapped him on the shoulder. "Not to worry, Jarf, not to worry. A week from now, you will be an unimaginably wealthy man."

* * *

Shela lay tied across her horse, the gelding picketed with Singer and Bastard, and their riders, in the temporary camp the Bounty Hunters had made.

Her stomach roiled from hunger, her tongue swelled for want of water. Her daughter had cleaned her somewhat, but as emotionally as the girl had behaved during the initial battle, Shela hadn't dared to let her know she'd regained her senses. No daughter should have to tend her mother this way, and she'd had to care for her baby sister, as well.

Hectaro had surprised her, keeping a cool head, not letting them provoke him. He'd figured out her ruse and not betrayed her. If she'd ordered him to, he'd have taken his sword from its sheath and freed them, but it wasn't time for that.

Vulpe seemed to have escaped. They certainly hadn't discussed killing him, and they talked about everything else. If Vulpe lived, he'd go right to his uncle and bring back help. If he were half the son she thought she'd raised, he'd have left one or two Wolf Soldiers to try to shadow them.

Now she feared her captors had found those Wolf Soldiers, as they picketed their horses and left to kill them while they slept.

If she were alone, then it was time to act.

"Lee?" she whispered, in the unlikely event there was some guard whom she hadn't sensed.

"Mother?" she heard her daughter's voice.

"Your Imperial Majesty," Hectaro interjected. "We're alone— I can't get to my sword—they bound us."

"Lee," Shela said, unable to see them, "free us. The unbinding spell."

She heard Lee incant, and felt the ropes slither away from her wrists and ankles. She bounced herself off of her saddle, then remounted as quick as she was able.

She winced at her sticky nethers. She'd have to be treated— she'd need a healer or an infection might leave her barren or worse.

"Are you well, m'lady?" Hectaro asked her, his eyes searching hers.

"I'm well," Shela said. "Where did they leave for?"

Hectaro stood and went for his sword, stuffed in the bedroll behind his saddle, laying in a pile with the others next to where they'd been tied. He had a swollen cheek from where they'd cuffed him. He pointed the sword almost directly south. "That way."

"Then who comes from the north?" she asked him.

Any city person might have missed it, not an Andaron, born on the plains. The dust trail of at least six horses, moving fast, not trying to disguise themselves, not running single file.

Her son had escaped after all.

Hectaro moved his horse between them and the two women and mounted it, as she'd expect a male to do. "No need," she told him, and touched his arm. "Those are Theran Lancers."

True enough, they passed to the east of a hill to their north, out wide in the open. They all recognized the uniforms immediately.

The warriors reined in and their sergeant, a fellow Andaron, made a fist over his heart when he recognized her.

"M'lady," he said. "We are sent by your son."

She sighed. Any mother would worry. "Where is he, and my brother?" she asked him.

"We haven't seen Duke Tali Digatishi in days," he said. "Vulpe arranged for this rescue. He is destroying his enemies now."

Shela's heart ran cold.

Her son, in battle, and warriors calling him by his first name? However he'd done it, he'd taken command of them. The boy was, as her husband, Yonega Waya, might say, his father's son.

"Bring us to him," she commanded him.

"Our orders are to keep you safe, m'lady," he informed her.

Not only had he taken command of them, they were loyal to him over her.

She raised a hand, white with power. There were times to be the Lady Shela Mordetur, mother of the Empire.

There was a time to be the Bitch of Eldador as well.

"You defy *me*?" she demanded. "Empress of the realm? Wife of the Conqueror?"

The Andaron's eyes went wide. "Of course not, your Imperial Majesty," he spluttered.

"On your *life*," she informed him, "bring me to my son."

The Lancers straightened. No one questioned her power.

"Immediately, m'lady," he said, and turned his horse. The Lancers took up a defensive ring around her, one in front, one to either side, and three behind, in a triangle shape. Lee reached Chawny up to Shela and mounted Singer, refusing to look at the young prince. When she seated herself the Andaron Lancer put heels to his mount and they cantered to the south. As they rode, she took Chawny in her arms and rubbed her nose on her baby's face. Chawny made pouty lips but wasn't about to betray them by crying.

Whatever her son had planned, she wasn't about to leap into it and betray him, neither would she let him fight his first battle alone.

The horses pounded out four daheer, none of the riders speaking. Already she could feel the skin tear around her nethers. She'd be sore and riding sidesaddle if she couldn't find a healer.

Perhaps worse if she couldn't find clean water or alcohol. Infection killed more insidiously than arrows.

Along the way she saw riders' sign, fresh in the gravel. She caught five distinctive tracks, then two breaking off to east and west.

They'd decided to circle around and entrap her son. She gave the Andaron sergeant the sign for wanting to go faster.

They thundered over a rise and found themselves at the edge of a battle.

She saw the signs of a camp, broken apart. Half a dozen horses ran free with Eldadorian saddles, more with mixed. Two Wolf Soldiers lay dead on the ground, one to the side of the camp, one at its center. A small Wolf Soldier squad with her son at the center of it formed in the middle, three unmounted Bounty Hunters trying to defend themselves from it, while another dozen Lancers passed in single file, their lances down.

Before she could even react, two of the three Bounty Hunters fell to the lancers, the third to two pikemen.

If they'd been dispatched so quickly—

They hadn't, she noted. The remaining two Bounty Hunters were fleeing to the east on their horses. Her power swelled, and she called the fire.

She wasn't at her strongest, but the ball of fire she threw at them scored the flank of one of the horses.

Her daughter's follow up knocked an Uman from the wounded animal's saddle. The last disappeared over a ridge. Vulpe was already sending half a dozen Lancers after them.

Five lancers, and an old man on a black stallion.

Little Storm!

* * *

Nina of the Aschire had never really taken to horseback riding. Her nature was to rely on her feet and, when in any forest, her hands. On the plains, however, one needed horses, so she'd learned to ride from the Empress.

Andarons rode fast and, as light as she was, she rode faster than most Andarons. She'd learned to relax, to move with the animal, to let the saddle support her without being bounced around in it.

In three days, she'd found herself in Thera, only to find the garrison turned out in search of the Empress, Lee and Chawny. She didn't care what her orders were, or who gave them. If Lee was in danger, that overrode everything.

She reached out for Lee with her mind and found nothing. She turned south, passing squad after squad of Lancers and Wolf Soldiers, and at one she even believed she'd seen Duke Two Spears. She didn't approach him—she barely knew the man and didn't want him to tell her to fetch the Emperor or to return to Galnesh Eldador.

Once she had to replace her mount—she'd simply worn the poor beast out. This part of Eldador was almost overrun with Angadorian horses, and she had no trouble trading at a Hostel. By the end of the fourth day, she was exhausted from riding and trying to reach out to Lee. She made herself a cold camp and pulled the saddle from her horse.

She immediately heard another mount, running alone, coming toward her from the west.

As Shela had taught her, she bound her mount's reins to the saddle horn and sprinted to the north, out of the rider's path. There'd be no hiding the horse from a rider, however she could use it to bring the rider into striking distance.

She ran as far as she felt she could sprint in three seconds, then threw herself into the dust, rolling in it, covering herself. She pressed her body flat into the Earth, and waited, barely breathing, waiting for the rider either to approach or to pass her by.

The rider seemed at first to want to pass to the south, then noticed her horse and arced in toward her. The horse slowed at about a third of a daheer, and came in at a trot.

She waited for the rider to rein in, take a look around, and then dismount.

Her power swelled. She'd have a buzzing headache later, but she'd be alive and with a horse to experience it.

The rider dropped like a sack of potatoes. Nina was wary. She waited several minutes, in case the other was pretending.

The other horse began to crop scrub through its bit.

Nina stood, approaching cautiously, ready to run if she had to. She finally stood over the prone body of the person who'd approached her.

"Well," she said to the open air. "That's a surprise."

Chapter Seven

Stranger and Strangers

"Nothing, your Grace," the scout reported. The Uman outrider was tan with dust, her horse so lathered it barely stood. Before realizing it, Tartan Stowe was planning for recovering the animal.

More important things to think about now, he thought.

"See to your mount," he told the woman. She nodded and dismounted. His second in command, Captain J'lek, a blooded veteran of the Wolf Soldier corps who'd been ordered to transfer to the Angadorian command, stood silent in his long, chain armor. His nose stood out like an axe blade, his eyes set like a hawk's under close-cropped, brown hair. Rumors spoke of his father as Supreme Commander J'her, however the Uman never broached the subject, so the Duke never inquired. If true, that made the Uman a spy, and Tartan had enough pokers in the fire in regard to the Emperor.

Tartan looked J'lek in the eye. "We've lost him," he said, simply. "He either kept going south, or came back through our lines."

"I could believe either," J'lek said. "I personally inspected every Man in the company and none of them is the one we're looking for. Supposedly this 'Jack' has a bull's strength and, despite his age, could overpower one of ours."

Tartan hadn't thought of that, but he filed it away. Where better to hide than in the ranks of those looking for you?

With cunning like that, Captain J'lek didn't need his father's reputation to distinguish him.

"We're for Angador, then," Tartan decided. If the Man was gone, then his original orders were to keep peace on the plains while other cities' garrisons emptied out into this campaign of Lupus'. The Emperor trusted him to keep the homefront, not to be at his right hand when he went looking for a fight.

"Might I suggest we go north, around the Lone Wood, then swing south?" J'lek interjected. He kept his face impassive—he might have been a statue. "There are a lot of refugees from Lupor out—bound to be some of them causing trouble for decent people."

Another good idea Tartan should have had. He nodded. "Let the company rest for today, we start fresh in the morning. Break out three kegs of that Koran ale we liberated—let the troops know they did what we expected of them."

"They didn't," J'lek said simply, coming as close as he ever had to questioning an order.

Tartan turned toward his pavilion. "I know it," he said, "but there's nothing for it now. I don't need them disheartened and looking to take out their anger on some unfortunate peasant. They tried, let them know we appreciate that they tried."

"Sir…"

Tartan stopped, turned at the waist, and looked J'lek in the eye again. He'd failed, he knew. He'd lost some of their respect. Now they'd think could question him. Now, they'd test his mettle.

Duke Two Spears had told him once that nothing ever went as planned, and the difference between a good leader and a bad one was how he handled failure and turned it into victory—if he could.

"You know," he drawled, his thumbs in his sword belt, "the Emperor tells a story of an Uman named 'Sammin' who, as his second in command, disrespected him in front of his men—do you recall what happened to Sammin?"

J'lek raised an eyebrow and held his gaze for a moment, then smiled a thin, spare smile and let himself look away. "Every Wolf Soldier knows that story," he said.

"And every Wolf Soldier knows the consequences of failure," Tartan said, "but these aren't Wolf Soldiers, these are Angadorian Knights, so give them ale and let them know we don't hate them."

"Immediately, your Grace," J'lek said. He made a fist over his heart, and turned on his heel. "Alright, you dogs," he roared, "we're done for the day. I want the jess doonar in place, horses quartered, and then I've three barrels of ale need to be drunk, if you're up to it."

There wasn't a cheer, but there was a chuckle, and Tartan settled for it. He entered his pavilion, where his wife was trying to catch herself a nap.

She slept a lot, and it displeased him, although he didn't say anything. If her dreams comforted her when she had nothing else to do, at least she was the kind of woman who'd follow him out on the trail, much like the Empress. Most wives would wait in the safety of a husband's palace.

Wives like his mother. Dead more than a decade, and he still missed her, that sweet soul whose soft hands had held him, and who'd left this world too soon. He remembered the day his father had informed them what had happened to her.

"The bastards killed your mother," he'd sobbed. He'd never seen Glennen cry before. His father had been like the god Adriam, powerful and wise. "They tried to get to me, instead they killed her."

"Mama?" he'd refused to believe it at the time. Mama couldn't be dead. She was…mama.

He'd already started drinking. Tartan would never see him sober again. Even at the King's funeral, he could smell the alcohol on the body, or at least imagined he could.

"They killed her," the King said. His sisters and his younger brother were already bawling. He had tried to stay strong. "I promise you, all of you, if I could have taken her place, I would have."

Probably said to make the children feel better, but his father had been invincible and immortal in his mind until that point in time.

"What will we do?" Alekennen, his eldest sister, had asked.

"I sent a man to vengeance," the King had said. Some Duke, some new favorite in the peerage. Tartan had seen him, all steel and horns. He'd killed a Bounty Hunter in court—not many could do that. Afterwards, Tartan and his brother Terran had acted out the battle with their wooden swords, taking turns at being Lupus.

Lupus had wreaked unholy vengeance on the people of Fovea for his mother's death. He'd killed thousands, and returned a hero, a legend, to slowly take the throne of Galnesh Eldador, while Tartan's father drank himself to death.

Tartan missed his mother and his father but, even worse, he'd felt cheated by Lupus for taking a vengeance that belonged to his family. It had taken him a long time to admit to himself that most of what Lupus had done had been necessitated by Glennen's failures.

Now Tartan sat and drank chilled wine, and watched his plain, common wife sleep. Good enough he'd been given someone who actually seemed to love him; one who could resent the Emperor for many of the same reasons as he.

The morning came red and bloody. The Emperor had once said that a red sky in the morning scared sailors, or some such thing, but Tartan didn't feel like remembering it.

His warriors had made short work of three barrels of Koran ale. Not enough for most of them to get drunk on, but the snoring had been impressive and the Duke hadn't slept well. His wife had put on an impressive display of not being awake for any of it.

He dressed as she arose and stretched, naked and inviting in their sleeping furs. Her three Uman maids were waiting to pack up the pavilion and its contents for the trip north.

The Emperor would have traveled with less, but then the Emperor's wife saw opulence as having three horses.

"Where to today, husband?" Yeral asked him, standing nude in their furs. Her maids immediately wrapped her in a cotton travel robe—one of the perhaps seven changes of clothing he could expect for her today.

"North, around the Lone Wood, then between the Lone Wood and the Bay, and back to Angador. Perhaps a month's journey."

He was ready to leave the pavilion and didn't need to see his wife's maids bath her. The thrill of that had left him long ago.

She raised an eyebrow. "Leaving this kinsman of the Emperor's uncaught?"

"He evaded us," Tartan admitted. "I can't be expected to turn over every stone on the plains. Should we be fortunate enough to overtake him, then so be it, but we'll likely never see him again.

"He's as like dead in a shallow grave by the hand of some farmer who wanted Little Storm," he added. "What man wouldn't kill him for a stallion of Blizzard's seed? I know I planned to."

Yeral smiled a wily smile. "I thought you were awfully eager to fulfill the Emperor's goals."

"I'm a loyal subject of the Empire," Tartan sniggered, bowing to her. "However, the Emperor keeps the spoils of his campaigns."

"Go!" she shooed him. "You have better things to do than

banter with me."

He whisked heroically out the tent flap and into the bustling army. J'lek already had the camp, the Wolf Soldier 'jess doonar,' half-disassembled and most of the men fed. Wolf Soldiers might be more efficient, Tartan thought, but Angadorians were not far behind.

"Rider to the north," he heard a scout report to J'lek. All heads in the vicinity turned to see a lone rider on a ridge two daheeri away, regarding them. The distance was too far to make out details.

"Well, that's a brave man," J'lek drawled. "Third, fifth and twenty-second squads of mounted archers—bring him in or bring him down. If that man escapes me, none of you will."

Tartan knew what *that* meant and none of his Angadorians seemed willing to risk J'lek's anger. Thirty mounted Men and Uman lit off for the north, breaking efficiently from the main force without the chaos that might have been expected from any other nation's camp. Horses in the jess doonar are quartered within its confines, but not to the center. They wouldn't be pilfered in the night, nor hindered when they were needed all of a sudden. The lone rider lit off with three squads in hot pursuit, two branching out to encircle him.

"They'll never catch Little Storm," Tartan commented to J'lek.

"Don't be too sure, your Grace," the Uman commented. "I know that terrain, and so do those squads, which is why I chose them. There's an open bowl on the other side of that ridge, and loose slag on every side of it. In rainier months it's a pond, but now it's a trap, and by the time he's through it, he's going to be outflanked by our mounted archers."

"Then we should have him!" Tartan felt excited. If he could wreak victory now—

"We have someone," J'lek said, "and it's not an Eldadorian—not armored like one, anyway. Not in an Eldadorian saddle and harness. But all of this 'Jack's' tack came from the royal stables, and why would he, knowing right where we are, stumble upon us through a wash like that, once he'd escaped to our north?"

Tartan nodded. Another important bit of information he'd missed, although he lacked the far-seeing eyes and the far-ranging years of an Uman. The race of Men ruled the Uman in Eldador, but this didn't make Umankind weak or stupid.

They hadn't even finished disassembling the jess doonar

before thirty horsemen returned with another in their midst. If it *had* been this 'Jack,' then he couldn't have been on Little Storm.

At a daheer away, Tartan knew it wasn't their quarry. He looked to be a Man, but a small one, on a small, shaggy pony, as well. Based on the height, he wondered if they hadn't caught a woman.

Wonderful, he thought to himself. He'd captured a curious Eldadorian out of Andurin. Wouldn't Groff be pleased?

When the three squads reined in, the rider they presented looked like a Confluni, bound by his wrists to the back of a saddle with no proper saddle horn.

"Confluni national," the sergeant of the third squad reported, making a fist over his heart for his liege lord. "Claims he's a prisoner and demands War's Wages."

"War's Wages?" Tartan looked at J'lek, who shrugged. Warriors demanded War's Wages when they were defeated in battle. Essentially, to be put down instead of kept as prisoners.

"You give dey War's Wages," the Confluni said, in broken Uman, "or War, he come after you!"

The sergeant cuffed him in the back of the head.

"How are you defeated in battle?" J'lek demanded of him. The Captain approached the pony's stirrup and looked up into the Confluni's eyes. The little Man's short black hair framed his yellow skin. He dressed in the leather of the Confluni National Guard. Tartan had seen their kind in the second attack of Thera.

But the Confluni didn't ride.

"I Confluni National Guard," the Man said. "I outrider for Confluni invasion force, land Eldador this week."

* * *

"Confluni National Guard?"

The little man nodded. Bound on the ground by wrists and ankles, the hate on his face shone like a beacon. He'd been armed to the hilt, as well—a scimitar, triple-curved bow, a spear that could almost have been a lance, a long sword behind his saddle and enough daggers to pepper two squads. He wore the leather armor and cap that CNG wore—that and his yellow skin betrayed him, or Nina never would have guessed his origin.

She'd had no idea whom she might have trapped, but if she'd been wagering, this would have come in with high odds.

"What are you doing in Eldador?"

"I demand War's Wages," he repeated.

Nina sighed. She knew of this ridiculous tradition. The Aschire had nothing like it. One fought until one could fight no more. If captured, you found another way to resist.

"I didn't defeat you in battle," Nina countered. "I owe War no wages, even if the Aschire had any fealty to War, which we do not."

"You Aschire?" the male looked suddenly extremely nervous.

It had bothered her from time to time to hear what people thought of her outside of the palace. "The Emperor's Attack Bitch," "The Emperor's *Spare* Bitch," "The Royal Watch Dog." Nina was seen to be cruel, terrifying, even evil in her single-minded duty to protect her charges.

She'd taken an oath, and Krell's daughter would betray no oath. That didn't make her evil.

However, if the legend of her had exceeded the reality of her, then why not make good use of it.

"I am Nina of the Aschire," she said, and stood. "Guardian of the House Mordetur."

She took a breath and invoked the alias she hated the most, the one she'd heard whispered after her so many times, even by warriors.

"*Mistress of Pain.*"

Now the Confluni's eyes were like Tabaars in the dusky light. He'd heard of her–he'd hear a *lot* about her.

"War's Wages," he demanded, struggling. "You take *now*."

"I wonder if it would make you more compliant," Nina speculated, pulling a dagger from her arm-sheath, "were I to relieve you of your manhood?"

She squatted back down to the man's level, at his hip, and laid her fingers on his thigh.

"No!"

If the man started screaming, and there were more of them, then she might end up in a fight she wasn't ready for or, worse, having to abandon this one. She extended her will, being careful to use the slightest amount of her power, to congeal the air around his mouth and nose.

He immediately began choking. The Emperor had explained to her and to Shela one day that sound existed actually as a movement of waves through the air, like the waves of the ocean, lapping at the shores of one's ears. When she thickened the air, it passed no sound, and from there she and Shela had created a whole new discipline in moving sound, and even light, from place to place, or stopping it.

"I can let you strangle, almost to death, then let you breath, and let you strangle again," she informed the red-faced Confluni, "and you'll live for weeks before your heart explodes. Or you can answer my questions, and I'll make your death quick, as you wish."

"But in the end," she said, and she leaned close, so he could feel her breath on his face, as the Emperor had taught her when interrogating a prisoner, "you'll tell me everything you know, everything I want to hear. The only question is how much I leave of you to bury."

She released the spell, and he gasped for air, coughing and puking down his shirt, and then she congealed the air again. It took three times before he gave in and told her what she wanted to know.

* * *

"He dies!"

"No, mother."

Lee watched her younger brother and her mother argue, almost as if she saw two strangers.

She'd defied her mother before, especially in her training to be a sorceress. Her mother had been gifted, and she no less, and both knew it was the discussion and the disagreement that would build her will and make her the sorceress she needed to be.

Little Vulpe had been singing at mother's knee since he could form words. He adored her, he worshipped her. He had *no* ability to cast; he could be her little boy. Sometimes Lee had envied him that.

Now he sat Marauder with his back straight and his hand on the pommel of the sword the Dwarves had made for him, as a gift to the Emperor when he'd announced his son. Not as strong as father's sword, nor as long, it was still *real*, and up to then his mother barely let him touch it. How he'd sneaked it along for this journey was beyond her.

But he was sure touching it now. In fact, he'd sheathed it bloody. Like a good Andaron, Lee recognized the red splatter at the sheath's open end.

"Don't you tell me—" Shela warned him, urging her gelding forward. She'd come within striking distance—deceptively far for her height.

"I *said* no," Vulpe told her, with the same command she'd heard in her father's voice. For one dazzling instant, she saw him as a miniature version of Lupus the Conqueror, without the blond hair, without the scar, without the eyes bluer than the sky, but that same set to his eyebrows, that same defiant nose, that same line to his jaw that said, "You are about to push me too far."

Even her mother reacted to it.

"M'lady, if I may intervene," Hectaro said, urging his mount up beside her.

What a disappointment *he* had been. Humbled, humiliated, licking their captors' feet like some dog—no more fantasies of conquering the world beside Hectaro! Even the sound of him galled her.

"You may *not*," Shela informed him. She was recollecting herself. Shela stood down Wolf Soldiers—only father really controlled her. Lee anticipated seeing Vulpe's little, red behind over a saddle and her mother with a switch in her hand, before long.

They were in the camp Vulpe had made to trap the Bounty Hunters and kill them. They'd gotten all of them but one, and only lost two Wolf Soldiers doing it. Vulpe, following his mother, had collected their one squad and added to it almost three more of Theran Lancers, whom he'd called from Thera on his own, to rescue them.

Lee had to admit that was a lot more than she'd expected to see from her brother, but then, he'd apparently had some help.

Grandfather was there. Grandfather, thinner now, and a little grayer, sitting Little Storm with new confidence, like any Andaron would. He had a falchion over his shoulder in a broad leather sheath, but he hadn't pulled it. No, grandfather wasn't a swordsman because grandfather didn't *need* to be. Grandfather was wise.

Hectaro simpered and lowered his head to mother. No big surprise there. Grandfather, on the other hand, sat right next to Vulpe, looking mother right in the eye, and unafraid.

He'd seen her and his face had lit up. He'd said, "Hello, little girl," and it had taken all of her will power not to leap off of Singer and run to his stirrup. Mother had other ideas what to do with him.

Shela glared at Vulpe. Even a month ago, he'd have already been screaming with his pants around his ankles and his mother holding a bloody switch. Now everything seemed different, and Lee was trying to figure out why.

"He kidnapped your sister," Shela informed him. "Do you have no *loyalty*, son? Do you not see he's manipulated you with this trick, not to save you but to capture us for himself?"

"Glynn Escaroth hid Chawny," Vulpe corrected her. "And took Raven with her. He went after her, and he just worked with me, to save *you*, mother.

"I've guaranteed his safety. He is with me. That means he is with you."

Lee couldn't argue with that. That was Andaron code as well as Eldadorian policy. The frustration sat clear on mother's face. She wouldn't betray her code, but she wanted grandfather to pay for what had happened to Chawny.

"Riders coming in," an Uman Wolf Soldier she recognized as Grelt announced, pointing to the north. All heads turned to see the dust over the ridge, a wide swath arcing back in the sky.

Men in formation, on horseback. Not single file, like Andarons, trying to disguise their numbers. Theran Lancers, announcing their presence in their own land.

When they topped the ridge, she recognized Tali Digatishi immediately, his mustachios flowing, the look of the unconquerable Andaron in his eyes and the set of a face dominated by his hawk nose.

Uncle Two Spears—mother turned back to her son with a triumphant look on her face.

* * *

Vulpe watched ten squads of Theran Lancers trot down the northern ridge toward them. He saw his mother's smirk and Hectaro's obviously worried expression. Hectar, Hectaro's father, had always had a calming influence on his own father. When the Emperor wanted to charge in, he always had J'her at his side, Rennin always wanted to follow behind him, Ceberro always wanted to lead the attack. Groff always thought it was a bad idea and Hectar always counseled patience. Of all of them, Hectar always had father's ear.

Hectaro was trying to do that now—trying to be the calm voice, just as Vulpe was trying to be his own father.

"Sit beside me, Hectaro," Vulpe ordered the older boy. Hectaro looked once at the side of mother's face, and then urged his mount forward and turned it, sitting opposite grandfather. Vulpe caught the look of disgust on Lee's face.

She used to like him. Well, things change.

Mother's smile brightened when she saw uncle Tali. She loved her brother. Vulpe had to assume that came in time, because unless he'd just found another rodent in his bed, Vulpe didn't get many smiles from Lee.

"Tali!" she greeted the Duke of Thera. The men who escorted them parted to let the two embrace, still on horseback, like Andarons.

"Shela—you're skin and bone!" Two Spears chided her, as he always did. "The mother of three should be fat!"

"I am the mother of millions," Shela said, meaning the Empire. "I have no time for eating. But I may have to make time to school this one."

She regarded Vulpe. He immediately felt like a deer staring down the shaft of an arrow, but he refused to do the usual head-down tactic that would have gotten him only a minor beating.

"A few men call you by your first name, and you think you can disrespect your mother, my sister?" he thundered. Tali Digatishi commanded men in two nations—he could just *look* at a person and make them want to cry. Vulpe felt that now.

No, he told himself. Grandfather was here; he had *men* now. Wolf Soldiers, and yes—they *did* call him by his first name.

Just like his father.

He straightened. "Duke Two Spears," he said, and inclined his head. "We welcome you. Your warriors helped me to save my mother, and I am in your debt."

"Ho, *ho!*" Two Spear's eyes widened, then he threw back his head. This was also Tali Digatishi—the fast living son of the Andoron Plains. Quick to fight and quick to laugh.

"Who is this one, who tries to be his father?" Two Spears continued. Vulpe saw the eyes of the warriors around him brighten, wanting to laugh at him.

Before he realized it, his hand fell on his sword's pommel.

Before he could stop it, every man and woman who'd fought with him did the same, Wolf Soldier and Theran Lancer alike. He'd grown up with that sound, the metallic clank of swords thumping scabbards. Say the word, he knew, and it became a blood bath. His twelve-year-old heart swelled. As he'd imagined it in the mirror a thousand times—the son of Lupus the Conqueror.

Two Spears' eyes widened, as did his mother's. His mother's face took on the indignation he'd seen her use with disobedient servants and defiant children. His uncle, however, wasn't looking at the warriors, or even at Vulpe himself, really.

His eyes were fixed on Vulpe's hip. "Prince Vulpe," he said,

"I want to see your sword."

No! that was going too far. Even if they took his command, Vulpe's sword was a gift from the Dwarves. He'd named it 'Fury,' he slept with it under his mattress, and he'd cared for the blade every day of his life that he could remember. He took it everywhere.

For Fury, he'd fight. Even his own uncle.

Two Spears must have seen the defiance in him. "Vulpe," he said, more softly, as he would to a shy horse, "I don't want you to give me your sword, please—just draw it."

Vulpe couldn't see anything wrong with that. He pulled the bloodstained blade.

Every warrior behind him did the same. The Therans clamored for their own weapons. Two Spears raised one hand, shouting, "Hold—hold your weapons. On your lives, no one draws."

He turned to his sister. "You see that?" he asked her.

Her brown eyes turned round as saucers. Vulpe didn't understand. She'd wanted to thrash him just a moment before, now she looked like she would take him in her arms and weep for him.

"He's barely seen his twelfth summer," she demanded.

Two Spears shook his head. He pulled his own Andaron scimitar and he threw it point-first into the earth before Marauder's feet. The stallion stamped and bobbed his head.

"He's blooded, Shela," he told her. "He's commanded men; he's fought with his own weapon. You know the way, as any other."

"He's a *boy!*"

He cuffed her. *No one* struck Shela Mordetur, Empress of Eldador, except for one man, and he wasn't here. Vulpe opened his mouth to save his uncle's life, knowing he would be too late.

But Shela just wiped the blood from the corner of her mouth, looked sadly into her brother's eyes, and then into his own. He didn't see the love of the mother who'd raised him right then. He didn't see the soft, giving woman who held him to her breast the first time he'd been thrown, the first time he'd been beaten learning to fight with this sword, the first time he'd cried in fear at a lightning storm.

He saw a more worn woman, who'd just put down a burden.

"He's come to man," Two Spears informed her. "And I swore fealty to his father, my blood brother, and you'll respect him and regard him as you would the Emperor."

He turned to Vulpe, inclined his head, and said, "Your Highness, the Theran Lancers are yours to command."

Chapter Eight

Fate

Glynn sang:

"For Fovea, Fovea, then must they live and die.
Fight the battle from within
With a champion from outside.
You shall be the weapons
The tools of men and gods
Who come too late for victory
And win despite these odds."

Vedeen nodded, smiling that passive smile she seemed to always have on her lips.

Raven wanted to smack that smile off sometimes, and this was one of them.

"Heard that," she said. "Been all over it. The Emperor conquers Fovea, we fight him. We lose, but we win, too."

"And doesn't that seem strange to you?" Vedeen asked. "That you should lose, but in losing, you should win?"

"No," Raven said. "I've read a thousand books like that. The hero dies and everyone realizes what he was fighting for - "

"Wait," Karl held his hand up, riding next to them. They'd ridden west of Metz and were turning north for Tonkin. From there, they planned to hire a ship for Outpost IX.

They'd left the Eldadorians they'd killed in shallow graves on the plains, including the hostage. He hadn't known enough to justify keeping him alive, although the thought of Karl putting him down made Raven have to force herself to look at him.

"You've read a *thousand* books?" he pressed her.

Glynn smiled her deprecating little smile. Even Xinto raised an eyebrow.

"I don't think there *are* thousands of books," he said, pulling his lumpy cloak around him. It seemed like rain and the temperature had dropped suddenly.

"Well, there are certainly books by the thousands," Glynn said, "however no one other than a high Duke or a King has access to them."

"The Emperor has a fondness for books," Vedeen said. "However, even *he* doesn't have *thousands*."

"Cast a truth saying, and see if I'm wrong," Raven argued. If one thing bugged her, it was to be called a liar.

Of course, these people didn't have a printing press and were a thousand years from one, she reasoned, so every book they'd ever seen had been hand-written. Probably no one here *had* read a thousand books.

Okay, maybe she hadn't—either. She did the math. If she'd been reading for twenty years, then fifty books a year, or a little less than one per week…

But then, school, kids' books—yea, could be a thousand.

"I would prefer not to drain all of my energy entirely," Glynn said. "Perhaps the good Druid might suffice—"

"I cast truth sayings on her all the time," Zarshar said. "For what she comes up with, I couldn't help myself. Go ahead, girl—how many books have you read?"

"I just did the math," Raven said, "and I could have easily read a thousand."

"No lie," Zarshar said.

"Unless you're lying," Karl added.

Zarshar bared his red teeth. Glynn help up her hand. "He is not," she said.

"You disbelieve me?" he growled.

"Well, you *do* lie," Xinto said. "In fact, you usually do it to hurt other people as much as you can."

Zarshar narrowed his eyes.

"You do," Xinto pressed him.

"Well," Zarshar said, finally, "you know I'm not now. She's read a thousand books. Maybe she's a princess or some high duchess in her own land."

"No," Raven said. "Where I'm from, we have a lot of books. I love to read."

"Waste of time," Karl grumbled. "Dusty tomes that smell funny. You want to read something, read the entrails of the next man you kill. That can tell you your future, you know."

"Yuck," Raven shuddered.

"I would not have thought you learned," Glynn admitted. "In fact, I am surprised you're even literate."

"Well, not in any language you know," Raven admitted. "That one I came here speaking, that Angron speaks."

"*King* Angron Aurelias," Glynn said, "and regardless, I must expand your teachings now to include the written word. If you are capable of it in any language, surely you are capable of it in the languages of Men and Uman."

"And, of course, the most gifted poets are Scitai," Xinto said, "so you'll have to learn Scitai."

"Sirrah," Glynn admonished Xinto, "I have no fear of a truth saying with *you*, and the most gifted poets are *clearly* Uman-Chi."

Karl snorted.

Glynn raised an eyebrow in challenge.

"We were discussing the passage," Vedeen reminded them gently. She sat straight in her saddle, her huge roan moving easily with the other horses, although a hand taller than any of them. She rode like a man, not sidesaddle like Raven and Glynn. Much as it would chafe the insides of her thighs at first, Raven wished she could do the same.

"Okay," she said, "We know I'm the *champion from outside.*"

"And how do you know this," Vedeen pressed her.

"Well," Raven said, "for one thing, I am from outside of Fovea. My lands aren't even in this reality."

"And yet, I spoke with your 'Jack,' and he used words more ancient than the Cheyak."

Vedeen and Zarshar had both informed her of this. Jack had spoken what she recognized as the Lord's Prayer, in Latin, and it had all but made Zarshar's head explode, while impressing the heck out of the Druids, who had been mouthing the words for thousands of years without even knowing what they meant."

In the name of the father, the son, and the holy spirit, Raven thought. How many times, as Melissa, had she crossed herself and said those same words.

That they should be so powerful here…

"Can I try something?" she asked.

"Absolutely not," Glynn immediately chimed in, straightening. Glynn was convinced that Raven's powers were a ticking bomb, and she always fought against the fuse.

"What do you want to try, dear?" Vedeen asked her.

"I want to say something more in that language," she said, "but I don't want to hurt Zarshar."

Zarshar perked up. To their north, Jahunga ran with their Toorians as their outrider guard, even without horses. To the left and right, mounted Volkhydrans on stolen Eldadorian horses road scout, while behind them their walking Volkhydrans formed the rear guard.

They'd become their own little army, Raven thought.

"You care so much that you hurt me, eh?" Zarshar rumbled.

There was a time to be leather thonged Raven, sword on her hip, dagger in her boot, throwing fireballs, and a time to be Melissa, all soft and gooey, and if Raven was learning *anything*, it was that.

She kicked her mount to pick its pace up and pulled up alongside Zarshar. While the others watched, she laid her hand alongside the giant, evil face, and looked into the devilish red eyes, almost at a level with her own, even mounted.

"Of course I do," she said, letting her eyes get all watery. "You're my friend, and I love you, big guy."

"War's whiskers," Karl swore.

Raven couldn't read the great, red eyes. Whether he would see this as an opportunity to exploit her, or an affront, was anyone's guess, but he loped along for several hundred yards, looking back at her, before he looked away.

"Speak your words," he said finally. "No slip of a girl can harm the Black Adept."

"Are you ready Vedeen?" Raven asked.

Vedeen nodded. The rest watched. Zarshar kept loping along.

She tried to remember some Latin words.

"E pluribus Unum," she said.

Vedeen shrugged. Nothing.

"Cogito, ergo sum," she said. *I think, therefore I am.* She'd taken a course in Cartesian philosophy.

Nothing.

"Nulla avaritia sine poena est," she said. There is no greed without punishment, from Seneca, a Roman from the time of Caesar.

Nothing.

Wait, she thought. Perhaps Monty Python had the answer.

"Pie Jesu Domine," she intoned, like the monks from the movie, "dona eis requiem."

Oh, sweet Jesus, grant them rest.

Zarshar roared in pain, falling to his knees. All of the horses started bucking in fear. Vedeen's mount reared, pawing at the sky, while Vedeen herself shrieked, standing up in the stirrups, her fists at her temples.

To her credit, Glynn kept her saddle. Karl was thrown, she and Xinto right after. They'd taught her to keep her heels down when in the saddle, which had made her calves ache until she got used to it—now she was glad. Her feet slipped from the stirrups, even as she pushed the reins away from her in mid flight, her ass flying higher than her head as she flew over the mare's mane. The bucking horse took off with the others, the Volkhydran riders taking off after them.

Landing chest first into the hard ground, Xinto *still* managed to grope her ass as he landed on top of her. Raven's nose filled up with the torn sod as she came to a rest on the ground. She rolled over, with the horny little Scitai next to her, looking up into the blue sky.

Zarshar was the first of them off the ground. He towered over Raven, his red eyes almost on fire, his red teeth actually foaming, and said, "Girl, as you love me—not that again."

Seemed like pretty sage advice to Raven.

* * *

She sat by the campfire that night, another creature like an antelope turning on a spit over it, the dog with its head in her lap.

Jahunga's turn to cook. She'd offered and been turned down. They didn't trust her to do a lot things, especially not now, but it seemed that, in this world, cooking was a man thing. She'd asked

Vedeen about it.

"Cooking?" she parotted. "Well, I suppose women do it more than males. I know Andaron men would starve to death with their kills around them, were it not for the women. However, Eldadorian males are measured by their cooking, and I actually find them, especially the Uman, more severe than the Andarons. A Toorian who can't cook his own kills is called 'part man,' and your Volkhydran, Karl, has probably cooked more than has been cooked for him."

"*My* Volkhyrdran?" Raven asked her.

"Am I mistaken?" Vedeen asked. "I'd considered coupling with him, but did not, for respect of you. The child would certainly be sound."

'What was it that her father used to say?' Raven wondered. 'Spank my ass and call me Sally?'

"I'm—um, er—I'm with Jack, not Karl," she said, finally.

"Ah," Vedeen said, nodding sagely.

Matchmaker action, Raven thought. She'd had this before.

It would be easier to be with Jack if she could actually *be* with Jack, or Bill, or whatever he was calling himself now. Personally, she'd really fallen in love with being Raven.

Raven could *handle* things.

"Goodsirs," she heard. She turned to see one of the Volkhydrans talking to Karl.

He was the oldest one—Forn. When the Volkhydrans needed to talk, they spoke to Forn, who spoke to Karl.

"What is it?" Karl grumbled. He did that. When they spoke to him, he acted like he couldn't stand them. They lapped that up.

"There's an outrider been shadowin' us fer an hour 'r more," he drawled. "Been waitin' to see what's he's about, seems he's about keepin' an eye what we're about."

Raven had to digest that. Glynn and Jahunga were already off their feet.

"And my Toorians missed this?" he demanded.

"My respects," Forn nodded to Jahunga, "an' it is that yer Toorians wouldn't know horse sign from horse shit. I don't suspect as it's much in yer jungles, anyway."

More for Raven to decipher.

Sorry, dude—jungle people can't tell anything about horses. Well, true enough. Jahunga nodded his acceptance of it.

"Where and how many?" Karl demanded.

"Jes' one," Forn said. "He's a whiley, though—we git closed to him once, and he lit off, showed up t' the other side of camp."

"You'll never catch him," Glynn said. "Either an Eldadorian scout or a Bounty Hunter hired by the Emperor to find us—either way, he'll torment you into chasing him, while his allies encircle us."

"Break camp and ride, then?" Karl asked her. He seemed uniquely worried. Raven really didn't know what Bounty Hunters were, but she'd heard them mentioned and there seemed to always be an edge of fear.

Jahunga shook his head. "This we cannot do," he said. "Move with them upon us, they start on our outriders and work their way in. Without the outriders they'll surround us like a lion pride."

Again, Raven couldn't argue with that.

She reached out with her mind, imagining keeping low, imagining keeping her power to the ground like little mice, scurrying through the dry grass.

She found a male three hundred yards from the camp, mounted, watching them; small, mean, dark—he wanted a reason to hurt them.

She found another, a woman, much the same. This one had a longbow and arrows.

Another to their south, another to their north.

"Girl?" Glynn asked her.

She roused herself from the spell, then felt embarrassed. She wasn't supposed to cast spells this close to Metz.

"I—um, gee, I'm sorry," she began.

"Too late for sorry, the damage, if any is done," she said. "In fact, you did a passable job reining in your power, much as you usually wield it like a club. Did you find this person?"

"I'm up to four so far," Raven said. "North, south, east and west. But that's just close to camp."

Karl looked at Jahunga across the fire. "That's something you do before you bring in an attack force," he said.

"That would be my thinking, yes," Jahunga said. "If they aren't about to attack us, then they're on their way."

"Who?" Xinto demanded.

All eyes turned to Raven.

"They're small Men," she said. "Black hair, yellow skin—they wear leather outfits and ride shaggy ponies. Does that help?"

Now all eyes reverted to Xinto.

"There's a shaggy pony from deep in Conflu," he said. "Some ride them—I don't know those people. You're describing Confluni warriors, but what are they doing here?"

"The Emperor of Conflu has approached the Silent Island many times since the second invasion of Thera," Glynn said. "They believe this is the side of Eldador that is, in fact, vulnerable."

"With thousands of Daff Kanaari warriors in Metz?" Karl scoffed. "I doubt Angron Aurelias ever got behind *that* plan."

"No," Glynn said, "he did not. However, with a sufficient force of Confluni…"

Xinto was already shaking his head. "No," he said. "Conflu would never take on the Empire alone. Then all of the retaliation would fall back on Conflu, should it fail. No, the Emperor would demand some powerful ally, someone with magic to counter Shela, should go with them."

"Such as the Dorkans," Karl said.

"Or the Toorians," Jahunga added. "Our shamans are *strong*."

"And without them, my people would lay waste to every village in your jungle," Zarshar said. "No, the Dorkans—definitely."

"Then our lot is with these people," Glynn said. "When this invasion force arrives, surely we must join with it."

"I don't think we're going to get that option," Karl said. "Those scouts aren't trying to contact us; they're following us until someone else can sweep in and destroy us."

"However with our own Ambassador," Glynn said, "we may well negotiate a peace, even an alliance—"

Xinto sighed. "I can at the least find this army and speak with its leader," he said. "Surely no one from Conflu will attack *me*."

"Take the Slee with you," Zarshar grumbled.

Xinto looked back up to the Devil quietly.

"Take the Slee," he repeated. "Best chance you have, if your friends decide not to like you. Let him know to slither in if you're not back out in half a day."

"I haven't even *seen* Slurn—" Raven began.

The Slee melted out of the night, a double curved bow in his hand, his spear and a quiver full of arrows over his shoulder. He dropped the bow and the arrows at Raven's feet.

"Well, maybe only three watching us, now," Karl said. "Where was this one, Slurn?"

Slurn pointed to the south.

"Any idea where that army of Confluni warriors is?" Karl asked.

Slurn pointed to the west, and hissed.

"Pretty far inland," Karl noted. "Had to find us by accident."

Slurn turned his yellow eyes to Raven. Much as he communicated anything, he showed his love for her. She had no idea where it came from, however she knew she felt safe with Slurn. She pushed the dog out of her lap and stood, crossed the camp and put her hand to the side of Slurn's scaly jaw.

She'd been getting stiff lately. She'd been hurt getting thrown. She'd stretched her legs too far apart, and fallen on her shoulder.

"Slurn," she gushed at him, batting her big, brown eyes. "Can you get Xinto to that camp and, if he needs you, get him out safely."

Slurn closed his eyes and hissed, "Ray—hen."

"That probably means, 'yes,' Forn speculated.

"I hate to think *what* that means," Karl added.

Slurn turned and was into the high grass in a moment. Xinto shot her a wink and was after the reptile-man.

What would come next was anyone's guess.

* * *

Nina of the Aschire road hard to the west—as fast as her horse could stand it. Up in the saddle, her legs aching, the sun beating her back, she searched the horizon for a sign of the Emperor's outriders.

It would take her days to get to Uman City and more days to get back. In days, a Confluni army could kill thousands and rout the inner earldoms of the Empire, even threaten Metz and Steel City.

She'd almost doubled back for Angador, but the Duke would either have the Emperor's kinsman and be sending his own riders to Uman City, or have given up by now, and either way he would be bound for Angador.

Better to let the Emperor know not to move his tens of thousands from his country, with an enemy already on the Andurin Peninsula.

There! She saw it to the northwest, horse-sign. Dust kicked up, and a lot of it—a strong force of horses.

She turned her mount and topped a hill, giving her some view over the land. She immediately saw the Wolf's Head standard of the

Emperor himself, at the center of a company of Theran Lancers.

What he was doing this far north was anyone's guess. Perhaps he had already been warned.

But no, as she approached, she made out the details of others there, first Duke Two Spears, larger than life on an Andaron stallion, then beside him his sister, the Empress herself, Chawny in a kirruk on her back. To either side of her, her children, Vulpe and Lee.

Her heart leapt, then another horse trotted up beside them, a black stallion larger than all of the rest.

She didn't recognize the Man, his hair and his beard longer, his stomach half the size, but she recognized Little Storm.

She drove her heels into the horse's side, pounding out the distance to her family and her enemy.

* * *

Had the world gone mad, she wondered?

Nina felt as if she'd woken up in a dream instead of from one.

Shela, Lee and Chawny had been captured by Genna. Vulpe had rescued them by collecting Wolf Soldiers and Lancers and setting a trap, and Jack, the Emperor's kinsman, had helped him.

Now Shela deferred to him, and Two Spears as well, and Wolf Soldiers were calling Vulpe by his first name, and saluting him.

What's more, Shela, the Bitch of Eldador, most feared woman alive, took direction from her son; her eyes looking like she'd buried him instead.

"Girl, are you sure?" Two Spears demanded of her.

She nodded. "Shela taught me how to interrogate a prisoner," she said. "The man came from a moving army of no less than fifty thousand Confluni, and they were waiting for reinforcements."

"Conflu could turn out that many," Shela said, "but to what end? We've crushed more."

"How?" Jack asked her.

Even his voice made her skin crawl. Nina yearned to plunge a dagger into his breast.

Shela's eyes narrowed and Nina could tell she felt no different. One of the Wolf Soldier guards whom she recognized from Shela's entourage, an Uman named Grelt, piped up, "Thirty thousand tried to overrun Thera more'n a decade ago, and the Emperor beat them with four thousand. Then they came at us with sixty thousand six years later, and Uman-Chi wizards, and we beat them in Thera again. Theran Lancers mowed them down; the Lady tore apart their wizards with her magic."

"I had help," Shela admitted. "Even Nina, here, was involved in that battle."

"So attack Thera again, with fewer troops?" Jack pulled at his grey and brown beard, looking past all of them. "No, I don't see that. That would just be stupid."

"They're waiting for reinforcements," Nina told him. Senile old man—she'd decided it. When she got him alone, he died. He couldn't be allowed to infect young Vulpe with his ramblings.

Vulpe would be a great man with the right guidance.

"Has *any* army been big enough to match the Emperor?" Jack pressed them. Now, Nina thought, he was just flattering them. "Has he ever been outnumbered so badly he didn't win?"

"No," Shela's fierce eyes told of her pride. "No, never."

Two Spears was nodding, however. "Even the Confluni wouldn't be so foolish," he said. "The old one is right. They've struck Thera twice and been beaten twice. The last time we sank most of the ships in their navy and burned Sarn to the ground. Lupus swore he would march to the capital of Conflu if they tried this again."

"When they went after Thera the first time," Shela said, slowly, "they attacked Eldador first, to try to draw the Wolf Soldiers out of the city. *Yonega Waya* pretended to send them, but sent the city militia instead. When they attacked Thera, they thought they faced the militia, and instead they faced the Wolf Soldiers."

"So if they make a feint at some city now…" Jack speculated.

They were all quiet. Now Nina could see it go either way. Attack a city as a distraction to go after another one, or attack a city, pretend to attack the other one, and then go after the first city.

Either way, a lot of Eldadorians were going to pay the price.

"We have to move before they're ready," Vulpe said, finally, his hand on his sword.

Nina recognized Fury, the sword she'd helped him name, which the Dwarves presented to his father on the day he was born. She'd hid it on him hundreds of time, and he'd found it as many. She was sure one day that he'd cut a finger off on the ultra-sharp blade.

Now she saw the blood splatter on the top of the sheath. Nina felt her mouth drop open as she looked into the face of the little boy whom she'd mothered, whom she'd held with skinned knees, whom she'd tickled until he gasped for air.

The face of the *man*, blooded before twelve years old.

There is no peace in the House of Mordetur, she told herself. No wonder they deferred to him. No wonder his mother looked as if she'd lost her son.

She had.

"Your Highness," Two Spears said, straightening, "we need to inform your father."

Vulpe looked immediately to Jack, whom he called 'grandfather.' The boy so desperate for his busy father had replaced him with this manufactured relative.

Jack nodded. "If your father sails off on some campaign with troops on his doorstep, he'll lose respect and maybe get stranded. The first thing they'll want to do is to cut off his supplies."

"If they know that he's campaigning," Two Spears said.

"Don't you think it's kind of a coincidence they picked this season to attack?" Jack looked him in the face, straightening on the impassive Little Storm. "Don't you people usually start your wars this month, because it's *called* War?"

"What of it?" Nina spat. These people talked and talked.

But now Shela was nodding. "Yes, we do," she said, and looked at her son. "Angron Aurelias all but paved a road for your father to start this new campaign. Now the Confluni are here, just as he's about to leave on it, right *after* Glynn Escaroth disappeared."

"Between Thera and Angador lie the most fertile plains in Eldador, and most of our grain and cattle," Two Spears said. "If the Confluni take or destroy those, our armies abroad will starve."

"A feint for Steel City," Jack said. "Then a direct assault on Uman City. That's what I'd do. Destroy that, and then park outside of Thera, and there goes all of the supplies in Eldador."

"We could ship—" Shela began, and caught herself.

They could ship through Galnesh Eldador, except they'd have to fight their way through whatever was left of that Confluni army, plus their reinforcements.

"Your Grace," Vulpe said, using the formal with his uncle. Vulpe the boy would have called him 'Uncle Tali,' or even Two Spears. Vulpe the man owed him better.

It still rattled Nina's brain.

"Two squads of fast Andaron riders, minimum armor, to Uman City. My father has to know what we know."

"Send them on different routes," Jack said.

Vulpe looked up at him. Marauder was more than a hand smaller than Little Storm, and Jack sat tall in the saddle regardless.

"You're at war, son," he said. "You have to assume that whatever you do, your enemy knows you'd do it and, whatever you know, your enemy already knows it. If they know you're on to them, then you'll want to tell your father, and they don't want that."

"One squad directly," Two Spears said, "one squad through the plains, and a third back to Thera, to approach by boat."

"Mother, you must warn the capitol," Vulpe said. "Hectar has probably already sent out a patrol—"

"I should return to my father," another boy said. Nina recognized Hectaro, Hectar's son. For the last year she'd been fighting a war to keep Lee away from him.

She shuddered imagining what they'd accomplished in her absence.

Vulpe nodded. "You'll take thirty Lancers and ride back to Galnesh Eldador with my sister," he said. "Lee can operate the Central Communications as well as mother."

"Lee has never—" Shela began, and looked at her daughter, who blushed crimson and looked down.

"Lee, you'll stay in communication with mother," Vulpe ordered her. Then he kicked his horse and moved right alongside of Hectaro, extending his tiny arm to the older boy.

Some would consider *him* the man, of at least eighteen summers. Hectaro took the prince's arm in his.

"On your life, guard her better than you did my mother," Vulpe said, the brown eyes hawkish.

Hectaro tried to look at him, and then looked away. "On my life," he murmured.

No doubt about it, Nina thought.

The world had gone mad.

Chapter Nine

Out of the Dark, into the Open

Yeral Stowe, Duchess of Angador, sat her palfrey and watched her husband as he directed his warriors. It seemed at once so simple and so complicated for him to control so many. Simple, because he gave the orders to his runners, who informed his majors, who informed his captains, who informed his lieutenants, who informed sergeants, who informed men-at-arms, moving a single command across four thousand in minutes.

Complicated to know what command to give, what order, how to tell if the left flank was exposed, or the march had lost a beat.

As a girl she'd seen Wolf Soldiers march on Uman City. She'd heard their heels drum the earth over an hour before they'd arrived. That thrum, that stomp, that terror had haunted her from that day to this.

Her father had told her, "You hear that, daughter? This upstart thinks that putting foot to Earth is no different than putting hand to steel. Well, the King may be a drunkard who's fallen for these ways, but your father will be the one who finally sits upon the throne."

A week later they were marching to Thera with their wrists in chains, and her oldest brother, Yor, marching in time with the Wolf Soldiers, them smirking to each other as he walked beside them.

Yor joined the Wolf Soldier guard years later and, as far as she knew, still lived. He'd fostered with the Emperor, competing with her husband for Lupus' attention, while Yeral served Shela Mordetur as a lady in waiting.

Her own mother had tried her hand as a seamstress, and then run off one day with a Volkhydran merchant without even a good-bye. They'd hung her father for sedition, then buried him at Glennen's feet, to serve his king for all time. The rest of her family, being reduced to common, would never join him there.

Her father had wrung one final promise from Rancor Mordetur before he stepped up to the gallows: do right by my family in my absence. She'd earned the favor of the Mordetur house, putting aside her blinding hatred for the horned goat who had deposed that great man. She'd learned everything she could about horsecraft from Shela Mordetur and she'd learned to bide her time and hold her bile.

She'd been the one to advise Hectaro to rub down his father's mare with wintergreen, to get Blizzard to seed her. No one but she had thought of that. She'd come up with it after listening to one of the Emperor's tedious stories of his greatness—how they'd eluded the Confluni in their own land.

That had been the work of a Bounty Hunter named Genna, now posing among her own ladies in waiting.

"Lupus told a captain once that fortune favors the bold," Yeral said to the demure looking woman mounted on the palfrey next to her. "Surely Desire blessed you for your temerity, that you should come back to me with an empty hand."

They spoke in hushed voices—the other lady could be trusted; she'd been promised a wealthy husband for her confidence. The lady whom Genna imitated now had wanted only her own Angadorian mare and 50 Tabaars when the journey ended.

"In fact, I fulfilled your contract, Lady," Genna informed her. "You wanted Shela Mordetur captured with as many of her children as I could include, then for me to return here, and I did so. You didn't mention bringing them."

Yeral felt her lip curl in anger and forced her face back to its ladylike serenity. Bounty Hunters are a tricky breed—in the end, they'd betrayed her father for their own good. This one counted herself among the best, and with her came a certain anonymity. Most people thought her dead.

"Play not your semantics game with me, good lady," Yeral

threatened her. "You were engaged and you knew your duty, or you would not have brought them so far—"

"Just my idea of humor," Genna interrupted her. "I failed in my mission, I returned to inform you. That is Guild policy. We've never had much luck with the Mordeturs."

Yeral smirked despite herself. True enough.

"No one could have predicted that her eleven-year-old would rally the army to his banner and take her back," Genna said. "In fact, he took one of my own men himself, a Fighting Bounty Hunter with more kills than I could count. It speaks well for my own son—"

Genna looked down. In her Uman disguise, she looked sadder still. Either she had lost a child, or planned to, Yeral decided.

Few enough female Bounty Hunters, fewer still with families.

"And now?" Yeral pressed her.

She met Genna's green eyes. "Well, I would as like to steal a horse and ride, except your husband has mastered the jess doonar, and they are simply too hard to steal from you. Seeing as you don't want him to know about my services, I think I'll be waiting for the next farm house, and then depart and steal or barter for my ride."

"Or you could remain," Yeral offered tentatively. "Tartan would never have approved our mission, however now with this Confluni threat emerging..."

That had the whole camp worried. They'd paid War's Wages to a scout of the Confluni army massing on the Andurin peninsula. If Lupus was campaigning with most of the armies of Eldador, it was a bad time to find so many here.

Tartan insisted that if 4,000 Wolf Soldiers could face thirty thousand outside of Thera, then why not 4,500 Angadorian Knights? Yeral believed he wanted to throw down the helmet of the Confluni general, the head still in it, at the Emperor's feet.

"You would like to take advantage of my experience with the Confluni," Genna finished for her.

Yeral nodded.

"And if, in the course of events, a certain Empress should present herself and her new-found warrior son to combat this menace..." Genna added.

Yeral smiled openly. Her husband caught her eyes and, believing all of her smiles were for him, returned it, and blew her a kiss from the back of his glove.

She'd earn those kisses soon enough. Genna knew her mind, however. With outriders this far flung, Shela would find them soon.

She wasn't the type of Empress to refuse the field. In that, Yeral had learned a lot from her. Be the woman at her man's side, be exciting, and watch him make all of your dreams come true.

Shela had told her that. She loved Shela in her way.

But she had her plans.

When she didn't respond, Genna nodded. She faded from Yeral's side, only to appear as a red-haired woman in leather, standing in their army's path, only an hour later.

Well enough.

* * *

"The invincible person, the Light of the West, Ymir Effecate Hagadashi Boohoori," the squire said, standing aside in his silks to let Xinto pass into the pavilion.

In the Western tradition, the noble remained in place, and announcements were made to those entering his presence or, in this case, hers.

Rare indeed to find a woman in charge of anything in Conflu, but Ymir Boohoori was considered special, the wife of the man who was defeated by Lupus the Conqueror in the Battle of Tamaran Glen.

Xinto's eyes adjusted to the gloom inside of the pavilion. Superior Scitai eyesight picked out details an Uman or a thin-brained Man would have missed. The dirt on the rug told of large feet and many of them. The leather woven into the walls of the pavilion wasn't deer or horse, but cow, died red, but clearly of a breed raised in the southern provinces of Conflu, nearer the capitol. The divan where Effecate reclined had been upholstered in satins lined with furs, again in the style of the capitol.

She came from the north, but she had spent more time in the Imperial Palace, at least recently.

Effecate Boohoori covered the divan and then some. Three young men in little more than a twist of cotton around their loins knelt by her feet, their heads down. The single piece of furniture was all but crushed under the weight of a woman whom, Xinto guessed, hadn't looked down and seen her own feet in years. Rolls of fat peeked out from purple and white silk twists in her sari, her long black hair draped down to the floor in a puddle, framing a face with three chins, inset brown eyes and a hook nose, sporting a mole with three hairs.

Singularly, one of the most repulsive women Xinto had ever seen. He forced a smile and bowed until the bright orange feather in his cap brushed the floor.

"Lovely lady," he said. "The noble presence honors me."

She nodded, and snorted as she shifted her body on the divan. A plate of fruits lay half-eaten by her head—apples and grapes. Xinto wanted to be rid of her before that vile mixture worked its magic on her intestinal tract.

"We are surprised to see you alive," Effecate said, finally. Her baritone voice sounded as graceless as a lowing aurochs. "We had received report that you had fallen afoul of the Emperor of Eldador."

"Is this, then, a rescue mission?" Xinto smiled through his beard, trying to be his most charming. "I am flattered."

She smiled through her fleshy lips. "Not that I would not have leapt at the chance," she complimented him, "however, no, Ambassador, we are here for…other purposes."

Xinto nodded. Confluni pleasantries like these could go on for hours. Normally, he would be content to exchange and banter, however, he knew Effecate Boohoori, and she didn't usually play to the normal etiquettes.

He had worked for her before. He could even be considered slightly responsible for her rise in power—not because he had inadvertently empowered the thin-brained Man who had killed her husband, but because she had paid him handsomely to spy on her enemies in Conflu, when Lupus the Conqueror came to power and made the rest of Fovea too dangerous for him to travel in.

"How might I be of service to you, then, gracious lady?" Xinto asked her. "What small service might I perform, to reflect upon what I am sure is to be a magnificent undertaking into these foreign lands?"

Effecate Boohoori smiled, her cheeks crinkling, and snapped her fingers twice at the young boys. One immediately picked up a lute and began strumming. Another began to dance, swaying his hips sinuously to the music, while the third reached up and began to rub the woman's bloated feet.

Xinto suppressed a shudder.

"Do you travel alone?" Effecate asked him casually.

"Not in these dangerous lands, no, great lady," Xinto said, and winced internally. He was trying to avoid words implying size.

She didn't react. "I am seeking to expand my fortunes here in

Eldador," she said, far too casually. She'd spent a fortune already by gathering so many. "I don't suppose you hold sway with any entrepreneurs, who perhaps don't share in Lupus the Conqueror's favors?"

Did he know of someone rich who could help her fund this invasion? Well, he did, but he wasn't ready to spill that yet. If she meant Glynn Escaroth, then she already knew the answer, having been spying on them for days. "The Emperor of Eldador has many enemies," he said.

"True enough," she said. She flicked a wrist at the dancing boy, and he slithered out of his cotton loincloth. Xinto felt his eyebrows drop despite himself. Court etiquette didn't lend itself to nude dancers of either sex. Certainly a noble lady might entertain herself, but not so openly as this. Xinto saw this as indication she was not, in fact, here as a member of the Imperial court. She didn't see herself returning to Conflu if she freely created this scandal.

What are you missing, Xinto? he demanded of himself.

"I'm informed," she said, as she actually reached out and stroked the young man dancing in front of her, "the Emperor is massing for an expedition outside of Eldador."

"I've heard rumor of the same," Xinto admitted.

"And I'm told," she continued, as the boy danced closer, and the other by her feet began to move up her legs, "he's had trouble with the security of his house."

Xinto smiled—that word had traveled fast. Lupus had turned out four Millennia, only to find his daughter in her bassinet and his prisoners escaped. Xinto had heard Confluni soldiers gossiping of this as he waited for his audience.

"Such persons, responsible for *such* humiliation, should of course fear the Emperor's wrath," the Ymir speculated.

"Such persons," Xinto countered, "would not act so, were they not able to fend for themselves."

Now the Ymir smiled.

'But were they to find common congress?" she asked.

Okay, Xinto told himself. *You know where I've come from; you want that Uman-Chi Enchantress. Well enough, but you know you've already got them. Why this show?*

What are you telling me, you aurochs?

"Let's assume they do," Xinto allowed her.

"Well, then let us assume there is a game going on," the Ymir said, "and a game within that, being played on the gamers, and surrounding that, even *another* game, that *no one* knows about, save for an Uman-Chi King, and I?"

Now Xinto's mind was racing. That was a lot of information, and if it meant what he thought, then that changed everything he knew about Glynn and her song.

"Well then, it comes to me that everyone better be in the *right* game," he said. "Because the ones that aren't, well…"

She smiled through her fat lips then waved him off. Not unlike a Confluni noble to end an audience once her piece was said.

Completely unlike one to roll onto her back for two young men in front of a departing guest—and that had Xinto wondering a lot about Ymir Effecate Hagadashi Boohoori.

* * *

Shela Mordetur lay naked on her stomach in a small tent with one oil lantern, Nina of the Aschire kneeling down behind her.

As a part of her pretending to be unconscious, she'd had to foul herself. Her daughter had moved her leather harness to one side but not properly cleaned it, nor her privates for a full week. The girl couldn't be blamed, and of course Shela could hardly have instructed her.

"How bad is it?" she asked her Aschire protégé, already knowing the answer.

Nina sighed. "It isn't good," she said, frankly. "You've a bad infection, Shela—this *must* hurt you."

Shela shook her head, her black hair swishing back and forth against her naked back. "It isn't bad," she lied. "It bothers me now when I relieve myself."

Nina grunted. The tent sides glowed as she invoked her healing power. The first thing an Andaron sorceress learned was to heal, and so the first thing Shela taught Nina was to heal. She felt the pain in the creases of her lower body as the broken skin was repaired.

It went on for several minutes. Shela turned her head as the tears rolled down her cheeks. The pain was nearly excruciating before it subsided.

Nina sighed again. "That's what I can do, my lady," she said.

Shela forced herself to ask, "Do you detect internal damage?"

Nina was quiet for a long while. She sighed, and then said,

"You've three healthy children, each of which will make you proud, my Empress. You've more than most people."

Shela lowered her head and saw where the tears soaked into the canvas floor of the tent. She'd loved her children, but in fact she'd wanted more, especially now that she knew she'd never have them.

"Don't," she said, and her voice caught in her throat.

"Don't tell the Emperor," she said, finally.

"Oh, of course not," Nina answered her. She felt the younger woman's hand on the small of her back, trying to comfort her.

A sorceress would treat many and know many secrets, especially among other women. In her tribe before she'd left it, then again among the *Waya Agiladia*, she'd had to tell other women their child-bearing years were over, that she'd need to cast the spells that would bring on menopause for another woman's safety.

None of them had ever been so young as she.

Her own fault, she admitted to herself. She'd had to come find her husband; she'd had to come get herself and her children captured.

She'd almost had to kill them all, and she would have if she'd been able. Arguably, this was better.

It didn't feel better.

Nina stayed with her for quite some time, not saying anything, just letting her weep.

* * *

Duke Ancenon Escaroth, newly of the House Escaroth, stood at the bow of his own ship, *She Sails Like a Cloud in the Heavens*, as she pulled in to the port of a city named 'Lupor.'

When it had been Kor, it had been an infested city of pirates and smugglers, where anything that could be imagined, no matter how vile, could be bought for a price.

Lupor already had her wharves clean and sparkling in barely three weeks, and Men, Toorians, Uman, even some Volkhydrans and Scitai were scurrying everywhere, making repairs to buildings that hadn't seen repair in hundreds of years, repaving streets and moving around those 'dumpsters' Lupus loved so much.

Surely Ancenon preferred cleanliness to filth; however Lupus, whom he'd seen personally up to his elbows in entrails, could almost be counted a fanatic. In many of his major cities huge, smoking buildings turned seawater into sparkling fresh, and pumped it into peoples' homes. So did they take wastes back out and into great vats, where of all things those wastes were reclaimed and used for some gas, 'meh-dane', which the Empire collected and stored in bottles.

If Lupus the Conqueror wanted to collect *that*, then he should invade Volkhydro after the harvest season, and he could breath of it to his heart's content.

He had wondered if this meh-dane was not the key ingredient in his 'chem-stree,' and experimented with it. If he lived to be older than Angron Aurelias, he would shudder at those days.

"Well, that is a face," came the usually chipper greeting from the dock. Ancenon looked down to see the familiar green curls and pale skin of Dilvesh, the Green One.

As he had so many times before, Ancenon Escaroth wondered at whom this person reminded him of, and could not decide.

"I was thinking of your liege lord," Ancenon complained. With one elegant leap, he flew from the bow of his ship to the dock beside Dilvesh, his magic carrying him gracefully. "You must ply me with wine now, and quell my sour stomach."

Dilvesh laughed and the two embraced. There existed an easy camaraderie between fellow members of the Daff Kanaar. Even with Lupus himself, Ancenon could actually let his guard down, allow himself to be a little more Ancenon, and less the former Prince of the Realm, High Priest to Adriam.

"He's not my liege lord," Dilvesh corrected him, turning to head down the dock. A little taller than Ancenon, the Duke followed him, both of their white robes swirling around their feet in the spring breeze, coming in crisp off of the Forgotten Sea.

"You serve his nation," Ancenon pressed him. He loved to match wits with Dilvesh, the closest among them to his equal. "You govern his new city."

"One of his new cities," Dilvesh pressed him, "or has he not begun the campaign yet?"

Dilvesh looked sideways at him, and Ancenon shrugged. As they stepped off of the dock into the wharf proper, six companies of Wolf Soldiers took up positions around them. Even the Emperor was not so closely guarded.

"Trouble in your command?" Ancenon noted.

"Not too much," Dilvesh countered, approaching the city's outer gate. The towers on either side had been broken once, and stood now at different heights. The gate between them had clearly been massive, with a triumphal arch now broken at either end. It was being remade with timbers from the forest around them, banded in steel.

The walls, once massive, with merlons and parapets, looked like an old gaffer's shattered teeth on top, where they hadn't crumbled.

So went Outpost III.

"It is in the nature of all things to resist change," Dilvesh added. "Some are better at it, I'm afraid."

Ancenon smiled. Were Dilvesh to catch fire, as Lupus had once said, he would do no more than fan himself and remark on the unseasonably warm day.

"I came when I received your message," Ancenon said. "Although I would not have been long otherwise. The outer islands are a wealth of new trade, and I was plying my wares. Now I see new opportunities in Lupor."

"One new opportunity, at least," Dilvesh agreed as they passed through the main gates. "Have you been able to find her?"

"Clear Genna?" Ancenon remarked. He frowned. "I can sense her to your west, a little north now, certainly moving in that direction. She's blurred, as with a host."

Dilvesh nodded. "The Trinity speaks of a great conflict, and I don't think it means of armed men."

"This child of Lupus'," Ancenon inferred. He sighed. "I spoke with Taffer Roo on the subject, when I was able to contact him. He assured me the timing is impossible. He certainly touched her before Shela, however the illness from her affliction would have killed an unborn child and, even had it not, the woman was clearly not pregnant at the Battle of Tamaran Glen."

Dilvesh nodded, and they continued to walk side by side. Everywhere, artisans and craftsmen were rebuilding, repaving and recreating this lost Outpost. Merchants were tenuously hawking their wares on street corners. Ancenon had never been here before and seen fewer whores, and not even a single dead body in the street.

"You've done passably well," he admitted with a wave.

Dilvesh wouldn't be distracted. "What if the affliction that crippled Genna forced her unborn child into some hibernation?" Dilvesh pressed him.

"What if aurochs learned arithmetic?" Ancenon asked him, smiling. "Sirrah, I am assured, there *is* no way. The timing doesn't work out. She would have had to have birthed, then, when we were training after the sack of Kattaran. We saw her every day then, and she did not."

"But she left that night before Lupus and Shela spent months recruiting, before she tried to get him killed by the Bounty Hunter in Galnesh Eldador," Dilvesh argued.

This was less fun, for the simplistic nature of it. "My friend, were you the product of a woman?" he demanded. "Know you nothing of these things? They gestate over ten months, or nine, some eleven, but never more than that, and no viable offspring before."

"You know very little of the poison used at the door to the vault in…that place," Dilvesh said, looking around him, his distress so intense he'd almost risked the wrath of Adriam by speaking the name of Outpost X. Now Ancenon gave him more attention.

They climbed the stone steps to some municipal building. The palace lay miles deep in the city. This was either a resting place or, preferably, one to provide them with horses.

Months at sea had not prepared Ancenon for long walks.

"Admittedly," Ancenon continued, as they stepped into a dimly lit building, through a solid steel door, "I do not."

He noted the Wolf Soldier guards didn't follow them in. Dilvesh didn't command them, they simply seemed to know better.

The smell of rot hit him from within. Ancenon stepped into a room full of beddings, some formal, some mattresses on the floor.

Uman women in the garb of healers moved amongst poor wretches, their arms and legs almost fluid, who lay moaning through shriveled lips and black teeth. Some lamented lost hair, some showed eyes that had flowed down their cheeks like fluid. Their skin was sallow and grey, some rotted away to where the bones showed.

Ancenon gasped.

"A previous 'Earl' of Kor discovered a wall which, if you touched it, this happened," Dilvesh said.

"Adriam's mercy," Ancenon muttered.

Dilvesh shook his head. "You won't find it here," he said. "Nor a cure with it. I've sent for the Empress but can't find her. Something is afoot in Eldador right now, and it isn't something good."

"How—how long, how old?" Ancenon was at a loss.

Dilvesh shook his head. "They lose their sanity in as little as six months," he said. "This sisterhood has been caring for these poor wretches for more than a generation. It seems none of them, regardless of race, ever dies, unless you cut them mortally. Even then, their blood spills out like a jelly, and it can take a week."

"This is the same poison, then...?"

"I'm sure of it."

"Are there, I mean, Sirrah, have you seen...?"

"I've seen no children," Dilvesh said, and Ancenon allowed himself another sigh. "However, I've seen whores with child, and placed my hand upon their stomachs, and known there is life inside."

"Vile," Ancenon gasped. "Vile, vile, monstrous."

Dilvesh turned and ushered Ancenon out the door. He allowed himself to be guided, though the sunlight did nothing to burn what he'd seen from his eyes.

The Cheyak were many things and, much as he revered them as his forefathers, he recognized them for their heinous capacities.

"I dread the fate of the spawn of these," Ancenon said, finally.

"Especially if one actually came to fruition," Dilvesh said, "as I suspect has transpired between Genna and Lupus."

Chapter Ten

The Eldadorian Land

Ten thousand Theran Lancers assembled on the Eldadorian plains, to the south of Thera and directly north east of the Lone Wood. The Wolf's Head banner and the green and white pennons of Eldador snapped on their wooden lances, stood emblazoned on tabards and shields and saddles.

Jack sat Little Storm at Vulpe's right hand. The boy never strayed far from him. He had an analytical mind, even if a young one, and he already knew about things like forage and supplies and training and how to build a defensible outpost on the plains. Jack and Two Spears—Tali Digatishi as Shela called him—advised him about scouts, and argued with him about tactics, and kept him from ordering a charge before his men were ready.

He'd wanted to charge when the first two thousand assembled. If pure bravery could win the battle then they should have. Jack knew better. Warriors were nodding and smiling to each other, proud of this Prince who'd taken up a sword to fight alongside of them in his father's name. Severely outnumbered, they'd be just as dead as any other soldiers, so they'd gotten Vulpe to wait.

Jack thought it insane to march at odds of five to one, even mounted, but Two Spears assured him they had the advantage, and this was Two Spears' world.

"Shela and three wizards from my own city will be our magical defense," Two Spears informed them. Three Uman with white hair and long, grey robes were huddled by the Empress and Nina of the Aschire. "Nina will stay with the Prince and be solely responsible for his protection."

"My father never—" Vulpe began.

"I had your father's back from the moment I met him," Shela admonished him. Jack chuckled and she glared at him.

"I'm sorry," he said, and bowed his head. "We say the same thing in my world—you must have learned that from the Emperor."

Shela smiled. "He says it all the time," she admitted, then turned her attention to her son. "Your father could barely do the slightest thing without me—and every time he strayed—"

Two Spears cleared his throat, a wide smile on his face. He'd warned Jack that when she didn't have her eyes right on him, Shela worried over the Emperor constantly and did everything she could to be at his side. Her abandoning the capitol came as a surprise to him, only in that it had taken so long.

"My life before his," Nina promised them, placing a hand on his arm. "I didn't spend so much time raising him to lose him now."

Vulpe made a face Jack had grown accustomed to—a kind of grimace that said, "I'm not a little boy anymore." For these people, he wasn't. Take the life of another, and you're a man here.

Jack had watched Vulpe cut that man down. He'd stood in the middle of a small squad of Wolf Soldiers, and he'd fought just as they do. Shield men held the line, men with long spears stabbed over their heads, and when Vulpe gave the word, the shields parted just enough for swords to slip out and stab. Vulpe could have stabbed at a tree or an ox for all he knew—it was pure luck his low height had come under the bounty hunter's guard, took him on the inside of his leg and sent blood spurting in a crimson fountain all over them.

But that made him a man here, and Jack was going to be damned if he'd die so soon after, because of it.

"We should have moved at dawn," Vulpe informed them, a scowl on his face. "We should be fighting now, not just outfitting. We should—"

Jack shook his head, and that quelled him. He'd discussed this with all of them before and, much as it was his idea, and he was a salesman, not a warrior, sales worked like any other battle, where the rules usually consisted of, "There are no rules."

"We've been gathering for a week," he said, "so they know how much strength we have. We know they caught one of our envoys to your father, so they know we sent for help. We see their scouts every day, and they see ours, and they know we rest in the day and train in the dusk light.

"You're safest against an enemy when they don't think you're up to anything. Logic says that we should wait for your father and his superior numbers, and crush them. They haven't run, so they plan to attack you one morning, soon, when they think you're not ready and they are. If they can kill or capture the Emperor's son and wife then they have a hell of a hand against the Empire."

"We should have called for the garrison at Galnesh Eldador," Shela complained. "Lee is back with Hectaro—we could have another four thousand Wolf Soldiers in ten days—"

"They'll attack in ten days," Two Spears argued. "Eti Kawnatay is right—we catch them entirely unaware, now, and half will be dead before they can pick up their swords. The rest of them will either surrender or run."

Two Spears had dubbed Jack 'Eti Kawnatay,' the Old Hunter. Well, the old hunter didn't think it would be that easy, however it still remained their best chance. If their envoy hadn't been captured, then maybe they could have waited, but not now. These people would be stupid to wait, and Jack knew better than to count on that.

It worried him. He didn't know anything about swords and fighting. He didn't know these people or how they made war, what they were capable of or what might limit them. Although he felt queasy about the odds, they claimed Shela's sorcery was so powerful she could kill most of them herself. That kind of made the whole thing irrelevant, then, didn't it?

Mostly, however, Jack wanted to know who these 'reinforcements' were. That, he felt, would be the key to everything. Another lesson from a life of sales, "Don't make your pitch until you have all of the facts." He'd learned to call that 'pitching in the dark,' and sometimes when you did you ended up beaning the batter.

Sometimes the pitch came back at you and hit you in the face.

In sales, you lost your commission. Here, the stakes were a *lot* higher.

* * *

Tartan Stowe stood on the Eldadorian plains, 4,500 Angadorian Knights behind him, watching an enormous army of Confluni marshal on a wide, vast plain.

Normally he'd expect to see as many head of aurochs, but this army had commandeered those. Farmers driven off of their land had come to him for his protection. They formed a side camp, where their daughters were plying his men for coin, and their sons were trying to decide if life might be better on top of a horse instead of staring at the arse of one, with a wooden plow in their hands.

Yerel stood to his left, J'lek to his right, and this scout who'd crossed their path, Jean, before them.

The woman had turned out to be a godsend, able not only to skirt the fringes but to penetrate this Confluni army. She'd spent a day within their camp, gathering information for them.

"You're sure?" Yeral insisted.

"As I stand before you," the woman said. She was in her thirties, gray in her hair, crows' feet at her eyes. She had the body of a dancer, in skintight leather, covered in daggers and a cross-pistol on her thigh. Tartan noted from her belly she'd birthed at least one child.

His wife regarded the side of his face; however Tartan remained focused on the army. He'd seen the Emperor do this—staring into the enemy camp as if into the face of an adversary, as if to read its eyes.

Tartan had *never* understood that, until now, with his own men at risk.

She'd found Glynn Escaroth, Xinto of the Woods, and a Man whose name he recognized, Karl Henekhson, in that camp, not as prisoners but as allies.

Karl Henekhson—the Hero of Tamara, the bravest Man ever to set foot on Fovean soil, had sided against Lupus the Conqueror with the stinking Confluni.

Tell his warriors that, and there would be no stopping them from attacking. He himself felt the rage. No one could more deeply betray the Emperor—not even he, himself.

It gave Tartan Stowe a whole new perspective on things. Did he want people to feel about him the way he felt about Karl Henekhson now?

"I will have his guts," Tartan swore, his own voice sounding strange in his ears.

He felt his wife's hand on his shoulder, delicate as a rose

petal. He knew her mind. If they could capture this one and hide him from the Emperor, they'd have a capable ally to train their warriors.

He'd have his head on a pike, Tartan thought. He'd throw it at the Emperor's feet.

"Love me—I won't do *this*!"

The thought shocked him.

"There's another army on their other side," Jean informed them. "Theran Lancers flying the Imperial banner and the Wolf's Head as well. Means that—"

"Someone from the Imperium is there," Tartan finished for her. You didn't get to sport the Wolf's Head unless you had a Mordetur among you.

"Duke Two Spears," Tartan said, and looked sideways at his wife, mounted on her palfrey. "I don't think the Empress will be outside of Galnesh Eldador with an army on the field, and I sincerely doubt she sent her children."

Yeral looked away from him. Jean grinned.

"Who knows what a woman will do for her man?" she said. She alone wasn't on horseback. She claimed she didn't need to be. For her age, there was no doubt she moved light on her feet.

"They train at night and rest all day," Jean said. "The Confluni have been getting up an hour before first light. They're getting ready for a fight—no doubt of that. The Therans, if they're smart, are just here to minimize the damage until Lu—the Emperor can bring his army up north."

Tartan nodded. Over one hundred thousand strong, he'd eradicate these Confluni, reinforcements or no. If Lupus the Conqueror had been successful against anyone, it was the Confluni.

"Dig in," Tartan said. As Lupus had told him, 'When you aren't ready to make your move yet, make sure your enemy sees you as too big to attack or at least not worth the effort.' "Establish the jess doonar, and keep a hot feed for the horses."

"Hot feed?" his wife questioned him. That meant a lot of corn, fresh cut grass, a lot of protein.

He nodded. "Two Spears is an Andaron," he said. "He's just crazy enough to attack that enemy and, if he does, then we're in it as well. We'll be making long, sweeping charges on their flanks while he engages them at their middle.

"Meanwhile, I want a detachment to the south looking for the

Emperor. If *he* takes the field, we're going to cut north and block this army's escape, or drive them unsuspecting into the Wolf's jaws."

J'lek nodded and, without another word, turned and left, Jean right after him in the other direction.

Tartan looked back into the camp. He felt sure they could see him, and he didn't care. 'Let your enemy know you're coming,' Lupus taught him. 'If they run in fear, then you win without fighting. If they stand their ground, make sure it's on shaky legs.'

"With the Hero of Tamara," Yeral began. Tartan held up his hand for silence.

He didn't want to hear her nattering at this point. He knew her mind without hearing her words. To her credit, she kept her peace and waited next to him.

Two questions ran through his mind, and the other one was, *Who are these reinforcements?*

* * *

Raven sat on the ground, on a big, soft fur Karl had given her, sharpening the edge of her sword and watching the people watching their army from the ridge to the south.

Supposedly the Eldadorians had a few thousand in that direction, and as many as ten to the northeast. Less than a third their number in all, but mounted.

No Wolf Soldiers, then. Wolf Soldiers fought on foot. According to Xinto, who had it from the woman who ran this army, the Emperor was about to put all of his troops on boats and ship them elsewhere to attack some other country.

Unless they cut the Emperor's own supply lines, of course. That was this army's mission. Be in the way of his food and his army would starve and fall apart. How many times had Raven heard, "An army marches on its belly?"

With a particle of her newfound magic, she reached her mind out to this person on the hill. He'd know if she invaded his privacy, but she could read what radiated off of him without tipping him off.

Male. Race of Men. Focused, angry, determined. He led others, perhaps even the Duke from the south, the son of the old king.

Glynn had wanted to offer this one his father's position as hereditary monarch, to sway the Fovean High Council to recognize the Duke as a King, and the Empire as illegitimate.

From what she'd learned of Rancor Mordetur, that would just make him laugh. He'd come and kill this Duke just to prove he could, and then go after anyone who made claims against him, so he could brag about it later.

From what she read of this Man, no one would ever get close enough to him to make the offer, anyway. She felt his anger, focused on them. If anyone from here approached this person, they'd be dead before saying a word.

"What do you see, child?" Glynn asked, approaching from behind.

When an Uman-Chi walked, they could do this thing where they seemed to glide around. Glynn did that all of the time here, now. She moved so quietly Raven couldn't hear her, and the hem of her new, white cotton robe hovered the same distance off of the ground, never moving.

It creeped Raven out.

Raven informed her of what she'd read.

Glynn nodded. "I agree," she said. "I think we might actually be looking at Tartan Stowe, the son the first King of Eldador."

"I thought that, too," Raven said.

Glynn glided over to her side. Seated, Raven allowed herself a glance at the hem of the white robe, and saw a white, silk slipper, planted firmly on the ground.

They looked and move like ghosts, but they were real enough.

"Local peasants tell a story of the Empress and the Imperial family being captured by the Bounty Hunter's guild," Glynn said. "What do you believe of that?"

Raven put her hand on the soil before her. Glynn believed the Earth was a living god who heard all of the secrets told upon Him and, if one could commune with Earth, one could know those secrets.

That struck Raven as pretty friggin' stupid, however she'd learned for herself that people had auras here, and these auras radiated like so many microwave ovens.

Those waves could embed themselves in the soil, and she could access them once she'd learned where to look and what questions to ask.

Hadn't Vedeen been telling them, over and over, their problem was not that they didn't understand Glynn's song, but that they didn't ask the right questions about it?

Raven shook her head to clear it and pressed her hand into the ground. For a moment, nothing. She imagined her hand at the tuner of a huge radio dial, and she turned it until she found the frequency she wanted.

The Empress, her daughters, stolen. A call for help from her son, him finding her, a battle.

Little Vulpe, calling Eldadorians to the Wolf's Head banner.

She looked up at Glynn, into her silver-on-silver eyes.

"Then you know it as well," the Uman-Chi said.

She nodded.

* * *

Thorn had never seen so many warriors in one place, and he'd spent his last fifteen years as a mercenary. He sat his Angadorian mare, Nantar next to him on a similar horse, overlooking a vast plain overloaded with tents, corrals, dog pens and warriors, training.

Daff Kanaari, Eldadorians, Wolf Soldiers, as many as one hundred thousand, rounded up and training, marching, making ready to move.

Already the harbor at Uman City sat clogged with Eldadorian Sea Wolves, square-rigged vessels wider, deeper and better armed than any on Fovea.

"He'll be upset," Nantar told Thorn, as if he needed to.

Thorn nodded. Black Lupus's horse climbed the hill where they sat with the Theran Lancer squad, ten messengers from young Vulpe, his son.

"The key is to make him hear the whole tale," Nantar said, more to himself than to Thorn. "Make him listen, not take off with this entire army, like he'll want to do.

Thorn wished Dilvesh were here, or Ancenon. They knew how to handle Lupus. Lupus would listen to their every word, still as a stone. Even Arath, were he here, might make Lupus listen. Lupus liked Arath, a general like himself.

Thorn and Nantar spent more time with Black Lupus than the rest of them, because the rest of them had 'great things' going on all the time, and Thorn and Nantar were warriors, like Lupus. When Lupus wanted to fight, when he wanted to drink, when he wanted to be a male, he sought out Thorn and Nantar.

Well, he would sure want to fight now.

"What news?" Lupus demanded, as soon as he was in earshot. His eyes traveled to the Theran Lancer squad that sat their horses to the left of Thorn and Nantar.

"Sees Far and Wide," Lupus' eyebrows swooped down toward

his nose like a falcon's wings, targeting the Andaron sergeant of the Theran squad. "What are you doing here? You're assigned to Thera."

To the last man, Thorn thought to himself. He knew them by *name*. No wonder they were so willing to fight for him?

"Your Imperial Majesty," the Lancer said, making a fist over his heart. "News from Vulpe, your son."

Lupus smiled a broad smile. That wouldn't last, Thorn thought to himself.

"Her Majesty, Empress Shela, was last month captured by Bounty Hunters, with your daughters. Your son escaped—"

"*What?*" Lupus already had his sword out.

"Patience, Lupus," Nantar said. "Hear it all."

"My *wife* and *daughters*—"

"Are safe," Nantar said. He kicked his horse up alongside Blizzard. The huge stallion was already pawing the ground, sensing his rider's agitation.

Lupus glared at the Theran Lancer, already sweating. He should have begun with, "Everyone you love is safe," as Nantar had told him, but he had his orders.

"Your family was on the road to Thera when attacked by Bounty Hunters. Your son rallied the Wolf Soldier survivors and sent for help from Duke Two Spears. Before he could respond, Vulpe collected two squads and rescued her himself."

Lupus straightened and the smile returned. Quick to anger, quick to forget, Thorn knew. Lupus' moods ran like the weather.

"My son did this?"

"I fought alongside Vulpe myself," one of the other men, another Andaron, said. In their own army, none dared speak out of turn. Here, it was different.

"You're a Wolf Soldier," Lupus said. "I know you—Thunderclap of the Swift Tails."

"I was sent to Thera to the Duke's service," Thunderclap said, "but I will remember to my last day, your son's blooding."

Now Thorn was surprised—he hadn't heard this. Vulpe, at eleven years old, had killed a man in combat. That made him a man himself. Now this Wolf Soldier called him by his first name, just as they did Lupus.

"My son *fought?*" the scowl had returned. Blizzard shifted under him.

Thunderclap nodded, his eyes greedy with blood lust at remembering it. "The old man, Jack, taught him to plan an ambush. We drew in our enemies like flies to our web, and we *struck*! Wolf Soldiers in foot formation, Theran Lancers circled back behind and charged in along the path of the advancing Bounty Hunters. Vulpe held the center of a Wolf Soldier squad!"

"Your Imperial Majesty, everyone whom you love is safe," the sergeant, Sees Far and Wide, said, finally. "But now ten thousand Theran Lancers stand between you and a Confluni army estimated at fifty thousand, camped on the plains of Eldador."

"Fifty thousand?" Lupus' eyebrows shot up on his head.

The sergeant nodded. "Vulpe commands the Therans, and has sent his sisters back to Galnesh Eldador with more lancers and Hectaro, son of Hectar. Princess Lee will operate your 'Central Communications,' and coordinate your major cities, however Two Spears, Vulpe and Jack all fear this army is here to destroy our supply lines, just as you leave on your campaign, and ask that you come and relieve them."

'Jack,' the messenger kept saying. Thorn hadn't heard *that* name before.

"It would be good practice for those green troops," Nantar said, still next to Lupus. "We'll destroy fifty thousand Confluni—it will barely b—"

Lupus held up his hand and quieted them all. Thorn recognized the look on the scarred face, the focus to the blue eyes. Thorn knew of two Men named Lupus, one barely more than a child in his heart, the other a cunning wolf. He tolerated a lot from the one to get these glimpses of the other.

"It's a trap," he said, his blue eyes sweeping them.

"What?" Nantar looked as if he'd been pole axed. "Lupus, if we leave your nation to those Confluni, your supply lines will be *cut*—"

Lupus shook his head. "Think I didn't expect a counter attack before we could get back?" he asked. "When we landed an army *this* vast on foreign shores, *someone* was going to say, 'Must be lonely on the home front,' and come in behind us. I left more than enough troops to handle fifty thousand."

"Then—" Nantar was dumbfounded.

They'd planned to have to argue Lupus *out* of attacking the Confluni, to let the Daff Kanaar take care of it, to pick an easier target for the campaigns, like Sental, rather than abandoning it entirely.

Now it looked like he would leave it all up to his eleven-year-old son.

"Nantar, what would you have me do?" Lupus demanded of him. He did this—he called them, 'interrogative questions,' making someone else make his point for him. Thorn hated it, but admittedly he'd used it himself with people too stupid to see things his way.

"We should send the Daff Kanaari soldiers to attack, at the least. Perhaps with an Eldadorian guard escort—"

Lupus nodded appreciatively. Thorn recognized the trap, the sarcastic look, the cat playing with its prey. "And will they win, Scarlet Nantar?"

"Of course they'll win," Nantar clearly saw the question for its obvious answer. "We've got—"

"We're Daff Kanaar," Lupus interrupted him. "We're Eldadorians. We're Wolf Soldiers. We win."

"Yes…"

Thorn saw it now, obvious after the fact.

"You think the Confluni, whom I've beaten *every single time* they've invaded, think otherwise?" Lupus pursued him.

Nantar looked down at the ground, then raised his head up grinning through his black and gray beard.

"We're supposed to go after them," Nantar said. "We're supposed to turn this army around, and then they'll come back with a spike up our arse and catch us between two armies, both ready."

Lupus nodded. Thorn smiled. He'd been waiting years for this, very patiently, but now he had it.

"Wrong," he said. Both looked at him.

"I knew this day would come," he continued, leaning back a little in his saddle, enjoying this. "I knew someone would finally point out your weakness, and exploit it, and I would be here to laugh."

"What?" Lupus was back to scowling. Good. Let him.

"It's too easy, Lupus," he said. "It's too pat. This is a trap, you're right, but these are the parts you are supposed to see, and you're supposed to say, 'Aren't I the clever Lupus the Conqueror, who out-thought you all again?'"

Lupus looked at Nantar; Nantar seemed to shrug inside of his armor. Both looked back at him.

"You think you're going to sit here, and send the garrison of one of your other cities, and first catch this army between your son and them, and then pull these troops back into the plains, and catch whoever marches out to take Uman City unawares?" Thorn pressed him.

Lupus looked at Nantar again, then back at Thorn, and finally nodded.

"*That's* what you're supposed to do," Thorn said. "And when you do that, they'll hit the city you leave behind, and *then* you'll come and relieve that city, and they'll be waiting for you.

"Meanwhile that army of fifty thousand is going to stay dug in and quiet, because you're right, fifty thousand isn't going to be able to attack you, but they can stand fast and defend for a long time, and while they do, every farmer on the plains is going to have his crops boarded up and his livestock hidden."

Lupus looked at Nantar again, and Nantar looked at Thorn. The Theran Lancers looked at each other; this was far past their meager abilities.

Thorn had said fourteen years ago Lupus would out think himself one day, and it had finally happened. Now Thorn stood here to point it out.

"So, we want to…" Lupus began, and Thorn could almost see his mind working out the problem.

"Thera must have nearly emptied out its garrison to provide ten thousand Lancers," Nantar said.

Lupus nodded. "He has one thousand foot reserves, but those troops are Eldadorian Regulars and don't see a lot of action. Thera's walls aren't much—you could take the city with a few thousand."

"And Galnesh Eldador?" Nantar asked.

"Four thousand Wolf Soldier guards, one thousand Eldadorian Regulars, Hectar to hold the city and the strongest walls on Fovea. No one's getting in there. Andurin has half its garrison still, Metz is pretty much cleaned out, except for a thousand home troops, usually Arath leaves warriors not fit to fight."

"Too far inland, I think," Thorn said. They both looked at him again. "Everyone knows Thera is second best to the capitol. Burn that to the ground and break the heart of the nation."

Nantar nodded, Lupus as well, then grinned.

"I know what we're going to do," he said, finally.

Chapter Eleven

Cats, Mice and Dogs

Vedeen knew they were coming over an hour before they arrived. These 'Theran Lancers' had gone to great efforts to conceal themselves, wrapping their horses' hooves, moving in long lines rather than many abreast, barely even talking to each other. Duke Two Spears' Andaron heritage, she felt, proved itself. Without her magic, she might never have known.

She'd never be without her magic, however, and she *did* know. She arose two hours before the dawn, Earth whispering into her ear of the coming storm.

She stroked the dog's head and rubbed the spot between the great, green eyes. Her slavering jaws hung limp, the tail still, the animal in ecstasy for the simple caress, and said nothing.

She had not come to fight. She did not side with these people. She might hear their song, but that did not make her one of them.

She fed herself, because there'd be no eating this morning, and she cared for her horse, because she loved it, and no one ever knew how a battle would go. She sensed them coming an hour before the dawn, spreading out on the other side of a hill to their west. The Confluni guards couldn't hear them, leaning sleepy on their spears, waiting to be relieved by the morning watch, and to commence their daily drills. Camp workers, cooks and artisans were barely stirring, catching final sips of sleep before the long day began.

The dog raised its ears, its tail thumping the ground. Vedeen wondered if she sensed them, too, but realized that their Raven had arisen with the other birds, and approached with that wide grin that the race of Men reserved for animals.

"You're up early," she said.

"I was listless," Vedeen admitted. No point in lying when the truth sufficed.

"Me, too—something's wrong," Raven admitted. She squatted quite unladylike before the dog, to rough her ears. Had Glynn been here, she'd have admonished her protégé.

Vedeen wasn't surprised to see the parts of a woman and didn't balk now, not that she'd have done the same.

"Wrong?" Vedeen pressed her. "Wrong how?"

Raven stood and hugged herself. She looked to the west, as if to see through the hill between her and the Theran Lancers. "Something...angry. Something close. I can almost touch it, like an outfit in the back of my closet."

Vedeen's interest had been piqued. Too late to help them now, she knew. "And if you reach out with your mind?" she asked.

"A jumble, like a crowded room—um, I'm not sure of the words. Like a stadium?"

This girl's gifts grew daily, more quickly than any she'd seen. Vedeen would have recruited her to the Druids, were there any point.

"Then perhaps you might—"

Raven's head swung around as if she had been slapped. Vedeen looked into her eyes, read her, and knew, *knew* she'd taken the next step.

"We're about to be attacked!" she exclaimed. A worker twenty feet away dropped an armload of pots and stared at her, slack-jawed. She spoke in the language of Men, and many Confluni knew it. "On the other side of that ridge, an army, a huge one!"

"Then what must you do, my dear?" Vedeen asked her.

She would not help, she would not advise, but she could observe and inquire to her heart's content.

Her hand turning white with power, Raven flung out her arm to the west, her palm open, a brilliant ball of energy flying from her to soar like an eagle into the sky. The very air seemed to tear as it passed, the dusk became day for its brilliance. Confluni stood blinking, who were awake so early, and the guards shouted and gripped their spears.

The ball flew over the ridge and exploded, a vast sphere of flame as if she'd found a way to ignite the air itself. The ground shook for the force. From a distance, horses screamed and Men swore. Three fireballs flew back over the ridge from the other side in retaliation. Raven was already sprinting, not from their path but into it, the dog at her side.

Vedeen watched them, then walked softly to her own skittish mount. She laid a comforting hand on his noble neck and he quieted.

The day promised to be long.

* * *

Marauder reared up as the dawn light exploded overhead. Vulpe, without even thinking, stood up in the saddle, his reins in one hand and his sword in the other, to balance himself and to take the shock of the beast's landing.

Many other Men and Uman were thrown, even some Andarons. Uncle Two Spears almost lost his seat and had to right himself and collect his dignity as his stallion kicked the air around them.

Little Storm stood unmoving, grandfather just like him, two yards away.

His mother raised a hand aflame with power and threw fire at the enemy. However it had happened, they'd been discovered. They had to move fast or lose the advantage of a surprise attack.

"To me!" Vulpe shouted as Marauder's hooves found the ground. "First through Sixth Millennia, to the center with me, Seventh and Eight to the south, Ninth and Tenth to the north!"

"Your Highness!" Two Spears shouted to him, as his own warriors followed Vulpe's orders. "They've seen us. We can't just attack—"

"One of their casters sensed us," Shela countered him. "If the army were ready they'd have stayed quiet. That was a warning call to wake up and get ready."

"She's right," grandfather added. "Two Spears let the buh—let him do this. No matter what happens, better to get directions from one source than two."

Two Spears wanted to argue, but he'd been supporting father for almost a decade now. Vulpe knew he'd rather kill every man on the field and lose Thera than lose that.

His father had drilled into both of them, "Better boldly down the wrong path than indecisively to nowhere."

The warriors had formed up into their squads in under a minute. The Ninth and Tenth were already moving, the Seventh and Eighth barely behind to their other side. Vulpe knew he wouldn't lead the charge, as his father had, but he'd send a full Millennia ahead and command from the middle.

"Forward!" he commanded, his heart racing, his eyes seeing red in the dawn. Another white-hot ball over their heads, and another, and another, this time exploding over their horses' heads but much closer, burning riders and bringing screams.

"Mother!" he commanded.

"On it!" she replied, and directed her acolytes. In these first stages, the very experienced casters would hang back, trying to get a sense of whom they were up against. The Confluni had no great wizards, but kept some crafty ones.

The First began the trot forward, lances raised, blowing trumpets now to tell of their coming. Behind them, dozens of women were beating kettle drums with huge mallets. The trumpets and the drums had been another of father's creations, and only his mounted warriors sounded the trumpets. Both were designed to spread terror before the charge.

Vulpe had to hope they'd work now.

* * *

Shela Mordetur watched the first Millennia trot off to engage, the Second one with her son preparing to follow.

She'd argued for the Fifth and lost. Then the Third. To her surprise, this 'Jack' had argued alongside of her, and it had been her brother, Two Spears, who'd defied her. "Bad enough not in the forefront," he'd said. "They'll forgive him that. Any less than the Second and they'll question his first kill."

He'd be getting another today, no doubt of that. The Second would see combat, not clean up like the Fourth. Shela watched Nina sprinting after Marauder. She leapt up onto his butt, to wrap her arms around Vulpe's waist as she had done so many times to his father.

Nina would bring him home safe, she knew. Shela had taught Nina more secrets than any other. Nina would, if necessary, spirit him away from the battle to her side, and suffer the indignity rather than the loss.

She'd not lose her son today.

Two of her acolytes raised their hands and called the lightening down upon the Confluni. More energy crackled over their heads. The same spell, over and over, an unworthy acolyte, if any. They knew where this one was now, tracing back the path of her attacks through the sky. She ordered the third of her acolytes, an Uman named Therbrand, to destroy this careless neophyte.

Therbrand raised an imperious hand, as over dramatic as any of his kind, and spoke the words to release balled energy. From the dimension of pain he called the Stinging Death, billions of tiny flecks, each too small to see; a swirling, whirling ball, to cast at the enemy.

He flung the ball over the ridge to find the other Wizard.

The Third Millennia trotted out behind the Second. The First must have, by now, engaged. She'd have to enhance their *sight*, to give them the ability to see the unseen enemy, and not endanger their own troops.

Swift as an arrow shot, along the path of the Stinging Death, an arc of pure energy caught Therbrand in the chest. He flew full thirty feet to land in a clump on the ground.

Shela and the other two ran to his side. Expecting a charred corpse, they found instead the old Uman, on his back, his chest gently rising and falling.

Slumbering. Shela read his aura, weak as a newborn babe's.

She had come!

* * *

Karl had tried to get his Volkhydrans to build a jess doonar once. They'd overpowered him and buried him up to his neck in the dirt. When they'd finally released him, a day later, he'd had to kill four to get their respect back, but he'd never asked them again.

The Confluni had simply told him, "No." They didn't do things that way, even though they'd been beaten because of them so many times.

He'd tried to show a few of them how to fight Wolf Soldier style, but they'd been heavily trained in their long, steady lines, and been so successful that, again, they just didn't see the point.

When a thousand horse thundered over the ridge to the east, they got the idea. Scrambling for their weapons and their shields, they would have loved to have walls to run to, stakes to hide behind, and ramparts to defend. Instead they drew a rope across the ground, and tried to stand at it.

Their archers might have saved them, except their arrows had been packed away for the night, close to the main cook fires to stay warm and dry and not warp in the humid spring.

In a wave behind the first thousand, another thousand topped the rise. This one had the Wolf's head banner near the center—a member of the Imperial family, announcing him or her self.

Karl pulled his own crossbow from over his shoulder. He'd likely get a shot in, maybe two. Killing Duke Two Spears wouldn't make the army crumble. Lupus' infrastructure allowed another to step immediately into a fallen general's place. Lupus himself had been separated from his troops and they'd fought on without him.

The first Confluni line planted their spears in the ground as the third Millennia of horse topped the far rise. This was too orderly, he thought. He looked to the north and the south, for the troops who'd come in behind them when these engaged.

Fire arced into their camp, destroying tents and killing warriors. Their shaggy ponies picketed close to the front were bolting and disrupting the warriors on the way to defend them.

"Sirrah, are you prepared?" Glynn demanded, gliding toward him. Raven had commented she was moving differently now, and he saw what she meant.

"Prepared to do what?" he demanded. "Witness the slaughter? Shouldn't you be, you know?" and he wiggled his fingers.

Glynn smirked a self-satisfied smirk. "If I announce my presence too early, then I surrender the tactical advantage of my being," she said. "I wish to see all of these troops before I am committed. Our Ravens holds the fore."

"Raven?" Karl asked her, but immediately knew that made good sense. They couldn't hurt Raven with their magic. In fact, they just made her stronger if they hit her. Raven *should* be trying to get them to attack her.

The thought of it, however, made his skin prickle.

"She has her protectors," Glynn answered without being asked. "Slurn, of course, who is ever at her side, and the dog, who will protect her from any rogue lancer."

"And you two have me, I suppose," Zarshar grumbled, appearing out of the mass of warriors. He reached out a long arm and spread his gigantic hand at the enemy. Lightening flickered at his talons and formed a single stream of pure energy, which slammed out past the Confluni and into the center of the advancing Theran lancers.

Warriors and horses screamed and fell. The line wavered just as it engaged the Confluni line. In many places they broke through, all of them wheeling their mounts to the left, driving their lances into the breasts of spearmen before enemy spears could touch them. Horses screamed, warriors on both sides swore and cried out. Fireballs arced out from behind the ridge, away from their previous targets and more toward the center of the army.

"Well done, Sirrah," Glynn said. "You have upset their charge."

Karl spat. "I didn't know he could do that," he said. Most Devils rend and tear, but he remembered now Zarshar, the Black Adept, cast spells as well.

"You see—we withhold our advantage unto our need," Glynn was smiling that little self-satisfied smile now. Behind her, he saw Raven running toward the enemy mages' new target. They must have detected her somehow, because they immediately redirected their fire.

"Don't be too sure of yourself," Karl said, and ran toward the combat with his crossbow out. The second Millennia would be close, and he wanted a shot at that person in the Imperial family.

He saw for himself, a boy in heavy armor, riding a huge, gray stallion, an Aschire seated behind him. He'd have thought he was mistaken except the boy was clearly shouting orders and distinguishing himself as being in command.

Lupus had a young son. Kill the boy and Lupus himself would wreak unholy vengeance on his head, if he had to give up or spend every resource that he had to do it.

Karl didn't kid himself that Lupus wouldn't take this personally. He'd been the second to receive the Mark of the Conqueror, Lupus himself being the first. Karl's glory, unwanted as it was, was a reflection on the Emperor. This would be, too.

Kill his child, and it went past personal. Lupus the Conqueror had a terrible focus when he wanted to.

Karl leveled the crossbow and lined up the crosshairs. He'd get one shot, then they'd all be on him. When Lupus' son fell, they'd go berserk for vengeance. The boy's armor looked almost impervious, but his face was left exposed.

He felt the tension on the trigger, he took a breath. Another horse, a huge stallion, kept getting in his way, the rider having a hard time keeping the beast in line. The horse was so large he could actually obscure the Prince's horse entirely.

No horse was so huge. This one was a black—suddenly, Karl recognized the animal, the mighty stallion, its wild-tossed mane.

Little Storm!

* * *

"Your Grace, they've engaged!"

The woman leapt into their pavilion through what should have been a guarded tent flap. For a moment, Tartan thought Nina of the Aschire might be back.

He recognized Jean, however. Outside, the camp had already begun to buzz, the sun not even up yet.

"The Therans have engaged the enemy," she repeated, her face flushed, sweat in her hair. She'd run a long way to get here.

Tartan sat straight up, casting the furs aside, revealing his breechclout and bare chest.

"You're sure?"

She nodded enthusiastically. Yeral was pushing herself up naked from her furs at his feet. "A surprise attack at dawn, and the wizards the first to engage. Never seen that before."

Tartan nodded. His guards were entering the pavilion now, embarrassed at the naked Duchess and the woman who'd gotten past them. Yeral pulled the furs back up to her chin.

"Tartan—must we?" she began to complain.

"Quiet," he ordered her. He'd been brusque with her lately, a product of his focus on this enemy and the things he'd learned. She subsided with an evil glare, drawing a smirk from Jean.

"Two of you," he ordered, singling two Uman out. "Help me with my armor. You others, find J'lek and let him know I want forty lines of one hundred. Two Spears will come right into their center; we'll sweep in at their sides and from behind."

The sergeant nodded and left with six other men. Two remained to help him on with his heavy plate and leggings. He wasn't as huge as the Emperor; he'd need help getting onto his horse when he was dressed out in field plate. He'd commissioned a broadsword just for a battle like this, and in his mind he was already swinging it.

"Do you want me to get you something to put on?" Jean was asking a blushing Yeral. His wife nodded and glared at him.

Leave it to a woman to pick now to want all female amenities.

She'd squirmed into a dressing robe and he'd gotten on his breastplate, cuirass and greaves when J'lek entered in his usual, knee-length chainmail and a steel cap, a sword over his shoulder.

"The men will be prepared in under ten minutes," he notified Tartan, making a fist over his heart. "I'm letting boys and girls from the refugee camp feed them mush in the saddle. The cooks, praise War, have been up for an hour."

Tartan nodded. The horses, as well, were fed an hour before dawn, on the off chance of a dawn attack. A lethargic or cramping mount could lose the fight for his rider. Andarons always fed their mounts before the dawn and then a half-day later, just for the reason those were times where no one ever fought.

He had his sleeves and gloves on and was out the tent flap before he realized he'd left without a good-bye to his wife. A look over his shoulder didn't show her chasing after him, just Jean with an evil look on her face, as if it were about time they got to killing.

His favorite horse, a big bay stallion with a full barrel and veined flank, stood by the lever for him. Hostlers attached cables to his breastplate, and he folded his arms across his middle as they lifted him to the the stomping animal's saddle. It snorted, impatient and quivering with energy for the regimen of high protein it had been on.

They'd sweep like a hurricane over the ridge despite their numbers, and surprise Two Spears with a victory this day.

Someone pushed a bowl of mush into his hands. He gave the horse his heels to move it forward as he led his troops out at a trot, this woman Jean loping along at his stirrup.

Behind him, his wife watched him go, in her bare feet and her dressing robe, having been denied two kisses that morning, with her dignity. Her lady in waiting laid a tenuous hand on her should as reconciliation, but she brushed it off.

If Tartan lived, he'd answer for these slights in her good time.

* * *

The dog whose name consisted simply now of *the dog* bound after the female on the horse, the one who stroked her head by the fire at night and who usually fed her.

Once again another rider approached her. Once again the dog turned on her back legs and launched herself at the offending rider. Once again she would bound three times and leap for the mounted warrior with the lance, knocking him from the horse he rode and following him to the ground.

She was away before the warrior could react. She'd been trained to do this almost from when she'd been a puppy, pushing targets from the tops of barrels, then maturing to young men and women on ponies, then to full mounted men. She'd lived with other dogs, males and females of her kind. They'd lain together as a pack on a hay-strewn floor, they'd eaten together and they'd played.

It had been a good time in her life. They'd called her 'Daisy' then. Once in a while a male of the race of Men had taken her to his personal quarters at night, and played with her and fed her and roughed her ears. She'd lain at his feet as he read by candle light, her chin on his instep, warding him as she did these.

The dog turned from the man on the ground as Confluni warriors stabbed him with their spears. She ran after the girl on the horse again, warding her. She liked this, this made sense to her. She warded the girl, she unhorsed the warriors. Later she might herd them—that was more her instinct than her training. The horses were irritating if they just roamed, they were more fun if they stood together in a circle.

She smelled blood, heard screaming and challenges—the angry sounds the two-legs made. She leapt over the body of a dying woman and her fur bristled as the girl on the horse used her magic.

The horse turned back. The dog sat on her haunches and she let it pass, catching her breath. This was the most men she'd ever unhorsed at one time—she could almost take her pick. She avoided their sharp lances as she'd been trained, she protected the girl.

When the girl on the horse took enough of a lead the dog chased off after her. She saw another warrior on another horse approaching her, and gathered herself again.

The noise, the smells, the horses—this was a really good day.

* * *

Xinto stood alongside Ymir Effecate Hagadashi Boohoori, her litter borne by twelve strong Confluni, sweating at the effort.

She'd been pulled from her pavilion to manage a battle already begun badly.

The Theran Lancers had battered their front lines in the first sweep of attack. Now commanders were trying to build up a shield and spear wall to face them, and to porter arrows to the north, where they'd be of some use in their defense.

"This *boy* has the nerve?" Effecate complained. She summoned a waiting commander with a wave of a plump hand. "You there, reinforce to the west and the north. When they've seen our archers, they'll come after them. I want five ranks deep to defend."

"Immediately, my lady," the man said, and bowed, sending a runner with orders. She sent instructions to reinforce the west, and to start a strategy of giving ground to the middle.

"Is that wise, Ymir Boohoori?" a commander asked with cast down eyes.

She sneered at him, the ugly face more twisted but the eyes more shrewd. "We'll draw them into the center, then once they've strayed deep, we'll close them off and riddle them with arrows."

Not a bad plan, Xinto thought, although they'd lose their own warriors in the process. Better to keep them out on the plains, however it was too late to build an embankment to fight behind, and their foot moved too slow to outpace the riders.

They'd already lost hundreds. Confluni healers were dragging warriors back from the front where they'd been skewered by lancers. It'd be a bloody day, no matter what else.

"Our wizards?" Effecate demanded.

"Holding back, per your orders."

Xinto's eyebrows rose. Raven had been engaged from the start of the battle. She had, in fact, warned them all. Vedeen was nowhere to be found, but Glynn and Zarshar were certainly fighting, and Karl and Jahunga had taken places among the infantry.

The Ymir saw the look on Xinto's face and answered him, "My husband nearly defeated the Daff Kanaar when he held back his magic until needed. I will do the same now."

Xinto nodded. He had no plans to fight himself. He'd make more of a contribution right where he was.

"Those reinforcements you were waiting for, then, gracious lady?" he asked.

She smiled and looked away from him.

Under Effecate's leadership, Xinto watched the Confluni line firm up while the archers took up a position to the north. Like waves of gray over an ocean of green spring grass, the Therans flew across the plains, slashed at their lines, pressing through and digging deep into their center, to retreat and be relieved by another wave.

The strategy left Confluni dead on the ground by scores. It also allowed Theran Lancers to break and rest while other waves struck, so only one third to one half of them were ever really in motion.

That seemed odd to Xinto—why break ten thousand warriors, as their spies assured them they had, into parts of six?

The wave with the Wolf's Head standard had begun another run at the center, the young Vulpe leading it, his captains at his sides. Effecate gave the order to draw them into the middle, the bowmen ready now. They'd spring their trap and see how this army ran with no one in charge of it.

The thousand horse swept into the center. The ranks of Conflu back-pedaled before them, many falling to the lances, into a second rank that stood firm in their face.

The thousand turned south to peel off and faced another wall of Confluni spearmen while, behind them, the gap they had pushed through closed.

"To the archers!" Effecate raised her voice in imperious command. She'd been successful, Xinto knew. There'd be no escape. The Theran horse was in turmoil.

Bugles blew to their north and south. Xinto turned to see two thousand more from either direction, a ripple of lances across the plains, one of them headed right for the backs of their archers.

"My lady, to the East! The East!" the commander who'd been routing her orders shouted. They all turned to see a wide swath of lancers thundering toward them in their impossibly heavy armor, mere moments from engaging—not Therans but Angadorian Knights.

No one stood between them and the center of the army, other than their own wounded. In one fell swoop, they were surrounded.

"My lady," Xinto began. Even with their superior numbers, they were undone.

A wave of fire tore the sky. Liquid magma dripped down between the Angadorians and the Confluni. Horses reared and warriors screamed out in fear at both sides.

At the mouth of Effecate's tent, four Uman-Chi stepped out onto the plains.

Chapter Twelve

Sons of the Emperor

Fire dripped from the sky between the Angadorians and the Confluni infantry, buying time for their commanders to form up a defensive line to their east.

Lightening hammered their western front, reopening the line that had trapped the thousand with the Mordetur prince. Another wave of Theran Lancers slashed their defenses, opening the breach wider, letting most of the thousand escape. Zarshar ripped the neck and head from a fallen horse and heaved it after them, having spent his magic.

To their north, the Therans swept across the edges of the Confluni ranks defending their archers. Runners sprinted to their commander to change his orders, to tell him to focus on the riders to the north, rather than the retreating Lancers.

Zarshar shook his head. Say what you wanted about the Eldadorian Empire, they could change their whole strategy on a moment's notice. One spoke to few, who spoke to many and, when a commander became isolated as they had done with this prince, another filled his place.

With this kind of training, his Swamp Devils would rule Fovea, however Zarshar knew no Swamp Devil, by its nature, would be a part of such an army.

They would *never* match the Empire. They might harm it, but they would never be more than a thorn in its largest toe.

The dog that had been their companion ran by him, behind the lines where he'd been ready to wade in and kill this prince himself. To his left he saw Raven, mounted bareback now on an Eldadorian stallion. The dog had clearly earned its keep this morning.

Karl Henekhson rode after her, a crossbow in his hand and a slack expression on his face. The Slee slipped behind them, unseen to those who didn't know how to look for him. In fact, Zarshar had barely caught him. Even among his own kind, he was slippery.

Karl reined in next to Zarshar, the look in his eyes unmistakable.

"You saw him, too, didn't you?" Karl asked.

"The gaffer, next to the prince?" Zarshar asked.

Karl nodded.

"Difficult to miss," the Swamp Devil said. "And not just a companion, an advisor, it seems. I wish I'd known the old Man had this sort of talent. They fight well."

"They fought well before the old man came," Karl said. The horse bobbed its head and snorted. Not fifty yards from them, the battle raged, mounted warriors clashing with their foot troops.

To the west, the fire in the sky subsided. Burned men and horses lay at the edges of a charred field, where the rest of the Angadorians waited for another chance.

To the south, their mounted warriors on shaggy ponies were trying to match their arrows for the swords and lances of the Therans. Hard to tell how that was going.

The ground shook beneath them, cracking in places. The enemy had discovered their Raven and were either attacking where she couldn't be, or using attacks like these, which focused away from her and affected them indirectly.

Men at the line stumbled and fell, lancers skewering them and trampling them. Their losses increased with every pass, and they'd taken few of their enemies. They couldn't overcome the reach of the lances.

Glynn slid up alongside of them, four more Uman-Chi at her side. "Sirrahs," she said, and indicated the others with a sweep of her hand. "Let me introduce the Caster Aniquen Demoran, his Grace, Haldan Evoprosee, his Excellence, Lelden Faire and his Highness Avek Noir, heir to the throne of Trenbon."

"A Swamp Devil, no less," Demoran said, looking him up and down. "I've not seen your like in over one hundred years. I think you're taller than they."

"I think you talk too much," Zarshar answered him. They all smiled like Uman-Chi could be expected to at some insolent subordinate. He'd pledged not to take Glynn's life—he had no such agreement with these others.

"Right now their Lancers are tearing up our lines," Karl said, moving his horse next to Zarshar. The Swamp Devil wasn't fooled. He knew that the Volkhydran sensed his next action and wanted to keep him from taking it.

"We've seen to the west," Evoprosee told them. "We'll let that quiet until they come again, and then take the rest of them. I believe our Glynn can handle the north, and young Aniquen the south, leaving the threat of Shela Mordetur to Lelden Faire and I."

"You'd do well to keep Raven close at hand then," Karl informed them. Again, the self-satisfied smile.

"Glynn's acolyte?" Aniquen didn't hide the disdain in his voice. "Admirable skills, but against the Empress?"

"She's *been* against the Empress while you've been hiding," Zarshar informed them, not because they didn't know it, but to throw it in their faces.

"She *is* endowed with an ability," Glynn said, as mousey as Zarshar had ever seen her. While they bantered, Confluni died in every direction. Their screams, which would have entertained him less than a year ago, actually irritated him now.

"We've heard she reflects magic," Aniquen said. "Or absorbs it in some way."

"Those who attack her with magic are struck powerless, not just their magical reserves but almost all of their life's energy," Glynn informed them.

Evoprosee nodded. Zarshar growled low in his throat, waiting to sneer at them if they hid behind the girl.

"Leave her to protect the Confluni Ymir," he said, finally. "I think we will be best protecting her person."

"Two of you against the Empress?" Zarshar scoffed. "I always wondered what the inside of an Uman-Chi looked like. I think today I'll know."

All five of them stiffened, shared a look, then glided away, moving in that way where they seemed to float. Zarshar had tried to master that once and failed.

It was a stupid trick.

"Well, you've made yourself some brand new friends," Karl informed him, as they left.

Zarshar turned to look him right in the eye. "What of it?"

Karl shrugged. "Nothing," he said, the scar on his face twitching once. He turned his head, spat and looked back into the Devil's eyes.

"Wish it had been me," Karl said, finally.

* * *

Tartan Stowe watched the field burning between him and the Confluni subsiding, smoldering remains of almost one hundred men and horses all that remained of his forward elements.

The Emperor had told him, "Don't attack in a mass, attack in waves. Minimize your losses if you're in over your head." He'd saved the bulk of his army that way.

Now he had to find a way to get his men across a burning field, against completely unexpected Confluni magical resistance, and engage an enemy that was ready for him.

"They aren't Confluni," Jean told him, as he spoke with J'lek.

"What?" Tartan gave her his attention, still at his stirrup.

"That was Lava Rain," Jean told him, her green eyes turned up to his. "An Uman-Chi spell. It's taxing, so they only use it from far away. By the time it burns down, they're ready to attack again."

"So no help there," J'lek said.

"No," Tartan corrected him. "A lot of help. They aren't ready to engage us—they're penned in on all sides. They want to hold us at bay until they've dealt with the Lancers."

Jean nodded. "You could sacrifice some warriors," she began.

Tartan shook his head. He didn't do that. Men could run in at the fore, to break ground, maybe die, that was a part of being a soldier. To be spent like coin for a tactical advantage—Lupus had looked him in the eye once and told him, "If you ever think you have to do that, look into your change purse, and ask yourself which coin in there will stand up and die for you, if the time should come."

But that's what an Uman-Chi would do.

"We have bugles?" he asked one of his subordinates, an Eldadorian of the race of Men, named Gheer.

"Um, well, yes, your Grace, I believe—"

"Sound them," Tartan said. "Ready the attack."

The man nodded and left for the buglers, whoever they might be. Tartan had always considered the bugles silly, but he saw a purpose for them now.

"Your Grace," J'lek said, his face as bland as ever, "if you mean to charge down the Lava Rain and take your losses…"

Tartan just smiled to himself. No, this would be better than that.

* * *

Shela climbed to the top of the ridge, two of her acolytes beside her. She'd left a guard on the one struck down by Raven.

Raven—*such* a betrayal. At her side, Raven and she would have remade the art of magic on Fovea. Now, the young girl would have to die.

Shela could spot her easily enough from atop the ridge, running back and forth on an Eldadorian charger. She even recognized the horse, one of their Andaron/Angadorian hybrids, a messenger's horse, built for stamina over speed.

One of Yonega Waya's dogs ran behind her. She'd warned him that those things were a bad idea, but he hadn't listened. He had this vision of a surprise for the next cavalry he faced, as if being skewered on his lances weren't a big enough surprise.

How she'd befriended the dog was anyone's guess. The children had kept one for a while, but it drooled and left a mess, and they never remembered to walk or feed it. The lives of princes and princesses are too full for such pets.

The flavor of the magic used against them had changed, which is why she'd climbed the ridge. Some things needed to be seen with actual eyes. Now she understood as she picked out the white-robed Uman-Chi Casters. They'd been betrayed, of course. Undone. The Silent Isle had made a fatal mistake, no matter how this battle went.

If they lost, then at worst Thera would fall. Her husband had been warned and could retake it.

"You both see her?" she asked her acolytes. She sensed their nod without turning. She felt her power coursing through her veins now, and employed it with less effort, much as a teakettle already hot comes to boil more quickly.

"The Uman-Chi will be attacking," she said. "They'll want to hit us on all fronts simultaneously. Expect one to come after us while the other attacks our warriors."

The Uman wizards sputtered. "*We*, my lady? Not to be a coward, but should we—"

She raised a hand. "We're as safe here as anywhere, Beltrum, they are Uman-Chi and their reach and their site is long. I want to see them as they attack, so I can defend us."

"Your will, mistress," the other said. So ridiculously formal. Either one had three times her years and a fraction of her abilities.

They never commit themselves, these Uman. They always keep a part of themselves outside of the battle. Not so, Shela Mordetur, Empress of Eldador. She, as her husband liked to say, wasn't afraid to get her hands dirty, right up to the elbows.

The Angadorians to the east charged, their bugles blaring. Foolish pup, Tartan—he'd lose his whole command. However it signaled the response from the Uman-Chi. The one to the east *had* to strike now, so the others did. Black energy in a wave pulsed out from the white-robed Uman right behind the center of their front line, straight at them on the rise. The other Uman-Chi, fifty feet from him, cast fire at the wave of Theran Lancers charging forward. To the north a flight of arrows flew toward their two Millennia, to split and multiply in mid air, and again, becoming a swarm of barbs to skewer their troops. To the south, the ground erupted before the lancers' charge, breaking them up into squads and single riders, leaving them divided for their own horsemen on their shaggy ponies to conquer.

Too many fronts for her, one woman, to fight. In her mind, she instructed Nina of the Aschire, as if she had to. The girl was already acting.

"Beltrum, the south," she commanded. "Cenyail, the north, Hell's Fire." Beltrum, for an Uman, had a creative mind and would assess the situation on his own. Cenyail still needed things pointed out to him.

She raised her left hand and met the black pulse from the Uman-Chi Wizard, then raised her right to drive out the air behind it. She didn't understand fully how this worked, but she'd discussed with her husband the 'is not,' the vacuum left when all of everything is removed from anywhere. He'd tried to explain to her how Water and Earth embraced in a void of space with no air, which struck her as gibberish because she breathed air every day; however he'd gotten her to experiment with solid objects and vacuum.

Move an arrow through the air and create a vacuum before it, and the arrow will stick in it like glue. Create the vacuum right behind, and it stops in mid flight.

Find a great mass in motion, and move a vacuum behind it, and do more than just stop it.

As with a teleportation spell, she removed all of the air in a great cone from behind the black pulse, not pointing it toward the Uman-Chi who'd cast the spell, but the other.

With a thunderous explosion, what her husband called "sonic boom", the black pulse swung around like a bird in flight and hammered into the unsuspecting Uman-Chi. The boom extinguished the fire directed at her own troops, and the detonation had horses rearing, warriors screaming and the Uman-Chi who'd cast the spell flying backwards across the ground.

Nina of the Aschire was already after him.

* * *

From out of nowhere, a sound louder than a thunderclap erupted from above the heads of their own soldiers. Duke Haldan Evoprosee watched his own spell annihilate Earl Lelden Faire before he could even raise a hand to defend himself, his skin melting from his bones under the black pulse.

'How very prophetic of the Swamp Devil,' he couldn't help thinking, even as he flew backwards and crashed ignominiously into a crowd of terrified Confluni.

Before him, sprinting as he'd seen those of her race do, an Aschire was putting arrow to bow and placing herself in sight of him.

He shook his head and righted himself with a small portion of his magic. 'No,' he thought. 'It would not do to be dead now, having so outrageously slain his fellow, even if the poor man was just an Earl.' He raised a hand to stop the arrow in mid flight.

It passed his ward easily and pierced his hand, the point mere inches from his own eye. The pain was nothing for the utter shock that so simple a spell had failed.

"To me!" he shouted, leaping quite uncouth to the protection of a dead horse's body. Another shaft embedded itself in his thigh almost immediately, and he reminded himself that the Aschire were second to none on Fovea in their marksmanship.

Well, second to one. The third shaft bound for his breast met another in mid air and was deflected. He dared to raise his head to see

Nina of the Aschire facing Xinto of the Woods, the famous Ambassador between all nations.

"We keep meeting like this," Xinto said, the rakish hat on his head bobbing a ridiculous orange feather as he spoke.

"This may be the last time," the Aschire growled at him. Haldan had it now—this was the infamous Nina, guardian of the Emperor's children. She possessed some of Shela's magic, or at least her teachings of it.

These little tricks popping up certainly kept one on one's toes.

"I'll kill squirrel as readily as anything else," Xinto replied, and quite slanderously. King Glennen had referred to the Aschire as 'squirrels,' while Emperor Mordetur had befriended them.

Haldan gathered his energy, first repairing his bleeding hand, and then readying himself to try a wall of force against this Aschire. As much as he'd love to just end her young life, she'd be of use in dealing with the Emperor when all of this had ended.

Faster even than his Uman-Chi eye could follow, Xinto and Nina drew and fired, the Scitai from one of the cross-pistols his people were notorious for, the Aschire from her bow. The two shafts passed each other in mid air above him, as he readied the wall for the girl, should she survive.

Nina spun on her heel and caught the arrow in her right hand—a neat trick he hadn't seen before. Apparently neither had Xinto, because it gave him just a moment's pause, and that moment found an Aschire shaft embedded in the front of his robe, his tiny body cast to the ground.

From behind Xinto, more than one hundred armed Confluni charged to his rescue. Haldan Evoprosee raised his hand to cast his wall of force.

Before him, a giant of a man, on a giant of a black stallion, pointed a lance at his midriff.

"Think that's what you want to do?" the Man asked him, in rough Uman.

It was a moment before he recognized the outworlder summoned by Glynn Escaroth, the one who'd called himself 'Bill.'

"Sirrah?" he was incredulous. He'd been swarmed with Theran Lancers now, his rescuers destroyed. He stood tenuously, the lance point at his bosom.

"I think you don't want to cast spells now," this Bill said. "I think you want to stand and be quiet."

Well, the last thing he wanted was that! However, the advice seemed sage, for what he saw about him.

To the north, ruin. Glynn had failed them, and the archers she'd tried to protect were overrun. To the West, with no magical support, the Lancers battered their Confluni allies, who could do little more than wave spears at them as they passed, in hopes of hooking an exposed leg, wither or fetlock.

To the south they'd fared better, and opened up a channel in the terrain torn up by young Aniquen. It was no wonder the Uman-Chi advised the King—he acted a marvel! Confluni poured south in retreat even now, through that opening, with no resistance.

They'd get away with more than half their army, if only Avek Noir held the east. He couldn't see to that side, although the sulfur smell in the air informed him that Lava Rain had fallen.

This Bill prodded his chest with the lance point. Clearly the Man meant to use the thing, and poor hospitality to those who'd brought him here! Watching the Man carefully, he began the spell that would take him back home to Trenbon, to report to his King.

"Stop him!" he heard. An arrow embedded itself in his shoulder, another in his upper arm. He spoke the last words through gritted teeth as he removed himself from this place, for the other.

As he transitioned, he heard the words, "Bill! What are you *doing*?" in the language of Men, then he was passing out at the steps of the palace of Outpost IX.

* * *

Avek Noir had sworn a solemn oath never to raise a hand to the Emperor, Rancor Mordetur and, for fourteen years, had lived by it.

When Angron Aurelias had sat him down in his private chambers in Outpost IX, he'd been updated as to the relative importance of such things.

"As far as we can tell," Angron had informed him, personally, "the Emperor has massed an army of over one hundred thousand, in order to march on the rest of Fovea."

Avek had straightened his back in the 'alert supplicant,' position, and turned his chin up in shock. "So many?"

Angron nodded. "Clearly, we are to blame for this. We—and this song of Glynn's."

Angron seemed close to weeping. He'd wrung his thin-fingered hands. "If we allow this," he said, "then Fovea is lost, us with it, as the Wolf's hunger surpasses even what we can imagine."

"What, then?" Avek had asked, but he already knew. As soon as the Emperor of Eldador had left, Angron had treated with the Emperor of Conflu. Those two met for one reason only.

Never successfully.

"We cannot defeat this army," Angron said, "so instead we shall starve it out. The Confluni will send an army of fifty thousand onto the Andurin Peninsula, and push south, into the fertile center of Eldador, just as soon as we are sure the Emperor is massed."

"Better not after?" Avek had argued, but no. After, there was no telling where this army would go. Were Conflu attacked, then it would be unlikely they would send a force so large.

"I have assured the Confluni that the Emperor will strike Sental," Angron said. "This army will be a ruse, however. The Emperor will not leave his nation while under attack."

"He'll destroy it easily with twice their number," Avek said. "He's done as much with far less."

Angron nodded. "And when he does, our Volkhydran allies will sweep into his port at Thera."

"He's staging at Thera?" Avek found that difficult to believe. He'd want someplace more quiet—all the world went to Thera now.

Angron shook his head. "He's staging at Uman City," the wise king said. "He'll see the trap, and he'll pull his troops away from Uman City, waiting for us to descend upon it. Meanwhile, as his Theran garrisons are emptied, the Volkhydrans will descend on that city, loot and burn it."

"Guaranteeing the Emperor will then crush the invaders from Conflu, then bring his monstrous army to Volkhydro," Avek asserted.

Angron nodded. "Where we shall be in wait for him, good Avek," he said. "Now, with limited supplies, fewer troops and his favorite city destroyed, he will seek a retaliatory strike and be met with the combined Fovean armies."

"Surely he'll know," Avek began, but stopped himself.

"He'll know," Angron said, "and he will come anyway, to prove he can beat us."

Angron had played the coward king to Lupus, because he knew Avek would report everything he heard to the Emperor to whom he owed fealty. Lupus, now, would be caught unawares, thinking the vassal of so many years would certainly not turn now.

Fourteen years was slightly more than the taking of a breath to an Uman-Chi. With more than three hundred years behind him, Avek remembered that day at Uman City, Outpost V, as if it were yesterday.

And so, for his king, he betrayed his oath. He reconciled himself to have no children, as they would be cursed anyway. He reconciled himself to lose all he had, be that the will of Adriam.

Little enough to do to stop this menace.

Now Avek faced the charging Angadorian Knights, some of whom he'd already killed, sealing his fate. He called the fire, the Lava Rain, to do so again.

This time they'd angled to the north, to skirt his defenses. He cast and, as he did so, to a single warrior, they stopped.

The Lava Rain fell harmless to the ground, out of the way of their charge, as the army backtracked to pick a new way west.

He tried to call the rain again, but it was too soon. He'd let his mind wander, been distracted, been fooled, and left depleted. His enemy had already found the path, and all that would stand up to them would be the courage of the Confluni warriors.

For however long that would last.

* * *

Seated on Little Storm, Jack looked down the length of his lance to see a flash and then nothing. A 'snap' registered in his head, like a metal rod breaking, almost as an after affect. He saw spots and realized that, whatever the magic, this Uman-Chi had escaped him.

"Goddammit," he swore, in English.

"Bill!" he heard to his left. He turned to see Melissa—Raven—on an Eldadorian warhorse, their dog at her feet.

The dog had a few scratches on her shoulders and her tongue lolled. She shook her head and flung slobber in gobbets all around her. She'd been busy. He'd heard warriors cursing the dog that had been knocking them from their saddles.

That made sense to him, in retrospect.

"What are you doing?" she demanded. The brown eyes looked tired and hurt. He'd been dreading this.

"The boy needed me," he said, simply.

Around them, the Theran Lancers under Vulpe were disengaging. He needed to break away with them.

"The boy?" she pressed him. Her long, dark hair hung in heavy wet strands. "Vulpe—you mean him? The one who called you 'grandfather?'"

Jack nodded. "He'd be dead," Jack said. "You don't know—they captured his mother."

"Bill, he's our enemy," she insisted. "After everything you've seen, everything you've done—"

Bill shook his head. "Have you talked to Vedeen?" he asked.

She knit her eyebrows. "What?"

He had to go. He turned his head to look over his left shoulder and made eye contact with Two Spears, then turned back to Melissa.

"She said something about how it isn't that we don't understand the song, but that we aren't asking the right questions.

"Talk to her, hunny," he said. Then he kicked Little Storm and the big stallion turned.

"Bill, no," he heard her telling him. "You're *not* going."

The ground around him began to smolder. Raven had been learning magic. Apparently she'd been getting good at it. Little Storm tried to lift a foot, then replaced it.

Any other horse would probably have gone nuts.

Jack didn't turn around. "Let me go," he told her.

"Bill," she said again.

He turned at that. "The name is Jack," he said, looking right into her soft brown eyes. This killed him. He should love this girl. She should be right beside him.

But he'd been told to protect her, that without him, she would fail, and once he'd thought about it, he'd realized what that meant.

"Don't go…" she whimpered.

"Stop it, Raven," he told her. "Stop it *right now.*"

Little Storm lurched forward. He turned his back to her without a good-bye. Ahead he could see the Prince looking over his shoulder at him. Little Storm started to trot and he heard the dog follow him for a few paces, then Melissa—Raven—called her back.

Good enough, he thought. She'd need the dog more than he.

* * *

Arath of the Daff Kanaar stood atop a hill overlooking a shallow bowl where Angadorian Knights had camped just hours before. The remains of their jess doonar showed disrespect for Earth.

Arath was not a religious Man, but he respected Earth deeply, for the secrets he had learned from the god, and for the many favors he'd enjoyed in his life, which Arath attributed to Him.

Lupus, for his many flaws, had always shown a love of Earth.

He destructed his jess doonar, healed the land behind him, covered wastes and washed out cook fires.

Arath smiled to himself, sitting his Angadorian gelding, Socks, named by Vulpe, the Emperor's son. He and Lupus shared a rivalry famous across Fovea, competition as the best general alive.

Lupus the more-famous. Lupus the more-celebrated. Lupus his liege-lord, truth be told.

But Lupus' plans had gone too far, and when that happened, Lupus knew who to call.

Now Confluni by the tens of thousands were marching double-time away from a crushing defeat at the hands of Theran Lancers and Angadorian Knights. Not good enough, Arath knew. From here they'd fortify, establish themselves, and be nearly impossible to dislodge. The bowl's natural defenses made a mounted attack suicide and an attack on foot costly. The remains of this jess doonar would only make them stronger.

Which, of course, was why Arath had come out of the north to meet them with 10,000 Daff Kanaar out of Uman City, under the command of Scarlet Nantar, who'd come on foot and stood in his armor at Arath's stirrup.

"You're ready for a fight then?" the Warrior in Red asked him, a huge grin on his face.

"Have to be in this line of work," he said. "What have we?"

"Ten thousand foot, forced march from Uman City after forced march from Metz. Made it here in spectacular time—just five days."

Arath frowned. "Should have taken ten," he said, "What good are they to me if they're exhausted?"

"Well, your Confluni are exhausted," Nantar said, "and we only did a few miles today. I marched the hell out of 'em the first three days then cooled 'em down the fourth. Yesterday all they did was sleep. Surprised you didn't hear 'em snoring."

Arath grinned. "So you claim my men are ready to go."

Nantar nodded. "In so many words," he said. "You're starting to sound like Thorn."

Arath snorted. "Where *is* your other wife?" he asked. "Can't remember the last time one of you wasn't in the other's shadow."

"He's taking care of Black Lupus, of course," Nantar said. "We know better than to leave him alone."

Arath nodded. They *did* know better. Lupus would do something ridiculous, just to prove he could, and then they'd all have hell to pay.

Below them, the Confluni were filling the bowl and building up the defenses of the abandoned jess doonar. "How long did you want to let them keep doing that?" Nantar asked him.

"Not much longer," Arath said. "I want more shovels in hand than swords, and more Confluni in the bowl than just these. We're going to be down in it, no point in having someone come up behind us, do to us what we just did to them."

Nantar nodded. "And the boy?" he asked. "Lupus' son?"

"The man, you mean," Arath said. He'd been contacted by Dilvesh, who'd been contacted by Lupus' oldest daughter, Lee, who'd been contacted by one of Lupus' wizards in Uman City. "Not only is he a blooded warrior now, but he—"

"I know, I know," Nantar said, motioning him quiet with one hand. He squinted up at the woodsman, and added, "Wouldn't you know the son would turn out like the father?"

"Usually it's the mother," Arath said. "Aren't your daughters more like you?"

Nantar's twin daughters, born at the same time as Vulpe, Nanette and Thorna, were notorious tomboys whom, as soon as they'd stood on their own feet, pulled off their dresses for breeches and the nearest sharp object.

"Living on the Andaron plains with Thorn's people," Nantar said. "Shela's advice, thinks they'll be more like me, not less."

"Mother Water should awake," Arath said. He noted the exodus into the bowl had become a trickle, and someone had finally gotten the idea to send scouts up the hills.

"It's time," he said. "Don't suppose we'll get any help from those brave Theran Lancers?"

Nantar smiled. "Return the favor?" he asked, incredulous. "Not likely. Now that they've warmed 'em up for us, they'll be getting contacted by a few fast-footed fellows I brought with me."

Nantar pulled the huge broadsword from over his shoulder. Behind him, his warriors were already assembled in the patchwork of squads that had come to be know as Wolf Soldier formation.

"Vulpe Mordetur," he said, "has other orders."

Chapter Thirteen

Wolf Soldiers

Admiral Geledar Taboorin of the Trenboni Imperial Fleet had taken it as a point of honor to come himself upon the Tech Ship flag ship, *My Lady's Lovely Way*, in escort of four hundred Volkhydran warships and twenty thousand warriors of the same nation.

Packed to the gills with their armor and their courage, the smaller, more maneuverable vessels skipped along the swells on Tren Bay, some of them recommissioned after years in dry dock, some of them converted back from fishing vessels, some of them barely painted and with green planks.

Thirty Tech Ships, the remains of a once-proud Trenboni fleet, fanned out before them, en route to Thera, the jewel of Eldador.

"Land, ho!" the Uman sailor from the crow's nest called.

"Where away?" the ship's captain returned.

"One point to starboard, beaches and shoals," the watch returned.

Taboorin turned to his Uman-Chi captain. "Isn't that awfully soon?" he asked. They shouldn't have made landfall until tomorrow.

"We may have caught a following current," the captain said. The expression on his face was clear, however. Unless Tren Bay had somehow become smaller, they'd come too fast.

Taboorin was old by Uman-Chi standards, in his seventh century. He counted himself one of the few survivors of the Battle of the Deceptions on the Trenboni side, and not for want of fighting.

Out-gunned and out-maneuvered, he'd escaped through Eldadorian Fire and a sky full of lightening to tell his tale to his King.

He didn't do that by taking anything for granted.

"Send out the *Red, Red Mist of Dawn*, and the *Warm Kiss of Life*, to investigate," he commanded. "To the rest of the fleet, ninety degrees to starboard and hold positions. If this is a trick—"

"Alarm, alarm!" the crow's watch cried. From directly before them, the scene wavered and what had looked like land became instead the square-rigged masts of the Eldadorian Fleet.

"Sea Wolves!" he heard the cry. His own blood ran cold. He saw the glistening brass funnels on the port side of three of them, meaning they were equipped with Eldadorian Fire.

"We're undone!" the Captain cried. "Crow's Watch, how many?"

"I've counted fifty masts," the Uman returned, his voice wavering. "And I've more to count."

"So many?" the Captain asked of the Admiral. The older Uman-Chi said nothing, taking stock of their situation.

That their plan had failed went without saying—no one had given them a promise of success, merely an opportunity at trying. In this case, they were to break for Chatoos if they could and Trenbon otherwise. It was foolishness to assume they'd reach either. They'd be no match for even half this number, and they'd never outrun the Sea Wolves.

Angron Aurelias' plan had been to get the Emperor to focus on Uman City while they took his jewel, Thera. If they were looking down the throats of a fleet of Sea Wolves now, then the odds were that, once again, the King had been outmaneuvered by the Man with only a fraction of his years.

Uman-Chi Tech Ships had commanded Tren Bay for centuries, and Geledar Taboorin had commanded Tech Ships. Now in fewer years than it took to train a good ensign, he wanted to run in terror from one of the race of Men!

"Any sign of that Confluni fleet?" Geledar demanded. The Confluni had dispatched a vast army to the shores of Eldador, and then departed for Outpost IX for refit and replenishment. Then they'd promised to help with the escort.

"None," the Captain said. "They may not have had time to overtake us, though. Confluni are poor sailors."

Admiral Taboorin nodded—no surprises there. The deck

beneath him swayed as their ship turned hard aport. The Tech Ships would break away from the Volkhydrans and give their charges a better chance to see shoreline.

Pointless—the Sea Wolves would run them down. Volkhydrans are brave, but bravery does precious little in the face of lightening and Eldadorian Fire.

"All ships to port," the Admiral ordered.

"To port?" the Captain challenged him. Already an Uman sailor relayed the order to the rest of the fleet, colored flags flying up a line behind the jib. Some of his captains had been in his service for thirty decades. They knew their Admiral; he'd gotten them out of scrapes before.

"I'm sick of running from the damned Emperor," Geledar Taboorin informed him. "He's of the race of Men, not gods. Stick him with a sword and he'll die like any other."

"Two hundred," the crow's watch reported. "Two hundred masts counted."

"My Lord, two hundred masts," the Captain said. "Certainly, we have *no* chance—"

Geledar Taboorin put his hand on the Captain's shoulder. "We had no chance the moment they spotted us," he said. "We had no chance the moment Angron Aurelias went back on his word with this bastard. By Water's soggy tits, Captain, an Uman-Chi has no chance when he's got sea water fifty feet over his head, and a sinking ship below him, and right now it seems to me that I can see the sun."

"Aye, aye, my Lord," the Captain said. "If nothing else, then we'll give them a fight for the histories."

"Or we'll make history," the Admiral said, then turned to his men and roared, "Who here wants to be with me to hand these Eldadorian bastards their first naval defeat?"

The Uman crew shook their fists and roared.

It was a start.

* * *

Raven seethed in anger on the battlefield, from within what used to be the safety of the Confluni army.

On every side, the Daff Kanaar pressed their troops. She'd never seen people die like this, not this close, not this bloody. She didn't realize all of the pain involved, all of the stink, the screaming and the loss of control.

She saw herself as having a job to do; she tried to focus on that. She wanted to put herself in the path of the enemy's spell casters, to trick them into attacking her, to drain them of their power.

When she could arrange that, the power flowed through her now, fulfilled her like a lover. The power sent her blood coursing like strong whiskey, running through her veins.

She'd been dumped by Bill, left to fend for herself. He'd sworn to her that he'd protect her here, be Galahad. He'd lied.

Every man who'd ever gotten past her guard had lied.

"Back," Karl shouted to the Confluni troops. They'd learned who he was somehow, they all listened to him now. Their leaders were mostly dead anyway—they needed someone to take charge.

"Fall back! Reinforce that line!" he shouted. "Pikemen to the front. Shields!"

Dumped. That friggin' muther. Who did he think he was?

"Hold the line! Hold the line!"

Daff Kanaar pressed them, shields and pikes, tearing up their lines, keeping them from forming an effective defense.

"Oh, stop it!" she howled, and felt her power swell.

Right then, one of the foreign wizards struck her, and amplified what she was already feeling.

Where she would have called the fire and cast it into the mass of Daff Kanaar, now she found a terrible focus with this swelling of energy. Now she remembered, of all things, those chemistry classes that she'd loved so much in college.

In her mind's eye she saw the air around her, actually *saw* it, oxygen, O-16, protons, neutrons and electrons forming molecules.

She saw the little bundles of balls, surrounded by electron dashes, speeding around like little solar systems.

Where they were random, she lined them up in a gigantic cube, encapsulating the people trapped within them.

Where electrons spun at one speed, she made them spin faster.

Faster.

Faster than sound. Faster than light. Faster than anything in nature could go.

Before her eyes, a cube of air four hundred feet across, four hundred feet deep and ten feet high converted itself from matter to energy, burning hotter than the sun.

The beings caught within didn't even have time to scream before the searing heat vaporized them. Stunned by what she'd done, she released the spell, the super-heated air rocketing upward, blasting a hole in the clouds above them.

The resulting sonic boom rocked them all, throwing her from her feet into the air. She instinctively built a cocoon of oxygen around her, a gelatinous bubble to protect her as she bounced through their army.

Behind her, to their east, a hill exploded, turning from a solid just to dust. Their commanders were screaming to the men—she couldn't hear what through the commotion and her own spell.

She bounced several times and came to rest on her back. Terrified Confluni warriors were charging to the west.

"Wasn't that a cute trick?"

"What?" she demanded.

There was Zarshar before her, stepping out of a dust storm with an Uman-Chi over his shoulder; male, one of Glynn's friends.

"I was waiting for you to do that," Zarshar informed her.

He had blood all over him. He'd reveled in this. The violence, the killing—this was like Christmas to Zarshar.

"You need to come with me," he informed her.

"But, the army, the, I mean—Karl," she stammered.

The Devil shook his head. Over his shoulder, the Uman-Chi hung limp in his white robes. He couldn't be dead, she thought, or Zarshar would have just left him.

"We're getting out of here," he informed her. "And you need to come with me."

She felt claws at her waist. She turned to see Slurn lifting her to her feet. As much as she could tell, he'd seemed concerned to her.

"Okay," she said, finally. If it got these two cooperating, the least she could do was come along.

* * *

It wasn't the shame-faced little boy who'd been caught playing with his sword again, who faced his father on the field outside of Thera, returning with a conquering army of Theran Lancers.

Nina of the Aschire sat proudly behind the many-times blooded Prince Vulpe Mordetur, who'd rescued his mother from Bounty Hunters, who'd outmaneuvered the Confluni and the Uman-Chi and who, outnumbered, remained victorious, much like his father.

Blizzard pawed the ground, his steel shoes striking sparks on the cobbled road outside of Thera's outer markers. The Emperor himself had come to greet his son, his wife and his Blood Brother.

"Your Imperial Majesty," Duke Two Spears nodded, from his own horse, then saluted, his fist over his heart.

Shela looked away nervously—she'd have a different discussion with the Emperor this night. She'd been told to remain in the capitol, much as she'd likely saved them all by disobeying.

This wasn't about that.

"Duke Two Spears," Lupus nodded. His eyes remained focused on his eleven-year-old son. Vulpe held his head high, his hand on his blooded sword.

"Your Imperial Majesty," Vulpe said, his young voice oddly commanding in its own way. Vulpe had represented his family well three days before when, on the field, he'd led charge after charge against the Confluni, then driven them into a trap set by the Emperor with the Daff Kanaar. It had taken all of them to convince young Vulpe that his father wanted him here, in Thera, not back on the plains, where battle still raged between the holdouts of a once-vast army and the most feared veterans on Fovea.

In the end, the old Man, whom Vulpe called 'grandfather,' informed him, "Son, you'll want to be a general one day. You'll want to replace your father. If you mean to do that, then you'd best learn how to take orders, or he'll never trust you to give them."

That had stopped Vulpe in his tracks. Shela had actually laid her hand on the old Man's forearm afterward, in clear gratitude for his wisdom. Nina had already planned his death up to that moment. Those few words had saved his life.

"Your Highness," Lupus said to his son. "I'm told I'm well-represented this past week."

"I did my best, father," Vulpe responded. She'd schooled him in this. Be humble. Lupus always credited those around him for his successes, do the same. He likes that.

"I had a lot of good advice," he added.

Nina felt the burning mass behind her eyes as she fought back tears of pride for this boy. She couldn't have loved him more if he were her own.

"The enemy?" Lupus asked.

"Twenty-five, maybe thirty thousand when we quit the field," Vulpe said. Two Spears had opened his mouth to answer and closed it, grinning, a sideways glance at the Prince. Vulpe ranked him; it was his position to speak to the Emperor.

"No more than Arath can handle," Lupus said, and directed his gaze to those around Vulpe.

Mounted on Little Storm, old Jack sat quiet, waiting, between Shela and her son. On his other side, a Wolf Soldier who'd served right next to Vulpe since he'd rescued his mother, a heavily tattooed Uman named Grelt, grinned in unashamed pride.

"Grelt," Lupus nodded to the Wolf Soldier. "I'm told there's a new commander for the Pack?"

The other Wolf Soldier who'd been with them, Drun, a Dorkan, slammed a meaty hand on Vulpe's shoulder, his forearm nearly knocking Nina from the back of his saddle.

"Aye," he growled for his fellow. "Vulpe fights like a lion. Those Confluni were pissing their pants and calling for their mamas when he rode up."

"He did well," Grelt said, more serious, looking in Lupus' eye. "I'd fight by him again," he said. "I'd kill any as wouldn't."

"I as well," Drun chimed in. "Be proud if you'd assign me to Vulpe's Millennium."

Theran Lancers chimed in. To his credit, Vulpe stayed quiet.

Lupus nodded. "Your Grace, your dagger, if you don't mind?"

Vulpe straightened. Nina felt the tears on her cheeks. She'd known this was coming. If the boy would be his father, then the boy would be *like* his father.

Blood ran from the corner of Shela's mouth, she was biting her lip so hard. Nina doubted she was aware of it. Her hand on his side, Nina detected the slightest tremble in Vulpe's small body.

Two Spears handed over the blade, a plain Andaron dagger. "For unmatched bravery, unquestioning loyalty, and service that does credit to Eldador, your Leader, and to the Pack, you are awarded our highest honor," Lupus said, raising the blade on high.

The sun glistened on the knife's edge. The weapon fell for the young face.

Vulpe met it on the keen edge of his own blade, Fury. To his credit, the draw was so fast that none of them could have stopped him. He even caught his own father by surprise.

The gasp from the Lancers behind them and the Wolf Soldiers next to him was almost an explosion. The father and son remained for a pregnant moment, sword to dagger and their horses side by side.

"No, father," he said.

"What?" a storm brewed behind the Emperor's eyes. "This is our highest honor—"

"I know," Vulpe said. He pulled his sword, and sheathed it, sitting straight in the saddle.

"I know it is, father," he said, as the Emperor's arm slowly lowered. "It's the highest honor a Wolf Soldier can receive.

"I haven't earned it," he said, and looked around him, mostly into old Jack's face. The man's smile bristled his beard as he nodded.

"I'm not a Wolf Soldier."

* * *

When Glynn had first sensed the presence of her Uman-Chi brethren in the Confluni camp, she'd been ecstatic. This spoke to her on every level—their companionship, their acceptance of her song, the King's participation in their mission.

When she'd noted that one of their number was Avek Noir, she'd been surprised. If *anyone* would be difficult to turn from the Emperor, it would be Noir. He'd been a Wolf Soldier, then come back with some manufactured fortune to rescue Outpost IX. No one failed to see the Emperor, then a Duke, had used Noir to his own ends, to buy himself the heir to the Trenboni throne.

No Uman-Chi should have been so shortsighted, yet here he stood with the rest of them.

She'd also been delighted to see handsome Aniquen Demoran among them. Aniquen's clever magic would be crucial in any battle.

Then she'd heard the plan, the trap within the trap.

"My Lords, prithee, you must speak in jest," she'd said, in the dim light of the Ymir's pavilion, a gaudy hovel for a slothful, obese woman. She pressed her knees together and laid her forearms wrists-up in the position of the open-minded supplicant.

"We most certainly do not," Haldan Evoprosee had informed her. Although Avek Noir ranked them all, he was oddly quiet and deferential to the Duke, an accomplished Caster over one hundred years his senior. "His Majesty believes the Emperor's own arrogance will lead him into the jaws of our deception."

"Your Grace, this army has not dug in," Glynn informed them. She'd spoken with Karl Henekhson. "It stands open on the plain between *two* armies, both mounted, and not even a fence of spikes between them."

"*We* are between them," Lelden Faire had informed her, his nose in the air. This had been the entire, productive portion of the conversation. They'd gone to great pains to assure her she'd done exactly as the King had expected, and proved his wisdom.

She'd tried to support these older Uman-Chi. She'd tried to defend the Confluni archers from a sweeping charge of Theran Lancers, and found her magic circumvented by the Empress. Admittedly, she'd never been in such a battle before, and she'd panicked and she'd acted too soon. She'd broken the Confluni's arching arrows into thousands upon thousands of dart-like missiles, and seen them burned away in their flight by a spell she recognized as Hell's Fire. She'd peppered her enemy in ash as the tiny missiles burned to nothing.

She'd been pummeled personally with balled lightening and fire while her archers defended themselves. That hadn't gone well.

The defense against the Daff Kanaari had gone far worse. This Eldadorian Prince may have outmaneuvered them; however his tactics showed his formal training. Nothing too creative, nothing too unique, sane waves of Lancers slashing at their lines from the safety of horseback and, with solid magical cover, he'd whittled them down.

To their East, the Angadorians with no magic had outfoxed Avek Noir and engaged a thin line of defenders in a much more bold and creative method, plunging deep into their ranks.

When they escaped south to a natural bowl, the Daff Kanaari had caught them and out-fought them with superior generals and better-trained warriors. With the aid of only marginal magical support, the Daff Kanaar had reduced them to a scant ten thousand.

Now they fought a running battle on the Eldadorian plains, trying to get to the Forgotten Sea where they could possibly negotiate or fight for ships to carry them out of Eldador.

Lelden Faire had been destroyed by their own magic. Avek Noir had descended into a useless funk, and Haldan Evoprosee had deserted them.

"Ymir Effecate Hagadashi," Aniquen said, "our magic is more than adequate to the task; however we cannot do all of the work for you. Your warriors must *fight*."

The woman snorted as one of her young boys fed her from a plate of fruit. More than once they'd walked in on her molesting them. Much as the race of Men could be vile, this woman seemed to revel in her perversion.

They'd have faired better with Xinto in his capacity as

ambassador for them, however that no longer proved possible.

"It's a trail of our blood, not yours, that they follow us in," she told them. "We counted on your support and sent fifty thousand. You send four."

"Five, your Grace," Aniquen corrected her.

"One I found myself," she said, and opened her disgusting maw for another grape. The boy fed her without expression.

"As be it," Aniquen said, taking the seated posture of the discourser, not the arguer, not that the woman would recognize it. "We are represented, and it was we who won your freedom from the Prince, then again from the Daff Kanaar."

When they couldn't defeat the Daff Kanaar soldiers and all seemed lost, Aniquen had cast a spell that forced the water from the hills to the southeast. They'd exploded in dust, choking friend and foe alike and giving the Confluni the cover to retreat.

Aniquen had swooned and Zarshar had carried him, limp as a newborn, as they retreated. They'd left their severely wounded behind, Xinto of the Woods among them.

Xinto had been a calming voice of reason, proven by experience. Jack had proven more wily and insightful. It must have taken more than she could imagine to turn him.

"You must contact your King and demand more troops and more wizards," the Ymir informed them, juice from the grape trickling down her chin.

"The agreement—" Aniquen began, but she waved him off.

"You've committed yourselves as we have," she informed him. "Lupus the Conqueror swore to drive to our capitol if we ever struck at him again. Your king has broken a treaty with him. Who in either of our nations will be left standing, if he survives?"

Glynn couldn't argue with the disgusting woman. She had entirely surmised their predicament. According to Avek, the king had planned to enrage the Emperor sufficiently to get him to attack Volkhydro, where a monstrous army awaited him. What now, if he came for the Uman-Chi or the Confluni instead?

Especially considering that, if they stood here defeated, then the invasion of Thera must be doomed.

* * *

Xinto of the Wood lay on his back on a battlefield, in bloody red dirt with a dead man for a pillow and his pain to comfort him.

His own people had abandoned him, not that he really blamed

them. His life slipped away, and none of their Wizards could help him, having been left too drained by the battle.

His vision clouding, Xinto wondered at what they thought they were accomplishing with this resistance of Glynn's. They'd certainly seen a good number of people killed, with more to come. They'd antagonized the Emperor. There would be no perfunctory invasion—Lupus the Conqueror had something to prove now.

He still remembered the boy on the huge horse who'd nearly run him down in the streets of Outpost IX, a messenger for the Dwarves. The first thought in his head had been that he'd be perfect for this mission of Prince Ancenon's. Short on brains and long on personal opinion, he'd be Ancenon's puppet and later thank Xinto for the opportunity.

He'd never asked himself how a stupid Man had tamed a stallion from the Herd that Cannot be Tamed, befriended the reclusive Dwarves, and crossed three nations in so short a life. Most people never strayed more than ten daheer from the house that birthed them.

What had Vedeen said? They weren't asking themselves the right questions.

Glynn sang of 'The One, who others wait upon.' He was waiting upon one now–the goddess Eveave, to take him to her bosom, to his last reward.

He didn't wait upon the Emperor. If Lupus found him now, he'd save him just to kill him one hundred more times.

Xinto stirred in the muddy paste his own red blood had made. His vision continued to blur. It shouldn't be long now.

Already the crows gathered overhead. They'd feast on his eyes. He hoped to be dead by then.

"The One, who others wait upon, To fight forever more."

That could mean anything. Typical gods—they couldn't just say, "Go here and turn the knob to the left." No, they had to speak their vagaries. They had to play their silly games.

The question, he reasoned, wasn't who the One was. That seemed obvious. The question, of course, was what waited upon him.

And in that thought, he got it. With that knowledge, he rattled the whole song off in his head.

The shock hit him so hard that, before his blood loss could take him, he succumbed to a heart attack instead, gripping his chest almost comically as he died.

* * *

Genna walked the remains of the battlefield. It had already begun to stink, and the birds to feast on eyes and entrails. Here she kicked a sword aside; there she stepped over the carcass of a horse.

If anyone ever guessed she refused to ride because she refused to be the reason why so noble a creature died, then she'd be mortified, but that secret was hers.

Hers and her dark, dark son's. In fact, she traveled West now to be near him, to rejoin him, now that she'd done as much damage as she dared.

Crossing the battlefield, she came across, of all things, Xinto's comical little cap, seated in a puddle of dark blood. Stuck into the center of that puddle was a brand new dagger, its hilt intricately carved and distinctive, its crossbar carved into the shape of two clutching hands.

She frowned. It was the type of unbalanced, gaudy thing she'd expect the Scitai to have. In fact, she strayed through here because she wanted to see the Scitai's corpse. He'd eluded her and started her on this journey—even if she couldn't kill him for it, she'd have liked to see him dead.

She pulled the dagger from the ground and it came away clean. Odd—not a grain of sand clung to the metal, much like the Emperor's blade.

She'd loved Lupus once. He'd betrayed her. She'd wept every day for a month when she'd discovered he'd blindsided her with his seed. Over the years, she'd had to admit to herself that she'd wanted his child. Why else give herself to him so frequently? She'd expected that son to be shining and tall, but that was not to be.

She hefted the blade. The metal looked almost black, and on closer inspection she found tiny jewels, wraps of wire, bits of wood and string and all manner of impurities carved into the hilt. It was as if the weapons maker couldn't decide on what to use, and had instead wrapped in a little bit of everything.

She shrugged and sheathed the blade in her belt scabbard. She'd give it to her son. It suited him. For the life of her, in proximity to her nethers, the thing actually seemed to warm to her.

She started off at a trot to the east. Some said the fumes of a new battlefield drove women insane, and in this case they might be right.

Chapter Fourteen

A Guardian Will Take You There

Thirteen battered Tech Ships of the Trenboni Imperial Fleet limped into the harbor at Outpost IX, escorting just under three hundred Volkhydran warships and fewer than twelve thousand weary warriors.

Admiral Geledar Taboorin stood at the prow of *My Lady's Lovely Way*, his arm in a sling and his face still covered in ash and blood, even after four days. He directed the ship himself, his captain having died, and other similarly trained individuals being scarce in their ranks.

'Victory!' the thought rang in his head. In his more than seven hundred years, he'd never fought so hard nor so well, his ships dancing in his command beneath him, coordinating a series of feints, drawing the Eldadorians out wider than they could defend themselves, then cutting their ships off at the knees.

Sea Wolves are faster, they carry more warriors, and they deliver more punishment in a one-to-one fight, armed not only with catapults but their considerable magic.

However a Tech Ships' enchantment is born of superior Uman-Chi Casters, and works at greater range. Admiral Geledar Taboorin had realized this at the Battle of the Deceptions. He became the rabbit to the hound and, from outside of the Wolves' strike circle, destroyed them.

When the Eldadorians had lost thirty ships they withdrew into four large fleets and formed a half-circle before the Trenboni. Were he to have pressed that, he would have had to come in close, and suffered. To have survived the fight at all, he knew, counted as his victory.

Now Angron Aurelias himself, with an Uman-Chi whom the Admiral recognized as Duke Haldan Evoprosee, a premier Caster of an old house and one whose magic had helped build this fleet, waited for him on the docks.

Taboorin had no magic, or he might have used his power to leap from the bow to the docks. As it was, he knelt on the deck and lowered his head to his liege lord for his fleet.

Angron nodded and, with his retinue, waited patiently for the Admiral to disembark.

My Lady was made fast to her space as the flagship of what remained of the fleet. Already another hundred masts had been commissioned. This violated the very laws of the Fovean High Council, laws the Uman-Chi themselves had put in place, but those would not see these lonely docks for years. In that time, many things would change.

Taboorin left his first mate, an Uman boatswain who'd served him personally for six decades, to commence repairs and see to the crew. None of them, bone weary as they were, would see a night in port for a week. *My Lady* had felt the scorch of Eldadorian Fire and the heat of magical lightening, even a few boulders from other catapults.

She wasn't the worst off in what remained of the fleet.

He left the ship, strode down the dock to where his King honored him by waiting, and knelt again before Angron Aurelias, his hand to his shoulder.

"Rise, Admiral Taboorin," Angron informed him. "It is We who must honor you, the savior of My fleet."

"Or what's left of it," Duke Evoprosee sneered, looking down his nose at Taboorin. The Admiral rose, stiff in his knees, to look the Duke in the eye.

He'd received the reports. "I didn't quit the field at first wounding," he answered, "and so my charges remain alive."

"My Lords, please," Angron said, raising his hand as

Evoprosee stiffened. "I'll hear nothing of loss today. If we can beat the Emperor on the Bay, then this nation is safe, and we ourselves are saved."

The King turned to walk back down the docks, where a litter would bear him back to the palace. Evoprosee walked to his left, while the place of honor, a step behind and to the right, was left for Taboorin in his glory. Much as he swelled with pride, he felt himself filled with caution as well.

"Your Majesty," he said, "prithee, do not overestimate this victory, for in it, we still lost a fourth of our charges and more than half of our fleet."

"More ships are in the offing," Evoprosee protested, and was silenced once again when the King raised a thin-fingered, pale hand.

"Can you repeat this victory again, with the resources you have?" he asked Taboorin, without turning.

"When my ships are repaired?" Taboorin asked, and sensed more than saw the King's nod. "Then I could defeat my own number and, with no other ships to protect, perhaps a few more.

"But the Eldadorian Empire's full navy, versus ours?" Taboorin shook his head. "No, your Majesty. We won the day when their losses exceeded ours, however had they persisted then, in time, we would have failed, and we did not see the Emperor's whole fleet."

"Then we celebrate nothing," Evoprosee said, as they approached the litter.

Angron remained quiet as he turned and leaned back into his seat upon the litter. He regarded neither of them, but looked south, to his enemies.

In the last decade, the King had worried himself thin enough where Taboorin feared a strong breeze might carry him away. The once-glorious white hair had come to lay thin and weak upon his shoulders. Where once Kings had begged his wisdom, now Dukes and Earls sneered at his side.

"Contact Glynn Escaroth," he said finally, to Evoprosee. The Duke folded his hands before him and nodded.

"It matters not now that we betray her position," he continued. "Let her know the names of some of our operatives in Eldador, the less reliable ones which we might lose with small cost."

"And your message, your Majesty?" the Duke asked.

The Uman porters lifted up the litter and gently carried him toward the palace. Taboorin and Evoprosee walked along either side.

"She is to inform them of our glorious victory on Tren Bay," he said, "and of the sad performance of the Imperial Fleet under Lupus himself."

Taboorin actually missed a step as he walked. The Uman porters traded looks of shock from what they overheard. Even as Evoprosee cleared his throat, Taboorin knew it would be quite a scandal at that evening's dinner banquet.

"Your Majesty, I obey even your slightest whim, but in fact we know—" Evoprosee began.

"We know nothing but what we can surmise," Angron answered him, rudely cutting the Duke off. "If I say the Emperor was himself defeated, then let him defend his honor, if he has any."

"Of course, your Majesty," the Duke said. "Shall I triple our guard and burn our ports in anticipation of the Emperor's arrival?"

As close to insolence as Taboorin had ever heard before the King. These times troubled him.

"If you wish to," Angron informed him. "However not before our Admiral carries me from here."

"Your Majesty?" Taboorin asked him. To insult the Emperor and then leave the security of Outpost IX made no sense to him.

"I am too long cooped up here," the King informed them. "I have not been to Volkhydro in three generations of the lives of Men. It is time to remind them of our greatness."

Taboorin smiled. The original plan had been to enrage the Emperor into making a bold attack, and then to catch him in his anger.

Surely their wise King had found another way.

"Your will be done," Evoprosee said. "I will make the necessary preparations, of course."

Taboorin grinned to himself. Wily if aged, that much was certain. Lupus the Conqueror would hear this challenge and not only rise to it, but seek to destroy its purveyor.

It would be bloody days in Volkhydro.

* * *

Empress Shela Mordetur, called the Mother of the Empire, the Bitch of Eldador and, perhaps, one of the most feared women alive, stood naked in a guest chamber in the ducal estate of Thera, her delicate hand on the cold, stone wall before her, her head down in the room's dim light, the curtains drawn on the real glass windows, the one door to this room shut.

The lash fell across her back, its leather kiss a hot line of pain from her shoulder to her hip.

She whimpered, tears flowing from her eyes down the perfect olive skin on her face.

She'd designed this room when she and her husband, then her master, had designed this place. She'd commissioned the high bed and the furniture; she'd carefully chosen the colors to accent the rest of the household and to make guests feel welcome. The estate was to have been their perfect home, the place for their children to be born, a place where every room had special meaning, every piece of furniture and painting an expression of their love.

The lash fell again. Her back exploded in pain. She cried out despite herself, the wall before her dotted with her tears. Her husband wasn't angry, he was furious with her, and she bore the brunt of his rage.

Normally he'd speak to her when she needed to be disciplined, tell her where she'd failed him, demand better behavior over and over. Sometimes the humiliation of the lecturing was worse to bear than the actual punishment.

Not this time. This time he was silent. Many said, "Fear the Emperor in his anger, be terrified of him in his calm." This was such a time. Dressed in his black leather pants and boots, his unadorned white cotton shirt, his blonde hair loose around his shoulders, his lips were pressed in a thin, pink line, his blue eyes as hard as diamonds. Her startling disobedience left him so upset, he couldn't speak.

The lash fell across her buttocks.

They'd ridden here with their son in quiet. She'd followed him to the stables with her brother, feeling the eyes on her, the quiet pregnant with suspense. It was the talk of the Empire that she would be subjected to his discipline. Some speculated as to why. She could crush him with her power. With a gesture and a thought, she would have Emperor Rancor Mordetur on his knees with his hair in his hands, screaming for her mercy. With an extension of her will, he would die in twisted agony between the time it would take him to pull back his arm, and for the lash to fall.

As it did.

As it did again.

She cried out and wept. His breathing was heavy. The fury

was passing. He might be rethinking himself, or he might be startled as to what he'd done to her already.

This was as bad as she'd ever been beaten by him. He'd dragged her here by her hair past the estate servants, ripped the leather travel harness from her body before he'd shut the door. He'd shoved her to the wall and pulled out the lash—something to be used on the aurochs by the herders.

He hadn't spoken from that moment to this, but he'd let his point be known with the lash.

"Maybe you need to spend a year with your people," he said, finally.

She gasped. "No!" she wept. "No, Yonega Waya. Please— please no. Not away from you. Never away from you."

Her tears and sweat ran down her breasts and belly, running through the stretch marks on her otherwise flat muscle, however faint. They formed puddles on the floor.

"You have no respect for me," he said. "My words mean nothing to you.

"I won't have this."

She wailed and spun on her heel, threw herself at his feet, her cheek to his boots. She'd die. She knew it. She'd die without him. She loved this man. As much if not more now than the first day she'd met him, she'd pledged herself to him. She'd faced down a god for him. She'd pitched her life to his path a dozen times, born the pain of childbirth for him. Left her people.

"No," she said. "No, no, no, no, no."

He was hard as stone. She knew he had it in him to make this decision. To put her on a horse with a thousand Wolf Soldier guards and to move her to her father's tribe.

She'd made such a bad decision. She'd do almost anything to take it back. And he knew—not about her being barren, but about what she'd nearly had to do to their children. She could see it in his eyes. That's where the anger came from. He loved his children almost as much as he loved her.

And she knew it was so, because had anyone else been guilty of what she'd done, that person would certainly be dead.

"Get up."

She stood before him, dust mixed with sweat on her face and breasts, in her hair. She arched her back and put back her shoulders for him, her eyes on his white shirt, stained with his sweat, avoiding his eyes because he'd put her right back against the wall if he thought she still defied him.

She didn't think he'd broken the skin on her back. He'd never done that. But he'd given her bruises that would shock her friends, if she let them see them.

His eyes ran over her naked body. She'd seen where Raven shaved her pubic hair away, and she'd done it with Nina's help. If this was the way of women of his world, then she'd do it.

She'd do anything for her man. Not because she feared him, but because she knew him. She knew his heart. She knew why he was so cruel to her sometimes, and he knew why he could beat her like he had.

Because if he didn't, then she'd simply defy him and, eventually, she'd discard him. There was a reason why her father had been willing to trade a powerful sorceress for a horse he could have stolen: because no other man would have her. No other man could keep her.

If he were a particle less controlling of her, she'd have been done with him long ago. Her man knew her like no other could, and kept her when no other could, because he'd rather be *dead* than lose her, and he'd proven *that* a dozen times, too.

"Do this again," he informed her, "and you're back on the plains, *Nasgiagev Dasqualodi Gatsinula*. Alone, with your father's tribe, until I decide to come get you."

Shela whimpered and started crying again. The solemn way he was saying it told her he was serious, that he'd do it. He'd let her go. If he couldn't keep her, he'd let her go.

"Never again," she said, shaking her head, her long, back hair waving back and forth across her breasts. "Never, I swear it. On my life, on my *life*, Yonega Waya. Never again."

He'd called her by her child's name, by the name she'd had when he'd taken her. She Runs Swiftly—because whenever any man came close to her and tried to be her friend, she'd run away.

He nodded. She just sensed his movement. He reached for his belt.

She dropped to her knees before him, pulling open the laces on his leather pants. She was still too tender for intercourse, not completely healed from her infection. He chuckled as she sought him out from his pants and took him in her mouth.

In fact, she didn't care for this, but she took it as a part of her punishment. In a corner or her mind, for what she was guilty of, she couldn't help thinking she might be due far worse.

* * *

Duchess Glynn Escaroth, Baroness of Britt and Caster, rose from her meditations with a smile on her face, having communicated with Duke Haldan Evoprosee from Trenbon.

Such a communication announced her presence like a beacon to every median Wizard in Eldador; however her location had been discovered for a week. Their army pressed east and had marched for four days, just under ten thousand strong and most of them beaten and demoralized under a darkening sky.

What they would do on the eastern coast of Eldador would be anyone's guess. She'd informed his Grace of their need and received only an indication of his vague concern.

Certainly not reassuring, however her King had come back to her side again, and she knew she must not fail.

"Karl, Jahunga, Vedeen," she said, pushing open the flap to their shared pavilion in the Confluni camp, "I've need of all of thee."

Karl and Jahunga both were sharpening Karl's blade. The warlord of Teher had purchased himself a breastplate and leggings and now looked the properly armed warrior. If he'd been irascible before, then he'd become even more foul since the conflict now called *The Battle of the Vice*, for the way their enemies had squeezed them.

Vedeen reclined on a pile of pillows, the dog's great head in her lap. Glynn saw the drooling beast's stain on her robes.

"And how might we help you?" Vedeen asked her, her sweet voice almost mocking.

"Probably more killing," Karl grumbled, and spat on the floor of the tent. He'd come to do that more and more, and Glynn had grown to mind it.

"There is more to life than this," Jahunga informed him, holding the sword by its handle. "Me, I've been a warrior my whole life and not done so much killing as in these last months."

Only two of Jahunga's Toorians and ten of Karl's Volkhydrans had survived the Daff Kanaar. They served as an honor guard now, a useless service to them.

"Karl and Jahunga," she said, "send your warriors home."

Both straightened. Karl narrowed his eyes. "Surely my

warriors fought better than your Confluni," Jahunga challenged her.

"If you think you're done with Volkhydro's help—" Karl said.

"Far from it, Sirrah," Glynn said, just as the first rain began to patter on the canvas ceiling above them. "It is because of their goodly service that I seek to dispatch them, gold in hand, to the homelands their hearts grow sick for."

"What benevolence is this?" Vedeen challenged her, grinning under her blonde locks.

"I am contacted by his Majesty, the King of Trenbon, and I am asked to purvey good news to all who would hear it."

"Well, we could use some good news," Karl informed her.

Glynn felt the smile grow on her face. "We are to spread a message, through your warriors and some few Trenboni agents in Eldador, of the defeat of the Eldadorian fleet under command of Lupus the Conqueror, at the hands of the Trenboni."

The three of them stood in surprise, the dog leaping to her feet and wagging her tail.

"In truth?" Jahunga demanded.

Vedeen clapped her hands. "What joyous news for you."

Karl spat again. "It's a lie," he said. All heads turned to him.

"Tech Ships can't move as fast as Sea Wolves," he said. "They don't have the warriors; they don't have the weapons—"

"I assure you, and will take truth telling if need be," Glynn said, "that two hundred Eldadorian keels faced less than forty Tech Ships and four hundred Volkhydran warships, and surrendered the Bay after losing thirty or more."

Jahunga picked up his spear and stabbed its butt end into the ground. "If we can do this—" he began.

Karl shook his head. Glynn sighed. She knew this one would be difficult, and she'd wanted to keep most of the plan away from him. Without convincing, however, Karl would not act, and she needed Karl's action.

So she explained to them the battle on the Bay, the Trenboni King's devices, the attempt on Thera and the plan now.

She'd have liked to wait for Zarshar and Slurn and Raven, however they weren't closely available and they could be told later.

"And now," Jahunga surmised for her, "you'd like to spread this false tale, based on a truth, to humiliate the Emperor—"

"You want him mad enough to attack anyway," Karl said,

interrupting Jahunga, putting a hand on his naked shoulder, "because you know now his smartest course of action is to keep his seat, destroy this Confluni army and try again some other time, when you won't be ready for him."

Glynn nodded, looking into Karl's eyes. "Precisely, Sirrah," she said. "See you a flaw in this plan?"

Karl looked back at her face, searching her, giving her that prying look all of his kind used, unable to penetrate her eyes. Lightning rumbled in the distance, filling the quiet.

"No," he said, finally, and looked away. "It's a good plan.

"We'd better get ourselves out of here, though," he added, and spat again, wiping his lips with the back of his hand. "Because the first thing he's going to do is grind this little army down to meat."

* * *

Standing out in the Eldadorian plain, the cold spring rain washing over her, Raven let her head hang down, let her hair fall before her in ropy twists.

Lightening pounded in the distance; she felt the shock run through her. Her essence descended into the living god, Earth, below her, and actually felt Him stirring.

Four days ago, Zarshar and Slurn had taken her away from the mainstay of the Confluni army. For four days, he'd kept her from eating, barely let her sleep, kept her walking in her bare feet, telling her she needed to reach down, feel Earth with her power.

She'd learned a lot here, about magic, about people, about herself. She'd been elevated, she'd been hunted, she been held and, finally, she'd been betrayed.

After four days, the weather getting worse the whole time, she'd found the god. Through Earth below her she felt Slurn's presence, to her left behind her, guarding her as ever he had, as ever he would until the day one of them died.

Slurn, not Bill, must be The Guardian Protector, and then it was Bill, not Slurn, who was the one who Eludes Prying Eyes. Vedeen had told them they hadn't asked the right questions about the poem, and she saw that now.

The rain beating down staccato on her head helped to focus her. The merciless cold braced her, her very soul shrieked to her now.

She could reach through Earth, and she could find Bill's feet on Him. She knew he'd gone to Thera. She could sense the convergence of power there.

Power—here, Power was a god, too. She could sense Him, grinning, wicked, embodied in Zarshar, who'd brought her here, who watched over her as she did this, as she committed herself to this new life and this new way.

She'd been held back because her mind informed her all of this was impossible. No such thing as magic, no such thing as spells. No such thing as God. Even when she wielded the power, she didn't herself believe it.

In church, what seemed another lifetime ago, she'd learned that the apostle Thomas hadn't believed Jesus had risen until he actually felt the wounds in His wrists from the crucifixion. Thomas didn't have faith, he needed proof. She'd been no different here.

After four days, she'd reached down and poked the essence of the god Earth. Now she had her proof; now she saw the places it could take her. She knew where she could go.

Raven's will reached out like an octopus and grabbed at all of the sources of energy around her. The storm, the lifeblood of the trees and blades of grass, the disembodied dead, even the essence of the god.

She took it, she bundled it up, she let it flow through her and she expelled it. She willed herself to move forward, not through space or even time but through reality, to a place she'd been before.

Back to the diner, back to the stool, back to the old woman in the sundress, smelling of Sunflowers perfume, cigarettes and coffee; she made it all real in her mind and, through her will; she spiked her presence into it.

She actually felt the stool beneath her butt, the scrunchy in her hair. She smelled the smoke from the Marlboros Eveave smoked, smelled the coffee in the cup before her.

"You are confident in your power," the goddess said, "if you seek to invoke Me."

The friendliness had left her. She didn't face the smiling grandmother now. She saw Eveave, the Taker and the Giver.

"Why?" Melissa demanded. Not Raven—on the plains, in the wet, she was Raven. Here, in the diner, she could still be Melissa.

"And what boon shall I hand to your enemies, to balance the benefit of answering that question for you?" Eveave asked her.

The first time, Melissa had welcomed this woman into her life.

The second, she'd recognized her power, but really hadn't thought that much of it.

Now she had an inkling of that strength, and she knew what it would cost to challenge it. If she were handed winning answers here, then her enemies would be given winning strategies later.

If she wanted to come out ahead here, she'd have to get something more creative than help.

The Emperor had spoken a lot about faith. Later, Glynn had wondered about that, too. If they knew of their gods, if they could speak to them, then they had no faith, they had proof instead.

But here, no one spoke to the gods—that wasn't allowed. These gods needed to import people from Earth, to speak to them.

"Who did you send back?" Raven asked her. "You brought us here—that's the take. What was the give?"

Eveave took a drag on her cigarette, held the smoke, and then exhaled slowly.

"I sent none," she said, finally. "Your God would not have it."

"Then there is still imbalance," Melissa said.

She reached down to her cup and, knowing it wasn't real, she still drank from the coffee, just to taste it. She hadn't had it in so long she almost lost her concentration over how good it was.

The scene wavered. Eveave smiled.

"Much to learn," she said.

"But there *is* imbalance," Melissa pressed on.

"Not for you," Eveave said. "But perhaps for your people. You are wrong if you believe I cannot tolerate imbalance. I simply see no reason for it."

"I think it's Bill, not me, who's imbalanced," Melissa said. She thought back to her sales training, to the things Bill had taught her about closing. The buyer had to not only see a win; he had to see a bigger win than yours.

You get that with the questions you ask. Vedeen had told them they weren't asking the right questions.

"I think that, if you're going to help anyone, it has to be Bill."

Eveave considered.

"Bill has changed sides," Melissa pressed her. "If I ask you to help him, then no matter what, that's balance."

"No," Eveave told her. "However, to your understanding, I see you might consider it so."

Eveave took another drag on her cigarette, and blew the smoke out through her nose in a very unladylike maneuver young boys were famous for.

"What boon would I give your Bill, in your opinion, that would maintain balance?"

Immediately, "Send him back—send him home."

Eveave smiled. "Even if I could, then he would not have it. You do not know this child of Men, young one, but I can tell you Bill has become Jack, and Jack is precisely where Jack wants to be."

That hurt her more than she could have admitted. She'd given herself to Bill, she'd loved him. He wasn't supposed to throw that back into her face; he was supposed to love her for it.

Eveave looked into her eyes and seemed to see all of this. Melissa didn't know how, but it made a lot of sense to her as Raven.

There were scary words to be associated with how she felt about herself these days.

"I think the boon is itself stated," Eveave said. "Bill shall have it. Balance, if ever it was disturbed, is restored."

"What?" Melissa shook her head. She'd missed something. She'd let her mind wander. Her feelings for Bill had distracted her, and she'd lost part of the conversation.

"In return for this service, you shall be rewarded, young one. Behold."

The waitress behind the counter handed her a menu. Melissa took it and opened it. Inside, she saw a map of Fovea, marked with places she recognized, such as Eldador, the Lone Wood, and Kor, which had its name crossed out and replaced with 'Lupor.'

She saw an 'X' just north of Lupor, on the coast, just within the Salt Wood. "You should be there," Eveave informed her, "and as quickly as possible."

The scene began to waver. She called on her will to hold it.

"That's another tough row you're hoeing, girly," Eveave informed her, "before you try that, you'd better ask yourself a few questions. Y'ain't been asking you the right questions yet."

In another moment the scene dissolved.

Raven fell to her knees in the rain, the mud splashing up on her naked thighs and her abdomen, soaking her drenched leather skirt. She expected to feel Zarshar's or Slurn's claws on her, but instead felt human hands take her shoulders.

She looked up, expecting to see Bill there. Instead she found herself staring into Karl's concerned brown eyes.

Before she could tell him what she'd learned, what she'd done, she slipped into unconsciousness.

* * *

Karl had constructed his own tent alongside of the pavilion where they all slept.

It was simpler and more like him, small enough to stay warm but large enough to move around and get dressed in. Holding a limp and drenched Raven, he fed her into it through the dropdown flap and followed her onto the furs.

Slurn had shadowed them all the way. Now he waited out in the rain. Zarshar had just bared his red teeth at them. He'd been standing there, watching her in the rain, when she'd fallen.

Something was going on between those three, and he didn't think he liked it.

Her leathers were drenched. He had a cotton over-shirt he liked. He covered her in it, and peeled the wet leather from her body. He'd never seen a woman who'd kept her stomach so flat— Volkhydrans tended to what they called a 'belt for the lean times.' As well, as he peeled off her harness, he noted that Volkhydran women, at least the ones he'd bedded, didn't shave away their pubic hair.

Why would anyone do that? He thought it must be incredibly painful. He'd shaved his face with a dagger when he'd had to—he'd never thought in his darkest nightmares to apply the blade elsewhere.

She stirred. The girl had incredible resolve. What would kill another woman made this one uneasy, and what would leave another Sorceress unconscious for days left her napping for an hour.

He quickly pulled the cotton shirt over her head, and then covered her naked legs with his bedding furs.

"Oh, ooo—ow," she complained. She batted her huge brown eyes and held the heel of her hand to her forehead.

He hung her leathers from a tent pole where they could drip dry. The rain pattered down on the tent canvas as he added his own furs to it. His past experience told him they would stink for getting so wet, but as he wore them, the heat from the sun and his body would dry them in a few days.

Naked, he slid into the sleeping furs beside Raven, just as she was awaking.

She looked him in the face and said a word he didn't know.

"What?" he asked her, in Uman.

"Oh, um—hello," she said. He could see her reaching under the furs, making sure she was proper. Her hand strayed to his naked thigh.

"Karl!"

"I soaked my furs pulling you out of the mud," he said. "And if you're wondering, yeah, I saw you naked."

She smiled and then pulled the furs to her chin.

Since becoming the Hero of Tamara, he'd had women throwing themselves at him. This one's refusal—her not caring who he was—he found refreshing. All felt new with Raven. She didn't care what he'd done; she cared what he did, what he planned to do.

He hadn't had that before. He'd learned to like it.

And, now, this 'Jack' had removed himself from the picture.

He wanted to lift that cotton shirt back up to her shoulders, to hold her down, sink into her. He wanted her fingernails in his back, to feel her resist, as women did, then yield, relent to his need as a male.

One had to be more careful with a sorceress. He'd heard stories—men turned into unnatural things.

As well, this was Raven and, truth be told, he didn't foresee any satisfaction in raping her.

"What did I catch you doing?" he asked her.

He saw the look cross her face. He shouldn't have done that. She wanted him to press her. War's whiskers, he was already naked.

"Oh, oh—no," she stammered. "I—I have to talk to Glynn—"

She almost leaped up out the furs. Karl put a hand on her breast, feeling it move beneath his fingers, pressing her back down to the furs beneath them.

Oddly, she subsided. She pressed her breast into his hand. He'd never had that before.

"Just tell me," he informed her.

She looked away, then back at him. "Zarshar took me out into the plains, and he told me—um, it's, well, he told me I needed to accept one god, at least one god from this planet."

That was stupid. "What do you mean, accept a god? How can you not accept the gods?"

She shook her head. "In my world, um, where I'm from, we only have one god, and not everyone believes in Him."

Even worse. "You don't believe in your god? What do you believe in, then? Who makes the sun rise? Who keeps the harvest and makes the game plentiful."

"None of that comes from any god," she said, looking into his eyes. "Well, not where I'm from—we don't, I don't know Karl. But Zarshar told me I needed to find one god, and so I reached through my feet, and I looked for Earth, and I found Him."

"Earth?" Karl found himself blinking. "You mean it—you actually reached down and you found Earth?"

"Well, yeah," she said. "I mean, aren't I supposed to find Earth?"

Inherent in his religion he had the primary rule of the gods—no contact. No one could violate that, but she spoke of other worlds. Other realities.

"What *are* you, girl?" he asked her.

Her brown eyes searched his. He pulled his hand away from her but she took it in her own, held the fingers in her tiny hands.

"I'm a champion," she said finally. "I think that's what Slurn and Zarshar have been trying to show me. I'm special somehow. Here, now, I'm part of a prophecy. I can touch your gods, and they can talk to me, and they do. I think Lupus does this, too, and that's why he's so successful here, and that's why I have to face him."

Karl looked skeptical. "*You're* going to match *the Conqueror*," he challenged her. "A tiny girl."

She smiled at him. "Yep, me—a tiny girl. And I'm going to need help, Karl. Not like Jack—I'm going to need help I can rely on. I need a man who can stand beside me for this, Karl. A fearless warrior.

"People say you're the bravest Man who ever put a foot down on Fovean soil," she said, and she moved her right hand from his hand to the side of his face. "Will you stand beside me, Karl?"

Karl chuckled. "Glynn really has her fingers in your mind," he said.

Raven chuckled back. "I don't think Glynn has an idea of half of what's going on," she said.

Before he even realized it, her hand was in his hair. Before he could react, her tongue was in his mouth. He hadn't encountered a woman who wanted this before. While his hands ran rough and hungry over her smooth, naked body, her hands were on him, too, and her knee rubbed the inside of his thigh.

"Yes," he sighed into her ear, her hair framing his face as their bodies moved together, "yes, Raven, I will stand beside you."

Afterward, he knew he'd never cried out so loudly, and he

wondered what the faces of his travel companions would look like when he saw them, after the rain stopped.

* * *

"Oh, like hell!"

The Sword of War cleaved through the table before them and into the stone floor beneath.

Thorn reminded himself that this had once been Black Lupus' war room, before he'd turned the whole thing over to Tali Digatishi, Duke Two Spears.

Tali held himself in check, a good Andaron to whom material things meant nothing.

It took him a moment, but he pulled the blade out of the stone floor. Of course there wasn't a blemish on it.

"Are you done with that?" Tali asked him, "or do you need us to bring in more furniture for you to destroy."

Black Lupus glowered at him.

"He's right," Thorn chimed in. "The damage is done—these rumors are everywhere, and you can't destroy enough furniture to make it go away."

It occurred to Thorn that almost every person in this room now—Tali, Shela, himself, Vulpe, Two Spears' wife Wanigey Digitolay—were Andarons. Andarons were running this Eldadorian Empire. Andarons were the strength of it.

Lupus had his 'Oligarchs,' but they'd betrayed him before.

The Uman, "Thebinaar", said, "Tongues are wagging all over the Empire about your first defeat, at the hands of the Uman-Chi."

Black Lupus seethed.

Thorn had never seen anyone take defeat so seriously before. Everyone was beaten eventually. He himself had to admit now he couldn't match Lupus with swords, pole axes or daggers. He'd *never* matched him wrestling—even Nantar couldn't beat him. Those thick, thick bones of his—you could hammer on him all day and he'd just laugh and come back at you.

But Nantar was *still* the greatest warrior alive.

"I think we need to change our plans a little," Lupus told them. Thorn recognized the wicked look in his eyes.

"You want to go fight them in Volkhydro," Thebinaar said to him, "where our operatives in Outpost IX says they're gathering."

"And where the King of Trenbon is so conveniently sailing,"

Two Spears said. "Yonega Waya, you must know this is a trap."

"You think?" Lupus demanded of him. "You think that's what they're doing? Because I wasn't sure."

"Yonega Waya, please," Shela put a hand on his arm, but he shook it off.

Then Wani, Two Spears' wife, stepped in. She took the sides of his face in her soft hands, and made him look into her eyes, even though he didn't want to.

"We love you, Waya," she said, her voice like a song. "And we know you'll destroy your enemies, and we know you'll stain Tren Bay red with their blood."

Strange words from one so soft, but that was the way of their women. An Andaron woman's blood ran hot, but her love ran so cool.

Finally, Black Lupus looked into her eyes. "Waya," she said. "You promised the warriors will stay home this year; that you will take Way Point late in the season and hold your surprises until next year when your enemies are weak, after they spend their gold for nothing, and their nobles scream about high taxes to pay for it all.

"That is a brilliant plan, Waya," she said. "Will you be undone by this decrepit Uman-Chi King farting on his throne? You've beaten them every time—will you let them trick you now?"

Thorn had told Tali he should grow fat with a wife so sweet, and he thought about that now. Wani, if she wanted to, could sing the birds out of the trees.

Shela stepped in next to him, pressed her body to his, and whispered into his ear, "Yonega Waya, my love, next year you'll take them all when they're weak, and you won't just take Volkhydro, you'll take every nation on Fovea, and lose half the warriors."

Black Lupus looked into Shela's eyes, and then Wani's. Thorn considered that it had been a long time since his own wife had flirted with him so shamelessly.

But it would have worked on him.

"They're gathering in Hydro?" he demanded of Thebinaar.

The Uman nodded. He hadn't been fooled. "It's the logical choice. Take that city and you own half of Fovea's commerce."

"We strike at Volkha," he said. "I want those hundred and fifty ships from the battle with Trenbon ready to go in a week."

"We'll only be able to move—" Duke Tali began.

"Thirty thousand," Lupus said. "I know. And then we'll only be able to leave twenty five thousand. That's all I need. Send

Eldadorian Regulars for now. Then bring the ships back and send more."

Thorn sighed. He'd go, too. Not enough he'd saved Lupus' whole nation. Not enough he fostered Nantar's brats with his own people. Not enough he maintained the moral of the troops, when no one else could.

Once, on the deck of a ship, he'd fought Lupus, and lost, been thrown down and at Lupus' mercy.

Lupus had treated him like an equal ever since. Thorn could do a lot for another Man with integrity like that.

Chapter Fifteen

The Road to Conquest

Tartan Stowe left the Battle of the Vice, as it was being called, with 2,500 mounted warriors, give or take a few dozen. Because the Emperor had taught them to use alcohol and witch hazel and 'conventional healers,' the only Knights who died after the battle suffered of their wounds in the two week march south to Angador, his duchy in the south, the bastion against Toor and producer of some of the finest horses on Fovea.

For two weeks he wondered what had become of the expert tracker, Jean who, as the battle roared, melted into the chaos and did not return. He'd hoped to make that woman part of his personal army.

For two weeks, he listened to his wife Yeral complain they had suffered more than any other, that they had turned the battle, and been less rewarded, not so much as thanked, for their efforts.

Now the noble walls of Angador, pennons snapping from her eight towers, took all of that away.

"Your glorious city, my Lord," J'lek informed him, as if he needed to be reminded.

"Once we're inside, we must contact Central Communications in Galnesh Eldador, and we should demand-," Yeral began.

Tartan nodded and just tuned her out. He'd done that a lot

these past weeks. She'd become more irascible since the Confluni had been sighted on Eldadorian soil. When he'd returned from the battle, bloody and victorious and feeling like a true son of the Emperor, her callous complaining had all but ruined it for him.

This wasn't characteristic of Yeral, and left him at a loss to deal with her.

"I want a week of liberty for these warriors," Tartan informed J'lek, interrupting his wife, then added, "in-city," when the Uman raised an eyebrow. "Send scouts out on three days ride. If anyone is seen coming—"

He interrupted himself when two squads of mounted warriors thundered out of his city's open gates. They flew his personal pennons, meaning they were either under his command or en route to him, the latter being more likely.

Tartan's eyes swept his towers. Sure enough, over the gate, a new pennon not his own.

"Ceberro," he said aloud.

"Your Grace?" J'lek asked him.

Tartan pointed. Behind him he heard thunder rumble. Late spring storms—bad ones. Interspersed with that, his warriors were passing the news about the liberty.

"Over the gate," he said, "where I'll see it, first thing, the fist on the anvil—Ceberro's personal pennon.

"Ceberro has returned to Angador."

* * *

"Your Highness," the Uman serving girl interrupted her.

Lee looked up from her writing desk in her new, personal rooms outside of the nursery, in the royal tower. She'd chosen the ones vacated by Alekennen, Glennen Stowe's daughter.

As a grown man now, Vulpe wouldn't sleep in the nursery. As his sister, she'd chosen him a room one floor lower than hers, once belonging to Tartan Stowe.

One floor lower, presumably to allow him to protect her from attack. She'd be damned if she'd stay in the nursery when her younger brother had left it. She doubted very much her mother would even raise an eyebrow.

Lee had only stayed there so long because she'd grown used to her brother's tagging along. She wouldn't have that any more.

"Yes, Kenne," she said. In Nina's absence, Kenne served her.

She was a slight girl, forty years old, a woman in Uman terms but with no children. Her husband served in the Eldadorian Regulars.

"Central Communications, your Highness," she said.

Lee sighed. How did her mother stand it? They'd developed a method where thoughts and images could travel between the cities, without the need of teleportation or messengers, however it all ran from here. Shela or another wizard had to assert her or his will to make it happen.

"Not Groff again?" she asked, standing, pushing the letter she'd been writing to her mother to one side. Groff had contacted her daily to keep abreast of the war effort, not that she knew anything. Meanwhile, his younger son, Grak, always stood in the background. Eighteen years her senior, Grak possessed Groff's severe features, his humorless attitude, and his hair already showed a widow's peak.

He'd taken her hand at banquet, and it was cold as ice.

"I am not so enlightened, your Highness," she said. She wouldn't be, Lee knew to make sure of that. Her father had taught her that her secrets were the greatest weapon their enemies could have, and this, after all, was war.

She followed Kenne out the door and down the stone-walled halls, a squad of Wolf Soldiers taking up her guard behind her. She knew their sergeant, D'leer, an Uman warrior in her father's service for years. No one less could be trusted to guard her person.

Up three gray stone flights, past her parents' chambers and one of her mother's remote studies, she found Central Communications, a circular room the width of the tower, a pulsing mass of blue and white and violet in the center of a sparse room. No chairs, several chalk boards, and a semi-circular table—her father's design with her mother's influence.

"Your Highness," Hectar greeted her. He'd come with J'her and his son, Hectaro. She nodded, entering through the one door and closing it on Kenne and the two guards.

"Your Grace," she greeted him back. She held her hand out for J'her, who always loved to kiss the back of it. As stern as a thunderstorm, she knew he loved her, and she was the only one who saw this side of him.

She curtsied for him, and treated the coward, Hectaro, to a dark look. She had nothing for him. Hectar hauled him around now just to try to squeeze him back into her favor.

"Ascenda, flagoona," she incanted to the Central Communications mass. The mass glowing purple and white rose up from where it hovered a foot from the floor and expanded, now with an image at its center of Tartan Stowe, his wife, her friend, Yeral, and Duke Ceberro of Vrek.

To their right, an Uman wizard who'd served her mother here before being transferred to Angador. He held the conduit open and had contacted Galnesh Eldador. Behind them, she caught the former Wolf Solider, J'lek, J'her's son. He'd joined the Wolf Soldiers after getting in trouble in Steel City, trying to win back his father's farm by killing the people on it. J'her himself had intervened on his behalf.

"Your Graces!" she greeted them. "It seems the orb is broken—I see Vrek and Angador at the same time!"

Tartan smiled, then Ceberro. Her father had never trusted the latter, and in her opinion trusted the former too much. Tartan, name him what they wanted, was a Stowe, and how could the Stowe's be happy as Dukes and Earls, not Kings and Princes? At least Yeral, once her mother's lady in waiting, had gone there to watch him.

"Your magic is infallible," Ceberro answered her, "we are, in fact, in Angador together."

"The southern cities are uniting?" Hectar asked, pretending at being shocked. "Has Toor attacked?"

Toor would never attack, she knew, but her father worried about the loyalty of his cities when he left them. She'd overheard him telling Hectar what to do if any or even all of them revolted while he was away.

She watched their eyes through the orb.

"The south is secure, as always, your Grace" Ceberro informed him. "We contact you to inform you that, to the best of our knowledge, this Confluni army is bound for Lupor."

She turned to Hectar. He was frowning, his arms crossed before him. "Not good news, your Highness," he said. "Lupor is recently conquered and may not be able to defend itself from their thousands."

"Our thinking exactly," Ceberro said. "And the Daff Kanaar have suffered heavy losses against them. Over one thousand dead in one strike by this Raven, and outrunning this army on the open plain."

"We believe even two thousand horse—" Tartan began.

"I spoke to my father of your bravery," Lee interupted him. He'd barely mentioned it, but Lee knew Tartan, having grown up with him, and knew his fragile ego. "He believes that, were it not for you, Eldador would have been cut in two."

"Really?" Tartan stumbled, then collected himself. "In truth, your Highness? I hadn't thought—"

She wanted to watch Tartan, but a sideways look from Yeral caught her eye. She seemed almost upset to hear this praise.

Yeral, too, was the child of someone deposed by her father. But—Yeral was her friend.

She decided to push it. "Your Grace, you are too humble!" she exclaimed, almost gushing. Hectar and J'her exchanged a look.

"My father refused to stop talking about your bravery and your genius," she gushed. "Your Angadorian Knights, invincible against so many times their number? He slipped many times and boasted about the enemy caught between his two sons."

Tartan straightened. Ceberro rolled his eyes.

Yeral fumed, then looked into the orb and collected herself, smiling sublimely at her husband.

More bad news.

"Your plans, your Highness?" Ceberro asked her. "Time may well be of the essence."

Lee turned her back to the orb and looked into Hectar's eyes, then J'her's. The effort of keeping the conduit open had started weighing on her.

"Cut them off?" Hectar asked J'her. As her father had said, rank was one thing, and ability everything. When it came to the defense of Eldador, J'her's voice stood second to the Emperor's.

J'her considered. "If they achieve the Salt Wood, they'll scatter and we'll get some of them, but never all of them. They could run what the Emperor calls guh—riyah operations on our villages and we'd be hard pressed to stop them."

"No chance the Daff Kanaar will overtake them?" Hectaro asked them.

Lee felt herself making a face.

"No chance of the Angadorians getting between them and Kor in time, either," J'her said. "We need to send out the Wolf Soldiers from Lupor, and then reinforce Lupor from Andurin."

Hectar looked straight into Lee's eyes. "You have to tell them not to go, but you have to make it their idea," he said. "Can you think of a way to do that, or do you need one of us—?"

Lee turned and painted on a smile.

"Your Graces, once again, the Empire is well served by both of you," Lee said, and saw them exchange a look.

Meanwhile, a self-satisfied grin spread across Yeral's face. Lee pressed on, watching her more than the two males.

"Can Angador's Knights get between this army and Lupor?"

Tartan turned his head to Ceberro, and the two spoke so low she couldn't hear them. However, the other Wizard could, and Lee communicated with him, instead.

Tartan: 'I can't get there in under two weeks.'

Ceberro: 'Even if she didn't know that, J'her does.'

Tartan: 'So why is she asking?'

Ceberro: 'She wants you to tell her no, so she doesn't have to refuse you instead.'

Tartan turned his head. "My lady, I am afraid, no. We advise that you contact Lupor itself, to be ready."

"We will be guided by your tactical wisdom," Lee said.

They bowed and she cut the spell, the orb in the center of the room returning to its original colors. Lee sighed, feeling giddy from the use of her power. Her mother had taught her that her might would grow like muscles from exercise and, in fact, every time she used this conduit, she'd felt that.

"That went unexpectedly well," Hectaro commented. Lee flipped a hand in his direction.

At her age, she didn't want responsibilities like this. Less than three months ago, she'd been playing dolls with her brother and 'mama' with her younger sister. She'd used her power to steal plums from the larder and imagined herself kissing Hectaro.

Now she found herself making decisions that could affect an empire, spying on girls she'd thought of as her friends, and wondering if her baby brother would be alive the next day. Now Dukes and generals looked to her for her opinion, and then insisted on using it.

"I can't imagine news any worse," she said.

* * *

"You were wise to report this," Emperor Rancor Mordetur informed his daughter, standing in the communications room at Thera.

Vulpe's mother, Shela, stood beside her husband, his left arm locked in both of hers, operating the conduit from this side. Vulpe had seen his mother run this magical orb before, but not from outside of Galnesh Eldador. He knew his sister could do it, but he had never seen her do it so confidently as this.

A lot had changed for an eleven-year-old boy, and fast.

"I'm bringing The Green One into this," Shela announced. "We need to know—"

"Dilvesh?" father said. "He's in Lupor."

Shela smiled. "As is your friend, Ancenon. They've already started the Central Communications conduit together. It must be finished by now."

Central Communications was a series of magical nodes, run by wizards – usually apprentices – to move speech and images between the major Eldadorian cities. It was an idea of Vulpe's mother, which she'd worked out with D'gattis and Dilvesh.

Vulpe could only think that the conduits, rather than the focal point in Galnesh Eldador, were simpler to create and maintain.

"I'll do it, mother," Lee offered. Shela smiled.

"Love, you've done enough already—"

"No," Vulpe's father commanded, without looking at either of them. "Let Lee do it. You're still recovering your strength."

He looked up. "This *is* all of the magic you're doing, right?"

Lee blushed. Nina said, "I know that look."

"No practicing new magix," Shela warned her. "Stick with what you know."

Lee bowed her head. Vulpe knew *that* look, too. She'd make the promise, but she'd never keep it. She was dying to be like mama.

Lee frowned to focus herself. It would take several minutes to get a response from Dilvesh, if he was even in Lupor.

Father turned to grandfather, standing opposite his mother. Those two had come to an uneasy truce, and now father was consulting him more and more.

"Your people have already been to Lupor once, haven't they?"

Grandfather nodded. "They were, but I wasn't there."

Father looked into grandfather's eyes. "But they know the city well enough to cause trouble?" he asked.

Father did that. No one could hold anything back from him. Vulpe had looked into those blue, blue eyes and spilled his deepest secrets before realizing.

Grandfather just shrugged. "I'd like to think they could," he said. "Karl, Jahunga—they could raise an army."

Father looked at mama, then back at grandfather. "When they decided to go there, did they have any special reason?" he asked.

"They needed a base of operations," he said. "If we could start something in Kor, cause you trouble on your border, then you'd stay home."

"Black Lupus!" they heard from the orb. All heads turned to see the orb divided in two parts, one with Lee and the other with Dilvesh, the Green One.

"Green Dilvesh," father nodded. "We believe as many as ten thousand Confluni warriors are coming to your city."

Dilvesh's pencil-thin eyebrows rose. "We've been following the battles," he said. "The Confluni are moving farther north."

Father looked at mother, then at uncle Two Spears. "Dukes Stowe and Ceberro in Angador claim they're for Lupor," he said.

"If Ceberro and Stowe are together in Angador," Dilvesh said, "I would be more concerned about that."

"I told you," Lee chimed in.

* * *

"Well, that didn't go as predicted," Ceberro commented to Tartan Stowe, sitting together in the Duke's personal study, a carafe of red wine between them on a table.

Ceberro had come here to Angador when he'd heard of the Battle of the Vice. He and the Emperor had made a very competent general out of Glennen's son, not that this came as any surprise.

Glennen had been magnificent on the battlefield, a match for the Emperor himself. Take that breeding with the training, and Tartan Stowe would end up the equal of anyone.

He'd certainly torn apart the Confluni with their Uman-Chi support, and with little help from wizards of his own. Even Ceberro couldn't be sure he'd have returned with so clean a victory.

Stowe just nodded. Ceberro could see him basking in the glow of the Emperor's praise, received through Lee. He still suffered from his father's abuse in those last days, and it left his ego wounded. Ceberro had tried to be the one who healed the boy, but the Emperor had stepped in. No one could compete with those opportunities, but then Ceberro had known better than to try.

He still woke up at night with bad dreams from the beating he'd taken at the Emperor's hands, that day thirteen years ago, when he'd challenged him for the right to be heir. It wasn't like him,

Ceberro didn't think it very manly to hold a grudge so long, but he'd never been so thoroughly beaten, so clearly defeated, especially when he'd meant so much to win. Lupus had destroyed him there on the sand and, before he could act on it, the King had gone and died.

Ceberro had been left no alternative but to throw everything behind the Heir. Civil War, possibly gratifying, would never have succeeded, not when Lupus could call on the Daff Kanaar. Even without them, Lupus could clearly count on Rennin and the upstart from Uman City to support him, along with his Aschire and his invincible Wolf Soldier guard. Groff remained questionable, but then Groff would never act until victory was clear. No, he knew what Lupus did to his enemies, so he became a friend, and waited.

When he'd declared himself an Emperor and his nation an empire, he'd waited for the Fovean High Council to step in, but they didn't. Then they'd seen the Battle of the Deceptions and the use of Eldadorian Fire, and knew better than to challenge Eldador.

He'd spoken to the other Dukes, which by then included Angador, Metz and the Aschire. Even Groff had liked the arrangement better, so Ceberro had applauded it.

Then this mad scheme had come. An outright invasion of other Fovean nations, in defiance of the Fovean High Council, provoked by a song from an Uman-Chi who opposed them.

Groff hadn't liked it, and had been allowed to keep most of his troops home.

Rennin fully supported it, and his troops went with the Emperor.

Tartan and Ceberro had been left behind to 'hold the home front,' but Ceberro's troops had gone with the Emperor. "Advise Tartan and expect blow back on this," he'd been informed, and had had to ask the Empress in private what 'blow back' was.

Expect the counter invasion of the Eldadorian nation. Well, they hadn't had to wait long.

"We're all lucky you're a genius," Ceberro said, casually sipping his wine. "Or we'd be on a knee before Conflu right now."

Tartan smiled. "I think not," he said.

Ceberro frowned. "You can't believe Vulpe won the day?" he countered.

Tartan frowned back, and reached for the carafe. "Vulpe, if he actually commanded those troops, ran a textbook attack on the

Confluni, and we both know who wrote the textbook," he said. "If I hadn't been there, then he'd have eventually withdrawn, but he would have contained the threat, and remember the Daff Kanaar were summoned. I made it less bloody; Ceberro, but I didn't win the day."

"Lee was right about one thing," Ceberro said. "You're too humble."

Tartan smiled and drank.

"If we aren't to be in the battle for Lupor," Ceberro pressed him, "then what are your plans?"

Tartan shrugged. "Scout the plains," he said. "You have the southern coast and the river, I have the plains. Nothing's changed."

"You believe the Emperor will still invade then?"

They'd both heard this new rumor, that the Emperor had been handed a defeat at sea by a fraction of his number in Tech Ships. Now the Emperor seemed to be shifting his attention to Volkhydro.

"Such a claim cannot go unanswered," Tartan said. "It's clearly a trap, so the Emperor will prove he can't *be* trapped."

"Or he'll fail," Ceberro said.

"Or he'll fail," Tartan agreed.

Better and better.

"In that event, have you ever wondered what you would do?" Ceberro asked him.

"Do?"

Ceberro took another drink. "What would you do, in the event the Emperor failed?" he asked.

Tartan frowned and put his drink down, leaning back in the comfortable chair.

"I think I know what you're asking me," he said, "so I'll tell you this, one time, and then we'll never have this conversation again."

Ceberro opened his mouth but Tartan just kept speaking. "There was a time when I believed Stowes, not Mordeturs, should run this nation, and if it became possible, or even plausible, to make that happen, then it was my right and my duty to see to it."

Tartan wet his lips, took a look into his wine, but didn't drink. "I have, since then, realized that a name doesn't run a nation, or an Empire, but a man does, and if that man has earned that right, then every one of any name should follow him, or earn that right himself.

"*Earn* it, Ceberro, not claim it for a name," he looked Ceberro right in the eye, and the Duke could see nothing of the recalcitrant boy who'd stepped into the Ducal throne of Angador—a city he'd created and then turned over to the King.

"I know you loved my father but, in the end, the things that made him strong, his passion and his love of Life, his willingness to commit everything and his inability to let go, destroyed him," Tartan said. "Can I say I'd have done better? That's not the question, Ceberro. The question is, 'Have I earned the right to try?', and the answer to that question is, 'Not yet.'"

"You know Lupus will never name you Heir," Ceberro said, looking Tartan right back in the eye.

"Who says I want it?" Tartan said.

They were quiet for a moment, then Tartan stood.

"Enjoy the wine," he said. "I've matters to attend to. You're welcome to stay as long as you like, but not to continue with this."

Ceberro watched him leave, having gotten his answer. He doubted Tartan would bring this to the attention of the Emperor, but he couldn't be sure. Instead, he might do well to sow some seeds of dissent between them, perhaps buying Angadorian steeds to keep them from the Emperor.

"Your Grace?"

He turned in his chair to see the Lady Yeral Stowe enter the study through a side door. Clearly she'd been listening at the eaves, spying on her own husband. He'd believed these two fully supported each other, however rumors could be unreliable and things changed.

"My Lady Duchess," Ceberro said, and stood to honor her.

She extended the back of her hand for kissing, then seated herself where her husband had sat, and picked up his glass of wine.

Ceberro sat, and picked up his own glass.

She sipped, ran a tongue over her lips, then looked seriously at Ceberro. "I must admit, your conversation surprised me," she said.

Not even shy about the spying, Ceberro thought as he dipped his head to acknowledge her. At least his own wife was discreet.

This woman's father had been utterly disgraced, and later executed, by the Emperor. Her family name was nothing. Many believed that Stowe had been paired with her to neutralize him.

"I think," she informed him, drawing out her words, "we have much to discuss."

* * *

Glynn sat sidesaddle on her Angadorian warhorse, one of the many they'd been able to collect after the battle ten days before.

Vedeen rode beside her on her original roan, in her manly saddle, their dog keeping pace at her mount's heels. Vedeen had said they weren't asking the right questions. Now their Jack, in leaving them, had said the same. Finally their Raven, speaking to the goddess Eveave, whom she'd somehow had the manna to *summon*, had sent them on a new direction, and once again implied they didn't understand the questions yet.

She knew she had to listen to the goddess, if to no one else, even as they hurried to the northern tip of the Salt Wood.

To her left, Avek Noir trotted his own mount, another Angadorian mare, keeping his own council. He'd asked to meet the two of them, but now took his time to choose his words.

So refreshing after Men who blurted out their first feelings.

"May we discourse of your protégé?" he asked them, finally.

"We must," Vedeen added. "I admit, the child concerns me."

Glynn found herself frowning, looking forward, considering. She finally said, "I concede concerns; however our needs are great—"

"You are aware," Avek interrupted her, a total surprise from one of her own kind, "of the first rule for an acolyte."

Glynn had learned the hundreds of rules for the acolyte as an exercise to progress in her training, so of course she knew the first.

"One learns at the capacity of discipline, not ability," she said.

They were right—she had to admit it. Any student could learn enough, almost immediately, to wield unimaginable power. Without the discipline to control it, the power became a threat to the Caster and to those around her.

"And yet," she asked, "how does one restrict the abilities of an acolyte whose gifts include resistance to magic?"

Avek nodded. "This *is* the problem," he agreed. "Normally her master would strip her of her power. I would not want to be the one to try to cast that spell on her."

"Nor I," Vedeen said. "We could ask her to abstain, however she's already wielded the power. She'll only crave more."

"The god does have an addictive nature," Avek agreed. "And for every disciple like the Empress who drinks deep and survives, there are many more like Raven who go too far and too fast."

"These arguments may matter little," Glynn said. "We have, unfortunately, lost one who was mentioned in the song."

Xinto's death had come as a complete surprise to her. First that he should be out-drawn by an Aschire, second that the protection of the goddess didn't extend to him. If the song was prophetic, then Xinto of the Wood should not have died.

"I'd thought that was pre-ordained," Vedeen said to her.

The horses plodded on while she considered that.

"For Fovea, for Fovea, then must they live and die.
Fight the battle from within
With a Champion from outside."

"In fact, my Lady," Avek said to her, "his death now that you believe you've collected the six weapons tends to verify your song."

Her heart constricted.

"You—forgive me, your Highness," she said, her voice incredulous in her own ears, "but you can't mean to suggest that we, the weapons of the song, are all doomed to *die*."

Avek regarded her with eyes that appeared brown to her, which would be silver-on-silver to anyone else.

"It isn't my song," he said, "and so I don't pretend to interpret it, however I may not be wise enough to see another way."

An Uman-Chi's way of saying this was *exactly* what he thought.

Glynn couldn't help but to find that conclusion very distressing.

"I believe it was, in fact, Lupus the Conqueror who limited Shela, until she became more adept," Vedeen said.

"Your pardon, lady Druid?" Avek said.

"Her slavery to him, willing though it was," Vedeen said. She was trying to rescue Glynn from a very embarrassing and disturbing topic of conversation, apparently.

"He encouraged her to some restraint. Without her 'Jack,' Raven is unrestrained."

"She has coupled with the Hero of Tamara," Avek noted.

"I personally find him a better match for her," Vedeen said, throwing back her long, blonde hair. "I admit I encouraged him."

Glynn arched an eyebrow. "Did you?"

Vedeen smiled her brilliant white smile. "They balance," she said. "He is the sword edge, she the file."

Glynn didn't see it that way, but kept her own council. She had other things to think of now. Avek, as well, remained silent.

Vedeen sighed.

Glynn watched Raven and Karl riding side-by-side, speaking to each other as lovers of the race of Men would. If she could encourage Karl to take a firm hand with her, then perhaps they could restrain their Raven.

Of course, if they were both doomed to die, then what matter?

Either way, this Raven's flight might be a short one.

Chapter Sixteen

Courage

Hectar took a moment to check himself in the mirror in his room, perfect and slim in his dark green doublet and tails, thigh-high boots gleaming black and his rapier at his side. His Uman servant, whom he regularly bedded, had brushed his long, grey hair out and down past his shoulders, giving him an almost regal look, as well as accentuating his widow's peak.

"Like a falcon," he thought to himself. The angular nose and the almost-golden eyes made him look the predatory bird.

"Love the servants and they'll make you look your best," Glennen had told him, years before. Probably not what he meant, however you never knew with Glennen.

In that end, Glennen had tried to love his share of servants, among other things, and then this 'Conqueror' had come along.

Before then, even if things hadn't been fine, they'd been under his control. Eldador hadn't been the military and economic juggernaut of the new age; however it had been almost completely under Hectar's hand. Glennen's idea of running things had been to sit his throne and growl at peasants and minor nobles. Hectar had financed the kingdom from his duchy, and done a damn good job of it.

He straightened, looked himself up and down one last time, and turned on one heel to march himself out the door to a meeting he'd requested with Lee, the fourteen-year-old now running Eldador.

By *Law*, it should be Tartan if anyone; however Glennen hadn't wanted that kind of monarchy. Glennen had looked fondly on Hectaro as his successor until 'the Conqueror.'

Now, rather than trying to put Hectaro in Alekennen's good graces, he pushed his son in the direction of Lee, and his best chances at a future. When Shela had come to him seven weeks before and told him to watch the Empire while she ran to her husband, he'd seen his opportunity and sent Hectaro to protect her. "Take your children, and mine as well, your Imperial Majesty," he'd told her. "Hectaro is death with his sword, and doesn't he ride one of Blizzard's get?"

He'd come back with a scowling princess who hated him and sniggering Wolf Soldiers who told a story of his being raped by a Bounty Hunter.

Now he struggled just to keep the boy's political future alive.

Lee Mordetur sat the Imperial throne with all of the dignity of a woman twice her age—back straight, hands in her lap, skirt of her dress spread out before her and, although her feet dangled, her heels stayed down as if she were riding it into the future of Fovea, much as she likely was. She'd brushed her brown hair back like her mother's, no ribbons or bows, a silver tiara worn as a decoration reminding the throne room she spoke with her father's power.

"Should be Tartan," Hectar told himself, as he waited at the doorway to the throne room to be announced. Courtiers might wait in the galleries, but not the Duke of the most powerful city on Fovea.

"His Grace," the liveried Uman announced from a podium beside the three Oligarchs, "Hectar Gelgelden, Duke of Galnesh Eldador."

Hectar threw back his shoulders and took a warrior's long, measured steps down the red carpet at the center of the throne room, ignoring courtiers and vassals. He smiled benevolently at the little girl who sometimes called him 'Uncle Hectar.'

"We are honored, and await your wisdom, your Grace," Lee told him, her voice a purr.

"We exist but to give it," he answered, and bowed at the end of the carpet, before the throne. "In this case, we come to speak for our beloved son, Hectaro."

The look of disgust that crossed Lee's face still surprised him, especially considering that, two months before; he'd had to chastise his son for complaining of the swooning princess' attentions.

"We listen," Lee said, formally. Her father had started that about six years ago. Translation: I don't like this subject.

"He is a young Man, and craves combat," Hectar said, forcing the smile. "As many young Men, his blood boils at the thought of missing the opportunities your father—"

She waved a hand and he cut himself off, his heart pounding in his chest. If she hated Hectaro now, she could disgrace him and there'd be nothing Hectar could do. This gamble could cost father and son everything.

"He wants to go to Thera?" Lee asked, quite frankly.

"If you'd consult with your father—" Hectar began. If not the girl, then certainly Lupus would honor his request, if she'd make it.

"Send him," she said. "I can think of nothing more perfect than Hectaro Gelgelden not being here."

Hectar smiled wide and bowed to the throne. Command of a company, perhaps even a Millennium, in victory, and no previous story of Hectaro and the Bounty Hunters would matter.

However who stood up in the gallery but his beloved son himself, two hands on the banister, a look in his eyes that could only be called fear?

"Your Highness—if I may?" he blurted, completely out of place and protocol.

As soon as Lupus had learned of the protocols of the throne room, he'd embraced and insisted on them. He loved anything structured, anything military. His warriors all marched in step, and so did he, once he knew what the drummer was playing.

His daughter could be expected to be no different. "We are *offended*," she said, and raised an eyebrow.

The unseen one hundred Wolf Soldiers who always watched over the throne room melted from hidden doors and from behind tapestries. Son of a Duke or not, a word from Lee and Hectaro would be in irons or worse.

Hectaro vaulted over the banister and then leapt to his father's side. Hectar closed his eyes and resisted the urge to take his brow between his thumb and forefinger.

"I beg your indulgence, your Highness," he said, and knelt, his head down. Lee rolled her eyes.

"Speak," she commanded him. "The sooner you're done, the sooner I'm done with you."

Like her father, Hectar thought, *she can turn a phrase on a knife's edge.*

"I beg to stay, and to guard your person, as your brother instructed me" Hectaro said, and looked up from the floor directly at the princess.

Any other girl might be impressed, but not the daughter of Shela Mordetur. Hectar knew her well enough to know she liked her Men blooded, not devoted.

"There's a surprise," Lee said, and the gallery gasped.

Hectaro turned his face back to the floor.

Lee kicked her feet, then caught herself. She allowed herself one look at her Oligarchs, then turned back toward his son with an expression Hectar had seen on Shela's face before.

Lee raised her hand majestically. "It seems to me," she said, "that his blood only boils for warm beds, good meals and a stone wall between him and his enemies. So be it—I'm assigning him to J'her, your Grace. Wolf Soldiers guard my person, he can learn from them."

"Your *Highness*," Hectar couldn't have been more stunned if she'd actually attacked him. "The—your Highness, your *Highness*— the Wolf Soldiers are volunteers, your Highness."

"And he just volunteered," she countered him. One look around the room showed him the sneers of courtiers and the exchange of knowing glances among the Wolf Soldier guards.

Hectaro stood to accept his fate. At least he had that in him.

"Your Highness," Hectar began again.

She let loose a long sigh. "He doesn't have to take the vows, not that he would. His cowardice cost a lot of Wolf Soldiers their lives. He wants to guard me? Well, they used to, so now he can. When father returns, Hectaro can go back to riding his horse and chasing servant girls."

"You are too kind," Hectaro said, and bowed low. Hectar could do nothing but bow after him.

The 'Conqueror' once had made a sarcastic comment about snatching defeat out of the jaws of victory, and Hectar hadn't really gotten that until now.

* * *

A week after she'd made love to Karl for the first time, Raven finally saw the great, green stretch of trees that marked the Salt Wood. Supposedly from here they would find the rescue they needed.

Where Bill—Jack—had been an occasional and gentle lover, Karl had been more energetic, more frequent and apparently used to forcing most of the women before her. She'd tried to educate him, to teach him how to kiss her and not hurt her jaw, to let her wrap her hands around him, rather than holding her wrists down.

One time when she hadn't been in the mood, he'd actually slapped her. She'd burned his shoulder in her anger right after.

After that he'd spoken to her about her power. "You know, a lot of really powerful sorceresses have males in their lives to guide them," he'd said, off-handedly.

"They do, huh?" she'd been able to guess where that was going. Glynn and Vedeen had been making excuses not to teach her anything new, so she'd been experimenting on her own. She'd found that a lot of what she'd learned of chemistry on her own world translated into magic here. She'd been able, for example, to take a lump of coal that their cooks carried and turned it into a huge diamond by rearranging its cell structure, just as she had her ruby. Afterwards, she'd been able to create a tiny vacuum in front of the diamond and shoot it over the horizon.

Which was a shame, because it was a very pretty diamond. She felt sure that, had Xinto been alive, he'd have jumped on one of the ponies here and gone after it. She missed the little pervert, who'd treated her body like a Braille novel.

"The Emperor and Empress, for example," Karl had continued. "You know, she was his slave once."

"I know," she'd said, not looking at him, riding side-by-side.

"Because if you learn too fast, your power unrestrained…"

She'd looked into his brown eyes, the scar on his face twitching guiltily. "You're all afraid I'm going to blow myself up or something?" she'd asked.

Say what she would about Karl, he admitted when he was caught, and he owned up to it. "Yeah," he'd said, "and take us with you. It's happened before."

"Yeah?" she'd been intrigued.

Supposedly a *lot* of those of the race of Men learned too fast; burned out and destroyed themselves. They'd all been terrified she'd do the same.

Pretty stupid, but there you go, she'd thought. She'd agreed to let him guide her, and that night they'd screwed like bunnies.

Now they were beating a path back to the Salt Wood with more than eight thousand Daff Kanaar warriors on their tails, hoping the goddess Eveave was going to pull them out of this situation they'd found themselves in.

It still bothered her that some price had been paid for this, and she didn't know what it was.

Even she could see the dust behind them from the Daff Kanaar army. No matter how far they had to go, they'd travel until they were sure their pursuers had made camp. The closer they came to the coast, the more sure she became that their enemy would either just march them into the ground, or pull some trick to make the Confluni think the Daff Kanaar had camped before they actually had.

Lost in these thoughts, she didn't even notice when Zarshar loped up alongside her on her Angadorian warhorse, and touched her thigh with a talon.

"Wuh—who, what?" she stammered.

"I said," he growled, through the slobber on his chin, with his black tongue lolling, "I'm going to scout out the woods with Slurn. If I'm not back by moonrise, I'll need you to send someone after us."

She shifted in her saddle—a proper man's saddle now. She was right about one thing—the leather *did* chaff her naked thighs.

"Why us?" Karl argued with him. "Tell Glynn or the Con—"

"If I tell that weak-minded Confluni anything, it'll be how happy I am to twist the heads off of her little play mates," Zarshar sneered. "As for Glynn, she'll just argue with me, and I'm going to do it anyway."

Raven smiled and shook her head. No one could keep peace between the Swamp Devil and the rest of them since Xinto had fallen, especially now that Bill had switched sides. It seemed to her that Zarshar questioned how much loyalty he owed them more and more lately.

Because he still seemed to care what she thought, Raven reached out and stroked the heavily muscled shoulder, looking as soulfully as she could into the red eyes.

"You'll be careful, won't you?" she asked him.

He growled low in his throat. "I hate it when you do that."

"But you *will* be careful," she pressed him.

She held his eyes with hers, until he had to look away. "I won't be killed today," he informed her, then looked past her to Karl, riding on her other side.

"Be careful of this one," he said. "She is far more evil than I."

"Don't I know it," Karl said, smiling. Raven swatted him.

Zarshar loped off to the horizon, Slurn behind him without a backward glance. She'd lost some sort of connection with her 'almost there.' She wasn't sure if it was her transition to more power, or her relationship with Karl, but the Slee kept his distance from her now.

"They'll be okay, won't they?" she asked Karl.

"He will," Karl remarked, watching after them, "but woe to whoever he comes across. He really likes killing."

* * *

Jack found Lupus in the captain's cabin of the *Bitch of Eldador*, his wife with him. Shela still wore an Andaron raider outfit almost exactly like the one he'd gotten Raven.

They were still in port in Thera. All of the wharves were full and there were nearly one hundred ships at anchor, barges moving warriors out to them.

Shela turned to cross behind the Emperor and Jack saw the bruises on the backs of her upper thighs and her lower back. She'd paid a heavy price for leaving Galnesh Eldador. Raven had told Jack the Emperor hit his wife, and that she expected it. His own wife drove him crazy and he'd divorced her, but he'd never raised a hand to her and he didn't think much of anyone who did.

Lupus looked up from a writing desk when Jack entered, Vulpe in tow, then back down at some parchment he'd been scribbling on furiously. One of the inventions he'd brought to this world was the ballpoint pen, and he used one now. Oddly, he hadn't figured out the pencil.

They waited for him to be done. Shela winked at them and stroked the side of Vulpe's face in the close cabin. Wolf Soldier guards tramped in and out, making reports about the fleet being ready.

"Your ship in order?" Lupus asked Vulpe without looking up.

"Yes, father," Vulpe said.

"Turned command over to your captain, did you?"

"Just of the loading."

He nodded, then looked up from his work and laid his pen down. "Come to explain to me why *you're* telling *me* you're not good enough to wear the Mark of the Conqueror?"

One of the Wolf Soldiers actually walked into the door without opening it. He muttered something and beat a retreat, everyone else in the room with him. In seconds it was just 'family,' much as Jack was family.

"Yes, father," Vulpe said.

Lupus turned his attention to Jack and looked him in the eye. "You here to take his side on this?" he asked.

"Really don't see there being much of a side," Jack said.

"The Mark of the Conqueror is the *highest* honor—" Shela began, but Lupus waved her off.

He looked at his son, and then at Jack. "Think I'm too hard on him?" he asked, surprisingly frank.

Jack knew that trick. Take the bait and Lupus would explode. Who the hell was he, right?

"I think you raised a boy who, when he had to, marshaled your warriors, made them his, and rescued his mother, and I don't think too many eleven-year-olds could pull that off," Jack said, honestly.

Lupus looked him in the eye and searched. Jack had to admit it was almost painful. He had this soul-searching gaze that made a guy's brain feel like it was being poked and prodded.

"But?" he asked, finally.

"But he's still eleven," Jack said. "And he doesn't want his own dad to cut his cheek open with a dagger, and at eleven years old, I don't think I would have, either, and neither would you."

Lupus turned to Shela, then his son. People said he loved his wife so much he didn't need words to talk to her, and Jack wondered if that were true.

He sighed. "You happy with being in charge of the Eldadorian Regulars?" he asked.

Vulpe straightened. "Father, I'm very proud—" he began.

"Don't give me that bullshit," Lupus said, and put a hand down on the table. "Talk to *me*, son—I know you did what you had to do, and there's no going back from it, but you think maybe you need to take a break from this?"

Vulpe, to his credit, didn't flicker. "Father," he said, "I just want to go with you."

Lupus smiled, reached out and roughed up his son's head. His son batted at his forearm and his mother smiled.

"You know morale of the army is very important," Lupus said. "How's about, before we go, you get up on the crow's nest of your ship and sing an aria for everyone? Something about blood and battles and invincible warriors?"

"I can do 'The Battle of the Deceptions,'" Vulpe exclaimed, and suddenly he was almost hopping up and down. "I know that by heart, I just need a flutist—"

"I'm sure there's a whole troupe of them at the Theatre au Thera," Shela said, "if you hurry and catch them."

Vulpe was out the door, then back in to make a fist over his heart in salute to his father, also his commander after taking a commission, then out the door and back in one more time to hug his mother, and then Jack. Jack gave him a solid thump on the back and the boy—the *man*—was out the door.

Lupus sighed and looked across the table at Jack. Shela pressed her side against her husband's shoulder.

"You mad?" Jack asked him. Better to find out; and he didn't think Lupus would lie.

"Nah," he said. "Don't like the way this all turned out, but there isn't a lot I can do about it. I wanted a better childhood for my kids than this. It feels like I'm dragging them into my life too early."

He meant he was pissed off at his wife, Jack knew, and he may feel he had a right to be, but that didn't change anything now.

"Be great if we had control of stuff like that," Jack said.

"Tell me about it," Lupus agreed.

* * *

Zarshar slipped through the standing pines in the Salt Wood, pressing through the northern tip to see what was on the other side, or here waiting for them.

The girl, he had to admit, was coming along nicely. She'd be a daughter to Power soon, a convert to the younger god. Already she'd been able to commune with Earth—something which only the most solemn of Dwarves were thought capable of, and then only after years of meditation. For her to do so by the force of her will showed how much promise she had.

The Slee had actually advised caution, and directly to him. His dedication to this daughter of Men overcoming his racial hatred, he worried that this one might suffer the fate of so many with the gifts of Power, and no long gifts from Life to perfect them.

At thirty, he was past what most Swamp Devils considered to be his prime, much as he had risen to the position of 'The Black Adept.' Back in his swamp, he'd likely have to fight just to keep his name of Zarshar. You earned names and titles among the Swamp Devils on the bones of your enemies.

Even still, he had mastered magic. Not so much as this girl, younger than he, but more than enough to crush his enemies, and more than enough to feel her touching him through Earth below, as she followed them. The Slee felt the same and hissed to him.

"I feel her," he whispered back, quiet by nature while hunting. He sensed more than saw the lizard fifteen feet in front of him. He had to admit, the thing moved almost undetectable in any terrain—a useful skill to have. Slurn could find their enemies, Zarshar could destroy them.

When this was done, he would gather his own people and he would make peace with the Slee. Together they would remake the south in their own image, Slee finding enemies and Swamp Devils destroying them. If the two races combined, then the Men and Uman on Fovea would soon be a memory.

"Two-legs to the east," the Slee hissed to him.

"How many?" Zarshar hissed back, crouching, the talons in his feet sinking into the ground.

"The ground shakes," Slurn informed him. "As many as one hundred."

Too many to fight—he needed to see if these were warriors or refuges from Kor, or perhaps a hunting party out of Andurin. Their path on the plains of Eldador had been no secret.

"Can you get close enough to see them?" Zarshar hissed.

The hiss in return was pure scorn. Of course Slurn could get that close. The thing slithered deeper into the brush, Zarshar crawling cautiously after. Slurn could keep himself concealed; however Swamp Devils were not so easy to hide.

Using a fraction of his power, he pressed a report into the skin of Earth for Raven to hear—a force of Men or Uman found, one hundred strong, investigating.

Slurn's next message came fainter on the wind. "Warriors, small, yellow skin," he said. "Bowmen, waiting for something, and an Uman-Chi among them—not one I know."

Zarshar had met a few Uman-Chi. They lived so long there were legends almost for each of them. They wouldn't regard the Slee as anything more than animals, and wouldn't make much of an effort to know them.

Zarshar drove his talons into the skin of Earth again. "Confluni warriors, an Uman-Chi. You should send Glynn and that fat thing that leads the army."

"Stop that!" Slurn hissed.

"What?"

"What you did, stop it—the Uman-Chi is looking right at me now—I feel its magic on my scales."

Power's bloody claws! Zarshar swore. A Caster, and a good one. They'd identified themselves. He didn't dare call for help or he'd be found. Even Raven's efforts were dangerous now. It wouldn't betray his whereabouts, but it would tell this 'Chi there was something here to look for.

This could get interesting fast.

Chapter Seventeen

The Right Questions

The light was dying in the dusk of the last day of the month of War. Vulpe Mordetur stood in the crow's nest of his ship, *The Dark Maiden*, his crew on the weather decks, the associated Eldadorian Regulars crowding the port and the Sea Wolves which had pulled in closer to hear him. It was always a major event when Vulpe sang and everyone wanted to hear him.

Nina stood next to Jack on the bow of the *Bitch of Eldador*, Wolf Soldiers lined up behind them. Admiral Jaspar, a Man from Kor who commanded the *Bitch*, stood behind them to one side with a couple of his captains.

"Have you heard him?" Nina asked Jack.

Jack, still dressed in his Volkhydran furs, a ridiculously large falchion over his shoulder and a pouch at his hip, crossed his arms and looked down at her. "I haven't," he said.

"I envy you," she said to him. That got a look of surprise. "There's no time like your first time hearing him."

"He's that good?"

"He's magical," Jaspar said from behind them. Jaspar had been a Koran pirate once—not a lot of things touched that dark soul.

"You—well, you'll see."

The ethereal call of the flute drifted out from the deck of the *Maiden*, then a violin or something like it played an eerie tune. Vulpe leaned out over the crowd, his middle pressed against the crow's nest's banister, and he looked out over the crowd.

You could have dropped a pin and it would have sounded like a shotgun blast, Jack thought.

> *"Alone, alone out on the waves,*
> *The Conqueror and his Wolve, they came.*
> *To face, to face the terrible wrath*
> *Of Tech-Ships come to kill the man."*

It was like a soaring eagle had picked Jack up off the ship's bow and carried him out over the waves. His mind filled with the images of a sea battle, Lupus standing at the bow of his ship, the salt spray on his face, his blonde hair streaming out behind him. Jack could smell the acrid smoke from burning ships, hear the screams of dying sailors, feel the ship rock beneath him as Men and Uman fought each other from the decks of their ships. The steam from where the water boiled, the Eldadorian Fire burning in it, actually stung his eyes.

> *"The ships did roll, the fires they burned,*
> *The warriors did shout, did scream.*
> *And all along, the Conqueror,*
> *Did breath his fire, did drink the steam!"*

Jack couldn't know how long the song went on. He went through all of it, the whole battle, felt his heart lift with the Emperor's victory, felt the tears run down his cheeks as he grieved the fallen on both sides.

Suddenly the song was over, and his feet were on the deck of the *Bitch*, and he was staring at the droplets on the toes of his boots and the wooden boards that were his tears.

"Oh, it's been a long time since I heard *that*," someone was saying.

"So amazing," said another.

"The gods, you know," he heard Jaspar telling his captains, "the gods give 'im that power. They 'ave to. How can we be defeated with the gods *sing* to us through 'im?"

Jack turned to Nina. His cheeks were wet and he wiped them on his sleeve. She didn't seem as affected.

"I," he began, and stammered. "I—don't know what to say."

"It's always like that," she said. She turned and pushed her way past the Wolf Soldiers, who seemed more than willing to give way to her. He followed.

"The first time is the best," she said, "because you aren't expecting it. But it's always like that when he sings."

Jack knew this was telling him something, but he couldn't really be sure what.

* * *

Duke Ancenon Escaroth could usually consider himself, if not a lucky male, then a male who made his own luck, and did it well.

He'd discovered Outpost X, created and lead the Free Legion, founded Metz and the most influential and important independent army on the planet, and finally become an advisor to the most dangerous Man in history.

Lupus might prove hard to control, but he left a trail of gold wherever he went. Ancenon bent his knee to Angron Aurelias, King of Outpost IX, but he did it as a wealthier person.

Angron had made an unfortunate decision. Ancenon, D'gattis and Avek had been clear—Trenbon did not have the strength to stand against Eldador. Their only reasonable path had to be to side with Lupus and ride out his short life, then replace him as the leading force on Fovea.

Ancenon had considered that a good plan. His King, apparently, disagreed. This left Ancenon Escaroth in the unfortunate position of being at odds with his liege lord in his effort to preserve the King's future.

His ship, *She Sails Like a Cloud in the Heavens*, hadn't even passed the Salt Wood before he found himself sailing into the path of a mixed fleet of Confluni warships, bound south. They'd hailed him and demanded that he surrender his vessel. He'd simply turned his ship to the east, to outrun them on the Forgotten Sea.

Without warning, the wind left his sails and the sails of the Confluni fleet. He'd been becalmed before, but this time Weather withheld her favor for a week, and he'd ordered his ship skulled to shore, terrified Confluni after him.

The Confluni had been trying for the Great Mid River, having left a huge army in Eldador and fearing to cross the Straights of Deception after. They'd only thought to cross his path because they hoped he could be coerced to use his magic to speed their ships. Ancenon found himself amused by the irony.

Now, standing on a white sand beach, Ancenon watched something watching him from the Salt Wood—something with a strange magic born of Earth that burned the very ground beneath him. Magic wielded like a bludgeon, where a dagger would have sufficed.

"Your Grace?" the Confluni captain asked from beside him. He'd noted Ancenon's distraction—it mustn't have been very hard.

"We are being watched, Sirrah," he said, "and by more than one. If you would be so kind as to summon the mainstay of your sailors, I think we need to consider returning to our ships."

"Our ships are becalmed," the captain protested. He was the usual squat, yellow-skinned and black-haired Confluni Ancenon had seen not change during his whole life. Challenge them and they fight—if they die, then they just didn't fight well enough.

"Better our archers against warriors crossing the surf," Ancenon informed him, not turning from the Salt Wood, "than our swords against them face-to-face in the sand."

He turned to the captain. "There is no disgrace in improving your position, Sirrah. The idea is that they die, not you."

The captain nodded. He ordered a stand of archers to cover the Salt Wood as his warriors collapsed their simple tents and moved their supplies to their ships. Meanwhile Ancenon watched the woods.

Every Uman-Chi knew other races couldn't read their eyes. He had his suspicions of Black Lupus, who'd searched his face on many occasions, and seemed to find something to focus on. Turning his face to his left now, he kept his eyes focused to his right, to a slightly less green patch in a stand of shrub, almost motionless, certainly not something anyone else would pay attention to.

Except that, every once in a while, it blinked at him.

Ancenon had been to the Slee Nation, and he'd seen Slee.

He also knew his new sister's group of vagabonds included one, and Dilvesh had informed him they were headed in this direction.

The thing watched him with that serpentine patience his kind possessed. They'd watch their prey for hours and not strike, either waiting to be hungry or just savoring the kill. This one's breathing didn't even disturb the grass around him.

The archers formed a semi-circle around Ancenon and he ignored them. He knew the benefits of surrounding himself with armed warriors. In this case he knew it wouldn't matter.

They weren't going anywhere.

* * *

Jahunga loped along at Magee's stirrup, a hand on her horse's side, missing his countrymen and remembering the fighting in the Battle of the Vice. It had been glorious, a tale for legends. They'd stood against Theran Lancers and Daff Kanaar, and prevailed, in that they'd been able to leave the field. Few if any were so fortunate.

"Sirrah, I wish I could entice you to ride," Magee informed him. Jahunga just shook his head. It would make him weak, and he needed to be strong, instead. The times he would soon find himself in would demand it.

Glynn opened her mouth to press him when she noted Karl and Raven riding back through the marching ranks of their Confluni soldiers to find them.

"What news?" Glynn demanded, as they reined in before her.

"Zarshar and Slurn are scouting out the Salt Wood," Karl said. "It's a trap. A stand of Confluni bowman and an Uman-Chi are waiting for us."

The news clearly upset Raven. "We don't know that it's a trap," she said. "They could be a relief force, or—"

Glynn shook her head. "We can't just assume that, not with so much at stake," she said. "I will consult with the Ymir, but I believe she and I and a vanguard of Confluni must treat with these, an endeavor which I fear will take time."

Karl looked to the West. "Time isn't something we have a lot of," he warned her. "You make it look like we're stopped here, and those Daff Kanaar are coming right up our arses, pikes and all."

Jahunga grinned wide. Karl had a way with his words.

"If you must engage them again, Sirrah, do you believe you can prevail?" Glynn asked him.

Karl shook his head, still looking west, then spat on the ground. "Not with these," he said. "They're demoralized and they're exhausted. They're trained well enough where they won't break, but warriors fight different when they know it's a last stand. Those Daff Kanaar will plow right through us and keep going to the sea."

"Then we must hope Eveave has treated well with our Raven," Glynn said, "and trust in Her—"

"It's exactly what she'd do," Raven said.

They all turned toward her. Around them, their army marched on like a sea of yellow faces.

Raven looked around her once, and said, "The Taker and the Giver—she'd give us a way out, and give them a way to block it."

Glynn nodded. Jahunga wondered at the young girl's wisdom. Those of his own tribe weren't so forthright. They had the same fire, but not her intuitive mind.

"You're learned well, my protégé," Glynn said. "What, then, would you advise?"

Raven bit her lower lip, but Jahunga knew the answer without her. She was wise, but he was worldly.

"I'll stay," he said.

Now he had all of their attention.

"Leave me five hundred," he said. "We'll make a camp like their jess doonar. That will make them dig their cleats in the sand. When you've settled with these ones on the coast, we'll come running, and you can cover us with arrows and your magic."

Karl shook his head. "And if those archers are there to pepper us?" he asked.

"Then, my good friend," Jahunga said, "we're dead anyway, and I'd rather be buried in the sun than have my body thrown in the ocean."

Karl's face split into a smile. He reached down and took Jahunga's forearm in his strong right hand, Jahunga doing the same.

"I'll send that Swamp Devil back for you," he promised. "I think he's craving some bloody mayhem."

"See that you do," Jahunga assured him. He turned on the heel of his sandal, his spear a comfort to him in his hand, to pick out his warriors. *The smaller ones*, he thought. *The quicker ones, who could run the fastest back to Salt Wood.*

He didn't plan to die here, after all, not knowing how all of this would turn out.

* * *

"*Forward, HARCH!*"

"Straighten up, you!"

"You think you're a Duke's brat to me? You're *nothing* to me! Nothing!"

"Stand up!"

"Sit down!"

"Why can't you do anything *right*?"

'Well,' Hectaro justified to himself, as he fell into his creaky bed, called a 'rack' with its too-thin mattress, its thin sheet and its pillow like a napkin, 'at least the food is good.'

And it was—Lupus prided himself on the food his 'Pack' ate. Plenty of meat, corn and milk with the fat not skimmed off. Every meal with bread with butter and vegetables until his stomach groaned. As much as you could eat in the fifteen minutes they gave you.

The first night he'd gone to bed hungry. The second he'd known better.

They were criminals and persons who'd run out of luck. Male and female treated the same. Some of them, he knew, had paired off, however mostly this was the Pack, the Pack *was*, and you, as they said, 'Didn't get your meat where you got your bread.'

Hectaro had found that pretty funny once he'd figured it out.

You came into the Pack with what you brought to it. They'd given him the tabard and the armor and the boots. He used his own sword, and he kept Bastard, his horse. He had a locker at the foot of his cot, with no lock on it. His second day there, he'd found a bag of silver inside.

He'd taken it and thrown it into the center aisle in their barracks. Every head turned. The sergeant for his squad stepped up and asked him, "What do you think that is, RIT?"

"I don't know what that is?" Hectaro answered him, looking him in the eye. "Someone put it in my locker, it doesn't belong there, so now whoever owns it can find it."

"You didn't steal that; get afraid you'd get caught?" the sergeant, a Man, demanded of him, invading his space, running an eye up and down his face.

"You wanna ask me that outside, sarge?" Hectaro asked him, holding his gaze. "I promise you, you won't like the answer."

The sergeant straightened, the barracks fell silent.

"I say he's in," someone down the row said.

"Aye," another, a Volkhydran who called himself 'Death,' said. "I'll fight aside him."

"And I."

"He's in, sarge."

The sergeant took a step back, a grin wide on his face. "You'd be surprised how many try to keep the silver," he said.

Hectaro grinned. It was a test—of course. Everything here was a test. The bedamnable tests were a test of how well you stood up to testing.

"And what happens to them?" Hectaro asked.

A green-haired Uman woman in a loin clout and nothing else stepped up and picked the silver up from the aisle, poured it into her hand and counted it, then poured it back into the bag. She had the body of a woman of the race of Men, full breasted and meaty, where Uman women tended to be slender.

The roots of her hair were dark, almost black, but she'd died it. Dark hair and dying were rare among the Uman.

"We beat 'em," the sergeant said, "the first time. We break their bones the second. The third, they get to swim home."

"None's made it," the Uman woman said. She turned and thrust her hand out to Hectaro, her breasts bobbing. "I'm D'leer, your new sergeant. You're a cub in my squad until I say otherwise. We guard Princess Lee in J'her's Millennia. That's fifth squad, third century, first Millennium—think you can remember that?"

"Five, three, one," Hectaro said, her forearm warm in his. She nodded, released him, turned and then spun on her heel to punch him in the face.

It likely would have worked on anyone else, but Hectaro had sparred with the Emperor, and he'd been taught that move. He ducked, the fist passed over his head, and he punched his new sergeant three times in her kidney, then flipped her. She landed on her ass, heels of her palms on the ground, legs apart, looking up at him.

"What was that for, looking at your tits?" Hectaro asked her.

She smiled up at him. The other Wolf Soldiers didn't swarm him—in the Pack, you fought your own fights. He'd learned that from day one.

"Too bad," he said, grinning down at her. "They're nice."

He reached down, she took his forearm. He expected her to punch him on the way up, but she didn't. She snorted, turned on her heel, and walked down to her rack in the barracks.

"Look at 'em all you want," she said. "You can't punch better than that; you'd better learn how to grow some of your own."

Hectaro chuckled. A few of the other warriors, his Pack-mates, then came around to slap his shoulders and welcome him.

Now, on his back in his rack, sore from a day of training, he thought back to that day. Since then, he'd come to really respect Sergeant D'leer, who'd been at the Battle of the Deceptions, the Battle of the Two Horses, and the Second Invasion of Thera, a personal guard to the Imperial family.

Yes, he could beat her butt at will.

No, he'd never break her. Not only that but he doubted very much he'd be a match for her leadership skills. Had it been her when the Bounty Hunters had attacked the Empress, instead of him, maybe Vulpe could have stayed a kid for a while longer.

War knew he wasn't one now.

"You've always got that look on your ugly face," he heard, from the head of his rack. He'd been so exhausted he hadn't even noticed her coming. He immediately recognized the voice, though— he heard it all day.

"If it's so ugly, what are you doing here looking at it, D'leer?"

She circled around so he could see her, dressed once again in her loincloth and nothing else. Most women in the Pack weren't self-conscious of their bodies, but most didn't display it like D'leer.

"It's mine to look at," she told him, half-a grin on her face. Her short, green hair framed her face. It was damp—she'd just come from the shower. "You're in my squad—I own every whisker on it."

Hectaro grinned and put his hands behind his head, stretching on his rack, arching his back. He wore only a loincloth like D'leer's.

She pulled that off of him without warning.

As the son of a Duke, he'd experienced sex before, usually with Uman servants. The two races couldn't breed—the Uman servants made good lovers, even if their women usually held their chastity as dear as the daughters of Men.

He'd NEVER had a woman be so forward with him. She actually regarded him, as if he were some stud horse, reached down and took him in her hand, played with him.

A young man, it was all he could do to keep his self-control.

"Ever had this before?" she asked him.

"Not like this," he admitted.

"Servants you've violated," she pressed. "My sister Uman."

He closed his eyes, fighting the feeling of her grip, both hard as steel and soft as silk, on him.

"Uh, huh," he grunted.

He opened her eyes and saw her smiling. She'd let her own loincloth fall. Unlike Men, Uman remained completely smooth below the neck.

"I was a servant in Trenbon," she informed him, as she stepped over his rack to straddle him. Other members of his Century, Wolf Soldiers from all over Fovea, slept feet away with nothing but air and night between them.

No secrets in the Pack.

"I was visited by a Confluni lord, who thought he would take me, experience me like some meal," she continued. He felt her directing him inside of her, felt her wet heat. "Beforehand, he thought he would have his fun. He brought…things."

Without warning she slammed down against him.

"I gagged him on one of those things," she said. "He died. I was thrown into a cell in Outpost VII with other Uman who made me wish I had just put up with the Confluni, and then the Daff Kanaar recruiter, Lupus, came."

She started to move. Hectaro couldn't understand what she was doing. All day, she'd beaten him like a dog, now she gave him *this*? Not just her body but her secrets—no one in the Pack asked the question, "Why are you here?"

"Lupus saw something in me, and I entered the Pack," she said. "Since then, I've killed Men and Uman, noble and common.

"But I've never had this."

She squeezed him with her muscles, and he exploded so hard he actually saw stars. She continued with him until she bit her lip, then arched her back and then bit his collarbone.

In the Uman culture, that told other women to keep away.

She straightened, blood on her lips, smiling at him, then slapped him.

Standing up, she stepped off of him, leaving him spent. "Get some sleep, cub," she told him. "I won't be riding you like *this* tomorrow."

* * *

When Glynn emerged from the canopy of the Salt Wood onto the white sand beach of the Forgotten Sea, it was to find the sun just rising to her East on the first day of Destruction's month, and her brother Ancenon watching her from a stand of Confluni archers.

She recognized the standards immediately—these were Ymir Effecate Hagadashi Boohoori's own warriors. How Ancenon had come among them was anyone's guess, however, they'd never be turned on their liege lady.

"I greet you, brother," she said from the saddle, taking the form of the mounted visitor, her head lowered and her wrists turned out, her arms spread wide and her back slightly bowed.

Ancenon touched his forehead with his right hand and then made a long, deep sweep of his right arm to the ground, leading from the wrist, of the welcoming brother. Behind her, Avek Noir would be taking a form similar to hers, even though the Heir could in fact demand the others defer to him in such a situation.

They were in dire straits, after all, and this would communicate their need for rapid assistance to Ancenon more quickly than words.

"I am told you have fought mightily in your new homeland," Ancenon chided her. "The Battle of the Vice was an historic conflict to be a part of."

"And we are sorely worn for it," she said. Behind her, the Ymir emerged from the Wood on her litter, Karl to one side of her and Raven past him. On her left, Zarshar trundled out of the Salt Wood with their dog next to him, her tail beating his legs, and Vedeen on her roan beside him.

"Sorely worn and greatly encumbered," Ancenon said. The Confluni around him were already bowing to the Ymir. "I think you shall find surcease in the vessels behind me, those of your new friend, if I guess correctly."

"I hope so," she said. "I am surprised you tarry—"

"War's whiskers," Karl swore. "Do you know there's over eight thousand Daff Kanaar behind us? Let's load 'em up while we still can, and then get those we left out on the plains."

"There's Daff Kanaar before you as well, Sirrah," Ancenon informed him, straightening, the purple hook-symbol standing out on his breast, "and when last I knew you, you were not so bold."

"That was a long time ago," Karl informed him, and then spat on the ground. "And if you're saying you mean to keep us off those ships—"

Zarshar grinned, baring red teeth and flexing.

Ancenon smiled a politic smile and stepped aside, making another sweeping gesture with his arm. "I assure you, none's the case," he said. "Your ships are your own, I ask only that you leave me mine."

Karl wiped his lips with the back of his hand and looked to Zarshar.

One vile beast, communicating with another, Glynn couldn't help thinking.

"We need to get those warriors off the field," he said.

"I'll go," Vedeen offered. "I'll move faster, and the Trinity might provide me with a means to cover our retreat."

"I'd rather send a few hundred archers," Karl said, but added, "however, never was a Confluni could shoot worth a damn. Go ahead—we'll wait 'long as we can."

Vedeen kicked her roan and yanked her reins to the left, the great beast charging back into the Salt Wood. Glynn couldn't help being surprised she'd volunteered so quickly. It wasn't like her.

But then, these were strange times.

* * *

Vedeen's roan stallion pounded out the daheeri back through the Salt Wood to the jess doonar, where Jahunga and a few troops would make a last stand.

The beast was wearing from her ill use of it, but she knew instinctively it could give this run and back. She'd known him from a colt, and he'd never faltered when the Druids had needed him.

She needed to witness this now. She'd had her theories, of course, but now she wanted to see things with her own eyes. She parted the trees before her as she encouraged the horse to greater efforts. Indeed, the Trinity of Earth, Water and Weather *would* help her in this mission.

She came upon the Confluni much sooner than she'd expected, already driven from their position on the plains. Now they were running terrified through the woods, toward the beach, leading the Daff Kanaar right back to where they'd find the rest of the army.

Vedeen shook her head. They'd be too late, she knew. In fact, she couldn't be completely sure that *she* would be back in time. Not if she didn't find the one she sought.

Even as she thought these thoughts, she almost overran good Jahunga in a fight for his life with none other than Scarlet Nantar of the Daff Kanaar—the greatest warrior alive.

Black beard, black armor, red hook-symbol on his breast, Nantar moved like a dancer, his sword almost an extension of his arm.

Jahunga with a wooden spear might stab or leap back, but the best the Toorian could hope for was to keep the other at a distance until he himself could break and run.

Jahunga was no coward—far from it—but he was a single Man, naked under a long white robe, against a blooded warrior in full steel. The fact he held the other at bay even for this long spoke of his extraordinary courage.

Finally Nantar feinted to one side, leapt to the other, and his great broadsword, a weapon so heavy Vedeen doubted she could even lift it, cleaved down upon the Toorian's shoulder.

The Y-shaped bone in the Toorian's ear flashed, and the sword bounced from Jahunga's shoulder as if from steel. Vedeen smiled, recognizing the aura of the kafeara bird. It would be a crafty warrior who warded himself with one of these.

Nantar struck again, and again the sword bounced from the other's naked skin. The robe was cloven, but the Man beneath gritted his strong, white teeth and pressed the other with his spear.

Nantar barely hesitated. Raising his sword as if to strike again, he spun the blade point-downward and slammed it into the hem of Jahunga's robe. Jahunga leapt to one side instinctively and was restrained and put off-balance by his own clothing.

Nantar shook off his gauntlets and stepped in with fists raised against Jahunga. The latter, unable to pull free of his robe, cast his wooden spear instead. It splintered on the other's breastplate, barely fazing him.

Jahunga was no weakling—the muscles stood out strong on his ebony body. Nantar, a little taller, still retained the protection of his steel, and he moved unencumbered, swinging his fists mightily. Jahunga held the other, grappled with him, tried to find a soft spot to strike or, as a last resort, to pull free of the white robe.

He'd almost done it, he'd freed an arm and was about to slide out the other, when Nantar finally closed a mighty paw of a hand on the other's throat. The fingers of a man who might be one of the strongest alive dug into the other's windpipe and pulled him off balance. Jahunga clutched at Nantar's face and eyes, pulled at his armor, finally tried to dig into the other's grip, as Nantar took the Toorian two-handed, strangling him.

Jahunga's death rattle was a terrible thing to hear. Beneath her, the stallion pawed the dirt. She had to extend her will to quiet it.

She could have saved Jahunga, she knew, but that wasn't what had brought her here.

Nantar cast the dead Toorian to the ground and looked to the East, a predator unsated, sniffing for its prey. He looked right through Vedeen, never seeing her as more than the trees around her and the bushes at her horse's feet. In a few moments, he moved on.

Other warriors came and went. Vedeen had to time this very precisely. If she dallied too long—well, the horse couldn't swim, and it wasn't time yet to return to the Lone Wood. She had business elsewhere after this.

When she felt sure she was reasonably alone, and she'd waited for as long as she could, she went to the scene of this most recent battle. There, she looked down on the fallen remains of a true son of Toor, and a piece of a prophecy whose parts really didn't understand it.

"We are well served, valiant sir," she said, and blessed Jahunga, that he would find peace in Earth, when the god in His nature took him. She saw what she needed to see, then she turned and left him, remounting her roan.

These persons had yet to ask themselves the right questions—of that she had no doubt.

* * *

Earl Arath of Metz walked his horse, following where Nantar had lead their warriors in an all-out assault against the Confluni stragglers who'd stayed behind to hold them.

He'd had a good chuckle when he'd seen their jess doonar—little more than a mound of dirt and some sticks in front of it. If it were that easy, then everyone would do it, as Lupus might have said. It took more than dirt and sticks to create their 'little city'.

Now he had them. The Confluni wouldn't have left these behind unless they were up against it between the ocean and his army. Most likely Dilvesh, the Green One as he liked to call himself, had come north with a few thousand Wolf Soldiers and caught them up against the Forgotten Sea. Between the two of them they'd crush the Confluni and still have time to make the celebrations in Volkhydro.

Musing, Arath was caught off guard when his horse's hoof clanged on something hidden in the grass. The stallion shied and Arath had to pull back on the reins to quiet it. His warriors gave them both a wide berth—foot soldiers maintained a healthy fear of horses.

When his horse settled, Arath dismounted to see what he'd stepped on, suspecting it was a discarded weapon. Sure enough, he found an ebon sword with a white-bone handle in the shape of a 'Y,' wrapped in a white cloth, where his horse had stepped on it.

The blade should have been bent and ruined, but it wasn't. It gleamed, unmarred, in Arath's hands. 'Must be Dwarfish,' Arath couldn't help thinking.

"What's that?" Nantar asked him, emerging from the brush.

"Something my horse stepped on," Arath said, shrugging. He rewrapped it and slid it into his bedroll behind his saddle. It was too long for his preference, but he wanted Dilvesh to look at it, anyway. Lupus had that Sword of War of his, and if this was something similar then he felt he should have it.

Lupus had too many advantages, anyway.

"They're all running to the sea," Nantar informed him. "I killed a Toorian around here somewhere—I was coming back to see if he had anything on him."

"A Toorian?" Arath looked around him for the traditional white robe and didn't see it.

"Yeah—never seen a Toorian with anything to do with Confluni, but if this lot could have a Swamp Devil with them, then they could have a Toorian, I suppose."

Arath had seen the Swamp Devil. Actually, he'd secretly hoped to come across it in the battle. Nantar would want to match it, of course, but not if Arath got to it first.

He sighed. "Ready for a final press on these?" Arath asked his Daff Kanaar brother as he remounted.

"Just waiting for you, your Excellency," Nantar informed him, a wide smile splitting his black beard. Arath shook his head. Nantar without his humor wouldn't be Nantar.

He kicked his mount into motion and led his army off to finish this battle once and for all.

Chapter Eighteen

Rather Unfortunate Mistakes

Ten days at sea saw the Eldadorian fleet past Trenbon and closing on Volkhydran water space. On the 8th day of Destruction the sun shone warm on the waves, burning them a bright blue. Fish leapt over the ships' wakes, some of them, including the 'Great Heart,' dragging nets to supplement their feed underway.

Shela watched her son's ship from *The Bitch of Eldador*, leaning on the rail of her husband's flagship. Yonega Waya, her White Wolf, conferred with his son now, coordinating the attack on Volkha. Faster ships, what he called 'cutters,' the *Stallion* and the *Mare* by name, preceded the fleet and had verified the position of the Trenboni and Volkhydrans outside of Hydro.

They hadn't gotten close enough to verify the land army, but no one doubted where that army waited now.

Her son—his sister should be helping him chose a new warrior's name. Her husband had wanted 'Vulpe.' He informed her it meant 'fox,' just as Lupus meant 'Wolf' in one of the languages of her husband's people. That suited the growing boy, but not the new man, a general among the Eldadorian Regulars.

She'd chosen Tali Digatishi, Two Spears, for her brother because he could throw one hunting spear at a gazelle, then another before the first struck, and see both hit the same, moving target. It marked his strength and skill, setting him apart from other Andarons.

Her mother, still alive then, had preferred some sort of bird-name. He'd been *Usdi Wohali* or 'Little Eagle' as a child. Shela didn't see much use in birds.

Which is why sisters, not mothers, decided these things. She wouldn't make the mistake of advising her son now.

Of course, now that the father had the son beside him, she didn't advise *him* as much either. Yonega Waya had this 'Jack,' his son, grim-faced Thorn and a few Eldadorian commanders around him at all times. Like Men, they argued and pointed, shook their fists and laughed at each other for farting, and cast contemptuous glances at women who offered their opinions.

If Raven hadn't betrayed them, Shela would have *her* now. She'd been convinced at one point Eveave had provided two to them instead of one, so when 'Jack,' took too much of the Emperor's time, she'd have the other.

Now her daughter sat the throne in Galnesh Eldador, the boy she'd cuddled and rubbed noses with six months before carried a sword over his shoulder and saluted his subordinates, and her one remaining female, Nina, stood three steps behind him and to his left, guarding him as she had Lee.

She didn't even have her baby to console her. Chawny would be knuckling her eyes for the wet nurse now, under her sister's care.

No wonder so many noble women stayed home from these things. In fact, for all of the battle and the glory, she found it boring.

"My Lady?"

She turned her head to look over her right shoulder and found a Lieutenant in the Eldadorian Regulars standing at attention behind her, trying hard to look off into space and not at the lower cheek of her behind where it poked out from her short leather skirt.

She should be wearing the raider's jacket to cover her, but the goddess Weather had given them a hot day.

"Yes?"

"Central Communications, my Lady," he said.

They'd opened a conduit on the *Bitch*—such power broadcast their exact position, but in fact that's why they'd done it.

She straightened and turned on one long heel. Normally she'd shuck the boots at sea, but learning to walk on the dangerous surface on the tall, narrow heels, if nothing else, gave her something to do. A sorceress spent most of her time relearning her focus, after all.

"With me," she said, absently. Of course the officer would guard her person right to the door of the executive cabin they'd converted for Central Communications. "What," she considered, employing her husband's dry wit, "would she do if she were attacked by a flounder along the way?"

Central Communications at Galnesh Eldador required a huge room in pristine marble. She'd spent weeks enchanting it, making the whole room vibrate at one pitch, allowing a Wizard or herself to create a channel between it and another room, more simply constructed, allowing whole groups of people, not just the magically gifted, to communicate on one caster's efforts. The room, then, did most of the work—the caster merely had to tap in to it.

The other rooms, which her husband called 'satellites,' could be aligned to that same vibration, what he called a 'frequency.' The idea had come to her when he'd tried to describe machines his people used to store data and run things called 'programs' on a server.

She'd never understood that, but it had inspired this.

She entered a small, clean cabin, whose center shone with a glowing sphere. In it, she saw her daughter's face, and knew at once that trouble brewed at the capitol.

So like her father, this one, she thought. They might appear calm to others, but Shela knew the angry set to the eyes, the scowl, not quite a frown, and the focus of a Mordetur with a problem.

"Your Imperial Majesty," she said, and curtsied, "may I present his Grace, Hectar Gelgelden, Duke of Galnesh Eldador."

Shela couldn't keep a smile back. She nodded to the Duke, dressed in his usual elegance, his hair gleaming on his shoulders. "My compliments, your Grace—you've perfected my daughter's court manners."

"But that I had," Hectar informed her, "but that I had. Her Highness has seen fit to increase the ranks of her father's Wolf Soldiers with none other than my son."

"What?"

Lupus loved and encouraged his daughter, but Shela couldn't imagine a good ending to his learning she'd altered his Pack.

"It was my intent to send him to Thera to sail out with the fleet," Hectar informed her, "and properly asked the Princess' permission. At that point she intervened and decided instead—"

"Oh, no you don't," Lee intervened. Now her scowl was pronounced. Shela noted, as any mother would, the circles at the young girl's eyes, and her hair in disarray.

This responsibility had been telling on so young a girl.

"I told you, 'Sure,'" she pointed an accusing finger at the Duke. "Your coward son, Hectaro, said he wanted to stay."

"My son is *not* a coward!" Hectar turned a shoulder to the sphere, and the connection wavered at her daughter's distraction.

Shela added her own power to it, and then communicated directly with her daughter, "Patience, child—Hectar is one of your father's most loyal Dukes, and there are even Wolf Soldiers who might listen to him over you."

Lee seethed and bit her lower lip, turning back to the orb.

"Your son has certainly distinguished himself with *me*," Shela insisted to Hectar. "My daughter may have seen otherwise, but I saw your wisdom in him when he held his tongue and bided his time with the Bounty Hunters who abducted us. When he was needed, like any Gelgelden, he was *there*."

Hectar straightened. They'd misjudged Hectar's needs, Shela knew. He'd been waiting for some acknowledgement of his son, and hadn't gotten it from Lee. Hectar had great ambitions for Hectaro.

Shela returned her attention to Lee. "So Hectaro preferred to remain in the capitol?" she asked.

"He said he wanted to guard *me*," Lee informed her, with a sideways glance at Hectar. "And I told him if that's what he wanted, then he could serve with the Wolf Soldiers."

"You gave him no option," Hectar objected. "You all but called him a coward in the royal court."

Shela sighed—this had already passed, apparently. "Has Hectaro taken the vows?" she asked.

Both shook their heads. "The Princess at least allowed him to be relieved of his Wolf Soldier duties upon the Emperor's return to Galnesh Eldador," he said. "I'm sure she's uninformed as to how long that might be."

Lee turned on Hectar. "What?" she demanded, sensing insult.

"Enough!" Shela commanded both of them, and in her mind added to Lee, "Patience, daughter—you've offended him and, like any man, he's just trying to shake some of the hurt off."

"Well, he doesn't have to do that to *me*," she insisted in her own mind.

"Who else does he have?" Shela asked her. Aloud, she said, "Well, what is Hectaro's opinion of all of this? Is he miserable in the Pack?"

"With your daughter's permission, you might ask him yourself," Hectar informed her. "He's been assigned to her protection, and is standing right here."

Lee turned the focus of the orb and, sure enough, there stood Hectaro at attention with a squad. Shela recognized the sergeant, D'leer, as one of the personal guard for the family. She'd been one of the few to turn down promotion because she preferred the Royals.

"D'leer," Shela addressed the sergeant. "How does he?"

D'leer gave him a sideways glance. To Hectaro's credit, he left his eyes focused straight ahead, as if he wasn't a party to and didn't care what went on around him.

"As good as any, Lady," she reported, her back straight. "He's had his moments, but the Pack accepts him."

"Do you want out of the Pack, soldier?" Shela asked him.

"No, ma'am," he responded, in that guttural voice her husband's soldiers used.

"He can't say otherwise, shamed as he is," Hectar complained. "You have to release him—"

Shela saw where this was going already. Her daughter had handed her an untenable situation. Either she left Hectaro in, and his Packmates would wonder about him, and his father become an enemy, or she released him, and the rest of Fovea would think him a coward.

Apparently Hectaro saw that too. Standing in the second rank with the swordsmen, he pulled his weapon and put it to his breast.

"With all respect, my Ladies," he informed her, "but if you order me out of the Pack I'll throw myself on it."

Lee's eyes widened. Hectar gasped. The Wolf Soldier squad kept looking straight forward, but Shela could still detect a few satisfied expressions among them, especially D'leer.

Lupus' Wolf Soldiers made for a strange breed. Every one among them came on a second chance. Some balked at it and a few deserted, but for the most part, these men and women formed a very special bond with Lupus at the center of it and, once in, they were Wolf Soldiers above all else.

"I think I'd rather not kill your son, your Grace," Shela

informed him. "Perhaps your son and my daughter know better than we what they need in their lives?"

"This is that Wolf Soldier training," Hectar began, and Shela interrupted him because she knew where he was going.

"You mean the training that makes them the most effective soldiers on Fovea, and the most vital part of Eldador's defense?" she asked him, before he could go farther.

She'd alienate the Duke before the Wolf Soldier guard.

He looked into the sphere, trying to focus on her eyes, and she saw the man's shoulders slump in resignation. "I suppose that's what it is," he informed her.

"I recall a dashing Duke who spent a good part of his life by the sword," Shela informed him. "I don't suppose you know the sort of Man that made of him?"

Ever vane, Hectar had to give her a half-smile for that. "I admit I might have forgotten for a while," he admitted.

"Think of the dread the rest of Fovea will feel for the Duke who was once a Wolf Soldier," Shela reminded him. "Think of the fortunes of the Duke who can call on the loyalty of the Pack? I have to think my daughter has added to your son's future immensely."

She could see she'd caught Hectar entirely off guard with that. She'd come up with the point on the spur of the moment, as her husband put it, but even she had to admit the argument hit home.

Rule stood on the shoulders of respect, and no one dared but respect the Wolf Soldiers.

"But only until your return," Hectar insisted. "I won't lose him to the Pack."

"Your decision on that, soldier?" Shela asked Hectaro.

He slammed his sword into its sheath and returned to attention. Looking straight forward, he said, "Once in the Pack, always in the Pack, my Lady, but I know I'm returning to my father's service when I'm done here."

"If he lasts that long," D'leer added. "He fights passable well, but I've yet to get a decent punch out of him."

Shela allowed herself a grin, which spread to all of them. "Well, then—I trust this issue is to everyone's satisfaction?"

She could feel her daughter faltering—the discussion had taken a lot of time and cost more of her energy when it went on more than one level as this one had. "I'll discuss this with your father, and then with you, my daughter," she promised Lee, using the private conduit.

"You will *not* do this again, and you will be certain to tend your herd with Hectar."

"I promise, mother," she responded.

"Have you seen to your brother's needs?"

"I moved us both to the royal tower," she said. "Chawny's in the nursery—she's doing okay. I see her a few times a day."

"You keep an eye on Hectaro, as well," Shela informed her.

Lee sighed in her mind.

"You're culling your herd of that one too early, daughter," Shela informed her. "Some warriors who weren't worthy have gone into the Wolf Soldiers, but not one has left it except on his back."

"Yes, mother."

"Your Grace," Shela said aloud, "I thank you again for guiding my daughter in what must be a trying time for you. Please be as generous with your advice to her as you have been to the rest of us."

"Ever at your service, your Imperial Majesty," he said, and threw a sideways glance at Lee. Clearly he counted himself the victor in all of this, and when a Man considers himself the victor, Shela had always found him easiest to manage.

She broke the connection. Her daughter could tend her own herd now. She'd have to speak with the Oligarchs in order to find out how this had progressed so rapidly so ill.

Later that day, when her husband had decided to take a break from his generals and advisors to eat, he asked her, "What have you been doing with yourself today?"

She considered telling him of her daughter's troubles, but instead settled on, "I spoke with Lee for a little while. She moved hers and her brother's rooms to our tower."

"Weren't you going to ask her to do that anyway?"

Shela nodded and stroked the side of his face, by the scar. "Seems Hectaro has also taken a short commission for himself."

Lupus frowned and nodded. "Good for him," he said. "I was surprised when his father didn't beg me to take him along."

"Yonega Waya!" she pretended to exclaim. "We have to leave *someone* home!"

He smiled and kissed her, and she let herself melt into that for a while. Simple enough to handle Men, when they consider themselves in control, she reminded herself.

* * *

Raven sat on the fo'csle of the Confluni ship that carried her and her friends across Tren Bay, the sun warm on her face, the breeze cool in her hair. She'd grown long and shaggy in these months here, giving her a wild look.

It fit her mood.

Their dog lay at her feet—it barely left her now. Vedeen sat to her left on the deck and smiled that benign smile of hers. To her right, the ship's wooden rails came to a point—she knew it was called the 'bow' in English, but she couldn't remember the local word.

That struck her funny, because she had already started thinking in the Language of Men, and forgetting her English.

Zarshar hovered at the bow, perched like a gargoyle, his black hair blowing out like a streamer. Behind him and across from her, Slurn had curled himself up in a ball, and next to Slurn sat Karl, sullen and alone, missing Jahunga.

Vedeen had returned to them with a story of how Jahunga had fallen to Scarlet Nantar of the Daff Kanaar. Karl had sworn a blood oath on the spot to avenge him, and barely said a word since. In a week and a half he'd barely touched her in bed and wouldn't talk about it. Glynn had informed her, on one of her rare visits, that this was the way of Men, to grieve such losses, and she must excuse him. Vedeen seemed to support her in that.

For her, grieving meant communicating. She'd been informed it wasn't up to her to tell another how to grieve, either.

She needed to talk to someone, too. She really missed Jahunga—he'd been a friend, the first one she'd made here who wasn't forced on her. However Glynn clearly didn't listen to her when she spoke of it, and Vedeen just agreed with everything she said. Zarshar thought it was great that Jahunga had fallen in battle, and Karl just wasn't talking.

Slurn and the dog really didn't give a lot back.

"There," Zarshar said, finally.

Karl's head came up. "What?"

The Swamp Devil's head didn't turn. "Straight ahead of us, just past the horizon, the Emperor's fleet. I know his woman's magic—the whole place reeks of it."

Raven stood and tried to look over the horizon. All she could see was water, blue as the sky. Their ship was near the front of the fleet. To either side and all around them, long wooden ships with single, triangular sails, some with oars, spotted the Bay.

"His fleet should be past the Llorando," Karl said, standing as well. "No way did we come that far, this fast."

He'd remarked on that before. They'd come to the Straights of Deception too fast. They'd crossed it too fast. They moved too fast when he could see the coast of Sental.

Glynn had told her of a spell Uman-Chi used to make their ships go faster—to make the front of their sails repel air, and the back of their sails attract it. They could do it to one, maybe two sails at a time. In their home nations, they'd found types of cloth that could hold spells, and used their magic to create fast ships that always worked that way.

She hadn't had any of that cloth, but Ancenon had. All she'd needed to do was to see it up close, and then to use her power to put its structure into her mind. From that she could make subtle changes in the structure of the canvas of their Confluni ships.

By the third day, their fleet was skipping across the waves. Glynn had commented that the cloth was rare, and so the effect was limited. When the cloth was pure, as it was when Raven changed it, the spell casting became that much easier, and the effect that much greater.

"What can I tell you?" Zarshar rumbled. "We're here. I'm going to tell Glynn we need to slow down or be ready to fight."

Raven focused on the water right at the horizon but couldn't see anything but more waves. The Swamp Devil was using his magic to sniff out other magic—she wasn't as good at that. Nina had told her a person's magic was their own—that it would give them abilities to do some things very well and some things less well. It depended on the mind and the god that favored them.

Raven knew what god favored her, but she'd been able to touch Earth, too. She could move her will through Earth and sense things through him—through the dirt they called his skin.

If Earth, than why not Water? Water was supposedly a wounded goddess here, but Slurn's people worshipped her. He thought she had power no one had tapped into yet.

As she had with Earth, she stood and forced her will down

through her feet, down through her body and the deck of the ship she sat on, into the water below, into the salt and H_2O, imagining all of the water molecules, swishing around randomly, refracting the light, keeping her from seeing through it.

She couldn't see through the water because the light refracted against it and made it act like a solid. She could look down and see deceptively far, if she moved to the railing, because with the light behind her the effect was less. What she needed to do was to line up those water molecules like a tunnel—then she could see through them like a telescope.

So she imagined that, for just a few seconds, every molecule would line up, like the lattice of a diamond, perfectly straight, rigid, becoming a tunnel she could look right through.

She imagined it, focused it in her mind, and willed it to be.

A *clang* like some gigantic metal door slamming shut rang off of the horizon. Fish flew up out of the Bay in a straight line from a point two thirds of the way to the horizon, for as far as the eye could see, some of them torn apart and bloody.

All eyes turned to the huge, clear tunnel she'd created, like a hole punched in the water a daheer away from the ship she sat on. Through it, they all saw the square sails of Eldadorian Sea Wolves, several hulls and some of the bronze tubes that warned of Eldadorian Fire.

Raven's vision wavered. The spell sucked the life out of her like a leech! She fell to her knees, clutching for support and finding the dog's back. The dog licked Raven's face as Raven released the spell, and barely heard a sound like a sonic boom as the water righted itself again.

She thought, *I really need to stop doing stuff like that*, as she fell across the dog and out of consciousness.

* * *

Glynn sat with her peer, Avek Noir, and the Ymir on the Confluni flag ship, where the Bay rocked them in a nauseating manner and the three boys who attended the obese Confluni female sickened her further with the acts she had them perform, some of them in front of her Uman-Chi guests.

Those of the race of Men, she reminded herself, were barely more than animals.

She'd just propositioned the Ymir for the second time today to redirect to Volkhydro rather than Conflu, where these troops could be added to the Volkhydran defense. Her brother had informed her how the Emperor's ambitions now lay there, provoked by her own King.

Of course, Ancenon did not accompany them. His own ship first ran out ahead of them for the Straights, then fell far behind as theirs surpassed him. Glynn reminded herself that, come what may, she mustn't let this canvas fall to the Confluni Ymir.

The Ymir had only just opened up her flabby maw to respond when suddenly a noise like a hammer on an anvil, magnified one thousand times, rang across the cabin, shaking the ship to its core.

"By Adriam's beard!" Avek swore, standing. The three boys cowered at their mistress' feet. Glynn reached out instinctively with her mind, seeking the powerful cause of such an effect.

Of course, she was rewarded with the unique flavor of her protégé's magic.

The Ymir struggled to right herself as an even louder crash shook their ship, followed by a sensation of speed that had the furniture moving across the cabin.

She heard Confluni screaming and calling out to each other outside on the weather decks. Avek leapt for the door before she could stop him and yanked it open.

A wave of salt water swept in, drenching all of them. Glynn shook the stinging salt spray from her eyes. Looking past it she could see the ship was in a spin. Other Confluni vessels were tossed upon inexplicably rough seas, under a clear blue sky.

Then, as quickly as it had begun, it was over. The Bay righted itself and the swells returned.

Her mind reached out and found Zarshar's.

"Such power!" he exclaimed. She questioned him, and discovered that, as expected, Raven had been blindly applying her power, ironically to enable them to see.

"And how many sails did you count?" she pressed him. No point in wasting what they'd learned.

"I couldn't be sure—the spell didn't even last a minute," Zarshar informed her, "but I saw more sails than I could count that fast."

Glynn bit back a sarcastic response. She'd clearly been spending too much time in the company of Karl Henekhson.

"Has the girl recovered?" Glynn asked.

She waited as the Swamp Devil checked. Meanwhile the Ymir's three boys were peeling her wet clothing from her body while Avek Noir had left to see to the crew. A better caster might have done more to protect them, however Avek Noir was not one, and she'd been caught by surprise.

"She breathes," Zarshar informed her, breaking her from her reverie. "If she has the black mind, it's too soon to tell."

Glynn acknowledged him in her mind and broke the connection. She'd have to go to their ship herself. She'd left a focus on their lower decks, then sealed the room where she'd created it.

Avek returned from the weather decks. "They lost a few ships," he informed her in the language of the Uman-Chi. "Can I assume this is the work of your Raven?"

"The girl is undisciplined," Glynn answered him. "We'd thought to pair her with Karl, hoping she'd benefit from his direction, however Jahunga's death has sorely affected him."

The Heir looked down for a moment, and then back up to her. "I've been contacted by Aniquen Demoran," he said. "His ship is safe – he claims to have been fortuitous in witnessing the event.

"Supposedly a great tunnel opened up through the Bay," Avek continued. As they spoke, the three boys were blotting the salt water from their mistress' fat rolls and ringing sea water from her long, black hair.

"They could see through it as it tore the fish apart," he continued. "Then it exploded and threw a huge wave in every direction. If they did in fact see the Eldadorian fleet on the other side, then its ships could have faired no better than ours."

Glynn nodded. She turned her attention to the Ymir. She could see no point in not using this opportunity to benefit them.

"Ymir Effecate Hagadashi Boohoori," she said, turning to the naked woman, sprawled out across her divan, "I regret to inform you we are discovered by the Eldadorian fleet."

The look of fear and loathing that crossed the woman's face was terrible to see. Glynn suppressed a smile, maintaining her calm.

"I *told* you this way wasn't safe," she drawled, pushing one of the boys away from her breasts. "Was this an attack by—?"

Glynn nodded. "Our Raven caught it at the last moment and deflected it," she said. "She's swooned, but you've lost as many as a dozen ships, while your enemy's power has been turned back on its fleet. We have a path to break, if we desire it."

"To the Silent Isle?" the Ymir asked.

Glynn smiled and shook her head. "I hate to inform you the Trenboni fleet has quit for Volkhydro," she said, "and we should do the same, and to their protection."

The Ymir sighed. "How do propose to guarantee my safety?"

"You forget, good lady," Glynn said, "that you carry with you Karl Henekhson, the Hero of Tamara. You could not *be* better guaranteed in Volkhydro."

The Ymir nodded and gave the order. The ship heeled to starboard, north to the Volkhydran shore.

Opportunity, Glynn reminded herself, is a dessert before the meal, rather than an entrée.

* * *

Nantar rode at the head of his Daff Kanaari army, listening to his old friend grumble as he had been for almost two weeks.

"Right out of my grasp," Brown Arath complained. "I had them, and they slid right out of my grasp."

"Yes," Nantar agreed with him. "They did. It is very unfair."

They'd broken off from Black Lupus' main army with ten thousand warriors. Now they headed up north to Andurin with eight thousand five hundred.

Nantar actually found it sort of amusing. They'd arrived just in time to see the fleet of Confluni ships travel over the horizon—nothing for it but to let the warriors take a day after the hard march, then turn them north.

They'd sent fast riders to Galnesh Eldador, and heard back just this morning that Black Lupus had taken off for Volkhydro, after his fleet had been defeated by the Uman-Chi.

Thorn had been right—they'd tried to take Thera with the Volkhydran fleet and, victory or defeat, the Eldadorians had turned them and saved the city.

Now Lupus characteristically had to get his own strike in, and had left for Volkhydro with 30,000 Eldadorian regulars.

They'd meet the combined Fovean armies. Nantar and Thorn both knew these warriors would come in handy, if they could be moved there in time.

What they'd come across, instead, was dismal weather off the Forgotten Sea, hard marches and cold camps on an endless walk.

Now they could actually see the outriders from Andurin. They'd called formation and had been marching tight for an hour, waiting for what came next.

The outriders pounded in, pulling up tight in front of their horses. Nantar counted five, all Uman, in Andurin's colors.

"Your business?" one demanded. Nantar gave him a casual look, then took another, and recognized the warrior.

"K'delden?" he asked. Arath perked up from being sullen on his mount. K'delden had been one of their Daff Kanaari warriors, rising to the level of commander of 100 after the Battle of Katarran.

"Lord Nantar," he said, and inclined his head. "Lord Arath, your Excellency. We've been waiting for you here."

"You have, huh?" Arath asked him. Arath didn't like it when *anyone* left the Free Legion, especially not anyone with a command.

K'delden nodded. "We have Sea Wolves waiting to port you and your warriors."

Arath and Nantar shared a glance. They hadn't even told anyone they were turning north. Lupus either had been watching them or shown great intuition.

"Port us?" Arath asked. "Where exactly are we going?"

K'delden passed Arath a scroll, sealed with the stamp of Andurin. They didn't actually take orders from Duke Groff, however they knew about Eldador's Central Communications, and Black Lupus might actually just be conveying advice through him.

Arath popped open the seal and pulled open the scroll. He read it, laughed out loud and handed it to Nantar. Nantar accepted it, read it once, and had to read it again—just to be sure.

He looked at Brown Arath—now he was the happy one.

"You must be kidding me."

***

Shela had been enjoying a rare moment alone with her husband when a hole ripped itself out of the ocean to her east. For a moment she saw a whole fleet of Confluni warships through it, then they were gone, and the Bay itself rose up to strike them.

She knew no magic to control Tren Bay. Perhaps if Dilvesh had been here—however there was no time to consider that. Their ship rose up on a huge wave, teetered, and then fell sickeningly down its other side, the crew scrambling to secure the rigging as men and cargo were swept into the water.

Lupus leapt to his feet, his first instinct for his crew. Before she'd met him—she assumed before he'd come here—he'd been a sailor, and since he'd loved the sea. He'd made of himself a passable hand on his Sea Wolves, and he knew the complicated rigging and how to manage its many sails.

"Up the mains'l," he bellowed. "Three quarter left rudder—you there, secure that line!"

Wolf Soldiers scrambled to obey him. Many ran to throw lines or flotation devices to those who'd fallen overboard. The captain of the ship, Admiral Jaspar, took command from Lupus and continued directing the ship's recovery. Shela stood in the doorway to their cabin, watching them, trying to decide what had happened.

She could smell the power that had been used—a strange mix of different gods. Whoever had done this had learned of Power, Earth and Water, and some other that she hadn't ever encountered—some application that defied magic somehow.

For a moment, she'd seen through the ocean, through the horizon, to a fleet that had to be daheeri away. Shela knew, even if she crippled herself, she wouldn't be able to channel the energy required to create an effect like that. More importantly, she wouldn't even know how.

As fast as it had come, the wave was gone. The sky above them remained blue as could be. *The Bitch* righted herself, tacking into the wind. Jaspar ordered that they deploy something that he called a 'sea anchor,' and that brought them to a complete stop, even while the Bay roiled beneath them. Shela saw the carcasses of uncountable dead fish, the gulls and other predators already converging on the unexpected feast. Wolf Soldiers paddled on their flotation barrels or hauled themselves in on the ship's ratlines in fear of what would swim out of deeper water to feed.

There were sharks in Tren Bay.

Lupus returned to her, blotting his face with a towel, the concern in his blue eyes telling. "What the hell was *that*?" he demanded.

She shook her head, her wet black hair clinging to her neck and to the sides of her face. "I have no idea, Yonega Waya," she told him. "Some use of power, less than what a god is capable of, more than any mortal should know, even the Uman-Chi."

"Angron Aurelias?" Lupus asked. Shela shook her head again.

"To what end?" she asked. "Where are the Tech Ships, swooping in to catch us unawares? Where are the—"

"The illusion!" Lupus exclaimed, and looked around him.

Nothing. All they saw on the waves were gulls and carcasses.

"By Power," Shela swore, and focused herself. The air shimmered, and around them the 'fleet' reappeared, dozens upon dozens of Sea Wolves, many armed with Eldadorian fire.

"Pointless now," Lupus growled. "If that was Angron then he knows—"

Shela stroked the side of his face. "Be of good faith, Yonega Waya," she said. "As I said, this was past the ability even of Angron Aurelias. Whatever we just witnessed, it's beyond what I know of magic, and if it came from anywhere, then it was from that Confluni fleet past the eastern horizon."

Lupus didn't look satisfied. She'd already told him of that fleet—they were waiting to see if it tried to sail past or turn around. They didn't think for a moment the Confluni would engage them, unless they saw through their illusion somehow.

Like this.

However, once again, where were the ships sweeping in over the horizon? Where was the follow-up strike? If they expected an illusion, they could have dispelled it at a fraction of the exertion.

Whatever had just happened, all they could do now was to wait here for it. They were alone, and didn't have the ability to send a few ships out to stir up their enemies. Their strategy, in fact, if they were discovered, was simply to stay out of weapon's range of whatever might chase them.

Lupus had a plan for Volkhydro and, as Shela had heard him say before, they weren't it.

Chapter Nineteen

Combat, in All of its Forms

Slurn had never seen anything terrifying about the ocean or Tren Bay. Some of his people saw those wide expanses of water and craved the closeness and the comfort of the shallow swamp, where one's claws always touched the bottom.

When he awoke on the deck of a Confluni ship, spinning out of control across the waves, the dark female whom he guarded laying slumped across the dog-beast, he knew a kind of terror he hadn't experienced since his early days after hatching.

"What was *that*?" Karl demanded, in the language of Men. "Who did—what? Did she?"

Vedeen leapt to Raven's side, where the dog-beast hovered protectively, not knowing whether to lay down and to comfort, or to jump out and attack. Slurn kept his distance, knowing his intrusion might set the thing off.

"Glynn wants to know if she's alive," Zarshar demanded. Vedeen reached for the girl's neck. The ship's spinning slowed, its deck awash with salt water, strewn with cargo, some of its crew hanging from the sides.

"She lives," Vedeen announced. "I know not how. She was the source of that magic, and it must have drained her mightily."

The dog-beast laid its great head down across the girl's midriff, where she lay on the deck. Karl knelt upon her long, black hair, his hand on her cheek.

"Raven," he called to her. "Raven!"

Vedeen placed a hand on his shoulder. "She cannot hear you," she said. "The energy is out of her—she sleeps now. She may in fact have the black mind—an anomaly—"

"I know what black mind is," he growled, then stood. "Stupid! Stupid! I can't believe how stupid—"

"You curse her while she lays sleeping?" Zarshar demanded, looking angry. But when, Slurn wondered, did their kind *not*?

"Not her," Karl said, looking up at the black devil. "Me—I'm the one supposed to watch over her. I'm supposed to be there, to guide her. First I let Jahunga die—now this."

Zarshar shook his head and turned away. A Swamp Devil would have contempt for any show of weakness, no matter how slight. Slee understood better, especially Slurn.

"Zarshar," he said, the Swamp Devil turned to him, the disgust on his face plain.

"Tell him it's not his fault."

Zarshar bared his red teeth. "Who's to say it isn't?" he asked.

Slurn's tail twitched in aggravation. "You know where we're going?" he asked.

Zarshar just looked at him.

"Then you know what that one has to do," Slurn continued. "He won't be able to do it with a mind full of rot and self-loathing."

Karl and Vedeen watched the exchange. The dog-beast growled low in its throat.

Zarshar growled back, drawing the dog-beast's hackles. "Karl Henekhson," he said, "Slurn asks me to inform you that you're not to blame, and on reflection I have to agree with him."

"It was my—" the Man began, but Zarshar shook his head.

"Jahunga was doing what any warrior does, and took a warrior's chances, doing it," Zarshar said.

"The girl has barely dabbled in her magix—no one would try half of what she's done before they'd trained for years. This one has toyed with her power for less than five moons."

"In truth," Vedeen said, "there was no containing her, and be it known that we tried. This was like to happen; it is just her bad luck it went so far and so badly."

Karl held her head between his calloused hands and shook his own. It was the nature of Men to grieve the fallen, Slurn knew. Karl, he believed, couldn't reconcile whether it was that time.

"When," he asked, then choked and swallowed. "When will you know—?"

Vedeen smiled her toothy smile and said, "Let the girl rest a few days. She's shown remarkable resilience up to now. Let us see if she rebounds from this effort."

Karl nodded.

"And before you go below decks and whimper," Zarshar added, his black tongue running over his red teeth, "keep in mind that we saw a whole Eldadorian *fleet* through that hole she opened up in the Bay. If they come after us, then you're going to wish you had her power to protect you."

* * *

Duchess Yeral Stowe sat in her personal chambers while an Uman servant girl brushed her hair and another did her toes. Light poured in through the open bay windows and puddled on the thick pile carpets at her feet. She liked the smell of fresh cut flowers and they surrounded her here.

Another Uman, a young man in her husband's livery, entered her room with a scroll in his hand. He knelt before her at her feet and held it up to her. She took the scroll without speaking to him.

Many noble women, especially in Eldador, had Uman lovers. There could be no issue from the coupling, although the parts all worked the same. She'd considered taking this one—he seemed devoted to her, or least devoted enough. Where her husband did perfectly fine by her when he showed interest, sometimes a woman likes to receive the services a lover will provide, and a husband might be shy of.

The Uman left. She popped the seal on the scroll, recognizing the mark of Duke Ceberro. She pulled the scroll open and read it, written in the Language of Men, which she'd made sure her personal servants had no command of. The scroll read:

Destruction 10, 97th year of the Fovean High Council
Duchess Stowe,
        I contact you in regard to our latest

*conversation, which I found both enlightening and
encouraging. In that vein, I have learned that the
Emperor has embarked on an invasion of the
Volkhydran nation with his wife and son, and left the
Empire in the hands of his daughter, Lee Mordetur.*

*I am gravely concerned that she is inadequate
to this task and, where we might normally rely on the
good influences of Duke Hectar Gelgelden, in fact Lee
has forced his son, Hectaro, to enlist in the Wolf
Soldier guard and come at odds with Hectar.*

*I can think of no better time for your husband
to fulfill his obligation to this empire and to travel
north, to Galnesh Eldador, there to assist and to
mediate for this embattled Princess.*

Your friend always,

Ceberro of Vrek

A week to arrive here, Yeral noted as she rolled the scroll up
and laid it in her lap, allowing the smile to cross her lips. She'd
known her alliance with Ceberro would bear fruit; he had the
connections in the palace at Galnesh Eldador her father had enjoyed,
and her husband would never have.

She'd never imagined they would bear so well so quickly, but
then it was said the sun never sets twice on the same Eldador.

"Girl," she said to the Uman brushing her hair. "Send a
message to the Duke my husband, and inform him we need to meet,
and soon."

The Uman girl nodded and left quietly. Yeral inhaled deeply
of the fresh flowers.

One day, she thought idly, she'd have to learn that girl's name.

* * *

Genedare, an Uman servant to the House of Stowe, didn't
quite walk and didn't quite run through the halls of the palace of
Angador, the city.

She'd been here for more than a year, serving first in the
kitchens, then moving on to the regular house staff when she managed
to assassinate three of those, and then into the Duchess' personal

retinue after six poisonings of the Uman serving there.

Such is the life of a Bounty Hunter.

Serving the Duchess hadn't provided much by the way of intelligence, however it had certainly been a boon for the mortuary. That is, until lately, when the Duchess began contracting with Duke Ceberro.

She found one of the Duke's footmen, an Uman like herself, and conveyed to him that the Duchess sought dinner with her husband this night, and the footman promised to convey this to the cook and to arrange dinner in the formal hall. The Duke had planned to eat there anyway, so if they'd done nothing, then the meeting would have occurred of its own.

The footman took the time to try to arrange a tryst with her, but Genedare resisted him. She had no problem with the occasional coupling which occurred among the house staff; however she simply lacked the time and didn't find herself attracted to the footman.

She moved past him and she found her way to the stables. She had to move quickly now—the Duchess was unreasonably demanding of her time and she didn't want to have to go on a killing spree to get her job back.

It spoke volumes that the Stowes never even noticed the killing she'd done already—they simply complained of the expense of training and rearranging the staff.

In the stables, Genedare found the stablemaster. He'd come here with the Stowes from Galnesh Eldador, He'd been a Bounty Hunter for more than two decades.

She walked up to him, a Man with long grey hair and a broken nose, his skin wrinkled with age, and he took her in his arms. They kissed passionately and he ran his fingers through her long, black hair.

He removed the message she'd placed there. She ran her hand into his pants and stroked him, removing a message he had for her.

They kissed again and parted. This had been going on for months. The whole palace spoke of what the Man must be able to do to attract so young and beautiful a girl.

When she was certain she was alone, she read the note, an acknowledgement that her last missive had been received.

No other instructions. At her level of service, she didn't receive updates, just instructions.

She sighed. That could change soon, she knew.

242

＊ ＊ ＊

Vulpe sat his horse, Marauder, next to grandfather's Little Storm and Karel of Stone's pinto pony, on a hilltop to the east of Volkha, the capitol of the Volkhydran nation. Behind them the Eldadorian fleet dropped twenty-five thousand Eldadorian Regulars on the shore.

"We've been detected?" Vulpe asked them.

Karel of Stone snorted. He hadn't come with the fleet, yet he'd arrived here before them. He was wearing his usual smile on his face, as if he found the rest of them funny.

"Unless they're blind," he said. "I have no idea what they think they're doing, though. According to your father, the survivors of their invasion of Eldador are in Hydro. They should be battening down and dropping the bars on their doors."

Vulpe watched the Volkhydrans moving in and out through the city's open gates. He'd expected bells ringing, warriors assembling, perhaps some sort of retaliatory strike, but nothing.

It was kind of a disappointment.

Nina loped up from the assembling troops to where they waited. Vulpe braced himself for what he knew she was about to do, as she'd done to his father a dozen times.

Sure enough, she sprang up onto Marauder's butt and wrapped her arms around his midriff. The surprised stallion snorted and sidestepped, bobbing its head in surprise. Blizzard, he knew, usually reared and tried to bite her.

He felt her cheek on the back of his head. "Your troops will be deployed in less than two hours," she said. "Your commanders await your orders."

Vulpe instinctively looked to his grandfather. The older man kept his focus on the city.

"Send an envoy," he said finally. "That's what I'd do. Give them your terms to surrender the city."

"And have them lock it up tight as a drum?" Karel challenged him. "If they're willing to let us just walk in there, then I say, 'Just walk in.' We can give our terms in person."

That sounded like a much better idea to Vulpe. He wanted to take the city with a battle, but if the Volkhydrans were going to make it this easy, then why endanger his warriors?

Grandfather shook his head. "We have a saying where I'm

from, 'If something looks too good to be true, then it probably is.' Something's going on that we're not seeing."

Karel sighed, Vulpe nodded. "Send in a thousand," he said. "Karel, will you lead them? Deliver our terms, and don't leave the city. Stay by the gate and—"

Karel nodded. "Fine, fine, lad," he said. He shot a dark look at grandfather. "I'm going to have a good laugh at your expense when I come back."

"See that you do," grandfather told him, without looking at him. "Try and bring the warriors back with you."

Karel shook his head and kicked his pony into a trot, turning him back toward the gathering army where he would pick his warriors. Vulpe sat quietly with Nina and grandfather for a while, watching the city, trying to see what the older man was seeing.

Nina kept holding him. It reminded him a lot of his growing up, how she'd always been there for him, looking out for him. He could barely remember a time in his life when he couldn't look around and see her somewhere near him, watching out for danger.

A man now, he almost wanted to shrug her off, however he'd seen her do the same thing with his father when she'd gone with him to battle, while he remained with his mother to witness the things he'd need to see if he ever intended to rule some day.

Now he'd been sent off with Karel, Thorn, grandfather, Nina and his Eldadorian advisors and sub officers to take a city. Even when he rode Marauder with an undersized lance into the Confluni horde in the Battle of the Vice, he hadn't felt his eleven summers so acutely. Then he'd just been part of a thundering mass raining havoc on screaming foot soldiers under his uncle's direction. He'd actually felt his Andaron blood surge at the wanton violence of it.

Now he was sitting back, calculating, giving orders that would affect the lives of others. Now he knew decisions made wrong here would cost his warriors their lives.

Father had grilled him and grandfather and their colonels under him on what he wanted, what he expected and what they needed to do, and he'd been emphatic on one point:

"No matter how much you strategize," he'd said, "and no matter how thoroughly you think it through, when the battle starts, plan for it not to go as you expected. A real leader isn't someone who makes a plan and executes it flawlessly. A real leader is someone who picks up the pieces when it all goes to hell, and wins the day anyway."

Those words played over and over in Vulpe's head. Sitting silent next to grandfather, watching Karel peel off a Millennium from his troops, the Fifth under a warrior named Gartheld Daggonin, he had to wonder how the pieces would fall apart, how he'd pick them up, and what he'd look like to the Fovean world if and when he failed.

* * *

Karel of Stone rode his pony, Trickery, ahead of ten columns of Eldadorian regulars, marching one hundred deep toward the gates of Volkha. They'd left their support more than five daheeri to their east, not that it mattered. These Volkhydrans were on about their everyday lives as if nothing in the world were wrong. He actually toyed with the idea of taking the city himself.

There'd been some changes made to the Eldadorian Regulars—something so secret that, outside of the Daff Kanaar, Lupus' family and those who were actually a part of it, it wasn't even known.

Karel would have called that a secret impossible to keep, however he ran their intelligence across Fovea, and no one spoke of Eldadorian Regulars, only Wolf Soldiers—the most feared warriors on the planet.

Lupus had spoken to him at length about 'counter intelligence,' seeding misinformation with information; giving little crumbs of truth to the enemy, and wrapping them in lies, so no one knew *what* to believe. With that, talk of Eldadorian Regulars performing close order drills and working with dogs was mixed with the idea that they would be disbanded entirely, or brought into the Wolf Soldier fold, or a million other things, likely and unlikely. When the topic of Eldadorian Regulars arose, there came so much else to distract from them that discussing them was pointless.

These musings were interrupted when the city gates loomed up before him, and the city guard stepped up with shields and pikes.

No matter how ambivalent the Volkhydrans might seem to be, the city guard still had to challenge such a large force marching up to their gates. Karel called a halt in order to let a wagon pulled by oxen, and a troop of hooded peasants with bundles on their backs, trudge into the city, their heads down as if they didn't even want to risk looking at these invaders.

The city guard marched twenty strong from the gate to the common market before it to confront them. Behind them, another wagon, this one drawn by a huge, furry draft horse, trundled out, circled by more peasants with more bundles, their heads also down.

Karel straightened on his pony, making sure they could see the silver mark of the Daff Kanaar on his breast. Even the bravest gate guard wouldn't outright shoot someone with *that* mark.

"Your business here?" the sergeant inquired of them, as he might any other traveler to the city.

Karel raised an eyebrow. Major Daggonin, standing next to him, grunted but just kept looking forward.

"Do you mean these thousand, or the *other* twenty-four Millennia that have landed on your shores?" Karel asked him.

The guard looked him in the eye, revealing no humor at the sarcasm, and said nothing. Karel sighed and adjusted in the saddle.

Behind the city guard, another wagon, pulled by oxen, and another troop of peasants with their heads down exited the city unquestioned. Karel looked to see what was in the wagon, however it was covered.

As the last one had been, as he recalled.

The sky was a bright blue—barely a cloud in it. Why bother covering their wares, then?

For that matter, what wares would farmers be carting *from* a port city like Volkha.

Karel turned his head and saw the wagon trail breaking off to the west. To the west lay Conflu. Absolutely no Volkhydran traffic moved by land to Conflu, Karel knew. No one farmed that land—the CNG saw to that.

Karel looked to the east where another wagon, covered, pulled by oxen and surrounded by hooded peasants baring burdens, approached from the road leading north to the rest of Volkhydro.

Exactly what one would expect—caravans from Ulef and Hydro approaching the port.

But then, why not enter through the northern gates?

"Well?" the sergeant demanded. The Man's irritation was plain. Behind him, the other guards traded glances and gripped their weapons more tightly, studiously avoiding looking at the caravans running in and out of the city.

"By Water's wet ass," Karel swore, ripping the collapsible

bow from his thigh. The bow immediately unfolded and tightened on its string as Karel pulled an arrow from the quiver hanging from his saddle horn.

The sergeant's eyes widened in surprise as he ripped out his own sword. Behind him his city watch raised up their shields and lowered their pikes against a charge. Without being told, Major Daggonin called, "To arms!" as the Eldadorian Regulars pulled their own swords and created a shield wall around themselves.

To every side, the peasants and the carts all stopped, looking on, hesitating.

Peasants, Karel knew, didn't hesitate when armored warriors pulled swords. Peasants ran away before they got caught in the middle of it.

"Got yourself a plan, then, shorty?" the sergeant sneered at him. "Because I think your thousand just put a foot in it."

Karel knew he and his pony were going to be the first casualties in this conflict if he didn't get himself out of it one way or another. The old gaffer had been right after all—this had looked too good to be true, and it was.

If he stood his ground, they'd likely attack him. If they retreated then it was definite—they had no reason to let this thousand go be a part of a stronger force when they could trim it off now. If he waited, then nothing good would happen.

"To the gate!" Karel bellowed, and launched two arrows into the sergeant of the guard. Daggonin immediately called for the charge, the Eldadorian Regulars moving forward with the telltale stomp of troops trained by Rancor Mordetur. Karel wheeled Trickery to his left and kicked him into motion down the ranks of the Eldadorians, arrows striking the ground around him. He turned in the saddle and launched retaliatory fire at what archers he could find. Covers flew from wagons and peasants threw off cloaks and bundles as the city's daily traffic revealed itself as a mass of Volkhydran warriors, waiting to converge on an overconfident advancing army.

Karel's sharp Scitai hearing picked up the drums and battle horns of Eldador—Vulpe had seen what had happened and was already coming to the rescue. It would take more than an hour for them to cover six daheeri, heavily armored as they were.

Karel shook his head. It would be a miracle if there were anything but bodies to recover here by then.

* * *

Jack watched the situation at the gates of Volkha explode, and the single Millennium take up a battle formation.

"War's Whiskers!" Vulpe swore. He'd likely picked the curse up from his warriors. "You were right, grandfather!"

"Wish I hadn't been," he said. "You better get your army moving if you don't want to lose that Millennium and see them close the gate on you."

Vulpe sent the order to his colonels, who relayed it to their majors. Faster than Jack could have thought possible, the army lurched forward, their war horns blowing and their feet stomping in unison.

The boom of kettle drums disrupted all of it. Jack had seen these—almost as tall as a man, born on wagons by draft horses, women with huge hammers beating skins pulled tight across them. They rang ominous from their hills to the city.

Jack couldn't imagine what the people in the city were thinking now.

At the gate to Volkha, all of those peasants and tradesmen they'd seen were suddenly armed warriors, and all of the carts loaded with wares were suddenly spewing armed Volkhydrans.

Karel of Stone was bravely leaving the scene, as fast as his pony could carry him, and a few mounted warriors were taking off after him. The pony might be feisty and Karel very light, but he wasn't going to get far before he got a sword in his back.

Jack didn't know exactly why he did it, but he couched his lance and drove his heels into Little Storm's side and, hearing Vulpe calling after him, lit off to the rescue.

The giant black stallion dug his rear legs in draft-horse-style and leapt into a full gallop. Amazingly smooth for so large a horse, Little Storm devoured the distance between the retreating pony and the advancing Volkhydrans, now five in number.

Jack didn't kid himself—he knew from personal experience that the distance he'd cover in just a few minutes would take an hour for their army. He had no skill with his sword—he could barely handle the lance, in fact. The best he could hope for was that the other warriors would break and run, and that didn't seem very likely.

He could stall them, and then Karel could get some distance. If they couldn't keep up with Little Storm, then he could play a dangerous game of cat and mouse until Karel had some legroom, and then run.

He closed on the pony, Karel looking wild-eyed, the pony's mane flying in the wind and the other five horses closing fast. He rode close enough to Karel to look him in the face, then he leveled his lance at the nearest warrior on the left.

The lance caught the armored Volkhydran squarely in the chest. Jack turned the weapon and pulled back on it in an attempt to save it, but the end snapped off like a dry twig, leaving him with little more than a large club. A warrior on his right closed in with his long sword drawn and held low, going for his horse instead of him.

Jack hauled on the reins and pulled the stallion hard over to the right, cutting across the other rider's path. The Volkhydran's horse, a stallion, reared in anger, the off-balance rider flying to the left side.

Jack turned Little Storm as if he would pursue Karel. The other warriors changed directions and came for him instead. Now, he thought, he might at least turn them away from the army; run them out on the plains, and then turn in a slow arc back to the protection of the Eldadorians.

No such luck. The slower horses stayed between him and the troops, on the inside of his circle. They couldn't catch him until the terrain got more rugged, but they could keep him away from his allies until then.

Jack toyed with cutting back to the city and trying to arc around in the other direction when arrows whipped out from behind the Volkhydran warriors. First one, and then the next, and then the third fell peppered with shafts in their necks and armor joints. Sensing they bore dead men, their horses started bucking and rearing, one taking off back to the city dragging a dead warrior by the stirrup.

Jack turned to see Karel and his pony on a tiny rise, barely a hill, with a bow in his hand. Jack didn't know the Scitai could shoot so well, but he was glad of it as he wheeled the big stallion to the right to go collect the errant Scitai.

Karel descended from the rise and dismounted by a dead Volkhydran. He knelt by the Man's waist and cut his purse from his belt. He weighed it in his hand and then he threw it to Jack.

"Here you go," Karel said, offering it up, hilt first. "Spoils of War. If you're going to go riding that horse to the rescue, you ought to be paid for it."

Jack took the pouch and poured the coins out into his hand, mostly copper. "Not so much in pay," he grumbled amiably.

Karel grinned his characteristic grin, climbing back onto his pony. "Like as might," he said, "you could add it to the coin I gave you when you left Galnesh Eldador, way back when."

Jack shook his head. "Guess you're a wise man, made a down payment on his own rescue."

Karel nodded, reining in next to Little Storm. Together they could see the Eldadorians slowly approaching the besieged city of Volkha, where the single Millennia had taken both sides of the city gate and were formed up in a circle, half on either side. Volkhydrans were throwing themselves at the warriors, but couldn't break their shield wall.

"You know, where I come from, we have a saying about Men," Karel said. "Would you like to hear it?"

Chapter Twenty

Perceptions

Melissa found herself back in a little park, by a little stream, dipping her toes in the cool, clear water. They'd just been done, and they looked *fabulous*.

She'd been here before. She remembered the two hills upstream. A doe munched clover on the nearer one, on her side of the stream. The sun beamed down warm and inviting, her skin was already browning under its glow.

She lay naked—she worried for a moment that someone would happen by—someone like Bill, the love of her life, or one of these new friends, whose names she couldn't remember right now.

But she got over it. So they saw her naked? None of them were bashful virgins.

"So this is what you do, now, girlie?" a familiar voice asked.

She remembered the timbre, the slight shake of age. She smelled the Sunflowers perfume without having to turn around.

"Hello, Eve," she said. "Are you going to go for a swim?"

Eve clicked her tongue at her. "No, and I don't think you have time for this foolishness, neither," Eve scolded her. "You been using your power too easy, and now you've hoed yourself quite a row."

"That's me," Melissa said, dipping her toes in and out of the water. A warm breeze blew across her body and gave her goose flesh. "A ho' with a row."

Up out of the water, a girl stepped onto the shore. She had a weathered face, snaggly hair, some of it missing. She had scars, and track marks on her arms. Deep black circles lay under her eyes. She dressed in a yellow t-shirt, tied at her hip, and a fluorescent green mini with no shoes.

"No, missy," Eve told her, "*that's* you, if I hadn't o' turned you from the path you was on."

Melissa sat up straight. She barely recognized herself. The girl smiled through dry, cracked lips, revealing a few missing teeth.

"What?" she demanded. She turned, but Eveave wasn't there behind her. She was alone here, with this image of herself.

"That's the you what was left of you," the goddess' voice informed her. "Mike broke you worse'n you remember. That first time, you was seen by a local boy who was waiting for you on that street corner and, if you'd gone back there to get money for another night's hotel stay, then he was goin' to turn you out."

The girl, this other Melly, knelt down by her toes, between her legs, and laid her dry, cracked nails on Melissa's shaved legs.

"Twenty bucks," she said, her voice a hollow sounding croak.

Melissa scooted back in horror.

"This what you want, girl?" Eveave's voice asked her. "This what you want me to put you back to? Cuz' if you need, I'll do it."

"N—no! God, no," Melissa gasped. "Why—why are you showing me this? What are you doing?"

And then the goddess Eveave stood there, to her left, not friendly Eve, but the imperial goddess, her lips pressed in a thin line of judgment, her eyes flashing with her power.

"You use your power without thought of consequence," Eveave stated, brooking no argument, pointing an accusing finger at Melissa's bare breast. "You float along; do you think I brought you here to watch?"

"N-no!" Melissa gasped. The other Melly touched her feet again. She tried to draw away, tried to stand, but the force of Eveave's presence kept her naked on her back.

"The time has come for you as My instrument to act," Eveave thundered. "You will be tempted, and it will be up to you to keep the balance on My behalf."

"How—how can I?" Melissa asked, before she could think

better of it. "You—the song! The song! We can't keep the people—the weapons—together. We lost Xinto, we lost Jahunga—Bill left us."

Eveave's lips remained in that firm line. "I am not here to provide you answers you already have," the goddess informed her. "However I am woeful of your ignorance, and of your unwillingness to fully analyze My word."

Melissa's mind raced. She didn't know what all of this meant. It was like listening from under water.

"Steel yourself, Raven," Eveave informed her. "Heed the companion whom I have sent to you. Enforce my will, enforce my way—achieve what you were brought here for!

"I am the balance," she thundered, expanding in size, towering over a shrinking Melissa. "I am *the way!*"

With that, Eveave was gone. The other Melly pushed away from her, sank back into the stream, disappearing beneath its surface.

The damaged smile and the sallow eyes haunted her.

Melissa looked around her. Suddenly this place had no comfort for her. She pulled her knees up to her breasts and hugged her legs. The wind blew cold. The doe stood up straight, looked around her and trotted off down the far side of the hill where it fed.

Raven—she'd been called Raven. Raven is what they called her here. Raven had discovered magic, a power within her. Raven had found a way to meld the science she'd come here with, to the magic she'd discovered since arriving.

She focused her will, and concentrated on understanding this place, this park, this stream, wasn't real.

* * *

"They *what?*"

Karl couldn't believe his ears, and yet the wizard had repeated himself twice.

"The Eldadorian army has sailed past us, and made landfall at Volkha," Avek Noir informed them. "I am contacted by our agent who advises your King, Gharf Bendenson, that the Emperor's son, Vulpe Mordetur, and twenty-five thousand Eldadorian Regulars have sacked the port and taken most of the city. What little resistance is left is centered at the palace, which won't hold."

Angron Aurelias watched them from behind Noir, from his litter, his ambiguous silver eyes telling Karl nothing.

They were gathered in the otherwise empty throne room at Hydro. Karl's cousin, Dragor, Duke of Hydro, presided over the Uman-Chi King and his casters, the obese Confluni Ymir, a Sentalan Chairman Ulminar and his people, a Dorkan Wizard of the Black Fist named Krendell, a gaggle of Andarons under Geeguh Digatish of Chatoos, and their own diminishing band, supposedly lead by Glynn.

They'd left Raven with Slurn and their dog in a tower Dragor had emptied for them. She'd barely moved in the two weeks since they'd come here, except to moan. Vedeen had called this a good sign—those with the black mind did nothing.

"I can still detect the Empress—" Krendell began, but Glynn waved him off contemptuously.

"You yourself said you couldn't detect their people, just her," she said. "We fell for a parlor trick, Sirrah, and one so simple it was beneath trying for anyone else. We summoned the Emperor, he played to our hubris, and now the Volkhydran capitol is lost."

"Not lost *yet*," Dragor insisted. "We still hold the palace—"

"Your King will make terms and quit the city," Angron interrupted him. The wizened old Uman-Chi's thin voice still commanded the authority of a King. "I have advised him through our agent, and he has agreed. The King of Volkhydro cannot fall to the Emperor, and the lives of his palace guard will be wasted in defense of the capitol. Meanwhile, he will send fast riders to Teher and Ulef and call out those garrisons."

"The garrison at Sarn, as well," the Ymir drawled from her padded lounge, "promises to relieve the city. We can deliver as many as thirty thousand."

"Volkhydro has no interest in swapping Eldadorian invaders for Confluni," Dragor said. Karl found himself agreeing. "Conflu is lucky enough to be *here*."

The Ymir straightened, but Angron held up his hand. "Your Grace," he said, "when the Emperor takes the city, he will have twenty-five thousand behind the walls of one of your strongest holdings. Unless you are interested in a siege of years, which he can relieve at any time with his own vast army, I must advise you to take what help you may, or at least defer judgment until your own King can advise you."

Dragor crossed his arms over his stomach. He looked sideways at Karl, then clicked his tongue.

"As a resident of Eldador," Vedeen said, "I can inform you in certainty that, if you report twenty-five thousand of the Emperor's troops, then you have seen less than a third."

"Less than a third," Geeguh echoed her. He shook his head, his long, black hair brushing his shoulders, his mustachios brushing his chest. "With an army so vast, how do we stand against the Emperor? How do we march from any city, when he commands the sea as well as the land, and can strike anywhere?"

"Rancor Mordetur can take any city of his choosing," Angron said. "However, he cannot take them *all*, Warlord, and this is his weakness. When the Emperor asserts himself *here*, he becomes vulnerable elsewhere, and our allies know themselves safe."

"Safe to strike him at his home," Krendell asserted. "I must agree with this plan of Angron's. Let Lupus take the city, and then let us march on him in strength. When he asserts more troops to relieve them, then we will strike at him in his home."

"*Then* we will have him," Zarshar said. "That is when my people can swarm up from Toor. Let the Empire be weak, and Swamp Devils *will* feed on its entrails."

As they had one hundred years ago, the Uman-Chi were rallying the people to their cause. Then the Foveans had been at each other's throats, this time they cooperated against a nation and a Man who didn't even exist before.

Dragor shook his head. "You're all eager to fight this battle in my nation," he said. "But my cousin's father and I are pledged to the defense of Volkhydro, and we have fought both with and against the Emperor, and we have employed and fought against the Daff Kanaar.

"And we have seen, time and again, with everything arrayed against him, the Emperor prevail and his enemies fail, even when he faces superior numbers and superior magic."

Glynn actually stepped up at that. "This is why," she said, "the goddess Eveave herself has seen to gift us, not just with prophecy but with champions, these, aligned alongside you."

She crossed the room and stood next to Angron. "This King, with the wisdom of nearly one thousand years, guides us. Surely, you must believe as he does, that we are blessed and *will* prevail."

"You lost four men out of five in Eldador," Dragor told her. "When you faced the Emperor's Regulars, you failed. Not Wolf Soldiers, Regulars. Theran Lancers and Angadorian Knights, then Daff Kanaar.

256

"The Emperor's warriors have Wolf Soldier training," Dragor said, and slammed his fist down on his throne. "How do we face *that*, except at terrible loss?"

Karl had had enough. Dragor and Karl's father had been sworn to the defense of Volkhydro, in his grandfather's tradition, but Karl had taken that oath, too.

"You know me, cousin?" he said, stepping forward.

It galled him. He'd run from this his whole life. The way the eyes turned, the way the room fell silent, for what he'd done, so long ago, not out of his bravery but, as he knew in his heart, in cowardice.

"I know you, cousin," Dragor said.

"Who am I?"

Dragor's eyebrows dipped. "You're Karl, Son of Henekh, son of Dragor, my grandfather, for who I am named–"

"No," Karl said, and put his hand on the hilt of his sword. "Who *am* I?"

"You're the Warlord of Teher, I know—", he began.

Karl interrupted him. "No," he demanded. "How do most Men, most Uman, even the Uman-Chi know me."

Dragor sighed. "You're the Hero of Tamara," he said. His scowl spoke louder than words.

"He turned the Battle of Tamaran Glen," Ulminar of Sental said. An old Uman even by Uman standards, he leaned on a wooden cane, his back bowed, his white hair limp and fine like Angron's.

"We must turn our armies over to him, and march on Volkha. By the end of that march, they'll have Wolf Soldier training. Before you're going to stop this war, you need to match the troops that can out-fight ten times their number."

He pointed at Karl. "There's the one who knows how."

* * *

Lee Mordetur sat the cold, stone throne of Galnesh Eldador, where her father had sat, and fought the urge to kick her feet as some boring Earl droned on about wanting to raise levies to protect his land.

Lee knew already that any Earl could raise as many levies as he wanted or was able, but this one wanted the Eldadorian state to pay for them, and the Shem Hannen had told her three times a day, every day since the end of Weather, that this movement by the Emperor was too expensive, and they couldn't spare any gold.

Of course, the more she couldn't spend it, the more they

wanted it, and the louder and more boringly they complained, as if they could wear her down.

Her little brother had more skill at this than they did. He'd even sing to her to get her to steal plums for him from the larder. If one of them sang now, she'd likely give him some wealth, just to break up the monotony.

To her left, Hectaro stood at attention in his Wolf Soldier uniform, his sword over his shoulder and his eyes set forward. She'd come to wonder what must go through his mind during these boring times at court. At least she got to sit down.

"And so, as you can plainly see, my elegant Lady," the Earl of Lee's Hope informed her. He'd even named his city after her. Her father called this 'sucking up,' but she didn't understand why.

She waved her hand. "Raise levies as you will, your Excellence," she informed him. "We cannot, however, recompense you. We are, after all, at war."

"It is because of the invasion—" he argued, but she raised her hand again.

"Perhaps you need the state to guarantee your loan from the Eldadorian bank?" she offered. She could do that. The Eldadorian bank could lend him coin, and then if he defaulted, Eldador would take his holdings as collateral and install a new Earl who could pay his debts.

Most Earls didn't like that. Dukes could make large land grants and sell leases to raise money. Earls usually had nothing but the taxes on their subjects.

"Perhaps I might be able to increase the taxes on my peasants?" he offered. "Higher taxes will drive many to my levies until they're lowered, and then those that remain will pay for them."

Lee actually had to take a look at the Shem Hannen for that one. Hectar hadn't come to court since speaking with her mother, although he'd stopped fighting her openly. She could sure use his advice now.

"The Emperor has always argued that high taxes limit wealth, not increase it," Haldarch, the oldest of the Shem Hannen, said. When her father didn't pay attention, he sometimes called this Shem Hannen, "Three."

It was a private joke throughout the capitol that he didn't know their names, and was too embarrassed to ask.

"An incomprehensible supposition," the Earl argued, then took a look around himself. Many of the courtiers went stone-faced. No one doubted that the Emperor's economic genius had built the Empire, even if they didn't understand it.

"We will consider, your Excellence," Lee offered. "However, I make no promise."

"Your least consideration is a blessing to a poor, old man," the Earl said. Lee thought that was a pretty stupid close, as he bowed his way out. He had some gray but he was neither old nor poor.

The Man stepped away, and Lee straightened to address the court.

"Before closing," she said, watching the Shem Hannen in her peripheral vision, "a declaration, straight from the Emperor, my father."

That got the whole court's attention. Eyes turned to her throughout the throne room.

"Let it be known, for those who are in need of wealth, for those loyal to the Eldadorian Empire or those who are fascinated with the lineage of the stallion Blizzard, a bounty—a contest, as well, if you will."

She took a breath, she licked her lips, and she announced, "A prize is to be awarded, one of the stallion Blizzard's get, as bounty to the first group or individual who can bring to this court ten horns, matched or unmatched, from the heads of Swamp Devils."

A murmur ran through the court. She herself questioned this. There was one mare left that was considered ridable from Blizzard. They'd managed to seed two draft mares, one of them Little Storm's dame, before her father left, but that was eleven months in the making, and years before delivery.

She called court closed for the day and stood to leave. There had been a secret exit built behind a mural of the first queen of Eldador—Alekanna or something—that everyone knew about because her father used it so often. She exited through there, Hectaro and his squad with him.

"We're going to my rooms," she informed them, absently. "I need a bath and I want to rest before dinner."

"Of course, Highness," D'leer informed her. "Shall I send ahead for your ladies?"

Her ladies. Since she'd started sitting court in Galnesh Eldador, barons had started sending her their daughters to be her ladies. More than anything else, they bickered and gossiped and practiced kissing each other, promising skills their future husbands would stay home from war for.

Her mother would have slapped them all silly if she were here. Where at first she'd liked the novelty of having ladies, none of them could cast, none of them rode and not one of them bore being trusted.

"I think you can handle my hair, D'leer," she said. "I'm tired and don't feel much like listening to them natter."

"Of course, my Lady," she said. D'leer had been with the family so long, she seemed more like a cousin than a Wolf Soldier, not that she had any cousins she knew of. Supposedly Uncle Tali had some bastards, but she never saw them.

She entered her rooms in the Family Tower, D'leer and Hectaro exchanging glances behind her, and she passed her sitting room for her personal baths. The Wolf Soldiers immediately took up positions at her door. She took a look at Hectaro, sighed and said, "Can you behave yourself?"

"My—my lady?" he stammered.

"I need to talk to you," she said. "If I let you in, can you sit behind a screen and behave yourself?"

"As you command, my Lady," he informed her.

She sighed. This might be a bad idea, but she needed someone she could trust to talk to now, and Hectaro had lived his whole life in the palace, and seen a lot more things than she had.

Some trick of her father's made water flow upwards in pipes from the ground and, more than that, made it flow hot if she wanted it. Her polished marble bath could be hot enough to scald her, as she'd learned after she'd moved here, and when she was done the servants didn't need to carry buckets to the windows, she just flipped a lever and the water drained away to nowhere.

She turned a knob to make the water flow now. D'leer set up a screen for Hectaro, her Uman eyes flickering to his beneath her pencil-thin black eyebrows. Some might think her mother would be furious with her for having a man in here while she bathed when, in fact, her mother had done more and worse in their Andaron tradition.

Her people were relatively frank about their bodies.

Hectaro stepped behind the makeshift curtain and Lee immediately shed her dress and kicked off her uncomfortable sandals. Steam rose from the water in the bath, and she closed the drain.

"You heard what was going on in court?" she asked him, knowing he had.

"Yes," he said from behind the screen.

She sank into the tub, about a quarter of the way filled with water already. She felt it soaking into her skin, into her muscles. She'd almost wanted to ride first, but she'd worn a nice dress and she didn't feel like changing.

Maybe tomorrow.

"Every Earl in the country is complaining they have no money and they want to raise taxes," she said. "Those Confluni, and the Daff Kanaar after them raided every farm they could find for forage, and then the Confluni burned even more of them to deny them to the warriors pursuing them."

"Father said that Earls always want to raise taxes, just like Dukes always want to lower them," Hectaro said. "Low taxes bring in more peasants, and then more money. But the peasants look to the Earls to protect them from raiders and brigands for free, and can't pay for themselves for years or more."

"So then if the Earls raise levies, they'll have to spend more gold—"

"They want the levies to raid each other," Hectaro said. D'leer had already opened a glass bottle filled with a green gel and started pouring it on her hair. The room filled with the smell of evergreen oil.

"They used to do that in lean times under Glennen," he said. "Glennen would let them and tell me the strong earldoms would survive, and he didn't need the weak ones."

"Your father doesn't let them do it," D'leer said, absently. "But then, he's not here."

"I can't see where this offer to bring in Swamp Devil horns will alleviate that," Hectaro said. "What gave you that idea?"

She shrugged, though he couldn't see it. "Father wanted it," she said. "I spoke with mother about your father, and then right after, and father wanted this. I don't think it has *anything* to do with starving Earls."

"It doesn't," D'leer said. Her thin, Uman fingers found their way into her thick brown hair, and her nails scratched her scalp as she worked the oil in. Lee spun the knob with her toe to turn the flow of water down as it filled up to where her breasts touched the upper part of her abdomen. She wasn't quite as well endowed as her mother, but then mother had three children.

"Did you see the Andarons in court?" D'leer continued. "They were pretty excited to hear there was a way to get one of Blizzard's foals."

Lee nodded. She knew her Andaron heritage, what they'd offered and what they'd risked to mix their herds with Blizzard.

"Eldadorians are happy with Angadorian steeds," Hectaro said. "If they're collecting levies, they want to raid each other, but they think they can get you to pay for it."

"So they want to get this past me?" Lee said.

"Apparently, yes."

She sighed. "So, what do I do?"

Hectaro was silent. D'leer worked the oil into her hair and then, without warning, pushed her head into the tub. Lee barely had the time to catch her breath, then forced her eyes to stay closed as the Uman worked the oil back out of her hair. Finally the fingers slipped away and she forced her head back up into the air, blowing a spray of mist as she did.

"Hey!"

"What you get when you have trained killers do your hair," D'leer informed her, the grin slight on her face.

"She doesn't do that when she does my hair," Hectaro informed them.

Lee surprised herself with the pang of jealousy that rippled through her. She hadn't thought she considered Hectaro to be anything now that he'd shown himself a coward, and yet here was this girl, who'd taken something she somehow considered hers.

"If you call delousing doing your hair," D'leer said, absently. She stood up and took a step back, the front of her uniform wet, waiting for Lee to finish her bath.

"You can't show any emotion," Hectaro announced from behind the screen.

"Wh—what?" that wasn't what she expected.

"With the Earls," he continued. "Yes, they're trying to take advantage of you, of your inexperience. If you show them any emotion, they'll think they've found a weakness, and then they'll all do it."

"You can't offend them, either," D'leer said. "If they decide to start withholding their taxes, then you'll have Dukes, not Earls, running to your door, and your father needs the support of his Dukes to fight his war."

"But if we let them raise levies, then they'll fight—" Lee began, and then she caught herself.

Her father had told her once of his own land—it stuck in her mind because he *never* spoke of his past—and how the politicians there had become greedy and corrupt, so they focused on almost nothing but their own power and wealth.

"Nobles who have no nobility," he'd informed her, "are worse than common thieves, because a thief only steals from a few people at a time, where a corrupt noble can affect hundreds. Eventually, it was their own suspicions of each other that destroyed the politicians, and let the common people get their leaders back under control."

Lee smiled to herself. She hadn't understood why her father had shared this with her, until now.

Her mother called him a wolf, after all.

"D'leer, send a squad to round up all of my ladies," she proclaimed, standing up dripping in her tub. She'd piled soft, fluffy towels by the wash basin here—another invention of her father's which he called 'terry cloth.' She took one from the pile and wrapped it around her while the Uman woman stuck her head out of the bathing room door.

"Why do you want your ladies?" Hectaro asked from behind the screen. "They aren't going to tell you any different—"

Lee pushed aside the screen for a startled Wolf Soldier/Prince. Hectaro's mouth dropped open to see her in nothing but her towel, her long dark hair limp and wet over her shoulder.

"I think it's time," she said, feeling closer not just to him but to her own father than she ever had before, "for all of you men to realize what we women have always known."

* * *

Lee's ladies in waiting flirted shamelessly with the court barons that evening, Lee presiding over them with an unquenchable grin on her face. Normally she detested the court barons; they had no morals and no property other than high-sounding names and a desire to live off of the Eldadorian state without working. They would take jobs teaching etiquette and riding from time to time, instructing the children of nobles and every girl knew never to be alone with them.

So the mead flowed at her father's table and her ladies flashed their pearly teeth and the clefts of their bosoms to lecherous nobles of varying ages.

As the night wore on, these noble daughters extracted oaths from these men to go to different earldoms, and to advise these Earls, in the name of the Empire, on how to better manage their money.

Of course, the court barons had no idea of how to manage money, and everyone knew it. Her father had become infamous when he'd elevated one court baron to the rank of Duke of Uman City, where he'd done, if not exceeding well, well enough to keep his title and for that port to prosper.

Later, he'd sent a court baron to Britt, and then the Baron of Britt to his death at the hands of the Dorkan Navy. That court baron remained a baron there still, technically subservient to Glynn Escaroth, who couldn't be reduced until her capture.

Why would the Eldadorian state, then, be sending *more* barons out to the Earldoms? The Earls would be speculating and gossiping and, while they did, they would have better things to do than to travel to the capitol, perhaps there to find the reason they were advised by court barons.

Hectaro had laughed richly when she'd told him the plan. He stood in a corner of the room behind her now, and she found herself sneaking looks at him as he stared off into space.

She might have misjudged Hectaro, she thought to herself.

Only time would tell.

* * *

Tartan Stowe had been surprised to hear not only that the princess, Lee, had come essentially to run the Empire, but that one of her first actions had been to alienate Duke Hectar Gelgelden. Hectar, as far as Tartan knew, loved the Emperor and counted him a good friend. Perhaps he'd been offended that Lee, and not he, sat the throne in Galnesh Eldador. Eldador under Tartan's father had looked to Hectar until the Conqueror had come.

Lupus liked to make his own rules.

Now Tartan and one thousand of his Angadorian Knights rode the long trail from Angador to Galnesh Eldador, where the Duke hoped his personal influence could heal any rifts that might be forming in the capitol. While Lupus made war in Volkhydro, someone had to see to things here. No one had been more the Emperor's student than he.

Tartan's wife had reminded him of all of this. As he rode, the Duke reflected at his good luck to have her. At first he'd been warned this marriage had been cast to nullify him. Yeral's family was disgraced, her father executed, and she, although a Lady, left unpropertied; barely more than a female court baron. The Empress had chosen wisely for him, though. Yeral had proven herself a good confidant with a sharp mind. Tartan tended not to want to play politics, taking too seriously the slights and too dearly the praises peers and courtiers laid on him. Yeral navigated all of it more clearly.

Now she remained with his brother, Terran, in Angador, charged with supporting Ceberro and guarding the south. In the unlikely event of an invasion from Toor, it would take weeks for Tartan to return here. Yeral, he knew, even if she couldn't command the armies, could support Terran and J'lek. In worst case, old Nevarre remained to help them.

As he rode, thinking these thoughts, Tartan felt very lucky indeed to be clear of the intrigue in his southern duchy. He took the opportunity to plan the words he might say to mend fences between house Mordetur and house Gelgelden.

Chapter Twenty-One

Conclusions

Slurn lay curled in a corner, in a stone room in a tower, in the palace at the center of Hydro, where Raven lay on a bed stacked with quilts, their dog at her feet, its great slobbering head across her lower legs.

His eyes watched her unblinking as they had for hours. His stomach rumbled at the rat he'd eaten, a smaller palace variety that had all but tumbled into his claws.

His exhalation didn't even stir the dry dust before him. Another female of the race of Men, a servant, had actually stared at him and decided he couldn't be real, and then retired. All of his attention remained on Raven, whose breast rose and fell as she slept.

The dog's head rose suddenly. Only a short second later, Slurn's predator senses detected that the girl had roused—she lay still but did not sleep.

Good for her that she'd learned not to start, as did the race of Men on awakening. That practice made them such easy prey.

The dog stood up on heavy mammalian bones, wagged its tail, turned on the bed to lick her face. Raven's eyes opened, not reacting to the dog's greeting, but staring at the ceiling, as if still wondering at the things she'd seen in her dreams.

Zarshar had informed them of the unimagined Power she'd wielded. Slurn had seen her enter the realm of the goddess, Water, and bend it to her will.

She'd created a channel in Water for daheeri. Clearly this one had the sleeping goddess' favor. This explained to him the adoration he felt for her. Without realizing it, he'd finally found the instrument of Water—the one who would face all other instruments and triumph.

Finally she rose, and looked right at him, Slurn not stirring or doing anything to announce himself, showing Slurn once again that *she* knew her people.

"Where—who? How long, Slurn?" she asked him.

He hissed, not even attempting to speak in the language of Men or Uman. "Ten days. You're in Volkhydro now, in the city of Hydro, in the Duke Dragor's palace."

She nodded, understanding him. This didn't surprise Slurn. They spoke the whispered language of the sleeping goddess.

"I—I tried a spell—that spell," she said, and raised a hand to her forehead. Her hair was greasy and lay almost in ropes from her head. She'd fouled herself in her bed, and Slurn could see she'd become aware of it.

"I need to clean up," she said. She pushed the dog from her and tried to rise. Slurn leapt to her side, his claws as gentle as a mother with her hatchlings, taking her elbow and the small of her back. He guided her to the adjoining washroom, and helped her to sit herself in a wooden basin. They scrubbed her with tepid water that had been kept here for cleaning, and wide, white cotton cloths and some evergreen oil.

She sat silent, her hands on the basin, turning when he needed and waiting for him to be done, collecting her strength. The dog attended them, running back between the basin and the bed, sniffing both of them in the nature of her kind.

Once he'd cleaned her, he fetched her leathers, and he dressed her. Finally he gave her the ruby she'd made for herself when she'd come into her power. Karl had tied a piece of leather around it so she could wear it as a pendent. She tied it around her neck so it sat in the hollow at the base of her throat. She didn't speak the entire time, and he said nothing to her.

It was not in the nature of Water to communicate.

Finally Raven turned to him, looked him in his eyes, took his snout in her delicate hands and held him. Inside, he melted—to be touched by Water's living instrument exceeded any thrill he'd ever known.

"She spoke to me again," she said, in the language of Men. "She told me the time was coming—that I had a decision to make. I've been wondering about that. What am I doing that no one else can do? We're about to find out now, I think. I've got a decision to make, and I'm getting scared that I know what that decision is."

A tear ran down her cheek. Her brown eyes shimmered for the ones she hadn't shed. Slurn's inner eyelid flickered sympathetically, as his eyes stared reverently into hers.

She took him in her arms, embraced him, her breasts pressed against his scales. In the history of Fovea, perhaps they were the first of their two species to do this.

From outside the room's one window, high up in the West wall, the sun suddenly streamed in. It didn't bathe them directly in its light; however it might as well have for how Slurn felt right then.

"I asked for help," she whimpered, "and I was told there's a price. She showed me what I'd have been without her, and when she saved me, I didn't know there'd be a price."

Slurn had no idea what that meant, however he quoted to her:

"They will fall, who walk with her
They will fall, who oppose her
They will fall, for the power
Of the goddess, who chose her."

She pulled away and looked back into his saurian eyes.

More tears, and then she nodded. The hardest thing any of them learned sometimes, Slurn realized right then, was that some things just have to be.

* * *

When Vulpe invaded Volkha, the armies under the Fovean High Council prepared to march to the West to relieve the city and to engage the enemy. No longer needed, the Trenboni fleet, or what was left of it, set sail south for the Silent Isle, to protect the Trenboni nation in case of retaliation from the Emperor.

Admiral Geledar Taboorin in his flagship looked not to the south, but to the east, where he could occasionally see masts over the horizon. Someone's large fleet was moving north, past them, back to Volkha.

There weren't too many large fleets on Tren Bay.

A military man and a strong advisor to the King, he'd ordered the Caster, Duke Haldan Evoprosee, to inform the King and request permission to return and to defend the city.

"Denied?"

The Admiral was incredulous.

"These are your orders," Evoprosee informed him. The effete Duke sipped wine from a crystal glass with a pinky finger extended, his white robes almost glowing in the gloom of the Captain's cabin, which he'd claimed for himself.

"Surely, I understand the importance—," Taboorin insisted, but was rudely interrupted.

Evoprosee wasn't even bothering with the proper forms.

"I must assert," the Duke said, "that you, in fact, understand nothing, and that we, the King's vassals, cannot pretend to his wisdom in this. You have your orders, Admiral, and need hear no more."

Taboorin straightened and, seeing no point in continuing the conversation, extended his forearms in a bare semblance of the appropriate withdrawal, and did so, leaving the gloom of the cabin for the sunlight of the weather decks.

Ten daheeri to the east, a mast peeked up as if to taunt him, and then descended back beneath the horizon.

He remembered a time when Uman-Chi fleets engaged other ships just out of their own curiosity, and answered to no one for it.

If Evoprosee represented the best of his own kind, then perhaps the time had come for those days of supremacy to sink beneath the waves.

Admiral Taboorin, in the back of his mind, began to compose the elegant speech which would announce his retirement.

* * *

Glynn Escaroth had always been familiar with the idea of a nightmare, however it wasn't until the march to Volkha from Hydro that she'd experienced one, and then not right away.

They'd spent a week in the Volkhydran city by the Llorando, Karl Henekhson slowly but surely usurping command of their international army, Geeguh Digatish at his side. It hadn't bothered her to see the armies called in to camp on the plains around the city—she'd seen armies before.

It hadn't bothered her to see them in war games, Karl dividing them into two sides, and those two sides into groups of ten. It hadn't bothered her to see warriors fight, to see them resist Karl, to see him bully and beat them into submission.

She'd seen all of that before.

When they'd left, her sitting her palfrey with Vedeen on her huge roan to her left, Raven on her Angadorian war horse and a man's saddle on her right, and their dog trotting beside them, she'd allowed herself to congregate with her fellows of the song, rather than with her people. She'd prefer the company and the wisdom of Angron Aurelias, but she would settle for the admiration of these lesser species.

That hadn't bothered her, either. She'd grown used to their boorish ways.

Three days march toward Volkha, and she'd heard a sound she hadn't been exposed to in almost a decade, however, and *that* had frozen the noble blood in her veins. Out of nowhere, tenuous at first and then with the confidence of fate, she'd heard the tread that had preceded the Wolf Soldier army, the stomp of thousands of feet, all hitting the ground at the same time.

A mathematical impossibility, embodied in the warriors who'd sworn their oath to the Emperor, filled the plains around her. When Karl heard it, his face split in a wolfish grin. Geeguh Digatish, the Andaron warlord whose name meant 'Bloody Spear,' had pounded him on the back. Their warriors marched a little straighter, their shields held a little higher, at the sound—not just Volkhydrans but Confluni and Sentalans as well—a combined army of nearly fifty thousand, and a supply train that stretched back to the horizon.

The following evening, when they practiced, they were moving back and forth across the plain like pieces on a game board. That night the pickets shone brilliant with pride.

In a fitful sleep, Glynn had seen her father beheaded again and again by the Emperor's sword. That night, she saw her brother spitted on an Eldadorian lance, the sadistic leer of the Emperor's Andaron brother chasing her through the bloody streets of Outpost IX.

Since then, awake or asleep, she saw those images in her mind, punctuated by the drumbeat of their army's tread.

Meditation, though achievable, gave her no solace. Food held no taste. The iron resolve of a Caster saw her through the calamity, however her heart yearned for the two males who had guided her whole life, replaced by the traitor Ancenon, now of her house.

"You are pensive, baroness," Vedeen commented to her, a smile as ever on her lips. A light breeze tugged at her beautiful blonde hair, picking up strands like pennons behind her.

Baroness now, not Duchess. She didn't want the accolades of the Southern Towers and House Escaroth.

"My sleep is disturbed," Glynn said, dismissing her. She'd come to suspect the Druid. The Battle of the Vice had come back to haunt her. Jahunga's questionable death reinforced that doubt. How had the Druid so easily warned Raven, and yet proved so useless in the fight? How had she found Jahunga so close to his being slain, and then escaped the Daff Kanaar so easily? Dilvesh, called The Green One, had proven one of the Emperor's strongest allies—this one must have some of that power to have replaced him.

"The coming battle, perhaps?" the Druid pressed her. To her right, Raven pouted in her own thoughts. The goddess Eveave had visited her again—an opportunity wasted on her inferior mind—and she puzzled fruitlessly over what she remembered of the words.

Now Raven traveled with a hand on her stomach, the tail of her raider's jacket spread out on her horse's behind, exposing her over-full breasts barely held in their harness. Flaunting her sexuality and a pouting lower lip—typical of Men.

"You will be casting for us, no doubt?" Glynn asked her of a sudden. Normally Uman-Chi protocol forbade being so forthright, however even D'gattis had argued that, with Men, a sudden thrust was sometimes called for where a parry seemed more elegant.

Raven and Vedeen both blinked and straightened. They couldn't see where her eyes pointed, so of course both thought themselves asked. This should play out interestingly.

Raven opened her mouth to speak, however she shut it when Vedeen answered, "I am here to observe. I never promised to act."

"The song—the prophecy," Glynn began.

"Surely you've realized I am not the One Who Fights as Does the Sun," Vedeen said, through her smile.

Glynn had grown so accustomed to these lesser races she'd spoken like one, too soon and out of place. She'd forgotten they did that from their own limitations.

"You can hear the song—" Glynn began.

"As can your King," Vedeen informed her. "I think he is not the 'one,' either."

Glynn had to allow herself a little smile. No, Angron Aurelias did not fight as does the sun.

Glynn sighed. "I fear to lose more before we've found that one," she said, finally, then turned her head, leaving no doubt as to whom she meant to address.

Around her, the drumbeat of feet beat the hard-packed Earth.

Vedeen's smile only grew, but Raven answered. "We found 'the One who Fights as Does the Sun' a long time ago," she said.

Glynn raised an eyebrow and gave her protégé her full attention. Perhaps this was some insight she'd been granted from the goddess?

Raven kept looking straight forward as she rode. "Eveave told me I had to be ready, that I had a decision to make, in Her way. I told Her we weren't ready, that we couldn't keep the weapons together. I wanted to tell her we didn't know what to do. She got real mad, and she told me to stop asking questions we already had the answers for."

"So, perhaps Vedeen—" Glynn began, but Raven cut her off.

"*No*, Glynn," Raven said, finally turning on her warhorse to face her. "It isn't Vedeen. Vedeen can leave us any time she likes. Vedeen doesn't even *help* us. All of the ones mentioned in the song felt like they had to come to find me, even you, and they all have to help whether they want to or not.

"Even Zarshar," Raven continued, and turned her face back forward. "You think Buh—um, Jack bound him with that agreement, then attacked us, and Zarshar couldn't twist that around if he wanted? He didn't even try. Vedeen let them attack us before the Battle of the Vice and didn't warn anybody."

The Druid's smile died on her lips, regarding the two of them. Glynn's attention flew between the other females, her mind racing to get to the place where Raven's seemed already to have gone.

"Vedeen," she said at last.

"I am here to observe," she answered, the smile returning to her lips, if not her eyes. "I cannot interfere."

"Take that attitude to the Emperor," Raven told her. "Go ahead. Go observe him, and tell him you were with us, and see if he just smiles and lets you keep your skin attached."

Vedeen actually showed her surprise with that. "The Druids have ever been the allies of the Emperor—"

"No," Raven said. Her sullen face more determined than Glynn had seen in her before. She had changed since her great casting—this seemed certain. Glynn had done the same once. She'd embraced Eveave and began great castings before singing her song.

Chaheff had told her long ago—the casting changes the Caster, as the Caster changes the world around him. She might be closer to understanding that now.

"Lupus doesn't touch your Druids because he needs 'The Green One,' and because Dilvesh is a member of the Daff Kanaar," Raven continued, oblivious to Glynn's musings. "That's not friendship—that's not even respect. As soon as he wants something more than he wants The Green One, he'll do whatever he has to with you."

Vedeen looked down and was silent. Raven had given her much to think about.

"And so—the 'One Who Fights as Does the Sun?'" Glynn pressed her. If she'd received insight from Eveave, then surely Glynn needed to evaluate it.

Raven put two fingers in her mouth and whistled. The dog's head perked up at her side. She snapped her fingers, and she pointed at Karl, ahead of her, carrying a lance now. He'd been practicing with Geeguh and the Andarons at charging.

The dog bound off toward Karl. The Volkhydran Warlord turned at the sound of the whistle, then smiled as he saw the dog approaching. When the beast didn't slow, the smile vanished and he kicked his horse into motion, to get out of her way.

The dog changed direction. Now the horse began to stamp and shift sideways. Others stepped away from Karl, opening a space around him like the reverse of a shadow, cast before the dog.

At the last second she leapt, her giant paws outstretched. Karl went for his sword but he was too late—the dog crashed into him and forced him from the saddle, the warhorse screaming and bucking in a circle dangerously close to the fallen Man.

The dog leapt from Karl and then focused on herding the spooked horse. Two Confluni footmen, smiling to each other, ran to the Volkhydran's side to help him to his feet, from the ground where the weight of his heavier new armor pinned him to the ground.

They could all hear Karl's swearing. One Volkhydran pulled

his sword and approached the dog, who turned on him with vicious teeth bared, taking up of all things a defensive posture over Karl.

Glynn turned to Raven. "Surely not," she said.

"I fear it was very obvious to me," Vedeen said. She turned to Raven. "When did you discover it?"

"As soon as I thought about it," Raven said. "How does the sun fight? It passively shines and takes down everything in its way, then leaves it alone. The sun doesn't celebrate its win, it just continues on, doing the same thing."

Vedeen smiled and nodded. Glynn's heart constricted.

When she informed her King that one of the beings mentioned in her song turned out to be a common dog, he would reconsider how seriously he should regard the warning.

Her mind sought to refuse this, but Caster's logic prevented her. Even as Karl sent a nasty look toward Raven and called his own warriors away from the dog, Glynn realized she would have to embrace this beast, and explain its importance to Angron, hoping the wise King would see as she did, that they were all the same in the eyes of the gods.

* * *

A month after he and eight thousand, five hundred Daff Kanaar warriors had departed Eldador for the north, Earl Arath of Metz looked out from the one standing tower in the remains of the palace at a city once called Katarran—now referred to as Luparran.

Black Lupus' vanity was exceeded only by his avarice, he reminded himself, even as he regretted the city hadn't been renamed 'Karath,'" as he'd wanted.

Hundreds of Uman and dozens of Dwarves labored below him on the reconstruction of the tumbled-down walls, the smashed and burned buildings and the ruined wharves.

A Dwarf with a golden emblem, a sun symbol with a hammer at its center, hanging from a gold chain around his neck and over a beard tucked in his belt, stood next to him. The Dwarf had introduced himself as Kvitch, Ambassador for the Simple People.

Invited here by his Dwarven kinsman, J'ktak, whom Arath knew as Black Lupus.

"How much longer until we're done here?" Arath asked him. Below, he saw Nantar working with some new and veteran troops. Recruiting was always easy in Sental—they'd been sending emissaries across the border, bringing the sons of farmers back.

"Years," Kvitch answered him. "Surely J'ktak told you this."

No, Black Lupus had sent him a scroll, asking him if he was willing to invade the Dorkan nation and retake this city. He had just assumed there'd be an army here. Of course, there hadn't been.

All of the glory to Lupus, all of the work to those around him, Arath grumbled to himself without speaking.

"I didn't even know Dwarves could *be* hired for work like this," Arath said.

A troop of five hundred Dorkan infantry had been marching down the road from the north for hours. Nantar planned to meet them with these veterans and new recruits outside the city walls. No point in letting them in and telling others how far they'd gotten.

"We can't," Kvitch informed him. "However, J'ktak is one of us, and we do this for him out of love."

"Little big for a Dwarf, isn't he?" Arath grumbled.

Nantar marched out to meet the Dorkans. The Wizards were apparently very upset that someone was working on the city they'd left to seed. Nantar was probably informing them this city, Luparran, was a protectorate of the Eldadorian Empire.

Yeah, Arath thought, *they should really like hearing that.*

Kvitch smiled through his thick beard, his stubby fingered hands playing with the chain on his breast. "I have to believe you know of the Battle of the Two Mountains and how J'ktak came out of the north," he said.

Of course Arath knew that. Everyone knew that. Of all of his secrets, that was one Lupus was freest with.

Anything to tell the world what a great general he was!

The Wizards shook their fists at Nantar. Knowing his friend, Arath didn't expect that to go well, either.

"You should be able to bring merchants and peasant workers in before month's end," Kvitch added. "We'll leave then. Your walls will be strong enough for a good fight, and your streets will be smooth and straight. I advise you to let people build their homes and businesses as they would."

One of the Dorkan wizards raised a hand, white with power.

Nantar didn't react—D'gattis, however, on the wall behind him, did. Lightening descended from a clear blue sky and struck down both Dorkan Wizards.

The Dorkan infantry scattered. Nantar ran them down.

'Third time that has happened—you'd think they'd learn?' Arath pondered to himself.

"Probably a good idea," Arath agreed out loud, turning from the tower's open window.

* * *

Before the advent of the Fovean High Council, most of the fighting going on along Tren Bay had occurred in or because of Volkhydro, and so it made sense for the place where peace might be parleyed for to be built there, as well.

That city had become the unwalled ruin called 'Medya.' It had been constructed more for meeting than for living, with wide barracks and a coliseum, staging areas and low-slung establishments that could be renovated quickly for visiting dignitaries.

Vacant for almost one hundred years, it now housed rats and peasants and a few herd of cattle. Believing the government no longer had an interest in it, regular Volkhydrans, especially those who didn't want to live in the shrinking cities and wandering tribes to the north, had relocated to this place under their own autonomy.

"I didn't even know this place still existed," Karl admitted, still on the back of his Eldadorian warhorse. Around him clustered the Santalan, Andaron, Dorkan and Confluni leaders, as well as Glynn, Zarshar and Raven.

"How can simple peasants manage themselves without nobles?" Glynn insisted. Raven shot her a look but said nothing. "They should be at each other's throats."

"They've been fighting someone," old Ulminar from Sental pointed out, a stick-finger with a long nail pointing to the northern edge of an outlying mansion. "See where someone tried to break in through there and was turned?"

Karl saw the scarred walls and nodded. Low-grade magic and the footprints of soldiers wearing cleats told him everything he needed to know.

The Uman-Chi already had Sentalans building them a palisade. Angron didn't need to be told what would soon happen here.

As the sun beat down on them in the middle of the month of Chaos, Karl squinted north toward the hills. He couldn't see them, but he had no doubt someone would be watching him from there.

Somewhere to the north, Vulpe Mordetur or troops sent by him would be waiting to meet them, not in the city but on the plains, in a one-to-one fight they believed they could win easily.

"Geeguh," Karl said, without looking to find him, "send ten squads of warriors into the city to see what the locals can tell us. Krendell, pick one of your junior Dorkan wizards to go with them—I need someone who can talk to them and report back to us right away."

Krendell sat a destrier of his own, a big, shaggy beast more like a draft horse than a charger. His purple robe draped across his giant paunch, hanging from his forearms with dagged sleeves. Sweat dotted his shaven head—his earrings and gold chains glinted in the bright sun.

"Why not send in one of your own Volkhydrans?" he demanded. "Surely you've an Earl or something—"

"They'd as like attack another Volkhydran," old Ulminar pointed out. "This city isn't supposed to be here. They're more afraid of their kinsmen than they are of you, especially if they've been attacked already."

Krendell nodded. He put a finger to his temple and made an expression of some great effort—more likely for effect than any pain it caused him—and quickly stopped and informed them, "It is done."

Karl nodded. He looked to the north. He would have liked a smoke trail, a dust cloud, perhaps to see a scout on top of a hill, but he had no such luck. Whoever watched him, if any did, they were good at it.

Karl wasn't sure what he would do if his enemy had bypassed Medya and were on their way to Hydro. They could have passed south of the advancing Eldadorians, and then he might lose two cities, both vital ports, rather than one.

That would not sit well with his people, his allies or the Fovean High Council.

* * *

Vulpe watched the Andarons enter the city of Medya from the relative safety of a cluster of hills to that city's north, mounted on Marauder.

Seated behind him, Nina observed, "You were right—they're scouting the city before they come too close."

Grandfather nodded from Little Storm. "Karl's no fool," he said. "I don't know who's running their army, but Karl wouldn't let them just march into the city. This is his nation—they're listening to him now."

"More than listening to him," Karel of Stone pointed out. He sat his pony with his wrists across the saddle horn. "Look at that formation—he hasn't just got them working together, he's got them in squads, and those Andarons have lances."

"The Emperor warned as much," Nina commented. Her voice was strained. She was making them appear to be an outcrop of trees on the top of a hill, or something like it.

Vulpe's army included four colonels—two of them were here. As well, Drun the Wolf Soldier, who'd been with him since he'd come to man, stood as he ever did at his side. He didn't go one hundred feet that Drun didn't find him.

Vulpe nodded. He'd questioned why they'd come here with no cavalry to face some of the toughest warriors in the world; especially considering they *knew* Uman-Chi were involved, and that meant every nation on Fovea was involved.

Now he knew better. According to his spies this army included over 50,000, with Andarons and Uman-Chi support.

He had twenty thousand Eldadorian Regulars. He'd left a little less than five to hold the city. At odds like this, no one would expect Wolf Soldiers to prevail—not against similarly trained warriors.

He'd been reinforced by ship two nights before. He'd expected warriors—he didn't receive them. He'd expected horse—he didn't get that either. Crates and crates of spears, and his father's *special forces*, never tested in battle. An experiment no one believed in, Vulpe included.

He'd expected the Emperor and hadn't seen him, either. His father had told him what he wanted, he expected his son to do it.

Vulpe smiled. Well—that was the point, now, wasn't it?

* * *

North of Vulpe, a Volkhhydran farmer and his children, three strong boys, tilled their field. They grew corn—this was good soil for it. His father's father had started a farm here, and his father had grown it.

They'd seen a lot of things change in Volkhydro. There'd come the peace, before which his grandfather had sold his goods to the armies that were always marching out to fight someone else's battles. They'd seen the coming of the new wars, when they did the same thing again. They'd seen the Empire grow and so many Volkhydrans leave here for promises of a new nation, but the farmer hadn't joined them.

He had a good life here. Strong sons and brothers, beautiful sisters and a wife who loved him. In this part of Volkhydro there weren't a lot of people who called themselves 'nobles,' so it was rare anyone ever came by to collect taxes.

So it was a real shock for him and his children to see a cloud of dust rise up from the hills to their northeast, then to hear the clatter of hooves carried on the wind. It wasn't long before they saw the forerunners of an army coming their way.

He sighed. The horses always came first, then the marching warriors. They'd heard from a passing merchant there were armies moving to their south. The farmer didn't care much about that—so long as the fighting stayed there, and it like would. Warriors fought for cities, not farms.

"Tell your mother," the farmer said to his youngest boy. "That troops 'r comin'. Get the dogs inside so as they don't bark at the horses."

He turned to the other boy. "Harvest what's near ready," he said. He knew a hungry army would raid him—he might as well get what he could. He himself would go move the aurochs to a gulley he knew of.

He sighed. He'd been through this before, he would again. Moments after his son ran in the house, his two sisters ran out in the direction of their nearest neighbor.

Word would pass—people would batten down. When it passed they'd get on with their lives.

These things happened.

* * *

Tartan Stowe entered the gates of Galnesh Eldador with one thousand knights, not to any cheering crowd as might the Emperor, but to dozens of confused looks and a few guards sprinting off in the direction of the palace.

He didn't do anything to stop them. He'd sent heralds a day before. He wanted the Princess to know he had come.

None of his knights spoke as he trotted down the main way. His eyes scanned the crowd for the Wolf Soldier escort he knew would soon surround him. J'her had been responsible for the security of Galnesh Eldador for over a decade, and he hadn't kept that post by letting armies wander the streets of the capitol.

He'd traveled barely more than a daheer when he saw the

Supreme Commander of the Wolf Soldier pack, seated on a gelding in the center of the main way, no less than fifty squads marshaled behind him.

"Your Grace," he said, as Tartan approached him, making a fist over his heart.

"Your Excellence, Supreme Commander," Tartan responded, and returned his salute.

"You are welcome here," J'her informed him. Tartan had a hard time believing it with so many elite troops arrayed in front of him. "Shall I escort you personally to the Princess, and offer your tired warriors the comfort of the barracks?"

Separating him from his warriors, and putting them outside of the palace gates, with him inside, Tartan thought to himself. He'd seen the Emperor do the same thing, but only with the warriors of those whom he didn't fully trust.

These were not good times.

"I am honored," he said.

"My warriors will escort yours," J'her said. "Of course, the Princess craves your wisdom as soon as she can receive it."

"I will help her in whatever way I can," Tartan promised. "I must also see his Grace, Duke Hectar. I would not presume to enter his city and not acknowledge him."

J'her nodded. "As soon as is expedient," he promised.

"Immediately, I think," Tartan said.

Tartan knew J'her—one of Lupus' most trusted Wolf Soldiers. When Lee had been a suckling infant, J'her had been one of those who stormed Outpost IX on the *idea* that they meant to capture Lupus' family. Now J'her could be relied upon to protect Lee from any threat, real or perceived. Coming here with his warriors, Tartan must have struck him as such a threat.

But J'her knew Lupus' business better than most Wolf Soldiers, as well, and a part of that had to be that Lupus the Conqueror needed the support of his Dukes right now, to keep the homeland safe while he expanded. A warrior would want to keep important men apart, to keep them from plotting or planning outside of the Emperor's designs.

A politician would realize the Dukes would do it anyway, and it was better to be in on those plans than the reason for them.

J'her nodded again, his Uman features set in the stern look of a soldier. "Of course, your Grace," he said. "I am at your service."

Tartan nodded to his lead knight, Lieutenant Radmon Rukh. "Go with them," he said. "Care for the horses and the men."

The knight nodded. All but 100 of the Wolf Soldiers peeled off smartly from the main, marching through the street with the Angadorian Knights behind them.

"His Grace, Hectar, is in his personal residence, just outside the palace gates, if you will accompany me," J'her informed him, lowering his head and sweeping his hand before him from his saddle. He straightened his back with a grin.

Tartan grinned back and shook his head, reining his horse in beside J'her's. "When your herald arrived, we were all surprised," J'her informed him. "You aren't supposed to be here, you know."

Tartan nodded. "I'd heard rumors of strange things in the capitol," he said. "Hectar and Lee were at each others' throats, then court barons had spread out into the earldoms as advisors."

Tartan grinned a wide grin. "A plan concocted by the Princess and Hectaro, Hectar's son," he said. "I didn't approve of it at first. Earls were petitioning for the right to raise levies, and seeking gold from the empire to finance them."

Tartan felt his forehead furrow. "They usually only want to raise levies when they plan to pillage each other," he said. That rarely happened under Lupus' rein. Under his own father, Tartan knew it to be more common.

"The Battle of the Vice and the invasion leading up to it was an expensive win for the farmers whose land it was fought on, and whose farms the enemy was chased through," J'her said. "The Emperor called that part of Fovea the 'bread basket' of Eldador."

Tartan shook his head. "Sounds like something he'd say."

J'her shrugged. "Court barons in the earldoms have the earls wondering if perhaps Lee is thinking of renaming some titles," J'her said. "She keeps them worrying about other things rather than coming begging for money."

Tartan smiled as they rounded a corner tower in the palace's outer wall and found themselves at the walled villa where House Gelgelden resided.

Where the walls in Galnesh Eldador were close-cut gray stone, the outer walls of the Gelgelden villa were sandstone, ochre in color. Where most walls had towers, the villa relied on platforms set behind the walls. Where almost any wall had gates, the villa sported an arch with a portcullis, no more.

Wolf Soldiers guarded the entrance. Tartan would have expected Eldadorian Regulars; however they might all be otherwise involved.

Both the Duke and the Supreme Commander dismounted, handing their reins to waiting Wolf Soldiers. J'her nodded to the gate guards and passed through without question. Their escort waited outside of the gate. Just within the portcullis lay a circular garden with a fountain at its center. The ground had been paved in brickwork rather than cobblestones, and white marble benches sat back among the plants that bloomed red and blue and violet around them.

Hectar Gelgelden sat on one of these benches, watching the humming birds that congregated around his blooms.

"Your Grace," Hectar said, without standing or even diverting his attention. "Your Excellence, Supreme Commander."

Tartan nodded and crossed the garden to the bench where Hectar sat. The older Man wore a green, crushed velvet doublet and hose, a rapier at his hip, and short riding boots. His long hair hung gray around his shoulders.

Hectar didn't acknowledge him, even then. J'her hung back as protocol demanded. Tartan ignored the Supreme Commander and focused on his brother Duke.

He sat, and waited for a few moments for Hectar to make his move. When that didn't happen, he cleared his throat and asked, "Is your son well?"

Hectar snorted and smiled a bitter smile. "He serves among the Wolf Soldiers," he said. "I'm told it improves his fortunes."

Tartan frowned. "The Wolf Soldiers are the most respected—" he began.

Hectar turned and slammed his hand down on his thigh. "Name me a Duke, an Earl, even a Baron who served among them," he demanded.

Tartan straightened. "Me," he said, simply.

Hectar looked him in the eye. "You *never* wore the tabard, slept among them, stood a watch," he said.

Tartan frowned. He said. "I marched among them, held a sword with them, trained with them and stood their watches. I'd have worn the tabard and been proud."

Hectar looked away and was quiet for a long moment.

"In fact," J'her said, grinning, "you stood more than one watch on the plains of Andoron."

Both Dukes grinned to themselves, for different reasons.

"When your father ruled," he said finally, quietly, "I all but ran his kingdom. I never aspired to the role of Heir, but always assumed it would be yours or mine.

"When Lupus rode in on his white charger," he continued, "with a way to make money from less, and a way to win battles with few, your father named him, and I was glad, because I saw a Man who controlled himself well, and who brought more power to Eldador."

"Father always loved you," Tartan informed him, "but he saw himself in Rancor Mordetur, and Lupus' victories as his own."

"Which I accepted," Hectar said, "until it became clear Lupus meant to run his own empire, his own way, and we who had served *so* long, and *so* well, were relegated to the role of vassals."

"Such as with your son," Tartan pressed him.

Hectar looked away.

"You've set your aspirations for your son," Tartan said, "and made no secret of it. The Princess adores him; he might then be marked as—"

"Vulpe commands the Eldadorian Regulars," Hectar interrupted him, and stood, walking to the fountain. Tartan followed him.

"He has the capitol of Volkhydro to his name," Hectar said, without turning. Tartan realized he was talking to J'her now. "He's pressing east, and will take Medya next, and then Hydro.

"Three cities before he's thirteen years of age—who do you think Lupus the Conqueror is grooming as his Heir?"

J'her's eyes shifted between Tartan's and Hectar's, before he responded.

"Your Grace," he said, "if you want my honest opinion?"

"Always."

He looked down, and sighed, and looked back up.

"I've seen Lupus the Conqueror wade into a Confluni army at the Battle of Tamaran Glen, and stand alone with nothing but his horse and his sword at the Second Invasion of Thera. I've seen him risk all when another man would have considered himself lucky to flee, and emerge stronger.

"Frankly, your Graces," he said, "I expect he'll outlive us all."

Chapter Twenty-Two

Clash

Princess Lee Mordetur sat the stone throne of Galnesh Eldador, watching Tartan Stowe stride up the red carpet toward her. Courtiers to her left whispered and speculated. Shem Hannen to her right stood grim-faced, waiting. She'd wanted to avoid this meeting, but her advisors had informed her she had to receive so important a Duke personally and formally.

Tartan was smiling, but she knew him well enough to recognize it wasn't real. He'd decided he had to mollify her, and that meant he wanted to tell her something she didn't want to hear. Duke Hectar Gelgelden had taken a seat in the gallery moments before Tartan's arrival. That didn't take much guessing.

Tartan stood in the open space at the foot of the throne. He inclined his head, and said, "Your Highness."

"Your Grace," she answered him, inclining her head as well.

There were 100 Wolf Soldier guards concealed around the throne room. One of them was Hectaro. Suddenly she wished she could see him, staring forward, pretending not to care what was going on around him, but actually listening to it all.

"I am come on advice of the Dukes Hectar and Ceberro," he informed her. "We are concerned of goings on in Galnesh Eldador, and of difficulties you're having, and wish to let you know we will help you in any way we can."

Wish to take it over for you, in your father's name, he meant. Lee straightened her back and forced herself to smile, as she'd seen her mother do. Shela did this when something had been said to anger her. Lee didn't expect they would take that meaning with her.

"Your help is, of course, appreciated," she informed Tartan. The Shem Hannen had informed her she could tell him nothing else. Send him away and it would be very easy for Tartan Stowe and his Angadorian horses to make trouble for the empire.

"Perhaps we shall meet in my father's advisory," she offered innocently. "You and Hectar could instruct me—much as my mother and father have?"

She kept that sweet smile pasted on her face. She'd been told to be more chatty with him, to flirt with and disarm him, before she made this offer. She couldn't, though. Suddenly, she couldn't stand this. She wanted to be out of here. She wanted to see Hectaro.

She wanted her mom.

Tartan smiled and inclined his head again. "Of course, your Highness," he informed her, "I don't mean to instruct you—"

"Don't be so *modest*, Duke Stowe," she said, the smile almost aching now. "You are of Eldador's highest and most respected house. My father regularly refers to you. I'm eager for your opinions."

Her father would have used that funny word, 'schmaltzy,' to describe this way of flattering him, but it had worked on Tartan before.

He grinned ear-to-ear, then got himself back under control and straightened. "If I may be excused to settle my men and take a little rest from a long journey, then, your Highness?"

She almost told him, 'Of course, Galnesh Eldador is yours,' as she'd heard her father say. In this case, she'd been warned such an offer would see Angadorian Knights relieving Wolf Soldier guards throughout the palace. Her father had done so with as many warriors at his first opportunity. Instead, she used one of her father's funny phrases, "Take your time, your Grace. I await thee."

He bowed out of her presence and finally turned to stride back out of the throne room. In the gallery, Hectar's expression betrayed both shock and indignation. Lee had to guess he'd expected something angrier and more forceful from Tartan.

When they met again, Hectar would be mean and pushy. Lee had been there with him, and she knew how to handle that.

She'd done it before.

* * *

Zarshar watched their Volkhydran warriors as they assembled a huge structure on the plains east of Medya. They carried timbers, dug holes, lashed them with strong rope and, in less time than he'd have thought possible, were assembling a platform which would rise fifty feet in the air. Raven would stand atop it with their other casters, and from there the spell casters would support their army.

Normally suicide for a caster to stand out so unsupported, but this was Raven, and Raven *wanted* to be attacked.

Slurn stepped up next to Zarshar. The two of them were inseparable now—if this song of Glynn's had done nothing else, it had accomplished that. They stood together, watching, waiting. The sun crossed the sky and the summer breeze blew in from the north. Zarshar had something to say, but he wanted Slurn to talk first.

Slurn hissed and the Swamp Devil finally nodded. "You know Jack, or the Mountain, or whatever it calls itself these days, is with them, don't you?" he asked.

"We all saw him at the Battle of the Vice," Zarshar answered, not turning away from the platform. He'd discussed this with Karl.

"If one of those mentioned in the song can turn against us, then either we don't understand it, or it means nothing," the Devil added.

Slurn's forked tongue flicked out to taste the air as he considered that. For months now, the song had been a central part of their lives. To say that it meant nothing…

"As well," the Swamp Devil continued, "Raven has convinced Glynn *a dog* is the One Who Fights as Does the Sun. What kind of prophecy relies on a dog?"

"Then why can't anyone sing it?" Slurn hissed. "Why can only certain people hear it? If it is treachery, then why not spread it far and wide?"

Zarshar bared his red fangs. "If just anyone can hear it, then it's just a song," he said. Slurn hissed and Zarshar nodded. "This makes it seem more like a prophecy."

Slurn shook his head. "But who would tell the lie?" he asked. "The Uman-Chi? Men? Who is trying to trick us into thinking we were following a prophecy?

"Magic strong enough to pull you from your Swamp, to draw me, to pull Jahunga from Toor and Karl from Volkhydro and Jack and Raven from another *world*—that is strong.

"That is the power of a god."

Slurn hissed, looked like he would leave and then turned back to him. He hissed the words:

"They will fall, who walk with her
They will fall, who oppose her
They will fall, for the power
Of the goddess, who chose her."

Zarshar said, "Not a very good omen, if you want to believe.

"We have a saying in the Swamp of Devils, Slurn. Death is the only promise Life keeps. A baby screams as he leaves his mother, because the first thing he realizes is that he's doomed."

"Fitting from a Swamp Devil," Slurn added dryly.

"The worst fear is of the unknown," Zarshar said. "What you can't face, what you can't admit to yourself. When you embrace your fate, you aren't afraid of it anymore. That doesn't mean you throw yourself on your spear. It means you know there is likely a spear out there, on its way to you.

"No—I don't believe in the song anymore, Slurn," he said. "I'm fighting this now because I've come to find faith in what we're doing."

* * *

Jack sat Little Storm next to Vulpe on Marauder, Nina of the Aschire sitting behind the Prince in his saddle.

The girl never let him out of her sight now. If Vulpe actually *were* his grandson, he'd be advising the boy there were things girls did based on opportunity.

Vulpe called him 'grandfather.' Warriors called Vulpe Lord General or by his first name, and meant it like when they called his father Lupus. Tough enough on an eleven-year-old.

"Why build a platform?" Vulpe asked him.

"So you'll attack it," Karel of Stone answered, from his pony.

He sat on the other side of the Prince, and Jack could barely see him.

"Why else?"

"So…don't attack it?" Vulpe asked.

Jack shook his head. "You have to attack it," he said. "If you don't, they'll have a strong point to rally around that you can't affect. What we really need to know is *how* to attack it."

"To know that, you have to know what it's for," Karel informed them.

"I sense strong magic from it now," Nina informed them. "It wasn't there before. Wards of some kind. I wish Shela were here—she'd know."

"Aren't we facing Uman-Chi kind of light for spell casters?" Jack asked them. All heads turned. "I mean, I know Nina's trained with Shela, but—"

Vulpe raised his hand. "Nina won't be fighting Uman-Chi," he said. "She's here to protect me. She's been doing it all my life."

She wrapped her arms around him and gave him a squeeze.

"Well, then— "

"When we need spell casters, we'll have them," Karel said. "We aren't stupid, Jack. We are Daff Kanaar. We know how to make war."

"But not about this platform thing," Jack said.

That shut them all up. They knew they were up against the Uman-Chi, and the Uman-Chi had the wisdom of centuries. Lupus had beaten them in the past, and repeatedly, but his secret had always been to take them by surprise, and he also wasn't here.

Jack sighed. "If they know about us, and they seem to, then the faster we hit them, the better our chances. They're still bigger than we are—we can't let them dig in, too."

Vulpe looked up at him, and suddenly reminded him of the kid telling on his sister for stealing plums almost five months ago.

"It's your army, Vulpe" Karel said. "So you can do with it what you want. Seems to me they have a lot of mouths to feed, after a pretty mediocre harvest this year. If we just hold 'em here, we have a good chance of them turning on each other and just going home."

"Will they do that?" Jack asked.

Jack couldn't really see Karel of Stone nodding, but he sensed it. Underneath him, Little Storm stood stock-still. "If there's one thing the Fovean nations have in common its mutual hatred of each other.

The Volkhydrans hate the Confluni; the Andarons hate them, too. Dorkans don't get along with Sentalans, Toorians don't trust anyone. Neither do Confluni. There's only one person I know who could keep them all together like this, and Nina claims to have killed him."

She had, Jack knew, because he'd seen it.

"My father doesn't want us to just hold them here," Vulpe said, not looking at the Scitai. "My father wants this army beaten, and that's what we'll do."

Jack's eyebrows shot up. For a second he heard Lupus' voice in the boy.

"At dawn?" he asked, also not turning.

"That worked for us before," he said.

Jack pointed out the outer buildings on the north end of Medya. "We'll move back west, then come at them right from there, use that as our anchor. Take those buildings tonight and set up protection for our archers, from the height advantage."

"Anchor on the right side?" Karel challenged him.

Wolf Soldiers usually tried to get some sort of anchor on the left, where their shields faced and their weapons didn't. For a Wolf soldier on the front line to hold off a warrior to his left, he had to break ranks with the shieldman to his right and open up their line.

"They'll see what they expect to see," Jack said. "When they come at us with almost three times our numbers and we don't run away, they'll be suspicious enough."

* * *

Angron Aurelias sat alone in the pathetic pavilion that represented the best that Volkhydrans could provide for him as a royal suite. In Outpost IX, they'd offered the Emperor several rooms, a sitting room, a library, art and a staff. Here, he was reconciled to an old bed in a single tent that served as meeting room and sleeping chamber, and a small wooden conservatory for his personal prayers.

The place wasn't even blessed to Adriam.

Ever the stoic, the King of Trenbon overcame all of these distractions and he focused his mind.

This ruse had been necessary if uncharacteristic for an Uman-Chi. He'd heard Glynn's song, and he'd known exactly what to do.

"They will fall, who walk with her
They will fall, who oppose her

They will fall, for the power
Of the goddess, who chose her."

Pick either side, and one is doomed. Pick no side, and be overrun. A word puzzle, one worthy of the superior Uman-Chi mind.

Pick both sides and survive.

Angron couldn't count the number of times the Emperor had been described as a force of nature. Get him moving in one direction, and he'd destroy everything in his path. Many had sought to stand in that path and weather the storm, and all had failed.

Angron had gotten the storm moving. He'd whipped up the anger, he'd put the Emperor on a path, and now he appeared to stand right in front of it.

But that wasn't the way to beat the Emperor. The Emperor, in the end of it all, would have some inconceivable surprise, and it would explode in all of their faces. Angron didn't need to know what it was to know it existed.

So instead he wouldn't stand in that path. In the end, he wouldn't weather the storm.

He would come in from behind.

* * *

Morning dawned red on 17th day of Chaos' month, coloring the spires of Galnesh Eldador for a Princess who couldn't sleep, cuddling another who simply missed her mother.

"Maaa maaaa!" little Chawny whined, knuckling her eyes. Lee could sympathize with her—she wanted mama, too.

She had to go to see Duke Stowe in the tower where she could speak with her mother. She'd already been informed the Empress needed her, so this made for a perfect time to bring Tartan back in on her father's side. Shela could talk to him, and to Hectar, as she had before, and assure them of whatever they needed to be assured of.

She stood and handed Chawny off to the wet nurse. She needed changing anyway. Chawny reached for her, making gripping motions with her fingers, tears on her cheeks. Lee's heart melted for her, but she couldn't stay. Mother didn't like to be kept waiting.

She almost brought the baby, but Hectar and Tartan would be there. She didn't want to look like a little girl with her baby sister.

She turned her back to the baby crying, D'leer and her

personal squad falling in behind her, Hectaro at its center. The tick of Wolf Soldier heels filled the hallways around her as she crossed the palace for the royal tower where Central Communications had been established.

She didn't speak the whole time. She had nothing to say. Her mind played over the words she might speak to Hectar and Tartan, but they all rang hollow in her ears.

She hadn't come up with anything by the time she'd climbed the steps and stood face-to-face with Tartan Stowe and Hectar Gelgelden. They exchanged pleasantries and Hectar nodded to his son, who of course ignored him. Together, they entered the chamber to face the image of the Empress.

* * *

Gharf Bendenson stood nearly as tall as the Emperor, and had more scars. He wore shaggy fur leggings and left his meaty forearms, breast and shaggy belly bare. He sat a gigantic horse nearly as big as Little Storm, with a retinue of warriors behind him, proud Volkhydrans.

Karl could have been one of them if he'd wanted, but now he thought they just looked stupid. From his own Angadorian warhorse, he regarded his King, then turned his head and spat on the ground.

Geeguh Digatish smiled wide next to him. Others didn't.

"This is *my* land, and I command this army," Gharf insisted.

He faced Karl directly, the rising sun putting Karl's shadow on him. Behind Karl, Geeguh Digatish, his own cousin Dragor, Ulminar of Sental and Zarshar backed him.

In Wolf Soldier formation, 10,000 Confluni warriors, another 20,000 Sentalans and 15,000 Volkhydrans and 10,000 Dorkans stood behind *them*, 10,000 Andaron horse with lances to their north.

Bendenson had brought 1,000, and his title.

"In battle, the Warlord of Teher leads," Dragor said, backing Karl. "That's him, not you."

"They *took my city*," Gharf roared, shaking his fist, spit flecking his red beard. Beneath him, his horses bobbed his head and took a few steps. "My warriors want *blood*."

"They'll have it," Karl promised. "But I've trained these warriors, and I've commanded them, and I'm not going to have you undo everything I've done."

"I'm your King," Bendenson informed him. "It's my *right—*"

"Bite his head off?" Zarshar asked, unusually calmly.

All of them went quiet.

Zarshar stepped forward. He could still look Gharf right in the eye, atop his horse. "One word from him, and I swallow your throat."

The red eyes flashed. Bendenson swallowed, then looked for support from Karl.

"I'm sworn to defend him," Karl said. "I think you'll find Angron Aurelias and a Chairman from Sental, along with some Ymir from Conflu by the platform. I think you need to talk to them."

"I'll talk to them," Gharf said. "And then to you, Karl son of Henekh, and you best be quite a hero when you face *me* without *that*."

Zarshar bared his red teeth, and Gharf shot him a look as he passed. None of them spoke until his warriors were out of earshot.

Karl stayed focused to the west. The Eldadorian Regulars formed up north of Medya, using the city to anchor their right side. If Vulpe followed his father's tactics then he wouldn't charge, he'd wait, and Karl knew every tall building would be loaded with archers.

If he charged them, he'd run right into the teeth of it, and if he didn't, then this army would tear itself apart. He knew Gharf Bendenson wouldn't stay afraid of Zarshar forever. Eventually he'd just demand the Volkhydrans flock to him, and most would.

Karl knew his brothers, and they wanted a fight. Those troops stood on Volkhydran soil.

"We'll march in five hundred squads across," Karl said, finally. "I don't see barricades—they expect a straight fight. I want to keep close ranks until we're right on them, then we'll break up and circle to the north—let them be surprised when they can't run."

"Arrow fire?" Ulminar asked him.

"Have the last row sling shields and pikes and walk firing as soon as we're in range," Karl said. "We have our shields—we'll get some protection from them until we can pin their archers down with ours."

Geeguh nodded. "I'll circle north," he said. "Flank them—even if they see us coming, they won't be able to do anything about us with no horse."

Karl put his right index and middle finger to his temple, and he thought about his woman.

"Yes," she answered him in his mind.

"Ready?"

"Ready as I'll ever be," Raven informed him. "Bunch of 'Chi up here and a Dorkan think they can boss me around."

Karl smiled despite himself. "Well, you'll straighten them out," he informed her.

"Where did you pick up that expression?"

Karl shrugged, then realized she couldn't see it. "Probably from you," he said. "You never say what you mean."

He sensed her breaking the connection. He lowered his hand and looked around him.

All eyes found him. He remembered a time when he hated that. Now he just didn't care.

He spat on the ground. "Let's march in on 'em," he said, finally. "See what they got."

* * *

"Here they come," Vulpe's senior Colonel informed him.

As if he couldn't see that.

"Form ranks!" he commanded. The order spread out through his troops. No different from Wolf Soldiers, the Eldadorian Regulars fell into formation. Shields fell into place along their lines—huge steel rectangles that covered the warriors from eyebrows to toes.

"Archers to the ready," he commanded. "Wait for my order."

"Horse moving to the north," grandfather informed him, sitting Little Storm. "Probably plan to flank us."

Vulpe nodded. "Special forces to the north then," he said. "Hold for my order."

"Those forces aren't tested," the Colonel asked. "I don't want to rely on them with no back up. Why aren't we marching out to meet them?"

Vulpe shook his head. "We let them, they'll come all the way," he said. His father had taught him that.

"I'm more worried about their magic," Karel said. "That's Angron Aurelias' banner flying over there."

"His Majesty will not fight," Ancenon informed them. "Although my other brethren will engage."

Dilvesh added, "They won't be expecting much resistance."

Ancenon had arrived during the night, and Dilvesh this morning. Karel of Stone had brought with him, among other things, a beacon for the two of them to home in on.

"You know about Raven," Jack asked them.

"We have studied the phenomenon of this female," Dilvesh said. "We know better than to attack her directly."

"It will suffice if we simply neutralize them," Ancenon said. "That alone will greatly frustrate their efforts."

"Do that," Vulpe said, "and my warriors can handle theirs."

Ancenon smiled, and turned his face to Karel of Stone. "So much like his father," he said.

Karel smiled that wide, happy smile that he had. "He's a hand full," he said. "But we'll know today if he's brilliant like his father."

"If one can call his father brilliant," Dilvesh said. "The Trinity speaks more about his luck."

Vulpe shook his head. They thought this was funny. His father had told him about this—how they relieved their tension and their fear by poking fun at each other. It wouldn't work for him. Vulpe needed his tension. He needed his fear.

They were crediting him with the fall of Volkha, now Lupha. He'd barely engaged and he knew it. Daggonin had won that battle and been named the governor of the city in reward for it.

Vulpe held tension and fear both close as the enemy marched in. The Wolf Soldier training was unmistakable. Karl Henekhson had been at them. His father had warned them of this, too.

He'd been anticipating it since Thera. He knew he wasn't supposed to swear, but by War's Whiskers, his father better be right about his so-called Special Forces, or this was going to be a *real* short battle and a lot of people were going to blame an eleven-year-old prince for it.

* * *

"It is not seemly we are kept waiting," Hectar complained, from Central Communications in the imperial palace of Galnesh Eldador. He'd dressed in his best blue doublet and light grey hose—even bought new shoes for this occasion.

Light brown with bright red bows and trailing ribbons, and high, thick heels. His rapier, belted rather than sheathed, shone to blinding.

Tartan, ever the stoic, said nothing, leaning against one of the long, curved table, looking to the spinning orb in the middle of the room. The local wizard, a woman of the race of Men and an acolyte of Shela's, explained, "We *are* at war, your Grace."

Lee sighed—the little girl was showing the wear. Her personal squad had come into the room with her again, Hectaro proud among them. Hectar had decided to humble himself and to admit this had been a boon to the young man, on hearing from a courtier in the throne room just yesterday, right after the meeting between Princess and Duke, the Princess had taken him into her confidences, now on the level not of an amorous young child, but as a young leader seeking council. If this be true, then Hectar's ambitions had been exceeded despite him, and he could *surely* solidify the union he'd been seeking between Houses Gelgelden and Mordetur.

The orb flickered in the middle of the room. All attention turned to it. Finally, Hectar thought to himself. There were things needed saying—on a moment he had to argue *against* Stowe assuming the throne and Lee, with his son's support, sustaining it.

"Her Imperial Majesty, Shela Mordetur, Empress of Eldador," the wizard announced unnecessarily.

Lee frowned and shook her head, her brown eyes searching the conduit.

"That isn't mother."

* * *

Geeguh Digatish found the lance uncomfortable on his arm. His horse balked at it waving around his head. Behind him, around him, squads of ten horsemen, Andarons all, thundered across the plains. Ten thousand strong, blooded warriors whooped in anger to terrify their foes, screaming for vengeances, screaming for blood.

He'd wanted to face Theran Lancers. He'd wanted to humble the infamous Tali Digatishi, who shared part of his name, who'd turned on his own people, who'd helped to found the rogue Wolf Riders clan and sided with another nation.

As far as anyone knew, Tali Digatishi cringed behind the walls of Thera. This would be a slaughter of footmen by mounted Men, but still glorious.

From the south, from the ranks of Eldadorian invaders, a force separated itself and ran north, right at them. For a second he dared to hope he'd meet *some* mounted resistance, but they were too small, too strange in their movements. Almost a daheer away, Geeguh had to force himself to admit what he was seeing.

Dogs. He sent warriors, and Prince Vulpe Mordetur sent dogs. Geeguh's rage burned inside him, he heard the angry screams from his warriors. A personal affront, a slap to his face from a boy half Andaron himself. Geeguh heard himself scream in anger.

Mordetur had gone too far. This wouldn't just be his defeat now. Geeguh would personally string the boy up naked and burn him for this. He'd wear the young man's sack in a bag around his neck when finally he faced the father.

Huge dogs bounded across the plain to meet him. He lowered the tilt of his lance. If he must kill dogs, he'd make it a bloody thing.

* * *

Karl Henekhson, Warlord of Teher, Hero of Tamara, watched the dogs take off to the north of the Eldadorian army.

He looked from their own dog, then to the others, and his heart froze in his chest. *This* was what she was here to tell them. They'd known, but they'd never assumed—never imagined *this* was what the Emperor would do with them.

Dogs by the hundreds, perhaps even a thousand, loped to the north, those telltale dewlaps flapping at their shoulders and jaws as they ran. Their own dog whined to see them, remaining close to him for some reason, where she'd normally stay near Raven. Drool hung from her jowls like strings. She knew what they would be doing better than he did.

And Geeguh Digatish would be caught completely unaware. He had no way to warn them.

"You see that?" Zarshar growled.

Their army marched in orderly squads to engage the enemy. Their own archers were firing arrows at will into the Eldadorian mass. Karl was about to order that they hold arrows—the enemy had their huge shields and were hiding behind them. Anchored to the city of Medya, they'd begun to look like a hedgehog wedged under a rock.

"Forget our cavalry flanking them," Karl said, and turned his head to spit. "If they get through that, then they'll be so confused and turned around they'll be useless to us."

"They don't wear armor," Zarshar said. "Or at least, not much. They'll be back on their horses—"

Karl waved him silent. It didn't matter and he couldn't worry about it now. He'd lost the advantage the cavalry gave him, and now he needed another.

He put two fingers to his temple.

"You see the dogs?" he asked his woman.

He sensed her affirmative. "We're trying to warn the Andarons now, but there isn't a Sorceress among them."

"Can you attack the dogs?"

He felt her pang of sympathy but pressed the issue of urgency in his mind. He knew Vedeen could likely open up the Earth around them, but Vedeen at the last minute couldn't be found.

Three balls of flame flew from their raised platform toward the dogs. They hadn't crossed half the distance before they were extinguished. Six more arced out from the platform, and also expired.

"They have Uman-Chi casters," Raven informed him. "Glynn thinks it's her brother, Ancenon."

"We have more," he argued.

He sensed her negative. "Easier to destroy than create," she said. "If he wants to just resist us, it makes him harder to beat."

Karl didn't have more time to argue. His army had come close enough to the Eldadorians where he could see faces. Warriors in front, a mix of all of the races, no different than the Wolf Soldier army, were shaking their shields and readying their swords.

The Eldadorians were unmoving. To the north, the howls of anger from the Andarons changed to surprise as dogs leapt at their riders and knocked them from the saddle. Some managed a little damage with their lances, however the Andarons were unready, and the dogs had been trained to avoid the weapons.

The Andaron charge stumbled. The Fovean army advanced. The first 500 squads passed onto a wide, flat battleground that circled the city. Without warning a flight of spears popped up from the Eldadorian regulars, moved back as one, and then flew forward.

The army came to a halt on his order. Like any Wolf Soldiers, the Foveans raised their shields and crouched behind them. Karl's runners delivered his orders to his designated colonels, they to his majors, they to his captains, and they to the lieutenants and sergeants on the field. This, he knew, was the real strength of the Wolf Soldier army. Not understanding this was why no one had been able to emulate it. It wasn't marching that made good soldiers; it was that this immediate communication, faster than a spear could fly through the air, made his entire army an extension of his will.

The men crouched, the spears landed and the sound of them breaking on the Fovean shields echoed across the plain.

Less than a minute later, runners reporting to him from his sergeants on the field, claimed these spears were soft iron with wooden handles, and they bent and broke on impact, so even where they didn't hit a man, they ruined his shield by piercing it and couldn't be thrown back, destroyed as they were.

He saw warriors trying to lift shields with bent spears in them. He saw a wave of motion through the enemy ranks—Eldadorian regulars seeking to rearm.

He put two fingers to his temple.

"Attack them, or try to protect us from the spears," he thought.

"I'll try," Raven said. She sounded desperate.

"Try?" he couldn't believe this. He sent the order for the front line to fall back. They peeled off smartly to the right hand side, the next five hundred squads marching in behind them. If the Eldadorians threw more spears, then he needed more shields to meet them, or his troops were going to see 5,000 warriors die with their swords still in their hands on the field.

If the Eldadorians threw now, it was going to be mayhem.

"What do you mean try?" Karl demanded.

"I'm up here alone with Glynn and Krendell," she informed him. Her concentration was so shaken she could barely communicate to him. "As soon as they realized Ancenon was on the other side, the Uman-Chi all disappeared."

Chapter Twenty-Three

Emperors and Kings

Geeguh Digatish leapt back onto his Andaron mount 'Free Air' for the third time after being knocked off by these damnable dogs.

Even as the Warlord raged at the enemy who wouldn't fight him, the Andaron in him appreciated the good joke of it, the humor behind the cunning of Emperor Rancor Mordetur.

They hadn't killed more than a few score, because the dogs wouldn't stay still and they wouldn't fight. They seemed almost to be grinning through hideous, wide jaws big enough to swallow a man's fist as they leapt, struck and ran.

To one side, several of them were herding spooked and angry mares and stallions. To the other, some sat on their haunches and panted, struggling to get their wind back, their tongues lolling and their black and brown coats heaving from the effort of moving their gigantic bodies.

In the center, Andarons tried to give chase with swords, to throw their lances like spears, to remount and to get out of the mass of dogs that, outnumbered, had stopped them cold on the plains.

Geeguh had hoped for some magic to save him, but none came. To the south, the Eldadorians had peppered the Fovean army with spears, and Karl had them shifting on the plains, trying to move fresh troops forward.

Geeguh had lent his faith to the Hero of Tamara. Karl had seemed to be the answer to the Emperor.

Apparently, Karl hadn't been asking the right questions.

His mount suddenly bucked up on him, doing what they called a 'crow's hop', all four feet coming off the ground at once as it bent it's back. Geeguh gripped the stallion's barrel with his strong legs, seeing many of the other horses around him doing the same. As one, every dog on the plains raised its head, and nearly one thousand tails started wagging as they took off in droves to the hills to the north of them, the very ones he'd hidden behind less than an hour before.

Andarons started running for their horses, happy for the respite. To the south, another flight of spears had the Fovean army scrambling for the safety of shields in the advancing second line. Karl's carefully planned squads shuddered as warriors desperate to save their own lives dove from the first rank, behind the second. The new front line bloated and more spears found their homes.

The Fovean army wavered. No magic seemed to support them. This day might be up to the Andarons to save—if he could get his troops turned south now, give Karl some breathing room to regroup, then work together to catch this still-outnumbered Eldadorian army between them.

"To the north!" someone cried out. Geeguh recognized a member of the Hunters tribe. He'd assumed the rank of captain in this new army. "To the north!"

There'd been rumors of movement to the north. Gharf Bendenson had called for reserves from Vol, Kendo and Myr, and local farmers to the north had stopped shipping them wares because someone moving a large force south was buying them.

No invading army *bought* wares. They took them and killed the farmers. Geeguh got his mount under control and turned its head around, expecting to see thousands of shaggy Volkhydrans come just in time to relieve their cousins. He stood up in his stirrups and looked to the north.

Maybe Gharf could lead that charge he wanted after all.

But Geeguh Digatish saw the snapping pennons of a line of Eldadorians—Theran lancers cresting the hill. Thousands strong, their dogs collected before them.

At the center, the huge white stallion that could only belong to one man, the warrior astride it with a lance in his hand.

The Andaron's heart froze in his chest.

* * *

Lee's heart froze in her chest. She stared into the orb at the center of the room called 'Central Communications,' and she knew before any of them what had found its way into their magix wasn't what she had called 'mama' all her life.

First of all, mama didn't have the strength to step *through* the orb like a portal, from somewhere else to here, and this thing did, along with the power to bring more with it.

Three Uman-Chi leapt out of the orb into Central Communications, a dozen heavily armed Uman warriors with them.

Tartan Stowe, Hectar Gelgelden and her Wolf Soldier guard reacted no slower. She found her person surrounded before she could even think of calling for them.

One of the Uman-Chi, an especially ancient looking one with white hair and an eagle on his breast, smiled like an old grandfather at her. The other two, one with scars on his face, the other shorter and mousier looking, flanked him. Their Uman guards took up a defensive perimeter.

The Communications wizard, Releya, raised a hand white with power, but the old man dismissed her with a flick of his wrist. She fell quiet to the floor, not even a whimper from her.

"Angron Aurelias," Hectar spat, moving with Tartan toward the Wolf Soldier squad as he spoke. "You go too far."

"Too far?" the old man asked him, his voice dripping with malice.

"Too far?" he repeated. "Your 'Emperor' sacks my city, sinks my ships, slaughters my allies, and *this* is too far?"

Even mother wouldn't have tried to stand toe-to-toe with the ancient power of the King of Trenbon. Lee tried to reach into the orb to find her, or Dilvesh, or anyone who might be on right then.

Nothing. The thing didn't even *feel* the same.

Angron turned his attention to her. "I'm sorry, little daughter, but your mother cast her net too wide with this. When I sensed it years ago, I saw how easy it would be to turn it to this purpose. I have waited since then to make this day happen."

Lee knew she had to get out of this room. She couldn't fight

Angron, much less three Uman-Chi. Her mother had never taught her the more complicated spells for translocation or a seeking, however she wasn't without her guile.

Powerful magic had been used to build Central Communications, woven intricately to tune this place to one frequency and to allow others to tap into it. With her sight as a sorceress, she saw those magix flowing through the marble walls like so many worms.

Picking a spot as far opposite the room's one door as she could see, she extended her will, she reached into the marble, and she unraveled them.

She let the magic run free.

"No!" Angron shouted, and raised a hand toward the same spot, taking the power, re-weaving it, containing it from the chaotic expulsion it would seek on its own, that would destroy the palace and a good portion of the city if she let it.

She struck another place, and another.

The other Uman-Chi were wide-eyed. They knew better than she what it meant simply to release such power from this place.

She had no warning before she felt the sword razor-sharp at her neck. From behind her, D'leer had two fingers beneath her eyes, her left hand over Lee's mouth.

D'leer, who'd been with the family for years.

"Your father will still want you, even if you're blind," the Uman hissed into her ear. She began to pull Lee from the rest of the Wolf Soldier squad. To her left, they broke apart to pass her.

Except for Hectaro, who plunged his sword in one fluid motion into D'leer's hip. The other Wolf Soldiers turned on him as one, D'leer screaming, *"Kill him!"* his father and Tartan Stowe running to his aid.

Lee pulled her head from the wounded Uman's grip. Hectaro punched D'leer in the face with an armored fist, even as another Wolf Soldier brought his pike down across the young man's back. Lee saw Hectaro's face twist with pain, heard his father call his name.

Tartan Stowe plunged his sword into one Wolf Soldier's breast, punched another in the throat, then turned on his heel to kick a third. Hectar wrapped his sword up with another, while D'leer and Hectaro both fell to their knees.

The Uman guards charged as the walls wavered under the Uman-Chi's efforts to contain the damage Lee had done. For a brief moment, Lee wondered if that had been too much. Her mother had warned her *never* to affect the magix that had been cast here, even with the best of intentions.

Her Andaron blood steeled her. Lee Mordetur would be *dead* before she'd be the captive of Uman-Chi scum.

A Wolf Soldier guard engaged an Uman. Another struck Hectar across the back of his neck with hilt of his sword, dropping the older man. Tartan stabbed that one through the neck, then abandoned his sword for the pike in the hands of the Soldier who'd struck Hectaro. As that warrior pulled his sword, Tartan heaved the weapon into the back of a distracted Uman-Chi.

The Caster actually exploded. All of them fell back, covered in the red entrails of the dead Wizard. The Uman guard was cast like so many rag dolls against the wall around the door where she'd hoped to escape. The room shuddered, however Lee could sense that Angron had the place almost under his control.

The orb wavered. Perhaps now she could use it to contact her mother!

Hectaro couldn't have been thinking that as he leapt to his feet, took her like a doll around the waist, and leapt for it. Almost every being in the room screamed, "No!" as the two of them passed into the brilliance of the altered orb.

The orb had been tuned to the room—the room had been taken out of tune. Lee extended her unskilled will, trying to meld with it, trying to commune with it, trying to discover some way to keep them alive inside of something that wasn't in anyone's control any more.

Still, she thought as her consciousness seeped away from her, better than being the captive of Uman-Chi scum.

She couldn't have been prouder of Prince Hectaro Gelgelden if she'd tried.

* * *

A flight of spears crashed into the combined Fovean armies, where the front and second ranks had crashed into each other in an effort to avoid the onslaught.

Chaos erupted. Karl actually saw two warriors end up skewered while fighting for a shield when the spears fell. Seeing the fight among the combined troops, the third and fourth ranks were backing up into the fifth, afraid they'd be the next targets if more spears fell.

"Hold the line—tell them to hold those lines!" Karl demanded of his runners. The word went out; the lines from the third on began to stiffen. Leaders took hold of their warriors. To the north, Karl saw the dogs had retreated from the cavalry. Maybe now they'd be able to get some help—

"Power's fury!" Zarshar swore beside him. Atop the crest of the hills to the north, the pennons of thousands of Theran Lancers snapped in the breeze. At their center, a gigantic white horse stood with an armored rider.

Drums began to beat to the west and to the north. Trumpets sounded. That meant one thing:

The Conqueror, come in person! No wonder the Uman-Chi had run—how far behind him could Shela Mordetur be? When the troops realized that, they'd be running for their lives, throwing their shields at the advancing enemy.

"Charge!" Karl bellowed. The runner boys looked up at him on his horse in surprise. "Send the order in—every rank, every division! Charge!"

They sprinted off to deliver his orders. Old Ulminar on a rawbone mare to his left, and Zarshar to his right, regarded him.

"That's Lupus the Conqueror up there," Karl informed them. "When they realize they're fighting *him*, this whole army will think they're through and run for their lives."

Zarshar grinned a wicked grin, showing his red teeth. "Unless they're engaged already, you mean," he said. "Then they'll have no choice but to fight for their lives."

"We still have the numbers," Ulminar said, turning back to the fight. "If he didn't bring his Bitch with him—"

"We'll deal with that if we have to," Karl said, and drew his own sword. "Right now, I'm more worried he's going to cut back through those lines of Andarons, most of them unhorsed and the rest with no lances."

* * *

Under Karl's verbal lash, the combined Fovean army crossed the battlefield and engaged the Eldadorian Regulars, through the teeth of another volley of spears. Two ranks of five thousand scattered or dead, he drove in with the third and fourth behind it, holding back the remaining five and a half for reserves, and for when he'd have to call back these.

"The one problem we never seem to overcome," Karl informed Ulminar, from the center of the army. "You have to go in with a first wave, and they're always likely to die. You can show up with as many troops as you want, but you can't fight with them all unless the ones in front can be pulled back or die."

"Normally we send in waves," Ulminar informed him. "But we've seen Wolf Soldiers engage, then move to the side as more troops come in."

They heard a whistle blow. There was a shudder from the front lines. Karl missed what had happened.

"As close as this is, there's nowhere to move them to. You essentially end up throwing the men at each other, and having the living walk across the bodies of the dead."

They continued to watch. The fighting had to be fierce. To the north, the Eldadorians had begun the charge forward, their dogs with and alongside of them, the Andarons mostly unhorsed and almost none of them with lances.

The whistle blew again. The front lines shuddered again. Again, Karl missed it.

"What is that?" Ulminar asked him. Karl admitted he didn't know, and once again put two fingers to his temple.

"Are you there?"

"What?" Raven demanded of him. She was weary, he knew. She was trying to find a way around the enemy's magic defense.

"Can you hear that whistle blowing?"

"No."

"Did you before?"

She paused for a few moments. "I could have—why?"

"Every time we hear it, the front line shudders. I'm about to commit another rank of warriors—what can you see from there?"

"Wait."

They waited. The din of fighting, metal against metal, against wooden shields, thundered before them. To the north, the dogs once again engaged the Andarons, this time with Theran Lancers right behind them. Even ready for them, the Andarons couldn't keep ahead of or out of the way of the dogs. Many of them fell; very few of the dogs died or were turned. As the Eldadorians swept in after the dogs, the Andarons fell by scores and hundreds. A good portion just ran out of their own fear.

Karl could see Blizzard with Lupus astride him, leading the charge, trampling the conquered with steel-shod hooves, now bloody up to his belly.

The whistle blew again, and the front lines shuddered.

"Oh—I saw it," Raven informed him.

"What's going on?"

"When the whistle blows, the warriors fighting on the Eldadorian front line all give a push with their shields, then fall back. The warriors standing in columns behind them all take a step up, and the next row fights.

"What?"

Karl could imagine it in his mind. The issue he'd just discussed with Ulminar—this let them refresh their frontline troops—they didn't have to die to be replaced. There seemed to be about fifteen minutes between whistle-blasts. This meant that, with 20,000 warriors lined up 1,000 across…

"A warrior only fights once every four hours, not allowing for deaths in the ranks, and then only for fifteen minutes," he heard in his mind. "If our warriors fought for that long they'd be worthless, and theirs would be fresh."

"War's Whiskers," Karl swore allowed. "We're actually outnumbered."

"What?" Ulminar demanded.

Karl turned to him on his horse and explained what he'd heard from Raven. "No matter how much I recycle my lines, they've got me outnumbered. We'll wear out hours before they do."

To the north, the Therans had engaged the Andarons and were already pushing through their lines. Karl moved two ranks from the back of his army to the north side, to provide shield wall protection against the coming charge.

The whistle blew again. His warriors in the third rank were lagging. He readied the fourth to replace them.

Zarshar seemed to be missing. Karl didn't need to guess where he had gone.

* * *

Zarshar loped through their long lines of squads, between pikemen and shieldmen, to race north and to himself engage the Theran Lancers.

Well—not all of them. He had a single one in mind.

He'd seen Blizzard and Lupus the Conqueror atop that hill,

waiting for him, and Zarshar knew right then this would be his last day. He'd never doubted the fight to take the Emperor's life would kill him—he'd tried to sell his life for that goal before. He'd been stopped, by none other than this 'Jack,' who now fought against him, and better than he'd ever hoped to.

He'd have liked to take Jack's life, but he didn't kid himself that he could wade through an army of Eldadorian Regulars. Here on the plains, in the heat of battle, there would be chaos, and Zarshar knew he would single out the Conqueror, and there take him.

Nothing mattered after that.

Zarshar loped out of the ranks of Fovean warriors and onto the plains, his long legs stretching, moving him faster than most horses could travel. Before him, Men and dogs swarmed about a battlefield, the Conqueror in the middle of it, his great sword red with blood. As soon as he saw a clear path to the Emperor, he roared his challenge.

Many heads turned. By now most of the lances were broken, most of the Andarons down, their horses scattered. A dog not unlike their own turned and leapt for him, his great jaws slavering, its huge paws extended. Zarshar plucked it out of the air and in one motion turned on a clawed heel and hurled it at the Emperor. True to its breeding, it knocked Lupus the Conqueror from his saddle.

His horse began bucking and kicking out his back legs. Lupus landed on his back on the plains, his warriors rushing to encircle and protect him. Another squad of them peeled off and charged for Zarshar, several with their lances down, the rest with swords out, to take the Swamp Devil before he could follow up his threat.

Too late! Zarshar sprinted for the fallen Emperor, his great long legs stretching to cover the ground between them. Trapped in his armor, Lupus shook his head and tried to roll off of his back.

Seeing Zarshar, he whistled one shrill note. Zarshar expected to see his horse, but instead one of the dogs ran to him, and Lupus gripped it by it great, spiked collar and spoke some word to him.

It leapt forward, pulling the Emperor up to his knees. As his warriors' horses pounded to his side, the Emperor regained his sword and made ready for Zarshar.

Zarshar was tempted to leap directly at the Emperor. Grapple him, he knew, and he was guaranteed the win. Lupus already had his sword ready, however, and Zarshar didn't want to impale himself on it. Instead at the last moment, he turned to the right, opposite the

Emperor's sword arm, and reached for the Man's face with his extended claw.

He should have felt sweet flesh curl through his claws. Instead the Emperor switched hands and met the claw with his sharp sword edge. Before he could withdraw his hand, the Emperor had claimed two fingers, sending them spinning away as the Devil passed.

Now Zarshar was behind the Emperor. He turned on his heel again, the Emperor having planted his sword in the ground to push himself up. Zarshar knew he had the victory now. He reached out with his good right hand for the Man's exposed neck.

He'd barely touched the blonde hair when a lancer's weapon crashed into the back of his steel breastplate. Zarshar lurched forward, caught the Emperor by the middle of his own back armor, and ended up actually pushing Lupus to his feet.

The Emperor turned, the horseman passed. Zarshar barely had the time to rip a handful of flesh from the offending beast's flank, and then the Black Adept faced the Conqueror.

The horse screamed. Lupus held up his left hand, a look of concern on his simian face. Zarshar could hear the other warriors reining in. Lupus himself squared off on the Swamp Devil alone—apparently wanting singles combat, or at least not to risk any other horses or warriors against the Swamp Devil.

"You seem ready for a fight," the Emperor told him, approaching slowly.

"Your last," Zarshar said, crouching now, his arms wide spread, the stumps where his fingers had been leaking brackish blood.

In fact Zarshar's magic usually protected him from steel weapons. It surprised him the Emperor's sword could cut him.

Lupus smiled. "A lot of people have told me that," he said. "They're all dead, and I'm not."

Zarshar took a swipe at Lupus' face with his injured hand, to distract him from a swipe at his leg with his right. Lupus fell for neither, and nearly touched him with that sword again. Zarshar fell backward then dropped to a heel and a palm, reaching for Lupus' ankle with a taloned foot, but again the Emperor defended himself with his sword, this time cutting Zarshar across the calf. Zarshar stood and ignored the pain.

Lupus was barely sweating. He began to circle to his right, to Zarshar's wounded side.

"Even if I fail," Zarshar informed him, "there will be others of my kind to come for you. We've been studying your *Empire*. If I fall, those who remain will take you."

Lupus laughed. "Those who remain?" he asked. "Are there any? I guess you've been away from home."

Zarshar's eyes narrowed. He took another swipe, trying to get a shoulder, a knee, something to twist the Man's armor, to slow him down and let Zarshar within the guard of that sword.

"Or didn't you know that I promised the first warrior who could come to me with ten horns from Swamp Devils one of Blizzard's get?"

Zarshar's jaw actually dropped. Every Andaron with a horse would be bound for the Swamp of Devils for a bounty like that. There would be whole tribes massacring his people to pool the horns and to collect ten, to improve their herds with Blizzard's seed.

Lupus lunged forward, and Zarshar responded just a second too late. The Sword of War plunged into his stomach. The Emperor turned it as he withdrew, pulling out a long rope of entrails.

Zarshar leapt back and felt the weird tug as his guts were literally ripped from him.

Lupus pressed the advantage. Zarshar raised an arm defensively to protect himself from the cutting sword, and saw it sheared away below the elbow. Black blood pumped like a fountain from the stump.

Zarshar roared and reached for the Emperor with his wounded hand, and Lupus trimmed that away as well, then took a portion of his right leg on the back swing.

Zarshar fell to his knees. He'd never been so easily humbled.

"My—my people," Zarshar stammered. He hadn't even realized he could care. He'd killed his own kind by the dozens, but to intimidate them into following him, not to collect their parts.

Lupus whistled for his mount. Blizzard, having collected himself, trotted up to Lupus' side. With a wary eye on Zarshar, Lupus sheathed his sword and reached for the stallion's mane, then stepped up into the stirrup and pulled himself up onto the stallion.

He regarded Zarshar from that vantage point.

"I don't need your people," he said, the contempt plain on his face, "and I can't control them, so I'm getting rid of them. Just like I did with you. You're the Black Adept, aren't you?"

Zarshar fell face first into the grass, feeling the life slip out of him. He twisted his neck around to see the mounted Man, wishing he had the strength, if not to bite, at least to drive his horns into the stallion's side, to take at least one thing from the Emperor.

He nodded.

Lupus nodded back. "Good," he said. "A lot of your people called for you or promised you'd lead them in revolt against me. Good to know I don't have to worry about that."

Lupus trotted away without a backward glance. He had other things to worry about. He hadn't even bothered to cut away a souvenir, to save the rent cuirass or take a horn. Lupus didn't even bother to finish him.

The battle, Zarshar realized as he began to die, hadn't been that important to him.

* * *

From her vantage point on the raised platform, Raven watched Zarshar fall to the Emperor. She watched the Fovean army hurl itself at the Eldadorian Regulars, grinding away squads by the score. The enemy wounded seemed far fewer. The Eldadorians fought amazingly hard when they knew they only had to keep it up for fifteen minutes, and then could rest for hours after.

A rank of Wolf Soldiers was 5,000 strong; a rank of Eldadorians could hold them with 2,000. When Foveans fell, they had to be replaced with men specialized in the correct positions—shieldmen or swordsmen or pikemen. All of the Eldadorians did the same thing.

By the time two thirds of their army had been killed or wounded, all of the Eldadorians had yet to fight. Now Theran lancers were slashing at their northern defenses, running in wide circles, picking them off with lances, which were being replaced by the Emperor's supply lines.

Meanwhile she'd tried everything she could think of against their enemies. She'd tried to make the molecules in the air spin into a super-hot plasma—they'd made it rain. She'd tried to shake the earth—they'd quelled it. She'd tried to bring down lightning on them, heat their weapons, even fired sonic booms in the air over them by spontaneously making whole volumes of air super-cool. Every time, she'd wrapped up something pretty as a package, they'd dispelled it before she could stop them.

At least Glynn was doing no better. She seemed upset that her people had spontaneously disappeared. She'd tried to coordinate her attacks right before and right after Raven's, but nothing had worked. She'd coordinated both their efforts with Krendell and that hadn't worked, either. They hadn't been attacked once, but they hadn't been able to get through, either.

"This makes no sense," Glynn admitted finally.

"That we came here at the request of your King, who abandoned us, or that most of my Dorkans are dead?" Krendell spat. He reached out to the sky and pulled down more lightning, but it dispelled harmlessly above their enemy.

"Rest assured Angron Aurelias fights the enemy in ways you could not imagine—" Glynn began.

"And yet, still, we lose," Krendell said.

Raven shook her head. "We can argue all day, but the fact is we're stuck here, and we can't get through. If we can't hurt their army, can we strengthen ours?"

That got their attention. Krendell looked to Glynn.

"We can imbue their bodies," he said. "Give them strength."

"I can increase the oxygen on our side of the battle lines," Raven said. "Maybe even rob it from their side? With more air for us and less for them—"

"Yes, try it," Glynn interrupted her. "I'll see what I can do to make our shields stronger. We'll last longer if we can't be touched."

Raven turned her attention to the battlefield. She imagined all of the air around them, imagined the spinning molecules and, as she focused, she lowered their temperature, created a giant heat sync in her mind and let the kinetic energy flow out of it. She saw the frost on the breath of their warriors, and knew she'd draw in all of the air from the plains around them, as the oxygen around their warriors contracted and created a vacuum.

She was about to tell Glynn and Krendell she thought it was working, when the platform lurched beneath her. Glynn reached down with an open hand, trying to reinforce the structure, when the whole thing slipped forward and began to crumble.

Krendell winked out of sight, a snap and a flash the only evidence of his being there. Glynn, fighting to keep the structure together, couldn't follow him, and Raven didn't know how. Together, the two women surfed the platform to the ground.

* * *

Shela Mordetur watched the tower fall. The stupid Wizards upon it had protected its structure, but had neglected its base. She'd done the same thing years before when she'd defeated the Uman-Chi in their own city.

Fools.

She'd left her horse a daheer to the east and walked in—she sprinted the rest of the way now. She'd seen Raven on top of that tower, and she'd seen Raven fall. She'd see her die now, a dagger in her heart as she'd promised her husband.

She approached the crumpled remains of their wooden tower cautiously. They'd left a rear guard, but the rear guard had stood under the platform to keep out of the sun. Many of them could be heard moaning. Most would moan no more. None of them seemed a threat to her.

As she approached, she recognized the faded blue dress she'd seen Glynn Escaroth wearing. She circled to the right of the pile of timbers on cats' feet, nervous she'd attract the attention of the enemy's reserves. Most of them were looking back at the twisted remains of the platform, but none of them were moving.

She admired the discipline—Karl Henekhson supposedly led them. He'd remembered his Wolf Soldier training.

The dress stirred—Glynn Escaroth still lived. Well—she could fix that.

She barely saw, more sensed the green blur of a Slee as it launched itself at her from the grass at her feet. Shela barely had time to raise a defensive spell as long, adamantine talons reached for her and dragged like nails down a chalkboard on her defenses.

The thing fell into a crouch and bared its teeth on her, placing itself squarely between Shela and the rubble. Shela raised a hand full of flame—these things feared fire, she knew from her time on the Andaron plains and in Wisex, their island city. She'd burn it, and it would run.

Instead it leapt at her again. She recreated her defensive wall, then dropped it when the Slee fell back. She raised the fire again, and she cast it at her enemy.

It leapt into the scrub and vanished. She'd seen Slee do this in their swamp as well—she'd never imagined they could do it on dry land.

She'd never seen one disappear so completely, either.

She sensed the motion behind her as the Slee struck again. Shela turned on a flat heel and released the flame, scorching the air as the Slee dived away at the last minute. It slithered back into the scrub, invisible again.

To the west, horses were coming toward the platform. She had to assume these would be mounted warriors. Yes, she could kill them all if she had to. No, she couldn't do that and defend herself from the Slee.

Her husband had wanted her to bring a few squads of Wolf Soldiers to protect her, and she'd demanded she could move more easily alone. Once again, he'd been proven right. She found it uncanny how he just *sensed* these things.

This time she didn't sense the motion when the Slee struck, it just launched itself from a bush right in front of her. She tried to raise her shield defense but couldn't do more than trap its tail. The Slee hung for a second in mid air, then dropped its feet to the ground and slashed at Shela.

Shela's leather harness ripped away, her breasts bobbing free as the Slee left eight red lines along her ribs. She gasped at the pain, stepping back, her heels slipping out from beneath her. The defense wavered, then came apart completely when her back hit the hard ground.

The Slee flew over her body and hit the ground behind her. She saw its tail whip over her head when it turned to make the killing strike.

She extended her will, and found the Slee's life entity. She took hold of it, wielding her power and, seeing the talons that reached for her eyes, she crushed it.

The ground shuddered when the Slee's body struck it. She felt the talons on her, lifeless, limp. She took a moment to collect herself, knowing those horses were getting closer.

Knowing she had to be hidden when they arrived, because drained and wounded as she was, she'd never outrun them to her own horse.

She pushed herself to a sitting position. Her ribs burned in pain. She applied her will to stitch the skin up where the Slee had torn it, leaving angry red scars. She could see the puddles of blood on either side of her. They'd be on to her no matter what.

The world swam for her. She'd lost too much blood. She

wasn't getting away from this—not this time. She pulled herself past the Slee, toward the scrub.

But the Slee was gone now—that seemed odd. She could have sworn she'd killed it. It was in the nature of these things that sorely wounded, they would slink off and find a place to die. This one must have done that.

Hearing the hoof beats, she reached for what she thought must be a branch, and instead found a discarded spear. It was a beautiful weapon—long bone handle overlaid with scales, sturdy shaft with a wicked barbed end. She took the thing in both hands and used it to push herself erect, getting a better perspective on the area around her, deep as she was in enemy territory.

The enemy approaching her was a single female in the white robes of a Druid. Her long blonde hair trailed behind her as her mount pounded to the precise spot where Shela waited, as if she had been drawn there.

"I don't know you, Druid," Shela said, leaning on the spear. She'd begun to sweat—she'd not be able to defend herself if this one had allied herself with the other Foveans.

"I am Vedeen," she said, extending a hand. "If you will allow me, I will take you to a safe place, Empress."

Shela nodded, and took the Druid's hand. Vedeen dragged her up into the saddle behind her with a surprising strength. Shela wrapped one arm around Vedeen's middle and lay her cheek on the back of Vedeen's shoulder.

The mount charged off, but Shela really couldn't say she knew to where.

* * *

A Volkhydran boy named Eric, a rare blonde sixteen years of age walked the battlefield after the Battle of the Foveans, as it was being called, where the united Fovean armies had been soundly defeated by half their number of Eldadorians, perhaps less.

The Conqueror himself had battled the Hero of Tamara. Eric could already imagine the songs the troubadours would be creating about a battle between such legends.

He'd never seen so many dead bodies. His startling blue eyes found Men, Uman, horses, dogs—ripped apart by lances, shredded by swords—the enemies who fought so hard against each other lay together so peacefully in death. If only they'd learned this lesson first?

When the Conqueror's son had invaded Volkha, the call had gone out to every Volkhydran city and town for support. Count Tezzen from Myr had responded with 1,000 Men, but came from so far north they'd missed the battle.

The grandson of an important commoner, a brewer named Terok, he'd come to represent his family as its only living male. He'd had an uncle, but he'd died before the boy's birth.

Fortunately he already stood taller than his mother, Aileen, and not much shorter than most Men. His father had left Aileen to guard a caravan and been lost with his uncle.

Most of the warriors were looking for survivors—allies to save and enemies to question. There weren't many of either. One spoke of a Swamp Devil killed by the Conqueror, and Eric had wandered off to find its body.

Supposedly he'd died where the Theran Lancers had overwhelmed the Andarons. Judging by the bodies, Eric had found the spot, but not the body.

Without warning, he tripped over a discarded sword and landed right on his face. In a cuirass and chainmail shirt, he made a huge clank when he landed, and snapped the sword he'd been given.

He'd liked that sword—a gift from his grandfather. He'd snapped it right at the crossguard. He pushed himself to his knees and threw the hilt aside in disgust. By his ankles he found the weapon that he'd tripped over.

He'd expected to find a simple footman's sword or an Andaron scimitar, and instead found a gleaming black blade with an exquisite steel basket around the leather-wrapped hilt. He stood and picked the weapon up, noting the perfect balance to the blade, four feet long.

If he'd been any shorter, he wouldn't have been able to keep it. Aileen had informed him that his father had been tall—he showed promise of the same. He swung the sword experimentally now, the whirring sound through the air telling him that, although discarded in a battlefield where horses had run, the blade remained true.

He tried to sheath the sword in the scabbard over his shoulder but found the weapon too long. In the end he drove the point through the scabbard. He'd get a new one back in Myr. Right now, the Emperor's army was marching on to Hydro, and all of the warriors expected the city to fall. King Gharf Bendenson had already ordered all reserves to Vol, to keep the Emperor from wrapping up the river.

This had been a dark two months for Volkhydro, but with the body of the Swamp Devil forgotten, the boy whistled to himself quite happily as he set off in search of Tezzen to show off his new prize.

Chapter Twenty-Four

Last Stand

Vedeen stood naked before the Green One, foremost among the Druids, bound to the center tent post in a pavilion to the west of Hydro, the next city in the Emperor's path.

She'd delivered Shela Mordetur to the Eldadorians, when surely Shela would have fallen to the Fovean army, or what remained of it. Karl had withdrawn from the field with barely twenty thousand and no horse after their platform had fallen. When that happened, Ancenon Escaroth and Dilvesh had rained down hell fire on what the Eldadorian Regulars hadn't already devastated.

True to Raven's word, she had earned no favor with the Emperor for her actions.

"Little sister," Dilvesh informed her, "you must understand— you were among our enemies, as no Druid should be, and clearly aided them—"

"I gave them no aid!" she insisted.

The pavilion had no furniture, just the tent pole at its center, planted in the ground. The pavilion had a peaked canvas top and four walls, capturing the month of Destruction's heat inside. The Green One, the Emperor, his son, his wife still leaning on that spear Vedeen had found her with, Thorn of the Daff Kanaar, Ancenon Escaroth, three generals whom she didn't know, and the Man whom she knew as 'Jack' only added to that heat in the close confines.

No woman should be so exposed before so many, she thought.

They'd let her ride with them for two weeks, preserving her dignity, gently chiding her to tell them her secrets. She'd insisted she could not—these were prophetic times, and she in her opinion the prophet who would tell it all. She'd known the truth of the song when Glynn first sang it, and it had spoken to her of her role. If she hadn't, then she'd have heard Jack speak in the 'oldest tongue,' the secret language of the Druids, and known anyway.

She'd explained this to the Green One, choosing her words carefully, as even *he* was a particle in the prophecy.

Today they'd dragged her out of her tent by her hair, stripped her naked and bound her to a pole. No Druid, as far as she knew, had ever done another so. The Trinity forbade it, much as this didn't seem to bother Dilvesh much.

"Let the warriors have at her," one of the generals said. He was a stocky Man, gray haired, armored like the Emperor, a scar on his face under his eye, horizontal, not vertical like the Mark of the Conqueror.

"A few dozen in and she'll tell us anything we want to know."

The Emperor's cold blue eyes told her he'd consider that plan if he felt he had to. Above all, however, she must not tell *him* what she knew. The gods revealed in their own good time—and that time clearly had not come.

"Black Lupus, you must not—" Ancenon began, but the Emperor raised a hand.

"Why turn on your friends?" Lupus asked, stepping forward.

The sweat ran down her body, from her temples to the insides of her thighs. The tent was stifling hot with its flap closed—however that was preferable to the leers that she'd receive, were it open.

"They are no friends of mine," she said. "Your own man, there, can tell you—I joined as an observer, nothing more."

Lupus nodded, looked down at her feet, let his eyes travel rather obviously up her body. The general's words rang in her mind.

She'd had no man in her life and wasn't eager to release her maidenhood that way.

"Why save the Empress?" he asked her.

He didn't seem angry, but it was said, "Fear the Emperor in his anger, be terrified of him in his calm." This was a man as cold and decisive as a snowstorm in the Great Northern Mountains, with all the fury behind it.

"I knew that, after refusing to help them in another battle, Glynn's fellows would turn against me. I thought I could ingratiate myself with you, if I saved your dearest one."

Dilvesh and Shela exchanged glances. She shrugged; he turned back to Lupus and whispered something in his ear. Most likely, he reported they couldn't read her, because as a Druid she was immune to truth saying.

"So this is two of them who've changed sides," Thorn said, looking sideways at Jack, and then at her. Jack didn't seem to react to that. "All for some song most people can't hear; some riddle the people who hear, can't solve."

"Except for her," the Emperor said, still looking at her with those icy blue eyes. "She's worked it out. She knows who the six in the song are, and she knows what's become of them."

I know whether you win or lose, you mean, she thought to herself, *and that's what you really want to know.*

Without turning away, he asked, "What sort of power does she have, Green One?"

"She's a Druid, like I am," he said, "though not so strong. She's the Guardian of the One—or she was supposed to be when I left her there. She draws on the natural Trinity."

"So we just can't let her parade around, and hope she doesn't change sides back," the Emperor said.

Shela looked at her, then at her husband. She pulled a long sickle dagger from her belt.

She saw the disappointment in the Green One's eyes.

"Make it quick," Lupus said, taking a step back.

Despite herself, she felt a tear run down the side of her face.

"*Ave Maria,*" Jack shouted, stepping forward, "*gratia plena, Dominus tecum.*"

Vedeen didn't know the words—no one really *spoke* the oldest tongue anymore, merely remembered certain of the phrases.

When Jack began, however, the casters among them, Shela and Ancenon and Dilvesh, spun their heads toward him and all stepped back. The Green One was wide-eyed, the Uman-Chi clearly shocked, his mouth open like a ragged hole in his pale skin.

The Empress had already raised a hand, white with power.

Jack went right at her. "*Benedicta tu in mulieribus*," he bellowed at her, pointing a finger at her breast, "*et benedictus fructus ventris tui, Iesus!*"

The Andaron screamed and fell to her knees, her fists at her temples. Vedeen's heart swelled for the power surging around her. She burst into tears.

Lupus pulled his sword and put his feet apart.

Jack stepped back from his and pulled a dagger from his belt. "*Sancta Maria!*" he cried out.

It was as if a giant had blown a great puff of air into the tent. It swelled at its walls, its roof expanded. Ropes meant to hold it to the ground and to the tent post started to twist against their braiding. The air pressure pounded the Druid's temples – it was as if madness were made whole and then corked into a bottle with her.

Dilvesh put his thumbs together and pointed both fingers at Jack. He spoke a word of power, but nothing happened.

Thorn pulled his sword and stuck at the Man's back, but the sword never touched Jack. It burned red and dropped to the ground, the woodsman swearing and holding his hands steaming before him.

"*Mater Dei!*" Jack cried out, taking a step toward Lupus.

The Emperor's sword glowed white.

"*Ora pro nobis peccatoribus, nunc,*" Jack continued, every word an accusation, spoken like a curse.

Vedeen's blood burned in her ears. The Empress screamed, her fists at her temples. Ancenon fell to his knees, his hair wrapped up between his fingers, moaning. The Green One cried out in hoarse agony, his cheeks covered in tears, blood running from tiny tears at his hair line.

"*—et in hora mortis nostrae!*"

The tent collapsed, its pole lines popping in rapid succession, then expanded again. As one, the people under the tent were swept away screaming into its sides, as if scooped up by an invisible hand. The canvas ripped from its moorings at the top of the center post, sending the other tent posts and the whole collection of people and rope bouncing in a cocoon of canvas away from where it once stood. Only Jack remained standing with the dagger in his hand, beside the naked Druid still tied to the center pole.

Jack looked Vedeen right in the eyes.

"Amen," he said.

* * *

The sky rumbled above them, black clouds gathered where there'd been blue sky before. Lightning struck the ground; horses both from the Theran Lancers and those they'd collected from the Andarons were screaming and rearing. Here and there she saw men and women either passed out or holding their heads, some beating the ground, some running. She could only assume these were the *barely gifted* among them.

Jack approached Vedeen with the dagger from his belt and cut the bonds at her wrists and ankles. Wolf Soldier guards were already sprinting to the spot where the pavilion had been.

Jack simply took her naked body over his shoulder and turned. He ran right at the charging Wolf Soldiers and informed them, "The Uman-Chi have attacked—the Emperor's down!"

He pointed to the canvas, rolled up almost 30 yards away.

The Wolf Soldiers responded without hesitation, turning to where the pavilion had landed. Vedeen could only hold on to Jack's belt as he ran, waiting for the shout from the Emperor.

He ran right to his horse, Little Storm, already saddled and waiting. Hers was nowhere to be found. She whistled for the beast but Jack didn't hesitate—he dumped her into his saddle and then leapt up behind her, pulling her into his lap. The old man was blowing like a whale, his beard wet with sweat and his face dotted.

"Hya! Little Storm!" he shouted. The stallion leapt from his picket, warriors trying to quiet the terrified horses scattering out of his way. Not far off, the white stallion Blizzard screamed a challenge after him.

Little Storm remained silent. Vedeen tried to right herself on the saddle, her breasts bobbing and her unprotected sex pressed uncomfortably against the saddle's crest. Jack turned the huge stallion north as soon as he could clear the outer limits of the jess doonar where the Eldadorians camped, west of Hydro.

"Why are you saving me?" Vedeen insisted. Finally she'd decided to crawl backwards into his lap. Jack wrapped an arm around her middle, a hand under her left breast, to keep her in place.

"Because I'm not going to just sit there and watch that bastard kill somebody," he said. "I made a promise before I got here. 'Stand beside her, and give her what she needs. She cannot stand alone.'"

"What—to Raven?" Vedeen's mind was racing. She heard the drumming of hooves in pursuit, but looked behind her to see her roan stallion, running with a picket line dragging from his halter. He ran alone - either the Emperor had been incapacitated, or he'd taken off in the wrong direction, neither of which seemed likely.

Lightening crashed into the ground to either side of them. Without warning the skies opened up in a deluge. If they could keep going then the Eldadorians couldn't use their dogs to track them and the horses' hoof prints would be lost. The rain soaked her hair and slicked her body. Jack tightened his grip on her.

The old man shook his head. "That's what I thought at first, too," he said. "But Raven never needed me to stand beside her. Raven needed me to let her be, so she could be who she was brought here to be, and not have me get in her way."

"Then who—what?" Vedeen had thought she'd embraced her role as prophet for this new prophecy—now she heard something that didn't fit in that template.

"You, Vedeen," he said. "I thought it might be Lee, or Shela—but they don't need me, they *have* protectors. I was brought here to be guardian protector, but I'm not here for the fight."

She turned in the saddle to face him. She looked into the weathered face, the old, wise eyes. Jack had the look of a man who'd worked a long time at a hard task, and finally accomplished it.

"I'm here for the clean up after," he said. "The war's been fought, and the battle lost. I'm here to help you pick up the pieces."

Little Storm pounded out across the plains, and finally to the road to Vol, slinging mud behind him. By then, Vedeen had no doubt they had eluded any pursuit, had there been any to begin with.

* * *

Glynn Escaroth had seen more changes in her life in the first eight months of the 97th year of the Fovean High Council, than she had in the 167 previous, combined.

From promising Caster to prophetic singer, to traded hostage, to hunted revolutionary, quickly to war lady and now, finally, to prisoner of those whom she had considered to be her allies.

She'd seen Angron Aurelias collect the mightiest army Fovea had ever seen, and then abandon it on the battlefield, herself with them. She'd seen that army fall apart under the bravest Man whose foot had ever touched Fovean soil, and seen him driven off by his own king, her protégé and their dog with them, but not her.

She'd been crushed under the platform that had fallen during the battle—a testament to the incompetence of Volkhydran craftsmanship. Her legs and left arm had been broken, and no healer had been able to affect her. The fingers of her left hand were lost, and her beautiful face scarred.

They carried her on a litter now, naked under a sheet, because she couldn't be relied upon to control her own wastes. Outside of the city of Hydro, to the west of the invading Eldadorian army under the command of Lupus the Conqueror, she could barely cast the spells that would minimize the stink around her.

Chaheff had taught her, when she'd been a child of barely one hundred, that when all is lost, then do not press on, but start again. An Uman-Chi is long of life, and should never fear a new beginning. In that philosophy, Glynn did not try to find a way to fight with her allies, who intended to do nothing more than use her body to trade to her King for renewed support.

Glynn closed her eyes, and stilled her mind, and began the ritual meditation she'd had learned so long ago, to collect her energies, as if a neophyte.

Once again, she stood by a little stream, and once again she poured the water from a pitcher she carried, and symbolically cleared her thoughts by pouring them like fish into that stream, where a huge, white one with sharp teeth devoured them all, looking up at her hungrily for more.

In the past, she'd nourished the fish, and it had left her. This time she knew she needed a new beginning, and tried something so unorthodox that no other Caster likely would consider it.

"What do you need, you ugly, white monster?" she asked it.

Of course, the fish existed as an image in her mind. To speak to it was irrelevant—she would simply manufacture conversation and waste her time. Every beginning Caster was tempted down this path, and every mentor discouraged it.

So why not find out why? Certainly time was hers to waste.

The fish poked its head up out of the water, and it looked at her with oddly intelligent eyes. "It's you who need, if you could know it," it informed her.

Her own words, as she recognized them.

"And what do I need, monster?" she asked it, already believing this exercise to be irrelevant.

"You need to fly, of course," he said. "You need to lift

yourself up, and raise your being as a shield over Hydro, as you did with Outpost IX."

She shook her head. "I haven't the strength," she said. "And should I try, then the Empress would be alerted to my presence immediately, and I'd be undone."

"You are undone already," the fish informed her. It seemed almost to be grinning now. "You missed all of the answers, Glynn Escaroth, because you never asked the questions. I need you not to question now, and then all will be answered."

Those were *not* her sentiments, she knew. Now she found herself intrigued. These actions, she knew, would end this life. A hard gamble to make on something that probably wasn't real.

"Perhaps you prefer the long life of a victim bound to a chair with a hole in the seat, to the short one of a hero," the fish informed her. "In that case, by all means, hover on a board over a pile of your own excrement."

That got her. She prepared herself, her insufficient energy, and once again she attached her lifeline to the little imperfection on her shoulder. She raised her being up above the city, became thin, strong, absorbing the energy of the sun and blanketing the city of Hydro.

She sensed the Empress immediately, and other wizards inside and out of the city. She sensed her so-called brother, who had betrayed her, and her King, within the city, who had done the same.

She lowered her being, and she embraced the city as a lover.

A familiar embrace, to be sure; an embrace no different than she had enjoyed with Outpost IX.

A thrill ran through her, even as she sensed the Empress' attack coming. She caressed the towers, the spires, the walls, the buildings and the roads. She knew now—she had it.

By Eveave's thin smile—she'd finally gotten it.

The question was not, "What to do to fight the One." The song answered that already.

The question she had yet to ask was, "What were they to do, once defeated?"

Shela's attack came accurate and merciless. The revelation so stunned Glynn that she barely even realized when Life left her body.

* * *

Geeguh Digatish had suffered a humiliating defeat to the Emperor and his dogs, and then another when what few warriors who had survived him were all informed the bounty now on Swamp Devil horns would be paid in the issue of Blizzard himself.

Andarons from all over Fovea were beating a hasty path to Toor, there to hunt Swamp Devils. Not only had that touched off a conflict with the Devils, it would likely lead to war with Toor. The Toorians were jealous of their jungles and had no love of horses.

Now he simply wanted to give his good-byes to Gharf Bendenson before he followed after them. He found the King at the litter where the crippled body of Glynn Escaroth had lain.

Instead of Glynn Escaroth, however, they found a long, white staff with a huge, green emerald woven into one end. He'd seen some sorceresses do this—take a large bole and, over generations, force it to grow around a precious gem, to create a staff that incorporated two facets of Earth. Such staffs could hold great power.

Certainly, if anyone could grow one, it would be an Uman-Chi. They would see the seedlings of trees grow to hundreds of feet in their long lifetimes.

"Where's the witch?" Geeguh asked Gharf. The Volkhydran appeared uniquely irritated.

"Who knows?" he spat back. "Her kin left, your kin left, Henekh's damn son failed us—why should I expect more from *her*?"

"I've never seen her with that staff," Geeguh commented.

Gharf looked him in the eye. "You want it?" he asked. "I was about to break it—I'm told your people have some magic."

That had to be sarcasm, Gharf knew. Everyone knew Shela Mordetur's heritage. He picked up the staff—the wood had been polished so smooth it was hard to feel.

"I've come to tell—" Geeguh began, but Gharf waved him off.

"You're leaving," he grumbled. "Go. I'm for Vol, myself. Dragor's going to lose his city, just like I did mine. This army's going to break apart, and I don't have enough Volkhydrans to lift the siege, so I'm sending emissaries to the High Council and trying to get another army to throw at him."

Geeguh shook his head. "Five years ago, even last year, I would have said that alone would guarantee your success against him. Now…"

"Now, if I were you I would get my Andarons out of Toor and back to Chatoos and Talen, because when he's done here, he's for there next," Gharf informed him. "And you're going to need more than that pretty stick to save you."

Geeguh, as least, didn't have that many warriors to collect before he left.

* * *

"Well?" Lupus demanded of his wife.

Shela shook her head. She'd detected the Uman-Chi presence over Hydro, and she'd attacked it. She'd defeated it too easily to know much about it.

"Gone," she said. She motioned with the back of her hand to wipe the sweat from her forehead, however there wasn't any.

"Any luck with finding Jack or the Druid?" Lupus asked.

Shela shook her head. She couldn't imagine what magic this 'Jack' had learned, however it had left the lot of them unconscious and, by the time she had been in any condition to pursue him, Jack and his new woman were gone.

Shela looked into Lupus' eyes. She hadn't wanted to kill the Druid, so she had to admit she wasn't all that upset that Jack had spirited her away. Yonega Waya, however, had been furious, and Vulpe devastated. She knew he missed his adopted grandfather.

She'd lost all contact with Central Communications, as well as with the wizards in Eldador. She'd tried some others she knew in Kor, now Lupor, however even these were inaccessible. They'd sent messengers, but these would take weeks to respond. Meanwhile, her husband had a city to conquer.

She'd decided to keep the harpoon she'd found. It was a pretty thing, and it fit her hand well. Her husband had his 'Sword of War.' Maybe, now, she had this.

Chapter Twenty-Five

The Right Question

Raven watched their dog sprint across the plain before them, hot on the trail of an animal that looked like a jackrabbit. The dog moved too slow to catch it, of course, but then, Raven wondered if that was the point.

Sometimes, it was just the chase. She could understand that.

She and Karl had traveled straight up the center of Volkhydro for four weeks, keeping low, keeping to themselves, only speaking to passersby when they had to, and then only as briefly as they could.

Then they'd heard Hydro had fallen to the Conqueror, and been renamed Hydrus, just as Volkha had been renamed Lupha.

"He's a cheeky bastard, that one," the old Volkhydran trader had informed them. "Seems he likes 'is own name, as he names all th' cities he conquers after himself."

"All of them?" Raven asked. Two wasn't really 'all.'

The old Man nodded. "He's got those two in Volkhydro, and that one to 'is east, Lupor, and anudder in Dorkan known as Luparran, as used to be Katarran."

Karl and Raven looked at each other, then back at the old Man. "He's already struck into Dorkan?"

"Jes the one city," the trader said, then turned his wrinkled face to spit. "But you can see as them Dorkans, they be mad as hornets and are massing their armies to meet the Daff Kanaar. Them's who's taken their city, a'ways."

Karl spat over the trader's on the ground. "So now Lupus is committed to a two front war?" he demanded.

The trader shrugged. "An' it seems," he said. "But news from Andoron issat every long-haired buck of 'em has lit off fer Toor and the Swamp of Devils, t' fetch a bounty of ten pair o' Swamp Devil horns, an' the first as does'll get hisself one o' Blizzard's get. That means as mebbe Sental and Conflu might come t' aid, if the High Council calls 'em, but as the rest o' Fovea got their own worries."

Raven actually had to take a moment to translate that. In nine months here, she'd come to think in the language of Men, and to be conversant in Uman. Her native English had become like a song she'd sung once in her life, but was in the process of forgetting. "Still, if Lupus has spread himself so thin—" Karl asked.

The trader shook his head. "You don't know what happened down south then, do ya'?"

Karl frowned. Raven perked up and answered for him, "In fact, we came from there," she said. "We were from Medya."

The trader nodded. "Then Life smile on you," he said. "But then you saw—Lupus outnumbered, not only victorious on the field, but as crushin' his enemies as he did. No one wants to take that on."

"So they die," Karl spat. "Rather than fight him, they sit and hide, and let him come to them."

The trader squinted his eyes and looked sideways at Karl. "Yer young," he said. "You want into Bendenson's army and to fight for Volkhydro, he'll take ya. Thing is, you work for 'im, you'll fight for free, where as the Emperor'll pay ya a good silver a month t'be on the Home Guard."

Karl's hand dropped on his sword hilt and the trader straightened on his bony gelding. Raven put her hand on Karl's forearm, stretching from her saddle, to quiet him.

"Don't ye be mad at me," the trader warned him. "What do ye expect a man t'do? Ol' Volkhydro ain't had no good jobs for years now, and here comes the Emperor, as conquers none other than th' Hero of Tamara, outnumbered on the field. Our own King don't even fight for any of his cities, but 'e runs away to Vol. Now we're supposed to go to him and fight for free, when 'ere's the Emperor, offers jobs and silver, and all 'e wants is for us to say we're Eldadorians now, when 'alf of us, we was tryin' t'be Eldadorians already? Don't seem like no argument to me."

It didn't seem like any argument to Raven, either. Nationalism is a wonderful thing, and it will keep warriors living in caves and fighting with sticks and stones if they have to. The Volkhydran King, however, wouldn't fight and couldn't feed them. He'd let his people live a worse and worse life, and then here comes a new guy, and these Volkhydrans *know* he can make things better, so why *not* be an Eldadorian instead of a Volkhydran?

Eldador would probably march right up into Volkhydro and barely lose a man.

Karl shook his head, and Raven wished the trader well for both of them. From that point on, Karl went from avoiding travelers to seeking them out, and for another three days they heard the same story, over and over.

Lupus had settled in the three southern Volkhydran cities. Gharf Bendenson was doing everything he could to try to build an army to fight him, other than pay those warriors or go fight for himself. Meanwhile, Dorkan had mobilized and was calling to the Fovean High Council for aid from the other nations.

None of them were offering, it seemed. By the fifth of Order, they were hearing excited reports that there was now free trade between Eldador and Volkhydro, and mills were starting to reopen.

That and some other disturbing news.

"Gone?" Karl demanded.

Now they spoke to a troop of fifteen young Volkhydrans under the leadership of a longhaired warrior who looked more like an Andaron than a Volkhydran. He had mustachios down past his jaws and carried a scimitar, but he dressed in furs. All of them rode those thin, fast horses that the Andarons had ridden in the battle of Medya.

"As I hear it, while they were fighting in Medya, the Uman-Chi left for Eldador and tried to kidnap Princess Lee right from the palace in Galnesh Eldador. Her own Wolf Soldier guard turned against them, and Young Prince Hectaro, disguised as a Wolf Soldier himself, took her through a magic portal, but no one knows to where."

That explained a lot to Raven. If Angron Aurelias was just using the attack on the plains as a distraction for the Emperor, then how better to make sure the latter presented himself than to make it one of these world-changing conflicts he loved to boast about. With Shela and Lupus in Volkhydro, the Uman-Chi could then get themselves into Galnesh Eldador…

But it hadn't worked. Somehow they'd either killed the Princess, or she'd escaped. Now no one knew where she was, and the latter seemed more likely.

"And now?" Karl pressed the leader.

The leader shrugged. "And now, there's a bounty on the head of anyone who was a leader of the Fovean army in Medya. Supposedly a hog's head full of gold, if you can believe such a thing."

Karl's eyebrows shot up his head. "Really," he asked, then turned his head and spat.

"Too little to go after an Uman-Chi," he continued. "Not enough to turn on a fellow Volkhydran."

"Well, you see, there's the thing," the other said. "As you can see, I'm not quite a Volkhydran, but in fact an Andaron who moved to Eldador about five years ago. And these Men here—they're from Lupha, and aren't Volkhydrans anymore, either."

Karl ripped his sword out of his sheath, the other sixteen warriors no slower.

The dog immediately leaped for their leader, taking him across the side, yelping as the Andaron's scimitar scratched her shoulder.

Raven tugged on her horse's reins, pulling it out of the fracas. She summoned flame and raised a hand white with power.

The dog landed on top of the Andaron, whimpering as she limped off of him. Four of the former Volkhydrans charged Karl at the same time, one on either side and two in the center. Karl's horse shied as he tried to reach for the nearest one with his sword.

The Andaron was back on his feet. "You two—to his rear. You three—after his woman. Somebody kill that damn dog!"

Then his head burst into flame, and he was too busy screaming to give any more orders. Power swelled in Raven's veins now as she looked for her next target.

Karl's mount crashed back to the ground. He managed a swipe across the breast of one of the warriors, catching the man's mount across the neck along the way, but that left Karl open on his left side, and the warrior there charged in with his sword held out like a lance.

Karl took the point in the ribs, even as their dog growled and turned, limping toward the attacker, trying to gather herself for another leap.

This time she just moved too slowly, and another of the horsemen simply ran the poor dog down. Raven heard the sick crunch of her bones under shod hooves.

That just pissed her off. That dog had been a loyal companion. Raven felt her upper lip curl, and called the fire again.

This time she burned the air around the offending Volkhydran, horse and all. Both screamed, and then saw a pain beyond screaming as they actually inhaled the burning air. The other horses shied, Karl's included, as she struck again, and again, and three warriors and their mounts fell screaming to the plains, kindling to the dry summer grass around them.

The smoke rose black, the mounted Men trying to control their mounts against the choking effects. Karl took another hit on his shoulder, plunging his sword into the breast of the man who'd struck him. The man fell, and his riderless horse spun and kicked Karl's square in the ribs. That mount reared, stepped back and then fell, Karl scrambling to get out from underneath him.

In his armor, it was impossible. The horse fell with Karl half-turned in the saddle. She saw him cough up a spout of blood right after. Raven had a hard time imagining his spine had survived it.

Ten warriors still faced her, and now she stood alone. She could stay and comfort her fallen lover, or she could run and live to fight another day. The give and the take, she knew. She felt her heart breaking as she wheeled the Eldadorian warhorse to her left and kicked it into a canter. Lighter than the armored Men and on a larger horse, she knew they'd never catch her, and she could only hope that she could summon the magic to eliminate them, or simply lose them on the plains. But either way, she'd seen the last of Karl and the dog.

She didn't like the idea of their dead bodies being dropped in front of Lupus the Conqueror, but she couldn't do anything to stop that. In the end, she knew she would live to regret it.

Lifting her behind out of the saddle, leaning forward for more speed, she felt the new swell of her belly graze the saddle horn.

She had more than her own life to think of, now.

* * *

Karl Henekhson lay on his hip and chest on the plains, blinking out the dust and smoke from his eyes, watching the butt of Raven's horse and the ten warriors chasing her across the hilly Volkhydran plains. It didn't take long before they all topped a rise and disappeared to him.

He didn't even bother trying to pull himself out from under his dead horse. He'd felt his spine snap, he lay in a puddle of his own blood where his armor had crushed his ribs. He wasn't going to be alive much longer.

To his left, he heard a whimper, and he turned to see their dog, its ribs smashed in, dragging itself to him. He had to smile, reaching for the animal, loyal girl that she'd been. Even though he'd never really bothered with the dog, and certainly never believed it was some part of the song, he didn't bear it any ill will.

Like him, she just didn't want to die alone. Finally he reached out far enough where he could grab one of the dewlaps at its neck, and dragged it the rest of the way to him. It licked his face, then lay on its side, panting, its life leaving it.

He'd certainly made a fine mess of this, he thought. Some hero. He'd let them all down, failed his country, his friends and his woman. She wasn't much of a horseman, and he knew most wizards couldn't cast from a running horse. Likely they'd be dragging her back naked in an hour or so.

The dog began that rapid breathing things did before they finally died. He stroked her side, his hand coming away wet with blood. It wouldn't be long for her.

He felt his own breath quicken. Even though the sun stood at its zenith, the land around him darkened.

It really didn't come as much of a surprise to him that he'd ended up a failure. For a little while, he'd hoped he had the numbers, the warriors, the ability to finally put down the Conqueror, but no one could do that. He warned them all in that hostel just south of Galnesh Eldador on that first night when they'd all come together. Stand in the Emperor's way and he'd just mow you down. The key to defeating Lupus the Conqueror was in taking what he wanted before he went after it, and then souring the victory for him.

They hadn't managed to do that.

The dog let out a long sigh, and then died. He actually felt like crying for it; another fool enough to follow him had paid for it.

Well, she'd followed Jack, actually. Jack had been the smartest of them. Jack had picked the right side. Jack would be at the Emperor's right hand now, the only one of them from their sad little party to survive this. Jack might possibly save Raven's life when they hauled her up naked before Rancor Mordetur, however he doubted it.

More likely he'd have to argue for her to have a painless death.

Even more likely Lupus would put the knife in Jack's hand, in order to test his loyalty. Then, most likely, both would die.

Karl felt his breathing go shallow. As he fought for air, the smoke and the dust becoming more and more intolerable, he turned to the left again. He wanted to lay his head on the dog, use its fur to filter his breathing.

But the dog was gone now, and a shield remained. He didn't recognize it, a thing all of steel, dull gray with light brown striping, the face of a dog with slavering jaws on its front. He dragged it to him, looked at the front, recognized the look of the dog they'd had, carved out of steel.

> "For Fovea, Fovea, then must they live and die.
> Fight the battle from within
> With a champion from outside.
> You shall be the weapons
> The tools of men and gods
> Who come too late for victory
> And win despite these odds."

His heart constricted as he realized it. He placed a hand on the front of the shield, stroked the cold metal face. Put two fingers on the warm, metal tongue.

He smiled one last smile, and said, "Good girl," before the goddess Life reclaimed Karl, son of Henekh, son of Dragor, Warlord of Teher and Hero of Tamara.

The bravest Man who'd ever set foot on Fovean soil.

* * *

Nina of the Aschire wasn't about to miss a sign so obvious as a plume of black smoke on the plains of Volkhydro. Loping along in her leathers, the wind in her purple hair, she couldn't be sure if she'd smelled the stink of burning flesh and hay before she'd seen the plumes. The hills here could mask sign until you were right on top of it, even for one with Aschire senses.

She crossed the horse sign on the way—ten in chase of one, running light, back across the tracks of two horses and a dog, one the same horse running light, and another running extra heavy—a big man in armor.

Raven and Karl, the two whom she'd been tracking for over a month, then one of them coming back without the dog. No way to tell if they'd overtake her—those chasing were pretty well encumbered and on Andaron horses. Those ran light and fast.

She followed the tracks back for almost an hour before she found the scorched dirt and bodies of a battle.

Six bodies of Men, five of horses decorated the scene, and the crows had already been at these. Nina smelled Raven's magic, so distinctive by its overstatement there could be no mistaking it.

She wasn't here. Neither was Karl Henekhson, neither was the dog. The two of these might have broken off from the rest, however if Karl had done that, it would have been to lead the warriors away from Raven, not toward her, and he would have left tracks.

The dog, especially—the dog would have left tracks, however she found none.

She found where the dog had been stomped by a horse, and she found the dead horse that had done it. She found where the dog had dragged itself, broken, to another horse's side. Sometimes a dog did that—looked for companionship in dying, even another wounded animal, however she recognized the dead horse as the Eldadorian she'd been tracking, and it had fallen and snapped its neck. Now it lay there with a sword underneath it, and a shield next to it—something that had been given to Karl, no doubt.

She picked both up. She knew nothing of either, however there were spells that could be cast to tie the owner of an object to that object, and to use the one to find the other. The sword was very similar to the Emperor's with a leather-wrapped handle and an overstated cross guard. A length of fur dangled from its crossbar.

The shield bore the face of a dog and was cast of pure steel. She'd expected it to be heavy; however she slung it over her back almost effortlessly and sheathed the sword within its handles. Funny that anyone should abandon such things, but then battles never really went the way anyone intended them.

She began a loping run south, back along the tracks of the one pursued by ten. If she ran across them, so be it. If not, then she'd be moving in the right direction, anyway.

Already she felt lonely for the little Prince whose bottom she'd powdered as a baby, and whose brown eyes and sweet voice beckoned to her even now.

Chapter Twenty-Six

Children of the Daff Kanaar

Waya Daganogeda, a twelve-year-old girl of the Hunter clan, and Chesswaya, another twelve-year-old girl of the Long Manes, played a game called 'chunkey' with two other 'yonega ukada' or 'white face' girls, in a space on the plains where they'd stomped down the grass, creating for themselves their own arena.

The game involved a round, gray stone almost as wide across as a man's hand, polished for hours until it was almost smooth as the water in a pond, which one team would roll along its edge, anywhere that the ground was flat.

The other team would throw their 'spears,' really just poles a little taller than they were, at the point where they guessed the stone disk would fall on its side. When the stone fell, the throwing team would get a point if the spear was within a hand's breadth of the stone, two points if it was half a hand's breadth, and five if stone was touching. However, if the stone hit the spear still in motion, that team lost two points.

Young warriors played the game all day and all night,

becoming deadly accurate with their spears. However, most of the young warriors had gone to Toor, hunting for Swamp Devils to bring to the Eldadorian Emperor, and the rest wouldn't play with 'agiosdi,' or little girls.

The two yonega ukada girls were Nanette and Thorna, their father Nantar of the Daff Kanaar, honored guests among the Hunters sponsored by Thorn, also of the Daff Kanaar. They dressed in breeches and vests like boys, though at fifteen summers Nanette already had a woman's body. Either girl had beaten boys almost men, and forced kisses from the more handsome of them until old Oolaysagee Chegeelee had switched their bare behinds. Even then they'd tried to kick and scratch him and had to be held arm and ankle by his women.

Little Dagi, as she was called, heaved her spear at the chunkey stone, called a nuyu, as it rolled in front of Nanette. The stone continued past the spear, then turned on an invisible axis and circled three times around where the spear had landed before coming to rest on its side, resting on the planted shaft.

"Five!" Dagi exclaimed, jumping up and down and clapping her hands. She wore the simple, sack-dress of a child of the Hunters, the hem embroidered in beads to say whose daughter she was.

"Cheater!" Nanette accused, already wanting to fight. "We said before, no magic!"

Chessa, come from the Long Manes, was fostered by old Oola himself, a sorceress of great promise. Oola had taught the Empress Shela Mordetur, counted best among the mystics of her age, and it had cost her father twenty horses to send her here to study under such a wise one.

Chessa, however, bore the rare, green eyes that marked Andaron women of exceptional beauty, and many speculated old Oola had more motives for her than simply to be his pupil. Willowy with thick, rich brown hair, Chessa promised to have the bucks all killing each other for her attention now that she'd come of age.

She stomped her foot now. "You don't know I used magic," she said.

"You didn't throw," Thorna argued. "You never throw when you use your magic."

"From now on you have to throw every time," Nanette agreed. Dagi looked nervously at Chessa—in fact, they all knew she'd been using her magic. Otherwise even the boys couldn't hope to beat

Nanette and Thorna.

"Then I don't want to play," Chessa protested, and kicked the nuyu. "It's no fun—no one can beat you."

"What if I promise only to use my left hand?" Nanette offered. Thorna nodded. "That should make it fair."

"Except that you are equally skilled with both hands," a voice informed them from outside the stomped down ring.

Fear gripped the hearts of all four girls. It wasn't unknown for tribes to raid for women in the War months. Mothers whose children had died in the winter, fathers whose tribes had more sons than daughters would pop up out of the grass with sacks and haul away foolish girls who strayed too far from their mothers' sides.

Little worry of that now, they'd thought, with most of the Andarons in Toor hunting Swamp Devils. Just their luck if some had stayed behind or come back early.

True to their fathers, Nanette and Thorna picked up the long wooden spears and leveled them at the new comer. Chessa tried to raise a spell of protection and, at the same time, to summon old Oola, failing at both. Dagi, having no weapon and no magic, did what Dagi always did.

Dagi lied.

"Our men are a stone's throw away," she warned. "You'd best be off with you, or we'll scream and then you'll see your own liver on a stick at our cook fire."

The newcomer chuckled and stepped out of the grass onto their playing field. He seemed to be of the race of Men, tall, stocky, in a white cloak like a shaman, his hair black down to his ears, streaked with gray like his beard. He held his hands out wide and empty before him, showing that he had no weapon.

The girls didn't relax, neither did they run, as one would expect young women to do. The four of them were, in fact, exceptional girls, although they'd yet to realize it.

"I only came to check up on you," the newcomer said. "These are troubling times, and certain children bear closer watching."

Dagi looked to the others, then back at the newcomer. She thought she might know the Man, however she couldn't say how.

"Which of you are the daughters of a Daff Kanaar?" the newcomer asked them.

Now the girls were all on their guard. The Daff Kanaar had

many enemies, who might seek hostages, especially now in these troubled times.

Nanette shook her spear. "You'd best be going, grandfather," she warned him. "My sister and I will see your guts in a moment."

The newcomer laughed his rich laugh again. The girls fought hard not to be lulled by it—the Man exuded such friendliness, such a feeling that all was right, that this thing happened just as it must.

"Well, those are the daughters of Nantar," he acknowledged, showing no fear of their spears. "No mistaking that. And these? Whose daughters are these?"

Chessa and Dagi exchanged a glance, and the former tried again to contact old Oola. This time she couldn't suppress a smile, as she found the old man's mind and warned him in a moment as to where she was, and what was happening.

Seconds later a war whoop rose up from the tribe, not a quarter of a daheer away.

The newcomer beamed. "Well done, Chesswaya," he said. "I knew you could do it, given time."

"Who are you?" Dagi demanded. With no weapon and no magic, still she remained the boldest of them. One warrior who'd tried to switch her for insulting his son had beat her bottom bloody; and still she'd cursed and taunted him. Finally he'd turned and switched his own son instead for not being more like her, and she'd cursed them both all the while.

"Know me, daughters of the Daff Kanaar," the newcomer said, tilting his head back and spreading his arms to the sun, "for I am thy savior, Steel, the Man-god, and I am come to recognize thee, and to report to thee a great thing has come to pass."

Nanette and Thorna both turned to the sound of whooping from the angry Andaron warriors who ran fast as they could to the rescue of four young girls in danger. Chessa let the power die out of her hand, and instead applied her will to test the substance of the one who had called himself Steel.

She knew in a second he wasn't lying, and fell right to her knees, Nanette and Thorna after her. Only Dagi remained standing.

"What thing?" she demanded, suspicious as ever. "What could you have to tell us, grandfather?"

Steel dropped his arms and beamed at the young girl. "I would tell you an age has ended, and another begun, and a prophecy sung by a young girl older than your oldest women has come to pass, as was foretold by the mother, Eveave."

"Words, words," Dagi challenged him. "Spoken like a crazy man. I suppose next you want to show us what is under your robes!"

"*Dagi*!" Chessa hissed, tugging at her hem. "Dagi, that *is* the Man-god, Steel!"

"So what if he is?" Dagi demanded, and took a step toward him, out of Chessa's reach. "You've come, Steel, you've met the daughters of Nantar, you've decreed a new age. What have you for Waya Daganogeda, eh?"

"Waya Daganogeda," Steel repeated, looking the young girl in the eye. "What makes you believe I wanted to see *those* daughters of the Daff Kanaar?"

Now Dagi frowned. She knew she'd been an adopted daughter, as many were among the tribes. Women and young girls could be traded as any commodity. Her mother, she knew, had been a Wet Belly once, until the Emperor had crushed their tribe to make his Waya Agiladia, and hence the meaning of her name—wolf's song.

"What Daff Kanaar is my father?" she asked him, and suddenly all was serious for little Dagi. She loved her adoptive father, but she'd rather know her own.

"Yours, and your sister's there, you mean?" Steel asked her, indicating Chessa. "Do you think it's any coincidence the two of you are thick as horse thieves? One Man came to the Andaron plains with three Andaron women, not knowing he in fact came with five, and your brother, his Andaron son, Agatani Chewla."

Dagi's mouth opened, then closed. In fact, she'd always felt a special bond with Chessa and the two, whose mothers were from lost tribes, Chessa's being a Drifter, had bonded just like sisters.

But there were certain names every Andaron knew, such as Yonega Waya, the White Wolf who sat the Emperor's throne in Eldador, and Shela, who was his wife, and Tali Digatishi, his blood brother and the Duke of Thera, who'd built the Theran Lancers from the cast off warriors of Andoron.

And Agatani Chewla, the Andoron name for Vulpe Mordetur, Prince of Eldador, a blooded man with three cities to his name at twelve summers.

The three of them born on almost the same day.

"We are the daughters of—" Chessa couldn't even say it.

Steel stood. The Andaron warriors were leaping high in the

grass now, close enough to see their brown eyes. They'd be on them in a moment, and wouldn't hesitate to kill the old Man, god or no.

"Daughters of the Daff Kanaar," he said, "the four of you are come to women, and there is a song to sing and only one can sing it to you—a Druid in Volkhydro. As was ordained, by the time you hear it, it will be too late—a battle will have already begun that will test the will of every Fovean. When you hear that song, you'll know what you must do to save this land, and you'll know who you must talk to accomplish that task."

Three Andaron warriors crashed into the little playing field, their scimitars drawn, to find four girls, three on their knees, and one crying who had never cried before. Old Oola only had to take one look at them to know they had seen something that innocent girls couldn't be prepared to see and, even though they wouldn't speak of it, he knew life as he'd known it on the Andaron plains had ended.

Such is the way of things.

* * *

The goddess Eveave lay back into the arms of Adriam, the All Father, who watched the machinations of the Foveans from on high.

They saw the One, War's instrument, rage over Fovea, unchecked and invincible.

"I admit," Adriam said, "you picked your own instrument well.

"My victory," she informed him, her lips a thin, red line "is complete."

"We could not have predicted Steel's involvement," Adriam informed her. "It seems the half-god had a part to play, as he saw it."

"It was Steel brought the Almadain to War's Avatar," Eveave said. "It was Steel who let the Guardian know who was his to guard, and why. It was Steel who wrote a song, and gave it to an Uman-Chi girl to sing it.

"Steel loves these children of Life. How could he *not* involve himself?"

Adriam nodded. He sensed, as well, Power, War and Chaos' machinations, and knew how pleased they were. They'd worried for the involvement of the greater gods, and now they thought themselves victorious.

Eveave sensed her husband's mind, and told him, "How better to hide overwhelming victory than in a cloak of utter defeat?"

The Fovean Chronicles will now take a brief intermission.

Please Enjoy:

Daddy's Girl
Not Your Father's Eldadorian Empire
Prodigal Son

Three short novels which run consecutively, which tell the tale of Randy's children.